'A rich and magical tale that is utterly compelling. The main protagonist – Fin – is cleverly drawn. He draws you into the story of two parallel universes – two very different Londons in which from one, a person vital to the existence of both worlds has been kidnapped. Unless Fin can find the Storyholder, the keeper of the Five Eternal Stories which weave the two worlds together their worlds will cease to exist. His journey is a long and very dark one that's full of foreboding but brilliantly told. This is a book that will remain etched in your memory long after you've finished it' *Lovereading.co.uk*

'A great fantasy with interesting and engaging characters and a relentless pace' *Total Sci Fi Online*

'Engaging, beautifully written, thrilling and with a cast of truly fantastic characters that are easy to believe in. This is a novel for anyone, of any age, who loves good stories. That's what it is all about in the end, the Stories' *Un:Bound*

D1430649

Also by Sarah Silverwood from Indigo:

The Double-Edged Sword
The Traitor's Gate

THE DOUBLE-EDGED SWORD

The Nowhere Chronicles

BOOK I

SARAH SILVERWOOD

Indigo

First published in Great Britain in 2010 by
Gollancz

This edition published in Great Britain in 2012 by
Indigo
An imprint of the Orion Publishing Group
Orion House, 5 Upper St Martin's Lane,
London WC2H 9EA
An Hachette UK Company

1 3 5 7 9 10 8 6 4 2

A CIP catalogue record for this book
is available from the British Library

ISBN 978 1 78062 059 6

Typeset by Deltatype Ltd, Birkenhead, Merseyside

Printed in Great Britain by Clays Ltd, St Ives plc

The Orion Publishing Group's policy is to use papers
that are natural, renewable and recyclable products and
made from wood grown in sustainable forests. The logging
and manufacturing processes are expected to conform to
the environmental regulations of the country of origin.

www.sarah-silverwood.com
www.orionbooks.co.uk

For Hayden: may all your days be magical

THE MAGI'S PROPHECY

Nine there are, and standing side by side
Linked by Love, Truth, Freedom, Hatred, Pride –
Their blood, it is the river's ebb and tide.

Here are two reflections of the same,
The dead bones of the one, the other's frame –
The Magi see the unravelling of the game:

This, their Prophecy.

The dark man comes to rule the new Dark Age.
His door admits those too who come to save.

Travellers from without, within
Bring honour, valour, hate and sin.
Light and dark and shades of each,
Will move through voids, the worlds to breach.

When life and death are bound in one,
The balance of all will come undone,
And love, the greatest damage cause
And forge the war to end all wars.

Eternal stories held unready shall bring
Black tempest, madness, and a battle for King.

The Magi cannot see the Prophecy's end,
Perhaps the Order of Travellers will defend.
Perhaps the stories will hold strong and clear,
The damaged keep us from the abyss of fear.

Don't fight these tellings: their passing must come,
But prepare, both worlds, for that which must be done.

When one plus one plus one is four.
All the worlds shall wait no more.

PART ONE

---◆---

The Somewhere

ONE

Finmere Tingewick Smith sat on the second step of the Old Bailey in the exact spot where he'd been abandoned in a small cardboard box sixteen years earlier. He sniffed, the icy November chill making his nose run. As happened every year he found himself wishing that his mother, whoever and wherever she was, had taken the plunge and actually stepped inside the building before walking out of his life forever. At least that way this annual ritual wouldn't be quite so uncomfortable. He shivered.

Watching his breath escape in a cloud of crystal mist, a vague sense of despondency washed over him. His jeans itched from the damp that crept through from the heavy white stone beneath him and he sighed. It would probably leave a wet patch in the denim and the streets weren't quite yet dark enough to cover it. Great. Just what he needed.

Various pairs of feet trudged by, most heeled, a few booted and some very polished, before finally a pair of well-worn but cared-for black lace-ups stopped.

''appy birthday, Fin.' The voice was gruff and warm and familiar, and despite the numbness and potential wet patch that was plaguing him, Finmere smiled.

'Hallo, Ted.' He felt a warm glow of affection in the pit of his stomach. His birthdays, odd as they were, weren't all bad.

''ere,' said Ted, ''old this and I'll light it.'

The cupcake had one blue candle standing proud from the

middle of it, same as every year, but this time the iced sponge seemed smaller – or maybe it was just that Fin had got eight centimetres taller this year. It was hard to tell. Ted sat down beside him, the smell of freshly smoked tobacco and soap cutting through the cold London air. The old man's spotless security guard uniform always made Finmere think of lavender. He wasn't sure why – it wasn't as if it actually smelled of lavender. But maybe it had on that night sixteen years ago.

The candle flickered into life with the crack of the lighter, and Ted grinned. 'Go on then, mate. Blow it out.' His face was thinner and more lined than it had been a year before, which made Finmere's heart tighten a little.

He took a deep breath and blew. The small light extinguished. 'Thanks, Ted. This is great.' The icing stuck to his clumsy fingers. He took a deep breath and started, 'Look, we don't have to keep doing this every year, though – you know, if it's too much bother ...'

'Don't be daft, lad! I like seeing you – don't see enough of you as it is, things being what they are. But that's the way of it. I just get to do as I'm told.' He paused, the corners of his eyes wrinkling fondly. 'I think about you all year, though, mate, not just on your birthday – don't you ever doubt that. Now go on, tuck in.'

It was gone five and the passers-by were growing in number as the city offices spat out their workers, done with them for another day. They were all hurrying down to the Tube or running for buses, and no one noticed the odd sight of the old man in uniform and the teenager in a hoodie munching a cake on the steps of the greatest law court in the land. As he chewed, Fin wondered if it was him or Ted, or a combination of both. He thought it was probably him. He'd always been pretty good at not being noticed.

'How are you, Ted?' It was funny how hard it was to find the right words. They got tangled on his tongue. Part of him

4

wanted to give the old man a hug, but he was too old for that now, especially as they hardly ever saw each other.

'Can't complain, mate, can't complain. I retire this year, you know,' Ted said. He stared down at his shoes for a moment or two. 'Sometimes it's hard to remember where all the years have gone. Time's a funny thing.'

Finmere wasn't sure if he was supposed to say anything. Sixteen wasn't old enough to really have a grip on the complexities of time, even when – or maybe especially when – your life was divided up into such strict chunks of it.

'Seems almost like yesterday I found you on this very step,' Ted continued, 'gurgling away, wrapped up in that funny little blanket of yours. Sixteen years. Blimey.' He looked across at Finmere. 'You still got that blanket?'

'Yeah.'

'Good. It's always good to know where you come from.'

Finmere wiped his nose with his sleeve. 'Is that why we do this every year?'

'Well, yes, p'rhap – and me and the boys in the big 'ouse like to see how you're getting along, of course.'

Finmere thought of the blanket, hidden safely away where it wouldn't get caught up in the confused muddle of his life. He supposed that once it might have smelled of his mother, and sometimes on bad days, even now that he was older, he'd get it out and press it hard against his face, searching for that elusive scent. Mainly, though, it just smelled of damp and the plastic bag it was kept in. He stared at the crowds bustling to get back to their homes and families. 'It's not really much to know, is it?' he said. 'A step and a blanket.'

Ted pulled a tin from his pocket and took a pre-rolled cigarette from it. The lighter flashed and the end burned. 'See this tin?' He held it out. It was battered and burnished with use, and if there'd ever been a picture on the front, it had long since worn away. 'I've 'ad this tin since I was younger than you. It belonged to me dad. I never met 'im, just like

5

you never met your old man neither. Mine died in the Great War. 'e left this on the mantelpiece, you know, for when 'e got back.'

Ted stared at the tin for a moment longer before slipping it back into his jacket. 'It made me mum feel like 'e'd just popped down the pub for a milk stout or two with the lads.' He paused. 'But 'e never came home. When she thought I was old enough, she let me 'ave it.' He grinned, revealing crooked teeth stained from a lifetime of tobacco, and leaned in and nudged the teenager. 'Maybe I'll give it to you, Fin, eh? When, you know … it's my time – 'ow'd you like that?'

Finmere smiled and nodded, though the thought added to the hollow ache that had been growing inside him as this birthday slowly rolled round. He couldn't help wonder why Ted didn't have any family of his own to give it to, why he'd want to pass something so special onto a kid he only saw once a year. Something he didn't really understand twisted inside for the old man. Ted's life was like a black hole in Fin's head – he didn't know if he was married, or whether he'd ever had children or grandchildren of his own, and if he had, what had happened to them.

Fin wiped his hands on his trousers. He wondered about a lot of things these days. Right now, for example, he was wondering whether Ted was losing the plot a little. They'd done the Great War in History, and it had finished in 1918. It was now 2010. And although the one constant in his life – whether he was at Eastfields Comprehensive or St Martin's School for Boys – was that Maths was the most boring subject in the world and he'd rather eat rats' heads than study it, Finmere was adept enough at subtraction to see that would make Ted just over ninety years old.

He glanced sideways at the old man. With his thinning silver hair and wrinkled face Ted could be anywhere over fifty, maybe even as old as seventy – but that didn't make sense. If Ted was retiring this year, then he had to be in his

6

sixties. Mr Carr regularly snarled at Jordan Brewster, 'I have only one more year of looking at your surly face, boy, and then the golden age of sixty-five will force our good-byes.' As far as Fin was concerned, anything over thirty was old, but he'd never heard of anyone working until they were ninety. Maybe Ted had just got his wars mixed up. Maybe he'd meant the Second World War. He must have.

He sighed again, then tried to look cheerful, despite the fact his toes were going numb in his trainers. Ted was watching him thoughtfully and Fin could feel the pressure of his gaze.

'You all right, son? You're ever so quiet tonight.'

Was he all right? He supposed he was fine – in fact, he supposed he was quite lucky, compared to some. He should be more grateful, he really should. To be anything else was just bad manners. It was just— Well, he was getting a little tired of not having a clue about his life, and why it had to be lived in such a convoluted way.

He shrugged. 'I'm fine, Ted, honest. And thanks for the cake.' He smiled. 'I'll never be too old for cake – and it's good seeing you every birthday, it really is.'

The old man flushed a little, making his face glow in the gloom.

'It's just …' Finmere continued, 'It's just sometimes I wish …' He searched for the right words. 'I wish I had some answers.'

Ted got up and stretched. He took a last drag of his cigarette and ground it out on the pavement. 'Sometimes, Fin, answers is overrated. You can trust old Ted on that.' He pulled Finmere to his feet. 'You ready to go see the old boys?'

Finmere supposed he was. He checked the back pockets of his jeans: they felt wet. Perfect. A wet arse was just what he needed while strolling through town. He twisted around, trying to see how bad it was, but his head wouldn't turn that far. Feeling horribly self-conscious, he forced his numb feet to push forward. His eyes followed the cracks in the pavement.

Somewhere in the distance a police siren wailed and white vans and black cabs beeped angry horns at each other, as if that would somehow make the capital's traffic move faster. The cold air burned his chest.

He felt Ted's arm, heavy and comforting, around his almost-level shoulder. 'Don't you worry, son,' the old man said. 'You're sixteen now.'

Finmere let his shoes scuff on the paving stones. 'How does that make a difference?'

'Stands to reason, don't it? Sixteen's an interesting age. Not quite a fully grown man, but not a kid any more, neither. It's like you're in the middle of two things and don't really belong in either. Anything is possible when you're sixteen.'

'I guess so.' Finmere's brain strained to wrap itself around Ted's answer.

'Sixteen: you – imagine that.' Ted chuckled a little. 'And then there's your birthday itself: the eleventh day of the eleventh month. Always been a funny date, that one. You can't quite trust it. It's a date things *happen* on. And you know what time I found you?'

Finmere nodded. 'Eleven minutes past eleven.'

'Yep, that's right. Just coming out for me first smoke of the shift, and there you was, just laying there. You didn't cry or nothing.' He let out a sound that was somewhere between a cough and a laugh. 'Amazing little thing, you was then.' He squeezed Fin's shoulder. 'And look at you now! Come on, then, pick up your feet and let's get to Charterhouse Square. They'll be waiting for us.'

TWO

They walked in comfortable silence against the flow of the pedestrian traffic, Ted carving them a path through the waves of people, Finmere following a step or two in his wake, heading deeper into the heart of the city. Turning off the main road, they cut up through quieter back streets where narrow, uneven flagstones were lit by the warm yellow glow of light escaping from corner pubs. When they came into the open space of Smithfield Market they followed the line of refrigerated meat lorries parked in a row through its covered heart, fighting the chill that blasted through the vast tunnel, until they emerged onto Charterhouse Street.

Taxis scuttled around like beetles, pausing to collect travellers, extinguish their beacon lights and then scurry onwards again. The temperature slid downwards as the twilight gloom was swallowed up by night, and by the time they turned into Charterhouse Square, Finmere could feel the tops of his ears stinging with cold.

He needed to buy a scarf. He should have got one the last time he'd gone shopping, but he'd forgotten, because last year he'd had his thick blue and cream school one for St Martin's. He had no clue where that was now. Packed in his red school trunk and hidden away somewhere until next year, no doubt, when the trunk would reappear. It would be dropped off in a black limousine, just after he was, at that very exclusive manor house school. Right now, however, he was living out of his green school trunk, the one he had every

9

alternative year when he was in State education, and Eastfields Comprehensive barely had a uniform, let alone striped House scarves.

Thinking about his red trunk and his green trunk, and his one-year-here-and-one-year-there existence, he decided it was pretty understandable that he was confused, even if that was a bit of an oxymoron or a paradox or some other word for something that shouldn't really make sense but did. An icy draught teased its way under his collar and he tugged his hoodie up a little bit more to cover his neck.

It wouldn't be so bad if he could even talk about it, but that was *definitely* not allowed, and he had never broken that rule, even though he'd been sorely tempted, especially since hitting secondary school. Or perhaps that should be secondary *schools*. Sometimes it just all got on top of him. It had been bad enough when he'd been smaller, but now when he changed schools he had to change the way he dressed and walked and even spoke, and the lies just got bigger and bigger. He felt like he was living with a permanent headache.

It would be more bearable if he could come up with one good reason for the old men to make him live this way, but he was stumped. It didn't make any sense – *nothing* made sense about his life.

Finmere was wondering more and more what would happen if he blurted out to either of his best mates, Joe or Christopher, exactly where he was on the *odd* years, when he wasn't at their particular school. And he had bigger worries too: now that he was sixteen would the old boys who paid for everything in his life just pack him and his trunks up and abandon him with nothing? Leave him back on the streets of London where they'd found him? They could do that; after all, he was, as the old nightwatchman had just pointed out, very nearly an adult. If he broke his part of the deal, maybe they'd decide his time in their care was up.

He shivered and glanced up at Ted, striding along in front of him. He looked kind, and he'd always been good to Finmere on their annual visit, but how well could you really know anyone you only saw once a year?

He pushed his hands down into his pockets and squeezed his fingers together until they tingled. He didn't think he really knew anyone that well, not even Joe and Christopher, and they'd been his friends since he'd been small. He wondered if they'd even like each other if they ever met. More than that, he wondered if they'd still like *him* if they ever met … they'd probably never forgive him for all his secrets, and he wouldn't exactly blame them.

'Where are you off to? We're 'ere, lad.'

Ted's voice brought Finmere to a halt – in his daze he'd almost walked past their destination.

'Sorry! I was just thinking—' He stopped and smiled. Ted was staring at him; it felt like the old man was looking right into his head, and Fin was glad his face was partially hidden by the darkness. He felt ashamed for his ungrateful thoughts. He'd seen plenty of homeless kids on the streets, kids with nothing whatsoever. He was lucky, he really was, and he'd best not forget it.

The gate squealed open. 'Come on then, son. You've got a lot of work ahead of you.'

Finmere nodded and followed him up the short path.

Anyone passing through Charterhouse Square would be forgiven for thinking that Orrery House was no different to the other imposing Georgian buildings that surrounded it. Even in the early evening darkness no lights shone out from behind from behind its shuttered windows, and there was no gilt sign attached to the gleaming door or railings declaring its purpose. There were in fact absolutely no outward clues that the building was any different to those housing the grimly serious bankers' and lawyers' offices that lined the four sides of the Square.

When he'd been younger, Fin had asked why there was no sign. After all, even Eastfields Comp had a sign – a big, tatty, graffiti-covered painted board – beside the main gate.

Ted had just laughed. 'Everyone who needs to know it's 'ere, knows it's 'ere, so why would it need a sign?' he'd said. 'Really, Fin, sometimes you say the funniest things.'

Standing outside the imposing anonymous black door so many years later, Finmere didn't think his question had been funny at all. There was something distinctly odd about an old folks' home with no sign outside. He'd been keeping an eye out ever since, and he had yet to find one other building like it that didn't proclaim its purpose. It was just what buildings did. They had signs outside them. It was part of how the world made sense.

He reached up and pressed the gold button. His heart fluttered a little and despite the cold, his hands felt sweaty. After a moment the door swung open.

'Ah yes, young Master Smith – not so young now, eh? Do come in.'

With the help of a sharp prod in the back from Ted, Finmere stepped inside and wiped his feet carefully on the doormat. The carpets throughout Orrery House were thick, perfect white, and had been for as long as Fin could remember. How they remained that way was a mystery to him. He couldn't keep a new T-shirt clean for a morning without dripping or dropping something dark and stainworthy down it.

His feet finally scrubbed to his satisfaction, he looked up and said, 'Hello, Mr Jarvis. How are you?'

'I am well, thank you.' Jarvis flicked imaginary dust from his spotless white butler's gloves that almost shone in the golden light spilling out from the chandeliers glittering beneath the high ceilings. 'Your birthdays come around faster and faster. It seems like yesterday you were here last.'

12

He smiled, apparently happy with the condition of his gloved fingers. It was a tight expression. 'But then, time can be like that, can't it? All over the place … and here we are again. And you've got taller.'

Finmere smiled agreeably and wished the adults around him would make more sense. He undid his jacket as his face prickled with warmth. The house was hot. The house was always hot.

'Normal routine?' Ted asked.

'Of course,' Jarvis replied. 'Judge Brown is currently detained in a meeting, but he said he'd be back to catch up with the boy before he leaves.' He turned and led them down the long corridor. The carpet whispered under his feet and Finmere imagined his heart and breath keeping time with his steps. Orrery House always made him a little nervous, but there was a part of him that loved being there. A step and a blanket might not be much to cling on to, but a huge, ornate, obviously wealthy building filled with people who had for some reason chosen to look after him – admittedly in their own very odd way – that was a lot more solid.

He took his coat and hoodie off and hung them in the cloakroom by the vast curving staircase. 'Where would you like me to start?'

'The third floor tonight, Master Smith. I don't expect you to get much more done this evening.'

'Okay. Well, I'll just go up then.'

'Good lad.' Ted grinned. 'It's always right to give something back.' He winked. 'I think I'll go and find meself a cup of tea. There'll be a sandwich ready for when you're done, lad.'

'Thanks, Ted.'

Finmere started up the stairs, clinging to the thick mahogany banister.

'Oh, and Master Smith?' Jarvis stood ramrod-straight in his perfectly tailed jacket. 'Make sure you're done by 11.45 p.m. sharp. There's no room for lateness tonight.'

13

Fin nodded. 'Yes, Mr Jarvis.'

The third floor lay in hushed silence when Finmere reached it. In an alcove a large vase of stargazer lilies were in full bloom and their sweet scent filled the warm air. Unnumbered glossy white doors lined both sides of the corridor and as Fin stopped outside the first one on his left, he wondered again at the building's aversion to signs of any kind. Surely these rooms had to be numbered somewhere? People couldn't just say, 'Oh, could you pop up and give that room on the third floor a clean. You know the one, somewhere on the middle on the left?' It just wouldn't work. It didn't make sense. Every door at his school – *both* his schools – had some kind of number or letter on it to separate it from all the other identical doors. That was how things worked.

He sighed. Maybe adults just got weirder as they got older. And if there was one thing he could say about the adults at Orrery House, it was that they were definitely old. Taking a deep breath and fighting his awkwardness, he knocked on the first door and opened it. 'Hello?'

The light was dimmer inside, away from the myriad reflected glass chandeliers in the corridor. A man sat in a wheelchair by the bed. He didn't move, or speak. Fin wasn't surprised. The residents of the house rarely spoke when he was there, and they were invariably wheelchair-bound. 'It's me, Mr Everclear,' he said, 'Finmere Tingewick Smith? I come every year? On my birthday?' The elderly man didn't answer.

Fin felt stupid standing half in the room and half out and his feet propelled him forwards until he was standing in front of the room's occupier, who looked at least a hundred years old. His wizened body made Ted look like a giant in comparison. The old man's hair was barely there, just a few wisps of smoky candyfloss drifting over his leathery liver-spotted scalp. His face was thin, his cheekbones almost tearing through the wrinkled, papery skin, and his eyes peered vacantly from under half-closed lids.

14

Fin tried to smile, but as usual he felt uncomfortable – and it was getting worse every year. Part of the problem was that he wasn't quite sure if the near-comatose guests could hear him or feel him, and worse than that, he had no idea whether they were even happy for him to be there. The thought that maybe somewhere inside, these old men just wanted him to go away and leave them in peace always made him feel a little like an unwanted intruder. Still, he thought, this was what the Judge wanted him to do, and it was only once each year – and surely the Judge would know what was for the best, far more than him.

Each room was the same: on the small table beside the bed there sat a leatherbound black book that Fin presumed was a Bible, a tin of mints and a pad of paper with a fine, expensive fountain pen on top. The pad in this room was blank. A shaving set had been laid out on a carefully folded towel, next to a small bowl of water.

He picked up the soft towel and carefully tucked it around the old man's scrawny neck before beginning to work up a lather with the soft horsehair shaving brush. There were no spray foams or gels here; they liked their shaves done the old-fashioned way at Orrery House. Very gently, under his breath, Fin began to whistle while he worked. He figured it was better than silence.

It was amazing how something as simple as shaving could make your arms ache. Maybe it was the concentration needed to keep his hand from shaking and allowing the razor to nick the wrinkled skin, but by ten-thirty his back was hurting from stooping and his fingers felt as if he'd been writing all day at school without a break. On the up side, though, he'd done nearly the whole corridor, and he was well ahead of schedule. After carefully wiping the left-over foam from Mr Soames' face, Finmere stood back and stretched his spine.

'I think I'm done,' he whispered. 'I hope you like it.' Mr Soames had actually dozed off half an hour previously, after giving Fin a gummy smile, introducing himself and offering him a mint from his bedside tin. After that, he'd snored his way healthily through the shave. The vibrations from his stentorian breathing should have left his drooping jowls covered in razor-cuts, but Fin had managed to keep his hands steady. After all these years of practice he had become skilled at this strange task.

After rinsing out the bowl and razor, Fin left the shaving kit in the en-suite bathroom and crept back into the corridor. He let out a slight yawn. He was about to go into the next unnumbered room when something distracted him: a sound, breaking the solemn silence of the third floor. He stopped and listened. It was *whistling*. Someone else was whistling, down at the far end – and whoever was doing it was just as bad as he was. Finmere chewed his lip. It would be far more interesting to shave whoever was the owner of that whistle than another sleeping resident. Fin tried to make a mental note of which room he'd reached – two doors down from where the central chandelier hung – and followed the sound.

At the furthest end of the floor the corridor curved round to the right, and a large landing with another, smaller set of stairs only slightly less grand than those he had come up. Fin peered over the banister to the floor below and then upwards. Nothing. No one. The place was empty. Slightly confused, he walked back the way he'd come and after a couple of metres, paused.

That was odd: the whistling was coming from an alcove next to the last of the bedroom doors. A large vase of daffodils filled the space. Finmere stood in front of it and stared. Flowers didn't whistle – and even if they did, he didn't imagine they'd be whistling 'She'll Be Coming Round the Mountain When She Comes' quite so badly out of tune.

Peering all around to check that there really was no one

there and this wasn't some dumb birthday joke, he leaned forward and listened to the vase, his face flushing at the thought of how stupid he'd look if Jarvis or Ted happened to come by and check on him. He felt a sense of relief to discover that the sound was coming from somewhere *behind* the vase, rather than from the flowers themselves. In fact, it sounded as if it was coming from behind the solid wall ...

His curiosity fully engaged, he reached out and gave the smooth plaster a tentative push. Nothing happened – not that he really expected it to. But the whistling had to be coming from somewhere. Orrery House was not like Mrs Baker's lodging house down in Bermondsey, where he could often hear the baby next door crying all night. The walls here were too thick for anything like that, and more importantly, there weren't any buildings on either side. Orrery House stood alone.

He stared again at the innocent white surface. Behind it, the whistler was in full flow, having moved on to 'Ten Green Bottles'. Maybe if he moved the flowers out of the way, he'd be able to get a better look, or at least a better listen. He was ahead of schedule, so he'd got a good ten minutes to spare. And it *was* his birthday, after all.

Firmly gripping the large crystal vase, he lifted it and turned to put it down carefully on the carpet behind him. He was relieved to see that it balanced okay. He wasn't in a hurry to find out if water would stain that perfect white wool. He stood up straight again and turned back round—

And swore out loud – not very quietly.

The alcove had swung silently open, and in front of him now was the entrance to a narrow, low corridor that looked like it opened out into another bedroom. *A secret bedroom.*

The whistling stopped.

'Harlequin? Is that you?'

Finmere swallowed, his mouth suddenly dry. His birthday was definitely getting more interesting.

17

THREE

Not knowing what else to, Finmere stepped through the archway. 'Um, no. It's Fin. Finmere Tingewick Smith.'

The low ceiling made him duck a little before it opened outwards and upwards, revealing a room that looked something between a study and a bedroom. It was much bigger than any of the others, and although the table by the bed had the obligatory tin of strong mints and the black book, there was so much more.

An old man was sitting in a wheelchair at the desk, his legs covered with a thick checked blanket despite the heat that was so stifling Finmere could hardly breathe. He looked up and stared for what felt like a very long time. 'Finmere, you say?'

Fin nodded, trying to keep his eyes on the old man rather than wandering to the mahogany bookshelves lining one wall that were crammed with large red and green leatherbound volumes, or the strange items that cluttered the shelves and desk. It was particularly difficult, because several documents were held down by a paperweight that looked remarkably like a skull of some kind. Almost, but not quite human, Fin thought. It had very, very large eye sockets, not like anything he'd ever seen in the science labs. Something about it made him feel mildly uncomfortable, like whatever had once inhabited it could still see out of those empty sockets.

'I know it's a stupid name,' he managed eventually. 'I didn't choose it.'

The old man's brow furrowed as he lowered his glasses and

peered over them. His beard may have been white, but there was nothing sleepy about the sharpness of his gaze. 'Stupid, you say, do you?' He paused, and then burst into snorts of laughter. 'Well, you may be right. But it could have been worse. You ask Ted what your name would have been if you'd been left on that step a day later. You ask him that!'

Startled by the man's words, Finmere lost his awkwardness and frowned. 'Do you know me, then? I don't remember you and I'm sure I would. You're so much more ... well, *alive* than the others. And I don't remember this room—' He looked around, and then upwards. Constellations were painted on the ceiling. Fin blinked. It must have been tiredness, but he could have sworn that the clusters of stars and planets were actually twinkling. 'I'd definitely remember a room like this,' he breathed.

'Oh, I know you, Finmere, even if we haven't met before. As for this room ... well, I'm not entirely sure it *is* here. Some rooms are like time. Funny places.' He wheeled himself a little closer. 'It's your birthday, isn't it? How old are you now?'

'Sixteen.'

The man in the chair grinned and leaned backwards, folding his hands. A black and gold ring glittered on his finger. He let out a little chuckle, then sighed. 'Sixteen, eh? That's an interesting age for you. It's almost like you're stuck between two worlds.' He laughed softly as if at a private joke and shuffled beneath his blanket. A flash of metal was quickly hidden beneath the wool, but not before Fin had seen it. What was that? It looked like the hilt of a sword, but surely it couldn't be?

'You've the adventures of childhood on one side,' the old man continued, 'and the dangers of adulthood on the other.'

'Ted said something like that earlier,' Fin muttered.

'Well, of course he did.' The old man smiled. 'Of course he did.'

Fin wasn't sure what to say next. Who was this old man? And how did he know so much stuff about him and Ted?

A shadow fell across the doorway.

'Finmere?' There was a long pause. 'What on earth are *you* doing in here? Out at once!'

Pulse racing, Fin turned to face the Judge. 'Sorry, I was just—'

'Sorry, Harlequin,' the old man interrupted, 'it's my fault entirely. He heard me whistling.'

Fin thought he'd never seen someone so ancient looking quite so cheeky before. The Judge, on the other hand, had turned so purple that Finmere thought his narrow head might explode.

'*Whistling?*' Judge Brown finally spat the word out. 'Really! What on earth *were* you thinking?' He glared balefully at the old man before gripping Fin's shoulders to steer him out. 'Don't answer that. I know exactly what you were thinking.' He pointed a long bony finger at the smiling figure under the blanket. 'And you should know better.'

The Judge propelled Finmere out through the alcove, muttering indistinctly under his breath. Just before the room disappeared behind him, Fin twisted his neck round and gave the man a quick smile goodbye. The old man winked at him, and then he was gone.

'Don't move. Stay there.' The Judge's voice was firm as he stood Fin out by the stairs and went back to pick up the vase. Standing in the bright white corridor watching Judge Brown replace the daffodils and seal off the room again, Fin wasn't sure quite how he felt. Embarrassed? Yeah, a little. Guilty? Yes, that too – whatever it was, it didn't feel good. He'd seen the Judge mildly irritated, and mildly entertained, but he'd never seen him so worked up before, so animated.

Away from the starry ceiling and back in the reality of the third floor, Finmere's heart began to knock against his ribs. He'd been too ungrateful, and he'd poked his nose in where he shouldn't have, and now the Judge was angry: properly angry.

Finn's face began to burn. 'I'm really, really sorry,' he started, 'I really am. I know it's rude to be nosy in people's houses when you haven't been asked to and I know you're probably really, really angry with me and I know you have every right—' Somewhere inside his head he could hear the stream of panicked words, but he couldn't quite stop them pouring out. '—and I know I'm just an abandoned kid and I should be more respectful—'

Judge Brown stared at him. 'What did you say?'

'I said I know it's rude to be nosy and—'

The Judge's hand flew up, silencing him. 'Yes, yes, yes, I heard that bit.' His face had returned to its normal paleness, apart from two blotches high on his cheeks. 'The last thing you said.' He peered at Finmere, his thin lips so tight they'd almost disappeared. 'Did I hear you say "*abandoned*"? Did you refer to yourself as an "*abandoned*" boy?'

Fin nodded slowly. His cheeks felt like they were on fire. 'Yes, sir,' he murmured.

The Judge let out a long rattle of breath. 'Well, good Lord, boy, what on earth ever gave you the idea you were *abandoned*? I've never heard anything so ridiculous!' He stared hard at Fin, as if he'd never seen him before in his life. 'It's quite absurd. Boys who are abandoned get left in *telephone boxes* and *bus stops*,' the Judge started again. 'They do *not* get left on the steps of the Old Bailey.' He sounded distinctly put out. 'You were most certainly not *abandoned*, Finmere Tingewick Smith. You were *placed*.' He drew himself up to his full height, looked at Fin and raised an eyebrow. 'And that, my boy, is a *completely* different thing.'

Still mildly panicked, Fin's vision shimmered a little at the edges and his thought slipped out in words before he could stop it. 'What's the difference?'

'*What's the difference?*' The Judge's normally deep, resonant voice was now in danger of shattering the crystals hanging from the chandelier above them. *'What's the difference?* What on earth do they teach you at these schools you go to?' His eyes were boring into Fin, who was wishing quite desperately that the thick white carpet would just open up and swallow him whole.

Fin shrugged helplessly. 'Maths. English. At St Martin's we do Latin, but I'm not very good at that. And there's PE and RE. Oh, and PHSCE.'

Judge Brown looked perplexed, as if Finmere was talking in a foreign language. He sighed and scratched his head. 'PE? RE? And PHSCE? Have all the academic subjects in the world been reduced to mere acronyms? I'm not even quite sure what they mean.'

'We have History and Geography too. And Science. I like them all,' Fin mumbled, immediately regretting the lie and hoping that the Judge wouldn't spot it. He was angry enough already.

'Well, I suppose they all have their place in the world, but I'm just not sure of their place in *your* world.' Judge Brown pulled back the sleeve of his red robe and glanced at his watch. 'Oh, is that the time already? Where does it get to?'

Fin didn't answer. He was staring at the Judge's thin wrist as it disappeared into the red sleeve again. He thought he'd seen two faces on the heavy gold bracelet in the brief moment he'd glimpsed it, and one of them had looked decidedly odd. Why on earth would the Judge need two watches? His head pounded and his mouth tasted metallic with tiredness. His ears buzzed. This birthday was definitely the strangest out of sixteen strange celebrations.

'So, are you mad at me?' he mumbled. If the Judge was going to punish him, then he might as well get it out of the way sooner rather than later. Fear rumbled in the pit of his stomach.

'Angry?' The Judge leaned forward and peered at him. 'Of

course I'm not angry – a little concerned about what they're filling your head with at these educational establishments you attend, but not angry.' He sighed and headed towards the stairs.

Fin followed him, trying to hear what the Judge was muttering.

'One thing is becoming quite clear, though, it's time you knew a bit more than you do. I think we need to have a chat, you know, about growing up ...'

Fin's heart sank as he followed the Judge down the sweeping staircase towards the ground floor. He was *definitely* too old for this. 'Um, do you mean about the birds and the bees? Because if you do, we've pretty much got that covered at school.' It'd been bad enough having to listen to Mr Clarke at St Martin's stumbling through exactly where babies came from when he was thirteen without having to go through the horror of hearing it from Judge Brown as well. Sixteen might be nearly grown up, but it definitely wasn't grown up enough. He didn't think he'd *ever* be that grown up.

The Judge stopped on the first-floor landing, his red robe floating around his gaunt form, and looked Fin up and down. 'Birds and bees? Why on earth should they be important? And what could I possibly have to say about them? I think that's best left to your biology teacher, don't you?' He turned and continued down the stairs. 'No, I'm talking about you, Finmere. *Your* life – that's what we need to have a chat about.'

The rollercoaster Fin's nerves had been riding on took another downward tilt. 'Uh ... tonight, sir?'

'No, not now. There's not enough time.' Judge Brown's brow furrowed and his mouth twitched at the edges, as if for a moment his mind was occupied with something very pressing and important. Finally he fixed his eyes on Finmere once more. 'Tomorrow afternoon at two. Come to my apartment at The Rookeries. You'll find it on the corner of Cowcross

Street. Ask the woman on the desk for the Rookhaven Suite. She'll send you up.' He paused. 'You might have to be quite insistent.' He glanced at his strange wristwatch again. 'Goodness me, where does it go? It's probably time for you to find Ted and have some supper before heading home.' He smiled kindly, the expression breaking the normal severity of his face. 'And happy birthday, Finmere.'

'But sir,' Fin said, fighting a yawn, 'tomorrow's Thursday.'

'And?'

'Well, it's a school day. Couldn't I come after, at about six?' School finished at three, but he was supposed to be having a kick-about with Joe and some of the other boys at half past and he wouldn't be able to explain where he was going without telling a lie. And lies, as he'd discovered over the years, frequently much to his cost, were hard to keep track of.

'Hmmm. No.' The wrinkles in Judge Brown's face deepened, and his expression looked to Fin like a mixture of thought and confusion. 'No, it has to be two p.m. What school are you at this year?'

'Eastfields Comp.'

The Judge's face cleared. 'Oh, that's simple then. You'll be here in no time at all from Tower Bridge. Twenty minutes on the Tube, I would think. If you leave school at one you'll be in plenty of time.' He reached out to shake Fin's hand.

He had already taken a couple of steps away before Fin's voice stopped him. 'But I can't just bunk school for the afternoon.' He wondered for a moment just how much Judge Brown understood about the way the world really worked. 'I'll need a note or something. You know – to explain why I'm not in class.' Not that most boys bothered – if they wanted to blow school off, they just did. But Fin didn't like to draw attention to himself like that. Teachers always blamed him for his yearly absences as if he was actually truanting, instead of just obeying his guardians. He didn't need to add to the grief by doing it for real.

The Judge pursed his lips. 'Hmmm. I'm not sure a note would be wise. Or entirely necessary. After all, I see children every day in the Oxford Street shops who should surely be in school. If they can do it, I don't see why you can't.' He nodded, the matter settled. 'I'll see you tomorrow. At two. Don't be late.'

And with that Judge Harlequin Brown marched off, muttering under his breath, his gleaming leather shoes whispering against the carpet until he disappeared behind his study door.

Finmere sighed for what felt like the thousandth time since he'd met up with Ted on the Old Bailey steps that evening. Thursday afternoon was Maths and English, and there was no way he was going to get out of them without being noticed. He was top of both classes.

He grimaced slightly, preparing himself for the detentions that were going to be coming his way because as much as he hated the idea of bunking school, he knew he didn't have any choice. He was far more nervous of Judge Harlequin Brown than he was of anyone – pupils or teachers – at Eastfields Comprehensive.

Standing there in the hushed silence of Orrery House on the night of his sixteenth birthday, Finmere felt as if the weight of the world was on his shoulders. He'd hoped that as he'd got older his life would get less complicated, but it didn't look like that was going to be the case, at least not this year.

He yawned, padding down the stairs into the basement where the kitchen was situated, and where no doubt Ted was keeping warm by the old range and smoking a roll-up without a care in the world. It must be nice to be Ted, he thought as the carpet gave way to huge slabs of stone. Ted always seemed so comfortable with himself and the world around him. Fin couldn't imagine anything worrying Ted too much. Maybe that was part of becoming an adult. Or maybe that was just part of being Ted. Thinking of Ted made him think of the old man in the secret room behind the wall, and that made him smile. This birthday hadn't been all bad.

He pushed open the heavy wooden kitchen door and stepped into the stifling heat at the heart of the house. The smell of freshly baked bread hit him with the rising temperature and he realised he was absolutely starving.

It was gone midnight by the time Ted quietly shut the front door of Orrery House behind them and walked with Finmere up the path and into the silent, empty square. The forbidding iron streetlamps sent down pools of yellow light that made the shadows of the trees and bushes appear even darker and more sinister. Fin watched his breath pour out in a grey mist.

'Let's find you a cab then, Fin.' Ted's voice was low and his head twitched from side to side for a moment before his shoulders relaxed. Finmere wondered if perhaps he too was a little bit spooked by the crazy shapes in the gloom around them that hinted at ghosts and monsters and all the things that Fin knew didn't exist but was scared of tempting Fate by disbelieving in them completely. He shivered. The freezing air felt even colder after the baking heat of the house.

Thinking of the house, he paused and frowned. 'Ted,' he said, 'why didn't we just ring a cab from the house? Surely that would have been easier?' He paused. 'And cheaper.'

Ted grinned. 'Always wanting answers, eh, Fin? Good job you and the Judge are 'aving that chat tomorrow – not a moment too soon, if you ask me.' The old man picked up the pace, striding towards the brightly lit main road, and Finmere had to trot to keep up.

How did Ted know he was meeting Judge Brown tomorrow? Fin hadn't said anything about it. Another odd incident to add to the barrage of oddness on a traditionally odd day. He was getting very tired of everyone else knowing more about his life than he did. Still, that was the way it had always been, and he really should be used to it by now. He watched as two black cabs sped by, reacting to the lack of traffic like caged animals given the freedom of the open plains.

Ted peered off into the distance as they approached the busy T-junction with Aldersgate Road. ''ere we are, Fin. We'll 'ave a cabbie stopping in no time at all.' He pulled a white handkerchief out of his pocket and wiped his nose. 'Cor, it's cold. This winter's going to be an 'ard one, Fin, you mark my words.' He grinned. ''ope you've got some long johns in that trunk of yours.'

Fin snorted. 'Yeah, right. That'd go down a storm at school.'

Ted waggled his eyebrows. 'Don't know what you're missing, mate. Nice and snug, long johns.'

Fin smiled. 'I'll take your word for it.'

They stood in companionable silence for a moment, Ted scouting for an empty cab, while Fin gazed up at the black sea of the night. Stars flashed and twinkled across the sky, dipping in and out of its inky surface. He thought of the room tucked behind the wall of Orrery House.

'You know my name, Ted?' He watched his breath dance away up to the smiling moon. 'What would it have been if I'd been left at the Old Bailey a day later?'

'Now what would make you ask a question like that?'

Fin lowered his gaze and found Ted watching him, and for a brief second he thought he saw something else underneath that amiable appearance he'd always known: something different. Something *not Ted*. And then it was gone, like a breath in the night air, and it was just Ted standing freezing on a London street corner and grinning at him.

Fin shrugged. 'I met an old man back at the house. He told me to ask you. He laughed about it.'

'As it happens, I suppose it is quite funny,' Ted said eventually. 'You know 'ow you was left on the steps on the night of the eleventh of November, and I made your name from the first three cases that was to come up against the Crown the next day?'

Finmere nodded. Ted had told him this on his seventh birthday, and he'd even shown him a copy of the court circular for that day: The Crown vs Finmere, The Crown vs Tingewick and the Crown vs Smith.

'Well,' Ted continued, 'if you'd appeared on the steps the next night, your name would have been Lesley Hogg Boyle.' He let out a laugh and nudged Finmere hard in the ribs. 'So 'ow's that for a name?'

Lesley Hogg Boyle. Life would have been awful at Eastfields Comp with a name like that. Sheer bloody hell. And it probably wouldn't have been that great at St Martin's either. Piggy Boyle, that's what they'd have called him – if he was lucky.

A yellow light appeared in the distance. Ted let out a long whistle and flagged it down. 'So next time you think your name's a bit odd, just think 'ow much worse it could've been, eh?'

The cab chugged to a halt at the kerb. 'That's what the old man said,' Fin muttered.

'Sounds like a sensible kind of bloke.' Ted pulled a twenty pound note from the pocket of his jacket. 'For the fare and tip.'

Fin took it awkwardly as he opened the taxi door and climbed in. 'Thanks for the cake and everything, Ted. I guess I'll see you again next year.' A moment of panic gripped him unexpectedly. 'You will still come for my birthday, won't you Ted? Even if you're retired?' The thought of not seeing the old man's familiar face again hit him suddenly like a low punch to the belly. He was as close to family as Fin had.

Ted pulled a roll-up from his tin and lit it. 'You don't lose me so fast, Fin, don't you worry.' He winked and pushed the door shut.

Fin leaned forward and pulled the side window down.

'Look after yourself, Ted.'

The old man grinned and then banged on the driver's door, letting him know he could go. Fin sat back in his seat as the cab pulled out into the road, and then twisted round to peer behind him. The space where Ted had been standing was empty. He watched for a couple of seconds, his heart sinking slightly, and then tiredness overwhelmed him and his mouth stretched wide in a yawn, his vision blurring.

'Where to, son?'

'Pardoner Street, Bermondsey,' he said through the yawn. 'Please.'

The driver nodded and fell back into silence. Finmere shivered and wished the cab was warmer. His eyelids burned and he let them slip shut. Just for a second.

Within less than a minute, he was fast asleep.

FOUR

Staring at the hands of the clock slowly ticking round to one o'clock, Fin stifled a yawn and really hoped that whatever the Judge was planning to tell him, it would be worth it. The day was not going well so far, and he hadn't even bunked the afternoon yet.

His eyes burned slightly and with the yawn refusing to die in his chest, he kept his head down, trying to be invisible. Not that invisibility took much skill in this class. Mr Settle was trying hard to get the life- and death-dates of Henry VIII's six wives up on the whiteboard, but every time he turned his back, paper balls flew across the room to the accompaniment of sniggers and muttered insults.

Mr Settle was new and Fin thought he'd feel a bit sorrier for him if he wasn't such a wimp. The Year Elevens were already feeling the strain of the exams at the end of the year, although most of them showed it by doing less work than their normal low output, or upping the aggro they gave out. To make matters work, Fin's class had KayleighTrent, who had point-blank refused to give Mr Settle her phone, or spit her gum out. For a terrible moment the teacher looked as if he was about to burst into tears, but thankfully he pulled himself together and gave her detention instead. He'd muttered something about calling her mother and Kayleigh had sucked her teeth and sworn at him and Mr Settle had pretended not to hear – either that or he was deaf, because Fin was on the other side of the room, and he'd definitely heard what she'd said.

Another paper ball bounced across the classroom and Fin looked back up at the clock. Four minutes to go until lunchtime. A knot tightened in his stomach. He was already in trouble. God only knew how much worse it was going to get.

He'd overslept after his late night at Orrery House and it was only after he'd got to school that he'd remembered that his Geography coursework was still under his bed. So not only was he ten minutes late getting to the class, but he'd then had to admit that he couldn't produce his work.

Old Boggy Marsh had sighed, a long-drawn-out breath of air, and peered over the top of his bifocal glasses before declaring that he would see Finmere at 3.30 p.m. sharp back in his classroom. 'Or Else.'

Fin's heart had sunk. An 'Or Else' from Mr Settle would mean nothing – no one gave a fart about what *he* thought – but Mr Marsh was ancient; he'd been at Eastfields for *ever*; twenty years at least. He'd taught most of the kids' mums and aunts and uncles. Mr Marsh was as much a part of Eastfields Comprehensive as the graffiti on the sign outside, that reappeared like magic every time someone tried to scrub it off. An 'Or Else' from Boggy Marsh was definitely worth taking note of. It wasn't like he was one of those teachers who would scream at you to reappear in their classrooms at break or lunch, *come hell or high water*, and promptly forget about it ten minutes later. Boggy Marsh remembered *everything*.

It was with a sick feeling in the pit of his stomach that Fin had taken his seat in Geography. Four hours later, as Mr Settle shouted over the din to tell them to pack away, that queasy feeling was still there.

'And don't forget,' Mr Settle repeated for the seventeenth time, or so it sounded like, as he slumped against the edge of his desk, 'essays due in tomorrow.' His words barely carried over the shrieks of the escaping horde of Year Eleven students. Finmere was pretty sure no huge pile of coursework was going to appear like a miracle on his desk the next day, but he was going to be in enough trouble this week as it was; somehow he'd find a way to do his when he got back from seeing the Judge.

Leaving Mr Settle to rest his head in his hands and wonder what fit of madness was upon him when he took the job at Eastfields, Fin fought his way through the sea of blue jumpers, kids battling each other to get to the canteen for some food or to the toilets for a cigarette. As he allowed himself to be caught up in the riotous crowd, he thought of St Martin's, where the corridors were oceans of calm, with everyone keeping to the left and no one running. They didn't even have bells to signal the start and end of lessons, breaks or lunchtimes. Fin couldn't imagine Eastfields trying to operate without bells. It was hard enough to get the kids into the classroom with them – it would be downright impossible without.

Finmere ducked left into the Maths corridor. The bank of lockers was almost visible at the other end. There were good bit and bad bits in both schools – Eastfields had girls, which was a definite plus, not that he'd gone out with many of them – well, two to be exact – but he couldn't imagine two places more different. No wonder his brain felt scrambled most of the time.

Crouching by his locker, he rummaged in his pocket for the small key. At least his door hadn't been dented yet this term – that was one advantage to being on the bottom row. It wasn't fist-height.

'You took your time. I'm bloody starving. Come on!' Joe's dark brown face was peering down at him. His shirt was untucked and tie loosened, just like Fin's was – like every self-respecting student wore their uniform.

'I thought you had detention with Dickface Davies?'

Joe laughed. 'Yeah, but I was never going – not at lunch-time.' He grinned, a warm, open expression that looked just like his mum's. Sometimes Fin went for tea at Joe's and Mrs

Manning would smile just like that – a little bit cheeky, but nothing nasty in it. Finmere wondered about his own smile, and if he looked more like his mum or his dad when he did it, but all he saw in his head when he tried to think about things like that was a grey, empty space with Judge Harlequin Brown floating in it like a dark shadow in the background.

'We've got him before break tomorrow,' Joe continued, oblivious to Fin's distraction. 'He can get me for it then.'

Fin had barely shoved his books in his locker before Joe was tugging him to his feet. 'C'mon, let's get some chips before they're all gone.'

Fin's stomach turned. He'd thought the day couldn't get any worse, but here it was – getting worse right in front of him. 'Look, Joe, I can't. I've got some stuff I need to do.'

'No worries. I'll come with you. But let's get food first. My stomach feels like my throat's been cut.'

Fin could feel his face redden as heat prickled his hair line. 'Um, this is stuff I've got to do by myself.' He shrugged help-lessly.

Joe's grin faltered. 'What kind of stuff?'

'Private stuff.' His throat dried. 'Family stuff.' There. The lie was out.

Joe's eyes widened and Fin could see that chips had been very much forgotten for a moment. 'Is this to do with your dad?' His voice dropped to a reverential whisper.

Finmere gave a slight nod. Why hadn't Joe gone to his detention like he was supposed to? At least then the lying could have been put off until later.

Joe closed the gap between them. 'What's he done now?'

Fin stepped away, pulling on his coat. 'Look, I really can't talk about it, Joe, you know?' He left the question hanging. 'But I've got to go. I'll see you tomorrow.'

'Where are you going? Don't tell me you're bunking off!' Shock killed off the whisper and Joe's voice was back to its loud best.

'*Shhh!*' Fin whispered, 'no need to tell everyone!' He tried to grin at Joe, but his face didn't seem to be working properly. 'Look, I'll see you tomorrow, yeah?' His feet felt heavy as lead as he started to push his way through the other kids, heading for the exit. He hated leaving his friend standing there looking confused and left out.

'Hey!' Joe called after him, 'hey, Fin! We're supposed to be playing footie after school! *Hey!*'

The hurt in his voice made Finmere flinch, but he kept moving. Joe would get over it by the morning – he was like that; he wasn't one to hold a grudge. He always saw the best in people. Somehow that thought made Finmere feel worse.

Rather than stroll out through the main gates where there were bound to be teachers on duty, Fin trotted round the side of the building, through the tunnel below Food Technology, nodding at the hardened smokers loitering there before scurrying out through the small side gate next to the bicycle racks.

Out on the pavement he pulled off his tie and shoved it into his pocket, then zipped up his jacket so that it almost covered his chin. Head down, as much for protection against the cold wind as for camouflage against being recognised by any staff who might have popped out for a quick pint, he strode in the direction of London Bridge Tube. It was a good ten minutes away and Finmere walked fast, anxious to put some distance between him and the school. He didn't know why he was so jittery: kids blew off class all the time. But he liked to keep his head beneath the teachers' radar. Life was quieter that way. It was easier to avoid awkward questions he couldn't answer.

Buses chugged out huge, impatient breaths of blue stench as they huffed and puffed slowly along the road beside him, occasionally pulling forward ahead by a few metres in a flurry of movement and then sitting idle in the long queue of cars and taxis while Fin overtook them.

Despite the detentions and trouble coming his way, and the catch-up work he was going to have to do, Fin couldn't help but feel a sense of exhilarating freedom as he took the steps down into the underground station. And anyway, he thought, checking his Oyster card was topped up, it wasn't as if skiving school had exactly been his choice. Judge Brown had pretty much told him to do it, which he figured was kind of like having that slip filled in showing parent/guardian's consent, just without him actually taking it into school.

FIVE

Fifteen minutes and one uneventful change later, Finmere climbed out of the warm belly of London at Farringdon Tube Station and paused to get his bearings before turning up Cowcross Street. He wondered whether it was something to do with having been abandoned there, but he never got lost in the Square Mile of the City of London. Wherever he was heading, his feet just naturally found their way. Or maybe it was just because the blanket he'd been wrapped in was safely hidden here, and that made it as close to an actual home as he had.

He walked the length of the street until he came to the junction with St Peter's Lane and stopped by the small oval sign hanging above a wooden door: he had arrived at The Rookeries. He smiled. At least this building conformed to the rules about letting people know exactly what it was – the only problem Fin had with this particular sign was that beneath the name, painted in flowing, understated letters, was the word 'Hotel'. The Judge had said he had an apartment here, but surely no one would have a flat in a hotel?

He bit his bottom lip and studied the grey brick building that curved up the full length of the tiny cobbled alley that was St Peter's Street. Large sash windows stared down at him, the polished glass glinting in the afternoon sunshine. Seeing no other real option, he stepped up to the door and pushed it open. If this wasn't the right place, then at least they might be able to tell him where he should be.

As he stepped into the reception area, he shut the heavy door quietly behind him. Standing inside the hotel, he felt quite uncomfortable, and suddenly very young. The high walls were panelled in polished wood. On his left, a fire roared and crackled in an ornate iron grate. Two wing-backed chairs with plump satin cushions sat on either side of the hearth, waiting for someone to be brave enough to sit in them. They looked old and very valuable to Fin's unpractised eye. A long ornate rug – Persian, Fin guessed – stretched out luxuriously from in front of the fire, almost reaching the receptionist's desk.

The desk was simply that: a large, leather-covered beast of wood standing on thick carved legs. Behind it, illuminated by the soft light thrown out from a large green lamp, two women concentrated on writing on thick sheets of paper, pausing only to dip their pens in an old-fashioned inkwell. The older woman occasionally looked over to check the younger woman's work.

Fin's scuffed school shoes tapped out his progress as he walked slowly across the stone-flagged floor, but neither woman looked up. After standing awkwardly in front of them for a moment, Fin coughed. The younger receptionist woman raised her head and smiled questioningly, putting down her strange pen. Finmere stared at it for a second. He thought only school kids wrote with pens like that, and even then, only in exercise books. As far as he could tell, as soon as you were an adult all your writing was done on a computer. That was his teachers' excuses for their own bad handwriting, at any rate. But the reception desk at the Rookeries didn't even have a PC, which was a little odd.

'Can I help you?' The woman's smile was a little tight, as if she was wondering how on earth a scruffy teenager had wandered into their beautifully antique establishment. She frowned as she took in his muddy black trousers, unpolished shoes and white shirt poking out from under his jumper.

'Shouldn't you be at school?' The older woman beside her still hadn't looked up, just muttered sums under her breath as she carefully wrote some figures down on the headed paper.

'Um, Finmere Tingewick Smith,' he said. The woman's face remained nonplussed. She had quite a disconcerting gaze, and Fin found himself picking nervously at the sleeve of his jacket and glancing up at the round mahogany-encased clock hanging from the wall behind the desk. 'Er ... Judge Harlequin Brown told me I had to meet him here. At two p.m. sharp.' The clock declared that he had a few minutes to spare.

The woman ducked her blonde head and ran a perfect fingernail down the page of a brown leatherbound ledger. She looked up. 'I'm afraid we have no one of the name Brown staying with us at the moment.' She promptly returned her attention to the work she'd been doing when he'd arrived.

Fin watched her for a moment, not quite sure how to proceed. But the Judge had said to be firm. 'I'm sorry,' he started, trying to keep his voice steady, 'but this is The Rookeries, isn't it?'

Sighing, the blonde woman looked up again. 'Yes, of course it is. Didn't you see the sign?'

Fin nodded. 'But is it the only Rookeries on Cowcross Street?'

She stared at him blankly. 'It would be a little confusing if there was more than one of them, wouldn't you say?'

'Then this has to be the place,' he said quietly, not wanting to be rude, but needing to stand his ground. He stepped slightly forward. 'Do you think you could check your register again, please? He's a Judge. Judge Harlequin Brown. He said I should ask for the Rookhaven Suite.'

'Well, that settles it.' She had obviously lost all patience with him. 'We don't even have a Rookhaven Suite!' She put her hands on her hips and glared at him as if he had committed a crime of some sort.

The elder woman stopped muttering and looked up. She

ran a cold, appraising gaze over Finmere, then she stood up straight and smoothed her skirt. 'Heather, be a dear and go and make us a nice pot of Earl Grey tea, will you?'

'But—' Heather tried to object.

'Now, Heather.' The old woman's voice was dry and clear and Fin recognised it as the kind of voice you just didn't argue with. Her steely-grey hair was pulled back so tightly into a bun that the corners of her eyes looked slightly misshapen. Or maybe it was just the thick line of make-up that gave that impression. She waited until the other woman had completely disappeared before stepping out from behind the desk and raising an immaculately plucked eyebrow. 'The Rookhaven Suite?'

She stared at him and Finmere swallowed and nodded, wishing the floor would open and eat him up. Then the clock on the wall softly chimed out two p.m. and the woman sighed.

'I suppose you'd better follow me.' Her body was stick-thin, and under her trim suit she wore thick brown tights and sensible black shoes. 'We wouldn't want to keep the Judge waiting, would we?' She turned and marched briskly across the rug towards a door Fin hadn't noticed, set into the wooden panelling behind one of the antique chairs.

'But that lady said you didn't have a Rookhaven Suite.'

'As far as that lady is concerned,' she said, twisting the door handle, 'we don't.'

Once again wondering at the strangeness and secrecy of the adult world, Finmere followed her through a long scarlet room with an enormous dining table in the middle, and another roasting fire filling a massive grate at the far end. A high corner table held a vase of bright lilies, and the scent filled the air just enough, but not too much. Fin counted ten carved chairs along one side of the table, and his eyes widened as he took in the glittering crystal glasses, highly polished silver cutlery and symmetrical fans of bright white linen napkins at every place setting.

'This is amazing,' he breathed. It was even more impressive than the dining room at St Martin's, and that was pretty stunning.

'We do our best,' the woman said, sounding all matter-of-fact, as she opened another door and ushered Finmere into what had to be the library or drawing room, or something else that he'd thought only existed in the Dickens novels he was forced to read in English, or those endless Victorian dramas they showed on TV every Christmas. Here there were several old-fashioned armchairs as well as two or three small desks, each with a lamp glowing next to a broadsheet newspaper and a small notepad and pen, in the identical place on each. Fin wondered how the people who stayed here ever plucked up the nerve to touch anything. Maybe they didn't. Maybe that's why it all looked so perfect.

Beside an open grate sat a small brass bucket of pine cones, and there must have been some already on the fire because if Fin had to rely on smell alone he'd have thought he was in a woodcutter's hut in a forest somewhere ... not that he'd ever been in a woodcutter's hut, but he'd loved fairy tales when he was little and he'd read enough to be able to imagine what that would smell like: warm, crisp and clean, just like this room ...

'Shut the door behind you, then.' She peered at him impatiently from beside one of the bookshelves.

'Oh, yes. Sorry.' Fin did as he was told. His palms felt slightly clammy, as if he were suddenly under the watchful scrutiny of Boggy Marsh rather than a stranger. He had a feeling that Mr Marsh would like this woman. He'd probably think she had just what it took to be a teacher back in the days he was always going on about, when teaching was all about discipline and chucking board rubbers at kids without any of this namby-pamby 'caring' rubbish.

It was only when the door from the dining room clicked firmly shut under his hand that the woman turned her arched gaze from Fin and back to the bookshelf. Stretching high, she ran her fingers along the top shelf until she reached the spine of a thick blue volume. Her sensibly trimmed fingernails gripped it and for a moment it looked as if she were going to take the book down, but instead she just tilted it towards her about forty-five degrees and then pushed it back. Her thin lips pursed with concentration to the point where they had almost disappeared as her fingers crept further along the shelf until she reached an old brown book whose spine was faded with age. She didn't pull that one right out either, but repeated the same tilting movement she'd done with the first.

Finmere stared. What on earth was she doing? She muttered under her breath as she searched out a third book then gave a relieved sigh and moved on to the more accessible shelves below. She moved more quickly after that, her hands a flurry of precise movements, selecting first one book and then another, in no apparent order, tilting each forward and then letting it slide back, until eventually she straightened up and smiled. It wasn't a warm smile, Fin decided, merely that of a job well done.

She smoothed invisible creases out of her skirt once again and ran a careful hand over her scraped-back bun to make sure none had escaped. Fin didn't think her hair would ever dare let itself get messy. Her bun was probably stapled into her head. For a brief moment Fin's head was full of a vision of her in an old-fashioned nightdress, fixing her hair firmly in place with a wall stapler like they used at school to put work displays up on the boards – and then thankfully it dissipated as he heard a series of clicks.

He looked around, trying to place the noise, when he realised that just at the place where the shelves met the fireplace, something was happening. There was a gap of maybe three centimetres, and the bookcase moving outwards slightly, as if the wall was letting out a small sigh. Fin was finding it hard to breathe at all. *A secret doorway*. Another *secret doorway*. His head was spinning.

With one hand gripped tightly round the edge, the woman allowed the bookshelf to swing silently open. 'Well, come on then.' She stared at Fin. 'I've got the accounts to do. I can't stand around here all day.'

Fin shook himself and stepped forward, peering into the newly appeared space. His eyes widened. He'd always thought that secret passageways would be dank and gloomy, and lit with spluttering candles or smoky gas lamps high on the walls, with maybe a rat or two scurrying past your feet. Instead, he was looking into a small square hallway. On the wall opposite was a coat rack and from it hung a long black mac, a red silk robe and a wig.

To his right was a thick wooden staircase that led straight up, then twisted to one side about ten metres up, and an old-fashioned Tiffany lamp hung down, giving out a very bright twenty-first century halogen glow. The hallway was warm, and not damp at all. The carpet was thick and white, just like the one at Orrery House. Fin felt a vague disappointment.

'And take your shoes off,' the receptionist added.

But at the first sight of the carpet, even before she'd started speaking, Fin had automatically started working the heel of one shoe off with the toe of the other. The woman nodded her approval. 'When the Judge has finished with you, you'll need to pull this lever here to get out.' She pointed at an old silver handle at the open edge of the doorway or bookcase or whatever it was. 'If it doesn't open immediately, that will be because there is a guest in the library and therefore the door will remain locked until the library is empty. Do you understand?'

Fin nodded, although, as usual, he was not entirely sure that he did. How was a door supposed to know that there was someone in the room? Secret cameras? Motion sensors, like in James Bond? It was all a little strange for a hotel that didn't even have a computer.

'If you have to wait too long,' she continued, 'then pull the lever twice in quick succession. That will call me from the desk and I'll clear the room. The door will work after that.' She stared at him coolly. 'But there is no need for impatience. Do not disturb me unless you have to wait a very, very long time.'

As she stepped back into the library she turned to Fin. 'As it is, most of our guests are out at meetings in the City all day.'

Fin thought he would happily wait in that small hallway until hell froze over, rather than pull that lever twice. 'Aren't you going to show me where to go?' he mumbled.

Her eyes flashed wide. 'I would have thought that would be obvious.' Forest fires could have sparked from the dryness in her voice. She pointed a too-straight bony finger towards the stairs. 'Upwards, boy. Upwards.'

And with that the door shut, leaving him facing a smooth wall, papered over just like the rest in a thick cream embossed with a pale golden fleur-de-lys. Of course, Finmere thought as he turned. Upwards.

The smooth wooden banister felt almost warm under his fingertips. Fin gripped it and began to climb the stairs. He could feel the thick carpet through his school socks, which for once had no holes in them. What kind of a place was this to live? Or maybe it was just where the Judge worked. Even so, it was still very odd: people didn't live behind secret door-ways in strange hotels where they weren't even listed. The world didn't work that way – or at least it hadn't, until he'd found the secret room in Orrery House the night before. Now strange secret passageways were popping up everywhere.

From the top step he followed a hallway to where it opened out into a larger area. There were four wooden doors, and a spiral staircase clinging to one corner.

'Um, hello? Judge Brown?' His voice sounded too loud in the quiet. He shuffled from one socked foot to the other. What if the Judge wasn't here? What if he'd got held up in court? That would just about finish Fin's day off – going through all that trouble at school, and not even knowing what it was that the Judge wanted to tell him.

'Hello?' he called, a little louder this time, trying not to sound too nervous.

'Finmere? Is that you?' Judge Harlequin Brown's voice floated down from above somewhere.

Fin smiled in relief. 'Yes, it's me.'

'Well, my boy, come up then. I'm in my study.'

Fin followed the tight curve of the narrow spiral staircase to the next floor. It made his head spin slightly. The Judge must be more sprightly than he looked if he ran up and down those stars all day, he thought – but then, the Judge's study was behind a secret doorway in a very peculiar hotel in the middle of Clerkenwell. Taking all things into consideration, Finmere was beginning to think that maybe there was more to Judge Brown than just the sombre, almost scarily serious man in a wig and red robe whom he saw once a year on his birthday.

The door at the end of the short corridor was slightly ajar, and Fin knocked.

'Come in, come in,' called the Judge, and Fin pushed it open and stepped inside.

'Good afternoon, your honour,' he said, wondering why his mouth felt dry. In the centre of the room was a huge desk, piled high with books and buff folders tied with pink ribbons. Small patches of the leather top came up for air between the mounds of clutter.

On the other side, Judge Harlequin Brown sat in a heavy chair. He peered at Fin over the glasses sitting low on his nose. 'Two o'clock exactly. Well done.' His eyes were sharp within their wrinkled surrounds. 'Time is funny enough without people being late.'

44

'Yes, sir,' Fin said, wondering as usual what on earth the Judge was talking about. Maybe time turned funny when you got old, but as far as Fin could see, it was pretty straightforward: seconds turned into minutes, minutes turned into hours, and so on, all very orderly and well-behaved.

'Pour the tea, Finmere. I need to finish signing these documents before we talk.'

As he nodded agreement, Fin glanced around. The room was hexagonal, and Fin thought it must be right at the top of the building, in the spire somewhere. He thought of the two women doing sums at that other desk so far below him and for a moment it felt like he was in another world. Then he spotted the teapot, sitting on a silver tray on a low table near one of the windows. He poured some milk into both cups, careful not to spill, and filled them with steaming liquid, pale and scented – the same tea the two women downstairs would be drinking: Earl Grey.

'Take a look out of the window.' The Judge didn't look at him but continued scratching signatures and notes on important-looking pieces of paper. 'I think you'll enjoy the view.'

Fin left the cups on the silver tray and wandered over to one of the windows. Despite the grey sky above, he grinned. It was amazing. The higgledy-piggeldy outlines of London's roofs lay spread out before him, arched, domed, slanty and pointy, clinging to each other or standing proud, the huge variety of clashing details reflecting the ages of the city.

He gasped slightly as his eyes fell on the familiar statue standing proud from the top of a building over to his left. 'I can see the Old Bailey from here!' he exclaimed. 'The statue of the lady with the scales.'

Behind him, Judge Brown chuckled. 'Marvellous, isn't she? So few people ever think to look up. They go through all their lives looking down or straight ahead. It's a continual source of surprise to me.' He tutted. 'Quite a waste. Can you see St Paul's?'

Fin's nerves were for a moment forgotten as he took in the glory of the London skyline, he cried, 'Yes! Yes, I can see the dome. It's fantastic!'

'That's good,' Judge Brown said softly. 'As long as you know where those two buildings are, you can't go far wrong. Sometimes in the evenings, when I have time to reflect, I like to stand at that window and look out. It gives me a sense of place and perspective. It reminds me of what's important.'

His sad tone made Fin turn round.

The old man was gazing almost wistfully out of the window, before he noticed Fin watching him and collected himself. Sitting himself firmly upright in his chair, he said, 'Well now, bring that tea over and sit, Finmere.' His voice was forthright once more, and Fin was glad. He liked to know Judge Harlequin Brown was stiff and serious and a touch dull. Anything else worried him.

He set the cups down carefully on a hastily cleared space on the desk and pulled a chair up so that he was facing the Judge. The carvings on the straight back dug into his spine slightly and he shuffled to get comfortable.

Judge Brown leaned forward, his thin hands clasped on the surface of the desk, one arm resting on a folder, and Fin's heart thumped a little louder as he looked at it. This one was tied with a black ribbon, not pink, and even though it was upside down he could clearly make out his own name printed on the top left hand corner. He swallowed hard. Were all his school reports in there? What other kinds of record would the Judge keep? Doctors? Dentists? Did he and all the other old men – those who were awake at any rate – study the file occasionally and decide whether Fin was still worth looking after? His stomach twisted in knots again and he thought he might heave.

'Now, Finmere' – the Judge settled his glasses slightly less precariously on the edge of his thin nose – 'you're sixteen now, and that's an important age. You're on the cusp of adulthood: between one world and another. Exciting times. But also' – he lowered his voice and looked around, as if checking they were alone – 'serious times.'

Fin frowned. Ted was saying something similar to him the previous evening.

The Judge took a sip of tea, then continued, 'And it is probably about time you knew a little more about who you are and where you come from.' He shook his head slightly. 'Abandoned indeed! Whatever possessed you to think such a thing?'

Fin shrugged, not sure what to say. 'I just thought … you know …' He let the sentence trail off, punctuating it with another helpless lift of the shoulders, but it was obvious from the Judge's perplexed expression that he didn't have the first clue as to what Fin had thought.

'Well, needless to say, you were most certainly *not* abandoned.' The Judge cleared his throat. 'You were *placed*. Here. Somewhere. Where you would be safe.' He stared with such intensity that Finmere had no choice but to nod. The chair felt very hard and very awkward under him. Safe from what?

'You see, Finmere—' He paused, and steepled his fingers. 'Things are either nowhere, or they're somewhere. Do you see? And you were left somewhere. Rather than nowhere. And we're none of us sure which of the two you belong in. Or maybe you belong in both.'

Fin didn't imagine that the Judge could be more awkward if he was in fact trying to explain the birds and the bees and where babies came from before they were found on the steps of the Old Bailey.

'Oh, it's all so difficult to explain – but I'm sure you're getting the gist of it.' He looked up hopefully. 'Aren't you?'

Fin's head ached slightly. 'Yes sir,' he said. He badly needed to make the Judge more relaxed, for both their sakes. 'Somewhere and nowhere.'

'Exactly!' Judge Brown exclaimed. 'I knew you'd see. You're a bright boy, Finmere Tingewick Smith. Your educators appear to have done you proud.' He let out a long, happy sigh. 'And now that you're sixteen, it's probably time you had this.' He untied the folder and pulled out a small item from a paper pocket on the inside. He slid it across the table and Fin picked it up and rolled it between his fingers for a moment, savouring the feel of it. He didn't think he'd ever seen anything quite like it before.The gold and black ring had a deep jade green stone at its centre and felt heavy in his hand, as if it were made of a metal mined so long ago that it carried the weight of its age with it.

'It was with you in your cardboard box – that's how we knew, d'you see? Ted saw it and brought you to me straight away. I knew we'd have to keep you safe.'

The Judge's voice had softened and Fin let it wash over him, half-listening, as he pushed the ring onto his middle finger. It was slightly too big, but he wanted to wear it. Now he had a blanket, a big strange house to visit once a year, and a ring. He didn't know if he wanted to laugh or cry at this sudden addition to the small collection of solid things he had of his own.

A memory clicked in Fin's head and he found it was whistling the tune 'She'll Be Coming Round the Mountain When She Comes'. 'I saw a ring like this,' he breathed. 'In the house last night.' The old man in the alcove had been wearing a ring just like this one, or very close, Finmere was sure of it.

Judge Brown raised an eyebrow. 'It wouldn't surprise me if you did. But these things can't be helped.' He leaned back in his chair, taking another sip of his tea. The lines in his forehead had relaxed a little.

'Well, I must say I feel quite relieved.' He smiled. 'Now that you understand everything I'm sure life will be much easier for you. In its own way.'

As he glanced at his watch, Fin dragged his eyes up from the ring to try and get a closer look at the strange face he'd caught a glimpse of last night. He couldn't see it though, and it didn't seem so very important now he had the ring: a new piece in the puzzle of his life. The reality of it was slowly sinking in. His fingers tingled.

'Good lord, half past already.' Judge Harlequin Brown clapped his hands together. 'You'd better run along back to that school of yours. I have a case to hear at three. Quite a serious one: double murder. Nasty business.'

Fin felt the muscles in his throat working as he tried to force out a small sound. He had so many questions to ask, there was so much that he didn't understand, but it was all just a blur in his head and his words were all jumbled up somewhere between his tongue and his lips.

The Judge stared impatiently at him. 'Well, go on then.' He pushed his glasses back up to the bridge of his nose. 'Time stops for no man. Or boy, for that matter.'

'Yes, sir, of course,' Fin finally managed to mumble. He stood up and then carefully carried the uncomfortable wooden chair back to where he had found it.

'Good.' The Judge flashed him a brief smile full of surprising warmth before lowering his head to the pile of folders and pulling one free from somewhere in the middle.

Fin looked at the top of the old man's balding head and the wisps of grey hair that drifted across it. He stared so hard that he thought he could make out small brown liver spots on the shiny scalp tilted towards him. The ring felt good on his finger, but Finmere could almost feel all his questions rolled up in its gold circle.

Eventually, he realised that Judge Brown was already lost in whatever words were written on the papers in front of him and he let out a small sigh. His heart and stomach felt as if they were trying to meet somewhere in the middle at the base of his lungs, and he took a deep breath to force them back into their respective places. He was used to having questions – he'd had questions all his life. He supposed he'd have to live with them for a bit longer.

The sick feeling still nestled in the pit of his stomach and the rest of the year stretched out like an eternity in his head.

He turned away and quietly walked to the door at the top of the stairs, pulling it almost closed behind him, just as he'd found it. He paused, his heart pounding in his chest and he felt a wave of anger at himself.

Why did he always nod so gormlessly and say he understood when he didn't? He wasn't like that at school, not often, anyway. Maybe he should have just put his hand up when the Judge had started going on about somewhere and nowhere – how hard would that have been? And what he'd said about knowing they had to keep him safe once they'd seen the ring in his cardboard box – what was that about?

He chewed his lip as he hesitated on the top step. There were three hundred and sixty-four more days before his seventeenth birthday and the next chance to find out anything. It would feel like forever. A small breeze came through the gap of the doorway and teased his hair. That's it, he thought; enough is enough. There was no way he could wait for another year. He had no choice but to go back.

He pulled himself up to his full height, trying to feel more like an adult, and pushed the door open. 'Look, your Honour,' he started, pleased to hear that his voice wasn't shaking too obviously, 'I know I said I did, but I didn't really ... understand ...'

His voice trailed off, not able to keep up with what his eyes were seeing. A ripple in the air on his side of the desk made some of the loose paper flutter and once again a cool breeze touched his face. Finmere barely noticed it.

'Judge Brown?' he whispered, creeping slowly forward, his hand unconsciously clenching into a fist, as if protecting the ring. He'd only been out of the room for a matter of moments ... and in that short time, something had happened. Something terrible ...

Judge Harlequin Brown had slid down in the chair. His

50

arms were hanging loosely on either side of his leather chair. A wet, red bloom was spreading outwards across his shirt, and Fin covered his mouth to stop from screaming like a little kid as he stared at it. There, embedded in the centre of the old man's chest, was the hilt of a gold sword. Black stones glinted down one side and right on the end a large red stone twinkled, mocking the blood it was spilling.

The world spun, and Fin could hear the rush of his own breath filling his head like the roar of the ocean. For a moment a dark, empty space opened up in Finmere's soul, and something reached out from it, as if to grab him— And then it closed, before Fin had even realised it was there.

A gargling sound came from the Judge. His head was lolling horribly, and it broke Finmere's frozen stance. He rushed to the other side of the desk and carefully held the old man's head in his trembling, sweaty palms. The Judge's glasses had fallen to the floor somewhere, but his wide eyes found Fin's.

'I'll get an ambulance—' The words rushed out, tumbling over each other. 'I'll ring the police … I'll get—'

'No time.' The Judge forced the words out, and as disbelief overwhelmed him, Fin's eyes burned with tears.

'But you're … We need the police …' He stared at the sword standing so proudly from the old man's ruined body. *Don't die*, he wanted to say. *Please, please don't die.* As his skin went first cold, then burning hot, he thought for one horrible moment he might pass out. The disbelief was draining away. This was all far too real—

The Judge reached up and gripped Fin's wrist. His bony fingers were icy. 'Listen, Finmere. Carefully.' His voice sounded damp, as if liquid were filling his lungs and throat. His eyes rolled downwards for a moment, then he gathered his strength and said clearly, 'Take the sword.'

'No!' Fin was shocked out of his skin. 'I can't—'

The cold hand tightened as the Judge's eyes bore into his with so much intensity that it almost hurt. 'Finmere, you

51

must take the sword ...' His breathing was ragged. 'Take the sword ... Find Ted.' He stopped, and Fin started to shake, but then the Judge mustered the last of his strength and finished, 'Ted will know what's best. What to do ...'

Warm tears dripped from Fin's eyes and onto the Judge's face.

He didn't flinch, but with the last of his strength repeated, 'Promise me you'll take the sword, Finmere.' His voice was fading. 'It's important.'

Fin didn't know if the old man was finding it difficult to focus on him or whether it was because his own vision was blurring so badly, but their gazes drifted apart. Finally he murmured, 'I promise.'

The hold on his arm was loosening but the Judge managed a gentle squeeze. 'Good boy.' The words were more air than sound. 'You've always been a good boy.' He smiled weakly and Fin could see blood between his teeth. 'Time for both of us to have some adventures, I think,' he wheezed. 'But mine ... mine will be elsewhere.' His eyes found Fin's for one final time. 'The sword, Fin. You must take the sword.'

His mouth widened for a moment and his body tensed, shaking slightly, then Finmere felt an awful heaviness sink into his arms: the dead weight of Judge Harlequin Brown's head.

The Judge was gone.

SIX

For what felt like an eternity Fin stood and stared at the body of the Judge. His feet were numb and his eyes twitching as he willed the Judge to move, for a finger to spasm, or for his wrecked chest to rise and fall once more with the effort of breathing. But there was nothing, and the only sound the thud of his own pulse echoing in his ears.

Suddenly Fin felt horribly alone, and from under the shock and grief surfaced the first pang of fear. He peered around him. The study was empty, and silent, with not even a clock ticking. Fin swallowed hard. Whoever had done this terrible thing had to still be here somewhere. He stared into the emptiness around him, but nothing moved. Could the murderer have got out somehow? Maybe through the window?

He looked at the thick glass panes. They were all closed, and the latches shut, so it wasn't likely, not unless the killer was a ninja or something – but this wasn't some cheesy action movie, this was real life. *This was actually happening.* In his mind Fin ran through those few minutes between leaving the room and coming back in. It already felt like hours ago. He'd only been outside the door for a couple of seconds – a minute at most – and it just wasn't possible that someone could have got in through the window, killed the Judge and got out again, not in that short space of time. And anyway, those latches didn't look as if they'd been open in a while.

He looked behind him. Maybe whoever it was had hidden behind the door and when Fin had come back in, the man had snuck out past him. That was more likely. It even sounded reasonable, although a small voice in Fin's head whispered that he was almost sure he'd have noticed if a man had slipped out of the room behind him. And the worst bit about accepting that as a possibility meant that the murderer could be waiting for him at the bottom of the stairs.

He suddenly realised that he was still standing frozen beside the Judge's chair, and he was shivering, his bones shaking and rattling in his skin, knocking his teeth against each other. He bit down accidentally on his tongue, and the flash of pain made his eyes water, but at least it pulled him out of the panic that was slowly threatening to eat him up. The metallic taste of blood tainted his mouth, but he fought the urge to spit. He had to get out of there—

Fin guessed he was on the verge of succumbing to blind panic. That wouldn't do: not when the Judge had given him instructions. Fin's heartbeat started to settle as he repeated to himself the Judge's words: he'd told him to find Ted. Ted would know what to do. Ted could definitely explain this to the police far better than Fin himself could.

He looked at the ornate hilt glinting wickedly at him from the Judge's wrecked chest. Whether he wanted to or not, he had to take the sword. He'd made a solemn promise to a dying man and he couldn't go back on his word, not now.

He swallowed hard, peeled off his jacket and spread it across the pink-ribboned files on Judge Brown's desk. He squeezed his eyes shut and put his hands out to grip the cold metal. As his hands tightened, he could feel every one of the gemstones digging into his sweaty palms.

'I'm sorry,' Finmere whispered one more time to the only guardian he'd ever known. He held his breath, shut his eyes and tugged hard. In the darkness behind his eyelids he thought of Joe and Christopher, and of the mysterious ring he'd just been given, and the blanket he'd been found in, and he tried very hard not to think about the way the sword slid out of Judge Harlequin Brown's body as smoothly as if his skin and flesh and bones were made of heavy butter.

Finally it came free with a thick gush of blood, and Fin jumped back, desperate to avoid getting any of it on his school uniform or himself. He didn't want to be tainted by this awful crime, and a small part of him was afraid that if any of the blood got on his skin it would never come off. He dropped the sword quickly onto his jacket, trying not to wonder if it might turn, snarling, and attack him now that it was free of its last victim. Something about the sword made him feel *strange* inside, as if he could taste something in his mouth, something he should know the name of, but he couldn't quite remember. There was something almost *familiar* about it, but that couldn't be right. He'd never seen anything like it before.

Under the thick crimson coating the gold shone with a yellow lustre that almost glowed, creating a small halo in the air above his extremely ordinary coat. The blade was odd too. Fin squinted, trying to stop the sword looking blurry. Both sides were equally honed, sharp from the tip down, and Fin was in no doubt that if he touched either side the blade would cleave his finger, right through to the bone below. He shivered. The longer he stared at it the weirder the feeling inside him.

A door tried to open in his mind, but behind it there was only a void of terrifying darkness and he mentally slammed it shut, glaring at the bloody metal lying on his coat. It was *strange*. He didn't have any other words that fitted it. And it had killed the Judge. The ache inside made him feel as if maybe the blade had stabbed his heart too.

He didn't want to look at the sword any longer. He quickly folded his coat around it, securing the bundle tight with the sleeves before reluctantly picking it up. As he clutched it tight to his chest, he was sure he could feel heat oozing through the cheap material. Was that the last of the Judge's warm life escaping, or was it coming from the sword itself?

Fin walked towards the door without looking backwards, not wanting to look at the Judge dead any more, afraid that he might not be able to remember what he'd looked like alive, but just as he reached the door, he froze. There was something wrong with the Judge's desk. *Something was missing.*

He turned and stared, a cold hand squeezing his heart. All the files lying there now splattered with the Judge's lifeblood were tied with pink ribbon. But the one tied in black, the one with his name on, that was gone.

He blinked hard.

No longer caring whether the murderer was lurking in wait for him somewhere, Finmere clattered through the doorway and down the narrow, curling stairs. The Judge's apartment had suddenly come alive with shadows: ghosts and monsters and men with knives, all ready to leap out at him. The more he panicked, the faster he moved, and the faster he ran the more panic gripped him, until, by the time he reached the end of the hallway where his shoes were waiting, his eyes were wide in terror, his breath was coming in ragged gasps and his face was flushed. Every bit of his skin tingled with the urgent need to escape.

Finally Fin forced himself to stop, and breathe deeply. He needed to calm down before his lungs and heart exploded. He pressed himself into the wall and stared back at the steps he'd nearly tumbled down in his haste to escape the murder scene. They yawned silently upwards, but nothing came down them after him: no monster. No killer. All the same, he stood and watched them carefully until his pulse had slowed to nearly normal pace and only then, a full five minutes later, did he risk looking down and bending to yank on his shoes one-handed.

With his jacket held tightly under one arm, he pulled the lever, silently willing the bookcase door to slide open. He knew full well that his face would betray him if she had to come and let him out. And with no killer apparently up there, why would she believe a teenager she'd never met when he said he had nothing to do with it – especially with the murder weapon hidden badly in his coat?

There was a slight grinding sound and the wall slid away from him, opening out on the pristine study. Finmere stepped quietly out of the hidden hallway and with his head down, scurried through the far doorway and into the dining room. The scent of the flowers seemed sickly now, too heavy, like gas in the air; if he breathed in too much, it would poison him. He didn't touch the chairs. He didn't touch anything. This building had let the Judge down and he didn't want anything to do with it any more.

At the doorway he stopped for a moment to get his bearings. He peered around the door carefully, until he had a clear view of the whole reception area. Beyond the rug and the armchairs he could see the desk. There was only one woman sitting there now, the younger one. Her blonde hair was falling across her face as she concentrated on whatever figures she'd been given to add up.

The silence ticked past in seconds in Fin's head as he hesitated. Somewhere near him the fire spat loudly, a small piece of wood exploding outwards. The receptionist didn't look up. Finmere gritted his teeth. It was now or never.

He willed his feet to move at a normal pace instead of breaking into a full pelt sprint as he stepped out onto the rug. His shoes moved silently on the soft surface. He kept his head lowered and his eyes fixed firmly on the heavy front door. Once he was on the outside he could panic as much as he wanted – but not until then.

The rug ended, and despite his best efforts to keep himself weightless, he flinched as his feet *whumphed* against the wood with every step. He felt vaguely sick, expecting alarm bells to start ringing out and shutters to slam down, trapping him and the murder weapon in that elegant hallway ... But nothing happened.

57

Although each moment felt like an hour, within a couple of minutes – and unable to believe his tiny sliver of luck – Finmere was pushing open the door and stepping out into cold, crisp London air.

As he let out a sigh that was very nearly a sob, Fin found his shaking body was already running to the corner of St Peter's Lane. He turned up it, his feet stumbling and sliding on the cobbles. Halfway up the narrow street his stomach lurched and leaped into his throat and he stopped and leaned against a wall, dry-heaving, retching until his tongue and throat felt like they'd been ripped away from the rest of his body. For the first time that day Fin was thankful he hadn't had time to stop for lunch. At least he hadn't spewed all over his shoes as well. He closed his eyes and leant his back against the rough wall, then slid down it until his knees were up under his chin, the bundled sword trapped against his chest. He shivered, chill despite the hot flush that turned his face scarlet.

The breath he was trying to get back got stuck in his throat as he opened his eyes and focused on the figure in front of him.

Joe was standing with his arms folded, staring down at him with a quizzical expression on his round face. 'So, are you going to tell me what's going on, or what?'

'What the—? What are you doing here?' Fin's throat burned with stomach acid, and his voice cracked a little.

'That was my next question. I'm here 'cos I followed you, that's obvious.' Joe crouched down against the wall beside him. 'But what were you doing in there? Is this to do with your dad?' Joe's smooth brown brow furrowed. 'You don't look too good, Fin. What's going on?'

He suddenly felt very tired. Finmere stared at Joe, completely at a loss. He couldn't decide whether he was glad or not that Joe'd followed him. It was good to see a friendly face, that was for sure, but just how friendly Joe would be when he found all Fin's story was lies – that was a whole different matter. For a moment a wave of self-pity threatened to engulf him ... and then he felt the shape of the sword through the jacket pressing against his chest. If Joe didn't want to be his friend any more, then he would just have to accept it – he'd told some huge lies, hadn't he? He wouldn't blame Joe the least bit if he felt angry and betrayed. But right now the most important thing he had to think about was doing what the Judge wanted, and that meant he had to find Ted. He pushed himself upright, relieved to find his legs were reasonable steady.

'Something bad's happened and I need to go and find someone,' Fin said, his voice feeling scratchy. He paused and wiped his mouth. 'Maybe you should go home, Joe. This bad thing ... ? I think it might get worse. And' – he glanced away, so Joe wouldn't see the pain in his face – 'and I haven't always been entirely honest about things I've told you.'

Joe studied him seriously for a second before shrugging. 'You want to tell me now?'

Fin shook his head. 'I can't talk about it, not yet. Not until we find Ted.' If he told Joe what had happened he was afraid he'd lose bits of the story – maybe bits that were vital, that Ted would need to hear, and he didn't want to let the Judge down like that. It was better to keep it all bound up inside, every detail safe.

'That's cool.'

Fin looked at Joe. He could see the curiosity eating up his friend, despite his silence, and he felt a wave of relief that Joe was there, followed by a warm rush of affection. 'I will tell you, just not now,' he repeated.

'Come on, then.' Joe grinned. 'I've got a fiver and I'm still bloody starving. You're not the only one who missed lunch.'

'Okay, but you'll have to eat while we're walking,' Fin said. 'I don't know how much time we've got ...' He didn't quite manage to stop his voice from wobbling.

SEVEN

Without his jacket, the cold November air blasted through Fin's school uniform until his skin was frozen, and a mass of goosebumps. The stone step of the Old Bailey felt damp again, but this time Fin didn't care if it left a patch on his trousers or not. That worry belonged to yesterday, his birthday; it felt like a million years ago. His eyes burned tiredly as he stared into the blur of Londoners, trying to spot Ted's familiar features somewhere amongst the mass of arms and legs and faces.

It was only two hours since Joe had found him outside The Rookeries, but it felt like days ago. The evening twilight was turning quickly to black night. Joe had wolfed down a big bag of hot chips dripping with salt and vinegar, but Fin barely touched his. There was a dead weight of grief in his belly and even the smell was making him feel vaguely sick again. He handed his paper-wrapped package over to Joe, who devoured the second bag as if he hadn't eaten in days.

When he'd done, Joe rolled up the paper and drop-kicked the rubbish into one of the street bins before turning round, grinning, and letting out a huge burp. Fin tried to smile back, but he felt more like breaking down. The busy world around him was making him uneasy.

As darkness crept up around them, they'd reached the Old Bailey, and Fin led Joe to the familiar place on the second step. It felt weird to have anyone there beside him, even his best mate. It was as if two of his worlds were colliding and getting all messed up – which, when he stopped to think about it, was pretty much exactly what was happening. It was weird, but then, everything was weird today ... weirder than weird.

After an hour sitting still in the cold, damp London air, even Joe's natural ebullience finally faded, and the two boys just sat unspeaking, side by side, hugging their knees in a vain attempt to keep warm, occasionally sniffing or coughing in the silence. They attracted more than a few curious stares, but as they were just sitting there, no one bothered with them apart from one bloke who dropped a pound coin into Fin's lap and told him to get some hot tea. Before the boys could explain, the man had walked off towards the station.

Above them streetlights flickered hesitantly, as if just waking up and not sure whether it was still too early to be on or not. On the other side of the street they blazed more confidently, and eventually the lights near Fin caught up.

Joe shivered, and Fin felt it vibrate through his arm.

'Is this the only place you meet this Ted bloke then?' Joe had kept his curiosity to himself as long as he could.

'Yeah,' Fin said, 'I see him here once a year. On my birthday. I saw him yesterday.'

Joe started to nod, and then he stopped and frowned. 'But your birthday's in the summer holidays – that's how we don't do anything for it. You're never around.'

Fin swallowed. The lies were setting themselves free, one by one. 'It's not true,' he whispered, a little croakily. 'I just made that up. Every birthday I have to come here and meet Ted, and then I have some stuff I have to do. I'm not allowed to talk about them – the things I have to do.' He sighed. 'So it's always been easier to lie.'

Joe sat silent for a moment, then his eyes widened. 'But why here? At the Old Bailey? Is this where your dad was sent down? This Ted, he's not your dad, is he? Has he snuck back from Rio? That would be so totally cool!'

Fin stared out at the anonymous faces that passed them.

61

He swallowed hard again and said quietly, 'I meet Ted here because this is where he found me, on this actual step, six-teen years ago yesterday. I was left here in a cardboard box.' He didn't mention the blanket. The blanket was his. It was private. 'Ted found me when he came to work. He's the night watchman here. This Judge and some old blokes in a kind of posh old folks' home have looked after me ever since. I don't really know why.'

He dragged his head round to look at Joe, terrified at the derision he expected to see.

His friend's mouth was hanging half-open, as if he had too many questions to ask and they'd all got tangled in a ball in his mouth. Eventually, he spat one out. 'So your old man's not a big-time gangster hiding out in Rio then?'

Fin's face burned with shame. 'No. I don't know who my dad is. Or my mum.'

Joe rubbed his hand back and forth over his short Afro like he always did when he was thinking hard. 'Well, I guess that means I don't have to worry about someone coming and blowing out my kneecaps if we ever fall out.'

Fin made a strange noise, a strangled laugh. 'Actually, I thought we'd fall out over this. You know, all these lies?'

'Nah, that's not worth losing a friend over, innit? I'm a bit surprised, but I've been told worse bullshit.' He paused. 'Yours aren't mean lies. There's a difference.'

For a moment the boys sat in peaceful silence, then Joe's back stiffened as another question surfaced. 'Hang on, then—' He stood up. 'If your dad's not a big criminal genius living in hiding, then where exactly do you go to every other year when you're not at Eastfields? You ain't exactly visiting a dad that doesn't exist, are you?'

Fin wondered how Joe would take the rest of the truth. No point hiding anything now, so there was only one way to find out. 'Well, this is going to sound strange—'

He stopped, the rest of the sentence cut off as his heart

leapt. Two familiar laced-up work boots were coming up the steps.

'Ted!' Fin leapt to his feet, the numbness and cold briefly forgotten.

The old man looked puzzled. 'Fin? What are you doing here?'

'Something— Something bad happened to Judge Brown.' Hot tears suddenly stung the backs of his eyes, but he angrily wiped them away on the back of his hand. He was too old for that.

Ted moved faster than Fin had ever seen him, running down the steps and positioning himself slightly behind the boys, as if protecting and sheltering them. His eyes moved swiftly, piercing through the darkness, evaluating the shapes and shadows, seeking out any potential threat. He had become that stranger Ted Fin had caught a glimpse of the night before, alert and watchful, no trace of the tired old man on the verge of retirement.

'We'd better get inside,' Ted muttered. 'Come on.'

Although he'd sat on the steps each birthday, and walked past the building, peering up in slight awe, a hundred times more, Fin had never actually been inside the Old Bailey. Its sleek, bright interior couldn't have been further away from the old-world elegance of The Rookeries or the cool sophistication of Orrery House. It was hard to imagine someone as old-fashioned as Judge Harlequin Brown working here.

Ted led them past a security guard, who winked at him, and although Fin had a moment of worry at the sight of a walk-through metal detector, Ted ignored it and unclipped the stretchy elastic 'No Entry' barrier in the middle and ushered the two boys through.

Joe let out a gasp of air. When Fin looked round, his friend was gazing wide-eyed up at the high ceilings lit with huge strips of halogen bulbs and then around at the people bustling around them. 'Wow,' he said, 'I can't believe I'm *inside* the Old Bailey. This is just too sick, man.'

Fin heard the slight Jamaican twang creep into Joe's voice with the street slang. Joe's mum's accent was straight South London, so he hadn't picked it up from her. He must have been hanging out with one of the gangs of older teenagers on the estate; it wouldn't surprise him if Joe was thinking about those guys now. Lots of the gang members had spent time in court, up before the Beak for all sorts. Fin didn't like the gangs, but he didn't say anything. He understood the need to belong to something, the need to be with others like you.

Ted ushered them down a corridor and opened a door on his left, waving the boys in before closing it firmly behind them. He pulled a chair from under the table and wedged it under the door handle, and only then did he relax slightly, his square shoulder dropping a centimetre or so.

In the bright light, the wrinkles on his face were deeper, his leathery skin almost a burnt red, but his eyes were still sharp and friendly. 'It's all right, Fin. There ain't no cameras in 'ere.'

Fin slowly put his bundled jacket down on the table. He was almost afraid to release it after carrying it so carefully for so long. 'Judge Brown told me to find you.' He swallowed hard to stop the tears coming back. He wouldn't cry, even though his throat was aching with the effort of holding the tears back. The Judge would not approve of such weakness, he was sure.

'You've done good, Fin: you've found me, like 'e wanted.' His voice was kindly. 'Now tell me: what 'appened?'

'I went to see him at The Rookeries – he asked me to skive off school to see him. He was going to answer my questions.' There was a tremor in his voice, and Fin fought to master it. He wasn't a kid, not any more. 'Judge Brown was working … there was a file on his desk, tied up with black ribbon and it had my name on … all the others were tied up in pink ribbon, that's how I noticed it.' The words were coming out in a stumbled rush, but Ted was staring at him intently, listening carefully.

Now that he'd started, Finmere needed to free the horrible story that had been trapped inside him. 'He gave me this ring.' Fin held up his hand so Ted could see it. His hand was still shaking. 'He – the Judge – said it was found with me in my cardboard box, and then he told me this stuff about somewhere and nowhere that I didn't really understand.' He sucked in a quick breath. 'When I got outside his study I knew that I needed him to explain it properly, so I went back in.' He looked at Ted, trying to focus on something other than the horrible picture in his head.

'I was only outside the door for a second, honest, Ted. And then ... then when I went back in' – his voice dropped and he moved to unwrap his jacket – 'he was sitting in his chair, and stabbed through the chest. With this.' He opened up the coat and the golden halo shone brightly through the dried blood.

An image flashed out of nowhere: the sword, slicing through air in front of him, the blade clean and bright, held in a strong man's grip. Biting back a gasp, he blinked it away. What was the matter with him? Was this what shock did, made you see things? He looked again at the stained metal on the desk.

'Blimey, Fin,' Joe said, softly. 'Is he dead?'

Finmere had almost forgotten Joe was with them. 'He told me to take the sword out of him and find Ted. And then he died.' He stared at Ted, wanting everything to return to the strangely abnormal normality that he'd been grumbling about only the day before, but now that couldn't ever happen. The Judge was dead, and the weapon that had killed him was lying there right in front of him. Nothing would ever be the same again.

Ted stood over the table, staring down at the golden sword.

His thick fingers rubbed at his chin; the twinkle had left his steely grey eyes.

Fin and Joe both watched him, waiting for him to speak.

'A double-edged sword,' he said finally. Joe looked at Fin, but Fin didn't know the significance of that any more than Joe did. The words meant nothing to him, so the weird feelings of recognition must be his mind playing tricks on him.

'A what?' Joe asked at last.

'A double-edged sword. One of the finest.' Ted picked up the weapon, examining it. 'This ain't good. This ain't good at all.' Taking a white handkerchief from his pocket, he carefully wiped the Judge's blood from the blade.

'Um, shouldn't you leave that? You know, for evidence?' Joe's voice was small.

Ted ignored him, almost as if he hadn't heard Joe speak at all, and looked carefully at the sword that he was turning this way and that in his hand. Finally he went on, 'A double-edged sword ain't made for killing. They was *never* made for killing.' He looked at Fin, who thought the weight of events had dug the wrinkles in his weathered face even deeper. 'And there was no one else there?'

Fin said, 'I know it sounds crazy, but it's the truth.' His heart raced. Surely Ted couldn't think *he* had anything to do with it? He hadn't thought of that—

'No, you ain't crazy, Fin.' He sniffed. 'They've gone and shown their cards now. We thought as 'ow they'd try something, but never for a second did we think as they'd gone this bad. We 'ad a meeting of the retired council last night. We were going to pull 'em in.' He sighed. 'Too late for that now ... Knight killing Knight? Terrible business.' He sounded as if the weight of the world had crushed his shoulders.

'Who's a knight?' Fin's head was starting to hurt, but at least it sounded like Ted believed his story. 'Who'd try something?'

'Whoever they sent to do this would've needed his own

sword to get back.' His gruff voice softened. 'This must be Harlequin's own – and 'e wanted you to 'ave it, son.' He smiled sadly at Fin for a long minute before holding the weapon out to him. 'And more'n that – you're going to need it.'

'But won't the police want it?' Fin asked. He didn't want the sword. It had taken the Judge from him, leaving Ted the nearest thing to family he had … and then there was that disturbing black space in his head that threatened to open up whenever he looked at it. That sword was trouble; he knew it.

Ted barked out a gruff, humourless laugh. 'This ain't police business, Fin. The police can't get where we need to go.'

Fin wondered why he wasn't all that surprised at Ted's answer. Nothing about his life so far had been normal; why should this be any different?

'We're going to 'ave to sort this one out, Fin – or rather, *you* are. My job's on this side, and the old boys don't travel so good no more. Me and Harlequin, we was 'oping to leave you out of it for a while – well, *I* was. Harlequin, 'e 'ad it in his head that you'd be getting involved quicker'n expected. That's why he wanted to talk to you.'

Fin looked at the sword again, and Ted nodded towards it. 'Take it. It's yours. But wrap it up again for now.'

Fin couldn't bring himself to touch it.

'The sword didn't do it, Finmere,' Ted said, quietly. 'This sword and the Judge, they've 'ad some adventures together. And so will you. Old Harlequin, 'e loved this sword. If metal could cry, this gold and steel would weep like a baby for what a man did with it.'

Fin slowly took the hilt. It felt warm, and the heat started to fill him from head to toe. Now that he was looking at it clearly, even through a haze of tears, he could see it was beautiful. His mouth dropped open a little as he took in the sparkling jewels, and the way the light glittered on the sharp edges. Something about it suddenly felt right – or *almost* right, at any rate, despite the black space in his head.

Joe sighed. 'I know I'm a bit thick, but are you getting any of this, Fin?'

Fin shook his head, still staring at the sword. 'No, not really.' He smiled slightly. 'Welcome to my world.'

Ted crossed his arms, and the brass buttons on his blue uniform glinted in the sword's glow. 'I'll try an' explain.' Looking at Fin, he nodded over at Joe. 'Although I don't know 'ow your mate 'ere will take it. He'd better 'ave a good imagination on him.'

'Oh— Ted, there's one more thing,' Fin interrupted, reluctantly putting the sword back down on his jacket. 'I forgot, but when I was leaving, the file with my name on it, the one with black ribbon? It was gone.'

Ted froze. 'Are you sure?'

'Yes, certain. It was definitely gone. Maybe they took it by mistake?' He'd been clinging to this impossible hope all afternoon. Why would whoever killed the Judge have the slightest interest in him?

'Bloody 'ell.' Ted quickly bundled up the sword again. 'Okay, we've got to get to Maggie's, and fast.'

'Maggie?'

'Your landlady? The woman at your boarding house? What d'you call'er? They'll be going there first, and God only knows what they'll do. Come on!'

EIGHT

St John Alexander Golden threw another thick log onto the fire blazing in the grate, though the room wasn't cold; he just liked the heat. As he leant on the mantelpiece and stared into flames, his white shirt billowed slightly like a sail.

Two clocks ticked out different times on the mahogany ledge, but lost in a world entirely his own, he didn't hear either of them. He stood so close to the flame that the sword hanging from his hip grew warmer, and the heat seeped into his dark-clad leg. If he stood here much longer it would get too hot to touch, even with gloves. Sometimes he thought the swords were just a little bit too sensitive to their surroundings. Maybe that was something else he could change in the future. Once all the worlds were his.

'Well, I think I've done it.' The voice broke St John's reverie and he turned. Behind him, Conrad Eyre's eyes narrowed as he tapped at the laptop keyboard. 'But I'm not sure it'll hold. The wireless signal's pretty weak.'

Conrad was still in his mid-twenties, and quite a lot younger than St John, but he'd been a Knight since he was eighteen, one of the youngest to be brought into their ranks in the history of the Order of the Knights of Nowhere. St John himself had been considered young when he'd taken up his sword at twenty. Most young men were over-eager for a life of adventure and excitement, so the old ones were keen to make sure that any new recruit was mature enough to accept and understand the risks and responsibilities the role entailed.

Since he'd been elected Commander of the Inner Council, St John had seen the advantage of surrounding himself with younger Knights: they were loyal, and they could be moulded. And St John had worked hard at instilling a new way of thinking: if the risks and the responsibilities were theirs, then the rewards should be too. He'd been slow and careful, and it had paid off.

He peered over Conrad's shoulder. 'Do your best to secure that signal. We may be in the medieval corner of town, but I want this place protected. We can't continue to keep it so heavily guarded any more. There'll be too much else for us to do.'

On the screen a computer image of the Tudor building in which they were standing rotated as lights flashed at various points.

'The red lights indicate body heat.' Conrad pointed to two red dots on the third floor. 'You see? That's us.' Several more red spots were visible in other areas of the high building.

St John's eyes narrowed and he rubbed his tightly clipped beard. 'And how do we know if those bodies are friendly or not?'

'Well, I've been working on that, and it's nearly done. I'm programming the system to recognise the unique vibration of each ring.' He held his middle finger up and his own ring sparkled sea-blue, like the stones in the hilt of his sword. St John's ring and sword stone were emerald. The sword and ring were presented together, both made of gold blended from all the worlds, or so the legend went. St John wasn't sure how much he believed in legends, but he *had* spent some time thinking about the Prophecy of late. It hadn't been in his thoughts when he'd started out this course of action, but now that he'd had time to reflect he could see very clearly that Fate was at work through him.

He was the man to rule the Dark Age. He could feel the truth of it in his blood. The destiny of all the worlds was his, and there was no way they could fail. That gave him quite a buzz.

'I scanned in the information from the hard drive at Orrery House,' Conrad said. 'They didn't even know I'd been there.' He shook his head. 'Stupid old men. I don't think they even use the computer you installed – they still log everything in those old ledgers.' He leaned back in the heavy wooden chair and stretched, running his hands through his slightly curly, slightly too-long hair. 'So, why did we set up here? This would have been much easier over in the Future Blocks.'

St John watched him and smiled. The younger Knight was proving a valuable right-hand man, and he was never going to be wise enough to threaten St John's position. The floor beneath his boots was covered with fresh reeds, brought up that morning by the old woman who kept her head down and managed the house. St John scrunched his way over them as he walked over to the narrow window and pulled the heavy cloth back to peer out.

The cool breeze wafted through: there was no glass in the windows of the buildings in this part of The Nowhere's London. At some point in the past, spotting a gap in the market, a visionary local glazier had tried to rectify the whole window/glass situation, but the city had awakened the next day to find that the glass had gone, just disappeared, as if it had never been there. This part of the city had grown from a late Middle Ages seed, a lost shoe or crown or head, and it didn't want to be messed with.

Far in the distance, at the edge of the smog-bound River Times, right down at the East End of the city, he could see the brightly lit dome and buildings of the Future Blocks. At night they glowed so intensely they lit up the city and touched the sky. St John smiled. As much as he felt at home right where he stood, he liked Future Blocks. He had plans for it. Like most things in The Nowhere, no one was entirely sure where Future Blocks had come from. *Some time, some place, I guess,* was the normal answer. *Like the rest of London. You want peace and quiet? Go live in the country.* As far as St John could tell, no one from The Nowhere's strange London Town ever did go and live in the country. They were city people, regardless of which time period they inhabited.

He let his eyes wander over the strange buildings in the distance. It had been a long time since he'd travelled to his own London, but the curve of the main building always made him think of the Millennium dome. It might have got mixed up with stuff from some other world, but Future Block owed something to Canary Wharf, of that he was sure.

He took a deep breath of the capital's smoky air. A million tastes and smells filled him.

'Politics, Conrad,' he muttered, still staring at the extra-ordinary skyline that had become so familiar. 'If we'd gone there, we'd have looked as if we had something to hide.'

He turned away from the soothing view and took the jug from where it sat on the solid wooden shelf over the stone fireplace. The pewter felt nicely warm and he poured the thick red wine into two goblets and handed one to Conrad. St John sipped his thoughtfully, studying Conrad as he fiddled with his computer.

'How do you feel about what you did today?' he asked at last.

Conrad looked up and frowned a little. 'Fine. It went fine. Everything according to plan. Why?' The slightly defensive tone to his voice made St John realise that the only concern the younger man had was that St John might think he'd done something not quite right.

Despite the fact that he'd chosen carefully, and gathered the men around him precisely for their ruthless qualities, St John did feel a slight ache inside. That afternoon Conrad had coldheartedly murdered Harlequin Brown, one of the finest Knights in living memory, a retired Commander of the Inner Council, the Guardian of Orrery House, and Defender of the

Order. Judge Harlequin Brown had been a man of impeccable honour, a kind and wise man, with a stain-free character. St John had always had a grudging respect for Harlequin.

When St John himself had been brought to the attention of the Knights of Nowhere, it had been Judge Brown who had raised concerns about elements of his personal history. Years later, after the first whisperings of trouble, it was Harlequin who had spoken out so vehemently against St John's election to Commander.

He'd respected Judge Brown precisely because the old man had seen so clearly right through him. And that was exactly why he'd had to die.

St John took a long sip of the heady wine. Its heat tingled against the inside of his mouth.

It was regretful that Harlequin had left them no choice but to kill him, but any slight remorse St John felt was tempered by the necessity of the deed. If the old man had just backed off and got on with looking after Orrery House, then maybe St John could have let him live. But that would never have been Harlequin's way.

He let out a silent sigh. Without Harlequin there would be no one to come against them in any ordered way, and even if any of the old men recovered enough, there would be no one to organise them. They would be too foggy and confused. He'd seen a recovery before: it took time to adjust, and by the time they were back to normal it would all be too late: the battle would be over before it had even begun.

As soon as he had what was needed here he was tempted to go and deal with the old ones anyway. It might be better to be safe than sorry.

St John smiled at Conrad and squeezed his shoulder, his ring sparkling in the half-light. 'You did well today, Conrad. I won't forget it. There isn't another on the council I'd have trusted with that task, not one.'

Conrad looked up, slightly flushed, and St John was pleased

to see the adoration obvious in his expression. He needed that. He knew only too well what familiarity could breed. 'It was an honour, sir,' Conrad said. 'You can always rely on me. To the death.'

St John smiled. 'Let's hope it doesn't come to that, eh?' He patted Conrad on the shoulder, picked up his goblet and left the younger man, going through to the small room that served as his private study. He slid the bolts across the thick studded wooden door, locking it from prying eyes, and walked over to his desk. Despite its size, the surface was clear except for one item: a buff brown file. He untied the black ribbon bow and opened it for the second time since Conrad Eyre had brought it back with him.

Leaning against the table, he flicked through the pages again. There were school reports, a photocopy of a passport with Harlequin listed as legal guardian, medical certificates and receipts for school feels and lodging costs, the most recent dated the end of October, for the house in Bermondsey that he'd sent Kane to investigate. There was also a chitty from Eastfields Comprehensive School for a new uniform jumper. Whoever the boy was, he was growing up.

There was nothing in the pages, though, that indicated why he might be important to the Knights. He frowned. But that didn't mean that he wasn't. Harlequin was not a stupid man, and there were some things he'd never write down. Still, if there were secrets in the house at Tower Bridge, Kane and O'Regan would dig them out, one way or another.

He scanned the reports, taking another sip of the wine. Why would Harlequin send the boy to two such different schools? It didn't make any sense. Still, judging by what the schools had to say in their tedious reports, wherever he was, the boy was well-behaved, bright and diligent in his studies. St John smiled wryly. *A good boy*. He couldn't imagine a child in Harlequin's care being anything other.

He stared thoughtfully over at the other side of the room,

absently tapping the folder with one finger. After a few moments, he stood up and crossed to a mound, covered with a tatty brown horse blanket. It still smelled of the stables, and thick, sweaty animals. He pulled it aside and let it fall to the ground, revealing an oval gilt mirror. Its edges were red bronze, a coloured metal St John had never seen, not in The Nowhere or The Somewhere. Strange carvings moved constantly, rippling under the iridescent metal border. St John found he couldn't look at them for long without making his eyes ache, and a dull pain would start thudding in the back of his head. But then, it was a magical thing, this mirror. It had come from the deep, dark East, and it hadn't been used in The Nowhere for centuries. Even once it was in his possession, St John had had to retain the Magus just to get it to work.

A thick chain was attached to one of the solid legs of his desk. It trailed across the floorboards and into the tarnished inky-grey surface. It hadn't reflected properly since it had been activated by the Magus, a serious look on his sombre face that clearly said he thought St John was a fool. He hadn't found St John's money or promises foolish, though, nor the luxury apartment in which he was currently housed on the other side of the city. St John wanted to keep him close until he was sure his services were no longer required. The Magi were notoriously difficult to find if they didn't want to be found – not that he could blame them

He stared into the gloomy oval. Wherever the awful place was on the other side of that surface, it was always a miserable, dark twilight, the colours of the world sucked out to leave only grainy shadows, midnight nothingness.

He tugged hard on the chain and heard the scuttling and scratching of disturbed beetles and bugs and whatever other vermin inhabited that mystical prison before she appeared on the other side of the cursed glass.

Her dirty yellow hair still glowed a little, as if fighting the stinking darkness around her, but it was fading, and falling free of the tight knot it had been tied in when he'd put her in there. Her eyes squinted against the sudden light, and St John wondered exactly how much she could see from the other side. Enough, he supposed, watching her shoulders stiffen and straighten a little. She looked tired.

He smiled. 'Are you ready to give them to me yet?'

Her face remained impassive and she pulled her knees up under her chin. St John couldn't tell whether she was on the floor or a chair of some kind, but the chain on her bare ankle rattled as she shifted.

'Well, you will.' He spoke calmly. 'You won't be able to stand it in there for ever. And believe me, I don't want to hurt you if I don't have to.' He paused, but she didn't show any sign of reaction. He didn't really expect her to – she might look fragile, but the Storyholder was tough all the way through. He wouldn't be surprised if he ended up having to summon the Truthfinders to make her speak. The Magus had been clear that they had ways of making *anyone* talk, Storyholder or not.

But he didn't want to do it yet, not while he might yet find an easier way to get the information. After all, he wasn't barbaric, and when all this was over he didn't want people to think he was a monster.

'In the meantime,' he added softly, 'maybe you can tell me why the Order is so interested in a sixteen-year-old boy from The Somewhere called Finmere Tingewick Smith?'

Her eyes flashed towards him, angry and insolent. So she had reacted to that name? He rubbed his golden beard. Now *that* was interesting.

NINE

With Ted carrying the wrapped-up sword, Finmere and Joe followed him back out of the Old Bailey and into the icy air. Once they were out on the pavement, Ted picked up his speed, turning right and breaking into a jog.

'Bank Tube, boys. And stay close.'

Fin fell into line behind him, allowing the old man to forge them a path through the pedestrians filling the pavements and overspilling here and there onto the road. Ted's steady pace was relatively fast, and within minutes Fin's body was hot, even without his jacket. As they turned down Cheapside, Fin could hear Joe's heavy breathing behind him.

Occasionally Ted looked back to check they were still together. Watching his back, the blue suit black in the darkness and his silver hair glinting like steel wire, Fin felt like he was looking at a stranger in Ted's body. Was there anybody or anything in his life he really knew at all?

His school shoes slipped a little on the pavement as he ran past the small turning into St Edward's Street, and Fin felt a slight ache as he glanced up it towards Postman's Park, where his blanket was safely stashed: he'd wrapped it in plastic and tucked it carefully behind the plaque for Olive Jones, a twenty-one-year-old waitress on a cruise liner who'd given her life-jacket to a passenger, a woman, saving her life at the cost of her own as the boat went down. All the plaques in Postman's Park were for ordinary people who had sacrificed their lives to save other people, like Henry James Bristow of

Walthamstow, who'd died after saving his little sister from burning. He'd been eight.

Sometimes Olive and his mother got all confused in his head. The cold air steamed in and out of him and for a moment Fin wished he could leave Ted and Joe and slip away into the peaceful tranquillity of that small, hidden-away park, just for half an hour, to read the ceramic plaques that lined the wall. It helped to remind Fin that despite his messed-up life and the terrible murder and the bloody sword, that there was still good in the world. He needed to press his face into his blanket, even if it did smell of damp plastic, and remind himself that he had once belonged somewhere, and for someone to have knitted him a blanket, they must have loved him, just a little bit.

But he was passing the turning and Fin's feet didn't slow, despite the longing in his heart. His shirt clung to his skin as he ran. This was no time to be feeling sorry for himself.

At the bottom of Cheapside, they joined the fast-moving throng and ran down the escalators at Bank. There was a train about to leave the platform and Ted held the closing doors open to get both boys on board, and then they were squashed into the warmth of the commuters crammed like sardines into the rattling and squealing carriages of the Northern line.

Fin looked up at Ted. Although his pace hadn't slowed at all in their dash to the station, his face was now bright red and blotchy, and large drops of sweat were dripping from his hair line. His breathing was hard as he tried to fill his lungs.

For the first time Ted didn't seem invincible to Fin, and the image of the Judge dead in his chair loomed horribly large in his head. What if they came for Ted next? What would happen then? Ted must have caught something in Fin's expression, because he flashed the same friendly Ted grin that Finmere had got used to year after year.

'Don't you worry, son. I might not be as fit as I used to be, but it'll take more'n a bit've a run to finish me off.' He coughed, his chest rattling, belying his words, but his smile was bright. 'I'll be right as rain once I've had a fag. You mark me.'

Fin smiled back, but he didn't really feel it. Someone had murdered Judge Harlequin Brown as if by magic, and if he could be killed so easily, then all bets were off for everyone else. No one was safe – not even Joe. He looked at his friend, suddenly realising he might have put him in danger, even if it was entirely accidentally. Joe was wedged uncomfortably in the armpit of a fat man hanging onto one of the overhead handles. He didn't look too happy about it. Fin wondered what he was making of all this.

'This is us,' Ted muttered, as the smooth voice from the speakers announced that they were at Borough Station. The doors pinged open, allowing the three to tumble out onto the platform, and Ted immediately broke into as much of a run as the busy station would allow, taking the long escalator up to the surface two steps at a time.

'Might as well be at football training,' Fin heard Joe mutter as he kept pace behind them. 'I thought old men were supposed to move slowly!'

Fin grinned over his shoulder. He was beginning to realise that Ted wasn't like other old men, just like the Judge hadn't been. Something about that made him feel proud.

It was only when they got to the door of 54 Pardoner Street and Fin had to rummage around in his jacket pocket for the front door key to the old terraced house that he had any real sense of fear for Mrs Baker. Until that point, despite Ted's worry and their mad dash across town, the idea of anyone wanting to hurt his landlady was pretty unbelievable, too weird for his brain to accept.

Fin had stayed there every other year for three years out of the past six; each of his years at Eastfields Comp. Mrs Baker was pleasant enough: she fed him and washed his clothes, but he didn't really *know* her. This was a boarding house, not a family home, and even when he was the only person staying there (which was quite often, because although it was clean, Mrs Baker's wasn't the poshest establishment in that part of London), she always treated him like a bed and breakfast guest, not family.

It had always been the same, even when he'd been younger. Except for meals, Finmere spent any spare time when he wasn't at school or with friends in his own room, where there was a TV, a desk and even a small fridge and a kettle. If he didn't get up with his alarm then she wouldn't come and turf him out of bed, like Joe's mum did, or the prefects did at St Martin's. It wasn't that she was lazy or unkind; she obviously thought it was perfectly normal for a small boy to get himself up and ready for school. He'd actually asked her about it when he was eleven, after he'd spent a night at Joe's place, and she'd looked at him as if he was slightly mad. 'It's only getting up, Fin, love. How hard can it be?' And then she'd laughed a little and walked away to brew up a fresh pot of tea.

He didn't really know much about Mrs Baker at all, Finmere realised as he finally found the key and handed it over to Ted. He didn't know where Mr Baker was – whether he was dead or divorced. He didn't know if she'd always run a boarding house, or if she'd done something far more exciting when she'd been younger. All he knew was that she sometimes sang old songs that sounded like they came from the forties, and that she loved to watch the soaps. That wasn't much for a person you'd known for three out of six years, was it?

His face flushed as Ted swung the door carefully open.

He'd never really asked her anything about herself. She was another part of his life, like Ted and the Judge, that he'd taken for granted …

'Follow me boys, and quietly.' Ted stepped into the hallway and Fin moved up behind him, his heart heavy. He'd spent too much of his life feeling sorry for himself about what he didn't have, not realising all the *good* things he did have. He was realising them now; he had to hope it wasn't completely too late.

They found Mrs Baker in the kitchen, slumped over the kitchen table. She raised her head as they came in, and Fin saw the terror in her eyes before she realised who it was.

'—ed.' The word was wet as she tried to speak, and Fin's mouth fell open. Who could do this to someone? And to a middle-aged woman at that …

'Oh, Maggie.' As Ted crouched beside her, Fin's chest started to close up. He couldn't speak. Mrs Baker was still wearing the old-fashioned floral housecoat that she always wore when she was doing the cleaning. Finmere wasn't sure that he'd recognise her if she hadn't got that on. His heart thumped, and he could taste sick at the back of his throat. Her face was swollen and her mouth was bleeding from the inside, as well as from her lip, where it was split right open. Fin ran to the sink, grabbed a clean tea towel and soaked it in cold water. Silently he passed it to Ted.

Joe had started picking up the pieces of broken crockery that covered the floor, making a pile at the other end of the table. Fin looked at the mess – the intruders had pulled out all the drawers and emptied the cupboards – and knew that what Joe was doing was only a small drop in the ocean … but at least it was something. He crouched down and joined in, though his eyes were continually drawn to the two adults.

Maggie flinched as Ted wiped her face. 'It'll take more than that, Ted love.' Her voice was slurred. 'I think they broke one of my teeth.'

'I'm so sorry, Maggie.' Fin had never heard Ted's voice sound so sad. 'This is all my fault. I reckon I've got rusty. I should've warned you we was thinking things were going bad, but we was 'oping we was wrong. We was too busy 'oping.' He sighed and took his battered tin out of his pocket. He lit one of his roll-up cigarettes and inhaled.

Maggie squeezed his free hand. 'It's not your fault, Ted, and don't you be thinking that. I'm a grown woman, and you can't be to blame for the deeds of bad men.' She dribbled a little as she spoke and Ted carefully wiped the blood away. 'You know that as well as me.'

She paused and shut her eyes. Fin watched them, fascinated. It sounded to him like Ted and Mrs Baker knew each other pretty well – why had neither of them ever mentioned that to him?

'They wanted to know about the boy, Ted. About Finmere.' She had lowered her voice to a whisper, but her breathing was so laboured that Finmere could hear every word.

He swallowed hard. Joe nudged him, his eyes wide. He'd obviously heard too. Fin felt a terrible, deep-seated empty feeling in his middle, worse even than the nausea he'd felt that morning when he realised he was going to have to bunk off school and skip old Boggy Marsh's detention. Why would anyone hurt Mrs Baker to find out about him? He was nothing, literally, a *nobody*.

'They wanted to know why Harlequin was looking after him. They said something about having his file. They wanted to know where he'd come from.'

Fin pulled himself to his feet, no longer pretending not to hear.

'I didn't tell them nothing, Ted – not a word.' She shrugged. 'Not that I know much, of course. That was smart of Harlequin. Luckily they weren't here long.' She chuckled a little, and Fin could see it hurt her. 'These thin walls finally came in handy, and that miserable old bugger next door finally did me a favour. He started banging and shouting about calling the police.'

She leaned heavily on the table and pushed herself to her feet. She looked around for a moment, and then reached down into a drawer hanging out on one runner and took out a packet of Nurofen. She dry-swallowed two, grimacing as she did so.

She looked at the two boys staring at her and tried to smile. 'They obviously haven't spent much time south of the river, eh? 'Cause if they had, they'd've known no one down here ever calls the police – and if they do, they sure as hell don't shout about it first.'

''ow'd they get 'ere?' Ted asked.

'Front door. Came and went that way.' She shrugged and looked around her. 'But next time, who knows?'

Fin wished he understood even part of what was going on, but he was still completely at a loss – it sounded just like Ted and Mrs Baker were talking in code, like the Judge. He felt his eyes starting to well up thinking about that last conversation and looked down at his feet, willing the tears to stop.

'You're right.' Ted looked around. 'They could come back at any time. This isn't safe, not for any of us.'

Mrs Baker looked around. 'You know what, Ted? I think it might be nice to go home now.'

Ted smiled. 'Let's get you back to the big 'ouse first. One thing at a time, eh?' He turned to Finmere. 'Right, Fin, get yourself upstairs and change into some jeans and trainers. Quick as you can. Joe, you 'elp Maggie 'ere with 'er coat and bag, eh?'

With too many questions on the tip of his tongue, but knowing this wasn't the time to ask them, Fin nodded his agreement, turned and ran up the two flights of stairs to his room at the top of the house. He didn't bother looking into the sitting-room off the middle landing; he didn't want to see that room wrecked too.

As he opened his door, his breath caught in his throat. His green trunk had been jemmied open and his belongings tipped out across the carpet. The same with his chest of drawers ... not that there was much for whoever had done this to see. What'd he got, after all? A few books. A couple of old board games. A battered iPod and an old computer that could barely chug out an essay.

He felt the ring on his finger and went ice-cold. If this had been the next day, he'd have left the ring here so that it wouldn't get confiscated by a teacher or nicked by one of the school yobs. And he had this feeling that the ring was exactly the kind of thing the men would have been looking for. That made sense: the Judge had given it to him, after all. He looked down at it. There was no way he was going to take it off for anything.

He rummaged in the mess of clothes on the floor and pulled out his jeans, a T-shirt, a long-sleeved shirt and the hoodie he'd worn the day before. He ripped off his uniform and re-dressed himself. Maybe now they realised he was just ordinary ... perhaps they might leave him alone now? He pulled his jumper over his head and felt an uncharacteristic surge of anger: actually, it didn't matter whether the men lost interest in him; *he* was interested in *them*. They needed to be punished for what they'd done to Judge Harlequin Brown and Mrs Baker, and if he could help Ted do that, then, he realised, he didn't care much about the danger.

He got onto his knees and peered under the bed, looking for his trainers. Next to one of them he saw his Geography exercise book, which drew him up short for a moment. It was like a symbol of a part of his life that had just ended abruptly. He stared at the book. He was pretty certain he wouldn't be going to school tomorrow ... He wondered if Ted would ever let him go back to Eastfields Comprehensive. In the gloom, the thought vanished as his eyes started to play tricks on him again. He'd been reaching for his trainer when his hand suddenly looked bigger, like a man's hand, the ring tight on a thick, tanned middle finger instead hanging loose on his skinny white one – and a split-second later it was just his own familiar left hand again, slim and pale. He stared at it.

What will be, will be.

Crouched frozen by his bed, he wasn't quite sure where the words came from – it wasn't something he'd ever said, although he thought it sounded like the sort of thing Judge Brown might have said. His heart thumped hard in his chest. The words had slipped through that doorway in his mind that had somehow opened again. Perhaps he should tell Ted about these weird feelings and thoughts; maybe he'd be able to explain them. He peered at the slightly open door in his mind. With a fear he didn't understand he gritted his teeth and mentally closed it. He pictured a bolt and drew it firmly across. Whatever was going on in his head, it could wait. Right now they had bigger things to worry about than his brain misbehaving.

He sat on the bed and tugged his shoes on. He still had his ring and his blanket, and Mrs Baker might be bashed about, but she was still alive. In some small ways, they'd already foiled these bad guys, whoever they were, if only a little bit.

'Hurry up, Fin.' Ted's voice sounded urgent, and Fin quickly knotted the second trainer and headed back down the stairs. He didn't look back.

Ted, Joe and Mrs Baker were standing by the front door.

'You ready?' Ted asked, and when Fin nodded, gave him a slip of paper. ''ere's the address of a caff, a kebab shop just round the back of Aldgate Tube. It's just down a side-street, next to a private cab office. Meet me there in an hour and a half.'

'What?' Fin gulped. *They were splitting up?*

'Don't argue, Fin. I've got to get Maggie safely to Orrery House.'

'Can't I come with you?' Fin hoped his voice didn't sound quite as desperate as he was feeling.

Ted shook his head. 'No, mate – but listen 'ere: don't go 'anging round that school of yours, all right? It might not be safe now. I'll explain everything I can at the caff, okay?' He looked at Fin. 'All right, son?'

Fin swallowed, and said, 'I'll be fine. Honest. Just look after Mrs Baker.' He smiled at the woman he barely knew, and she smiled wanly back.

When she pulled open the front door, Fin saw the effort took all her energy. 'You know who we need to find, Ted?' Her quiet voice sounded tired, but a bit clearer, as if she'd adjusted to the swelling in her battered mouth.

Fin thought she looked like an old woman, and wondered just how old she really was. He'd never really thought about her age before. But he still didn't understand a word she said as she told Ted, 'Fowkes. We need to find Fowkes.' She turned into the cold, busy night. 'Frightening though the thought is, he's probably the only young one left we can trust.'

TEN

When Ted entered the Oval Room on the top floor of Orrery House, Jarvis was pouring thick, strong coffee for the six old men sitting in the high-backed chairs placed along the sides of the long table. Ted's heart sank a little on seeing so many empty spaces. He'd hoped to find more awake and competent, but everywhere they turned, luck was against them. *Maybe it was Fate, finally turning against them. The Prophecy at work.* He squeezed the thought out of his head: he'd never been one for superstition over strength of will and he wasn't about to start now.

At the far side of the hushed room, Maggie stared into the various glass display cases lining the walls. They were filled with some of the rarest and most intricate orreries ever made, depicting both Zodiac and solar systems, fine gold and bronze and jewelled representations of the movement of the planets around the sun. Some of the beautiful models were ancient, two millennia or more old, and not made for such rough hands as his, but Ted loved looking at them; they brought the child inside him back to life, though that child had been gone such a very long time ...

Maggie looked up as he closed the doors. The blood had been washed off her face, but the swelling was dreadful. There was no time for childish wonder now, Ted thought grimly to himself.

'Keep that coffee coming, please, Jarvis,' Simeon Soames piped up cheerfully. 'The effort of getting out of that damned wheelchair has almost sent me back to sleep.'

Jarvis promptly refilled the espresso cup, careful not to spill the rich liquid on his white-gloved hands, and stepped backwards.

Ted stood at the head of the table and surveyed the elderly faces around him. 'Gentlemen,' he said firmly in his best English, 'we find ourselves in unthinkable times, and I don't think we can 'i— we can *hide* from it no more. The Inner Council 'as turned against us. St John Golden's gone 'is own way, and 'e's taken his Knights with 'im.'

A hunched man on Ted's left peered over his bifocal glasses and popped a mint into his mouth. Lucas Blake had been a good Knight until the Ageing got him, five years ago. 'Are you saying Golden has actually broken with the Order?' His voice sounded incredulous even as his eyes watered with the strength of the peppermint that helped keep his senses, and himself, awake.

'Of course that's what he's saying,' Freddie Wise snapped, his hand gripping the top of his ebony walking cane. 'I don't know why you're so surprised. He was never a good'un.' He sighed and sipped his coffee with a surprisingly steady hand. 'You youngsters, you thought he was just a hothead. You thought he'd calm down. But Harlequin knew. He tried to tell you.' He gestured to Jarvis to refill his cup. 'But none of you ingrates listened. And look where it got us.'

A heavy pause settled on them, filled with a fear none wanted to share.

'But now Harlequin's dead,' Ted said, eventually. 'And we can't bring 'im back.' There was a longer silence after that.

'He was a good man,' Lucas Blake said quietly. 'The Order will miss him. We need more men like him.'

'Something's very wrong, and it's more than them killing Harlequin – terrible as that is – and taking Finmere's file.' Harper Jones rubbed his sagging face wearily. 'I've had the most awful dreams – as if all the worlds were suffocating on top of me.'

'Me too.' Lucas Blake looked up, and in his eyes Ted could see the young man he had so recently been. He saw other things too, unspoken words that he felt singing inside his own thoughts. Words like *Prophecy* and *Legend*. Maybe there was some truth in this after all ...

'And I,' Freddie Wise added dryly, 'and it's not just us. The catatonic ones are dreaming too. They're moving and twitching and calling out. Isn't that right, Jarvis?'

'Quite so, sir. It's unheard of.'

Freddie looked up at Ted. 'I think I'd like to take a look at the map.'

Cardrew Cutler groaned. 'Do we have to? It gives me such a headache.'

'It gives everyone a headache, Cardrew. But I still want to look at it.'

Ted looked around the table, making sure they were all in agreement, then went over to the light switch by the door. He reached for the tiny catch on the underside, which clicked as his fingers worked it, and the casing rose upwards, revealing a button that glowed with a thousand different colours all at once. Ted pressed it and turned back to the table as the middle section rolled smoothly away, revealing the map underneath.

Ted, Maggie Barker and the old men stared into it in wonder. Even Jarvis' eternally chilly demeanour cracked a little as he gazed on it, for it was a mesmerising sight.

The map was not really a map at all, but an orrery of sorts: the True Orrery, showing all the Londons of all the worlds, layered over each other, each one in detailed colour and yet at the same time almost transparent.

Ted could make out a tiny red double-decker London bus that was blocking traffic on Westminster Bridge, its headlights bright in the winter darkness. Below that was a layer of another London, where late afternoon summer rain was falling on a slightly narrower bridge which was slightly to the left, a little way along the river. There was no bridge at all on the layer under that, but a strange ferry station, and below that …

He blinked.

If he tried to look too deeply into the layers that went down and down, far deeper than the table legs that apparently held them, his brain was likely to explode. The map wasn't made for staring at too long, or for trying to understand; it just *was*. He let his eyes watch it without looking, and then the map just went back to being a teeming mass of light and movement and colour.

Freddie Wise was still staring at it though. 'Look,' he said, softly, 'there.' He pointed towards the very corner of the map, where a thick grey cloud, denser and more oppressive than any natural rain cloud should be, had formed on the edge. As they watched, they could see it was moving, ever so slowly, towards the skies of London.

'Is that in all the worlds?' Lucas Blake whispered.

'Worse than that.' Freddie leaned back in his chair. 'There's no separation. Where the cloud is, you can't see the layers. It's as if they don't exist any more.'

Ted looked again. He was right.

'What does it mean?' Cardrew Cutler asked.

'I don't know – but it surely can't be good. The worlds each have their place, and it looks like the cloud is changing that. I think it's blurring them together.'

Ted went back to the wall and pressed the button again. The thin sheet of highly polished wood rolled back, covering the map. The room seemed dull for a moment, until his eyes readjusted.

'The Knights can't do that – we can't affect the balance of the worlds. So how is that happening?'

'What does Golden want?' Lucas asked.

'Power,' Ted answered. ''e's always wanted power.' His heart thumped in his chest as he worked out what was happening.

90

'*The stories*,' he said suddenly, looking around the table, 'the balance of *everything* lies in the Five Eternal Stories.'

Freddie looked shocked as he worked out what Ted was saying. The two old friends' eyes met. 'The Storyholder,' Freddie started, then stopped, his face appalled. After a moment he whispered, '*They've done something to the Storyholder.* Only she can affect all the worlds like this.'

Cardrew Cutler popped another mint into his mouth. 'Aren't we all avoiding something?' He peered around the table, his eyes finally resting on Freddie Wise. 'Even you, Freddie, with all your science and logic, you must be thinking it too.' He tapped a gnarled finger on the table and the words carved there glowed slightly. 'The Prophecy.'

Ted felt the atmosphere in the room crack slightly. So it wasn't just him and Lucas Blake who'd been thinking of the ancient words. They all had.

'The Prophecy is just an old poem written by a people we know nothing about.' Freddie's voice was soft. 'And we have never managed to work out exactly what it means.'

Simeon Soames shrugged, and Ted saw him wince with the effort. 'But you've got to admit, Freddie, if it wasn't for the Prophecy, the Order wouldn't even exist. The Prophecy is the *reason* for our existence. It's what we were formed to protect against, and although we all treat it like an old religion, and our role has changed almost beyond recognition over the centuries, maybe – just maybe ...' He let the words trail away.

Ted wasn't sure if he'd left the words unsaid simply because the old Knight was too tired to finish the sentence. Still, it didn't really matter. He'd made his point. Even Freddie was silently rereading the softly glowing words. Ted's own old eyes were drawn to them, even though he knew the passage by heart.

Nine there are, and standing side by side
Linked by Love, Truth, Freedom, Hatred, Pride –
Their blood, it is the river's ebb and tide.

Here are two reflections of the same,
The dead bones of the one, the other's frame –
The Magi see the unravelling of the game:

This, their Prophecy.

The dark man comes to rule the new Dark Age.
His door admits those too who come to save.

Travellers from without, within
Bring honour, valour, hate and sin.
Light and dark and shades of each,
Will move through voids, the worlds to breach.

When life and death are bound in one,
The balance of all will come undone,
And love, the greatest damage cause
And forge the war to end all wars.

Eternal stories held unready shall bring
Black tempest, madness, and a battle for King.

The Magi cannot see the Prophecy's end,
Perhaps the Order of Travellers will defend.
Perhaps the stories will hold strong and clear,
The damaged keep us from the abyss of fear.

Don't fight these tellings: their passing must come,
But prepare, both worlds, for that which must be done.

When one plus one plus one is four.
All the worlds shall wait no more.

Ted sighed, and it was echoed by the other old men. *The Prophecy*. No one had really believed in it, not for such a long time, not even Harlequin. The Order might have been started originally to guard against it, but over the centuries they'd become more of a police force, protecting The Nowhere from people or things slipping into it from The Somewhere. God help them all if there was actually any truth in the ancient words. He pictured the cloud spreading over the map and bit his lip. *The unravelling of the game.*

He met Freddie Wise's eyes again and saw his own fear reflected in his steady gaze. They were all far, far too old for this.

ELEVEN

They stopped off at Joe's flat on the Brickman Estate so Joe could get changed and leave a note for his mum, and got to Aldgate Station in plenty of time. It wasn't hard to find the little Turkish café and by eight-thirty they were sipping steaming mugs of sweet tea. There were a couple of the drivers from the small minicab office next door there too, tucking into sticky pastries.

Fin had been pleased and relieved to see that both businesses adhered to the generally accepted signage policy, even if, in the case of the taxi company at least, it was just a dirty backlit yellow square hanging over the street that said 'minicab'. It was still clear what the place was. The café was better, the Turkish-style writing decorated with grapes and grape leaves and big blue eyes to ward off evil. Just as it should be, Fin thought.

Ted put two polystyrene boxes on the plastic tablecloth and sat down. 'Get those down you, lads.'

Fin lifted the lid on a doner kebab laden with chilli sauce and mayonnaise. His stomach growled hungrily. 'Thanks, Ted,' he said, picking up a fork.

'Yeah, cheers, Ted,' Joe added, mumbling through his already full mouth. Ted hadn't even raised an eyebrow when he'd seen Joe sitting alongside Fin in the café, though Fin had been a bit nervous about the old man's reaction. But there'd been no stopping Joe – he was well up for whatever came next and there was no way Fin was leaving him out of it, he'd made that quite clear. He could deal with the lies – he could see Fin had his reasons – but if Fin sent him home now, that really would be the end of their friendship. Secretly Fin was relieved.

Ted sent Joe to the counter to fetch the teas and told Fin, 'It's okay, son. It ain't no surprise to me that he's 'ere, Fin. All boys love an adventure.' His voice had softened. 'Worrying about danger, that's for grown-ups, and you two ain't quite there yet.' Fin wondered just how much danger Ted was worrying about. Quite a lot, he decided, judging by his expression.

Ted looked out the window, his brow furrowed. Although they were still in the heart of London, the street outside was quiet. Finmere watched him while he ate, until finally he turned back to the boys and leaned forward, resting his elbows on the table. Around them the minicab drivers chatted and laughed and read foreign newspapers. None of them were paying any attention to the two teenagers and the old man in the security guard's uniform.

'Time to listen up,' Ted said quietly, his gruff voice more of a growl than a bark. 'There's some things I've got to tell you, stuff that Harlequin wanted to explain to you this afternoon, Fin. You're going to find some of it a bit 'ard to get your heads round.'

Fin's heart thumped in his chest. He leaned in, matching Ted's pose, and Joe did the same. They looked like conspirators, Fin though wryly. 'Go on, Ted. Whatever it is, I'll believe you.'

'Well,' Ted started, 'I'm just going to say it plain and straight.' He took a deep breath. 'Sometimes what you see ain't really everything there is to see. This world, our world, it exists, of course it does – but it ain't the only one. There's other worlds too. Ones we can't see so easily.'

'What like Mercury and Mars?' Joe interrupted, and Finmere kicked his shin under the table. Joe always had been too literal. As Fin glared at him, Joe rolled his eyes back.

'No, not like the planets. More like …' Ted paused, trying to find the right words.

'You don't mean like parallel universes?' Fin frowned as Ted burst into a grin. Something quietly clicked into place behind the firmly shut door in Fin's mind, so subtly Fin didn't even feel it.

'That's exactly right, Fin! Parallel universes. Pretty much like that.' Ted winked. 'You're a clever lad; we've always known it. So, these worlds – they're all a bit like ours, but at the same time, they're all different. It's not easy to explain. They're all kind of layered on top of each other – that's what we *think*, at any rate. Most of the worlds we can only imagine, but the closest one to us is different. We know about that one. It's called The Nowhere.'

Fin caught his breath. Was that what the Judge had been talking about? Things being nowhere or—

'What's our world called then?' Joe was fiddling madly with his short curly hair, thinking hard. 'Just Earth, like what we call it?'

Ted shook his head. 'No. Our world is called—'

'The Somewhere.' Fin finished the sentence and both Ted and Joe stared at him.

'How did you know that?' Joe asked.

'The Judge was talking about things being somewhere or nowhere. I didn't know what he meant.' Fin looked up at Ted. 'But it was the worlds, wasn't it? That's what he wanted me to know about.'

Ted gave a grim smile. 'Judge Brown, 'e was in charge of the Order of the Knights of Nowhere. You see, there's an old Prophecy in The Nowhere that foretold the coming of the Order.' He sniffed. 'It's like our worlds was *meant* to be linked by the Knights, whether for good or bad. That's what they reckoned in The Nowhere at any rate, when men from 'ere first showed up. The Prophecy used to be like a religion with them back in the old times, even though I'm not sure how much they believe in it these days either.' Fin wasn't sure Ted was making much more sense than the Judge had.

'Still, for four 'undred years the Knights've vowed to defend both worlds, and stand ready in case of dark 'appenings.' He sounded as if he was reciting a well-practised speech.

'The Knights, see, they've got these swords, and they can use 'em to cut through between the two worlds. It's a skill as sets them apart from ordinary people. Their double-edged swords symbolise the alliance between the worlds.' He frowned. 'And Harlequin Brown was murdered with one.'

Fin was only half-listening. The two voices were stretching out, almost as if he was hearing them under water. As he relived the events of that afternoon, so the pieces slowly started coming together in his head. *The study had been empty apart from him and the Judge. He'd only been out of the room for a few moments. And he'd felt that slight draught.*

'And that's how they killed him.' Fin's throat was dry. 'They came through from The Nowhere, and then went back again, as if they'd never been there at all.' He looked up. 'He was killed by a Knight.'

'Exactly,' Ted said. 'It's a terrible business.'

Joe's face was crunched in on itself. 'How did people find out about this other world, this Nowhere place?'

'The two worlds are so closely linked that there are weak spots between 'em. We're sort-of on top of and beside each other, I reckon. Sometimes these weak places, they opens up into gaps for a moment or two, and that's when things slip through. There's been legends and rumours about 'em in places all across the city. You can still hear 'em, if you listen in the right places.'

He looked up and smiled at the boys, his eyes twinkling. 'Jack the Ripper – 'e escaped to The Nowhere through a gap that tore open, just for a moment, and 'e might've got away with it if 'e hadn't killed a poor girl over there, just like 'e did over here. The Knights caught 'im and 'e was 'anged at Smithfield in The Nowhere.'

Joe's jaw dropped. He'd been fascinated by the legendary London killer ever since he'd watched a particularly gruesome film about it. 'Who was he?'

Ted tapped his nose. 'Ah – now that'd be telling.'

Fin wasn't sure if the old man was winding them up or not. All he knew was that his own head was spinning as he tried to keep up and make sense of it all.

'Anyway,' Ted said, 'all the weak spots aside, there was – or I should say *is* – one doorway that's always open, and it was when that doorway was found that The Nowhere was discovered, back in about 1615. They tried to wall it up at first; problem was, doorways like that, they're meant to be open, and walling 'em up, well, it don't always work. The doorway eventually wore its way through the bricks.'

Fin's tea had gone cold, but he sipped it anyway. 'Where is the doorway?' he asked.

'Right under the streets of Clerkenwell, in one of the back walls of the prison that was last known as the 'ouse of Detention. Been closed to the public since 2001, and that took some doing from Harlequin, let me tell you.' He shook his head, his smile rueful.

They sat in silence for a moment. Even Joe was still as they digested all this information.

Fin stared at the network of broken veins spreading across Ted's rough and red face. 'Are you one of them?' he asked at last. 'Are you a Knight of Nowhere?'

Ted shook his head. 'No – some people just ain't meant for it.' He smiled sadly.

'So where does Fin fit into all of this?' Joe swapped his polystyrene box with Finmere's and started to eat what was left of the cold kebab.

'Some seventeen years ago, a young Knight was murdered in The Nowhere. They was black times for a while.' He looked

98

at Fin. 'About a year later, you turned up in your cardboard box, and that Knight's ring was in there with you. Not his sword, mind, just the ring.'

Blood rushed through Fin's head and he heard the echo of Ted's next words even before the old man spoke them: 'Harlequin and the rest of us, we thought Baxter, the dead Knight, we thought he must be your father.'

Fin's head reeled and he clung to the sides of his chair as his world turned upside down. His skin tingled: *A father. With a name and everything. Baxter* ... Questions filled him from the toes up, too many to even think about putting into words. What had he been like? How old was he? How did he die? Something banged hard against the locked door in his mind. What was so important behind there? And why did it scare him so much? And what did it have to do with Baxter maybe being his father? *Father.* It was unreal—

Ted leaned forward and it was only when the old man gripped Fin's hand firmly in his did Finmere realise how badly he was shaking. 'But we don't know nothing for sure, Fin.' He squeezed Fin's hand a little. 'After that, the Knights elected a new Commander, a man called St John Alexander Golden. A lot of us, well, we thought 'e'd unite the Knights after the troubles – and 'e did, for a while.' He looked from one boy to the other. 'But now 'e's gone bad, and 'e's taken the young Knights with 'im – 'e's doing some terrible things, and we've got to stop him.

'It's the Prophecy, you see. Maybe this is connected and maybe it ain't, but we can't take no chances. It's what the Knights were made for, after all.'

Fin felt as if herds of elephants were stamping about in his brain, but right down in the very core of him, his whole being was singing: *a ring, a blanket and a name: Baxter.* He had more questions, but he'd already had a lot more answers than he'd ever had before. Pieces of his personal jigsaw were slotting into place and for the first time he was starting to feel as if he did belong somewhere. Or maybe Nowhere. He fought the twin urges to giggle and cry.

'But what can we do about that?' The words tumbled out of him. That was one question that Ted could answer.

'Son, you 'ave to break into the 'ouse of Detention and go through to The Nowhere. You 'ave to find a man called Fowkes and tell him that the Knights 'ave taken the Storyholder. He'll know what to do.'

Fin frowned. 'Who's the Storyholder? And who's Fowkes?'

'All in good time. It's always best not to know too much until you really have to,' Ted said with a grin. 'But I can tell you: it's your destiny, Fin. I can feel it in me water. Don't you see?'

Fin stared at him. He wasn't sure he saw much at all.

'If Baxter *was* your dad, and your mum was from The Nowhere, then you're the first person to truly belong in both.' He sat back. 'That's why Judge Brown arranged your life thataway: your life's always been split, one year in one place and one in another, to get you used to the idea of two different worlds. And to see 'ow well you could keep a secret.' He smiled. 'And you done us proud on all counts, Fin.'

Fin could feel white noise in his head trying to take over. There was too much to think about and he didn't know where to start. He certainly didn't feel special – if anything, he'd always felt the complete opposite of special.

He started sorting the information into piles in his head. The Nowhere. Baxter. The doorway. What was it Ted had said? They needed to think about the important things and right now, the most important thing was how they were going to get into the House of Detention.

He looked at the piles behind his eyes. Some sheets of paper were hovering, uncertain of quite where they belonged. His internal eyes were drawn to a piece of cream paper floating forward from a stack at the back of his mind labelled 'School'. Reaching out, he mentally grabbed it. He blinked.

'My best friend at St Martin's, Christopher Arnold-Mather, his father's in the government,' Fin started, almost gabbling in his haste to get the words out before they vanished from his head. 'He's the Minister of Cultural Affairs.'

Joe stared at him as if he'd completely lost the plot. 'Like, *really* relevant, Fin!'

Fin ignored Joe; he was just being funny about St Martin's, and the mention of Christopher as his best friend there.

'Minister of Cultural Affairs, you say?' Ted's eyes had narrowed.

'This House of Detention place, it sounds like it could come under something like that, doesn't it?'

Ted nodded. 'Go on.'

Fin smiled. 'I've got an idea, but we need to get Christopher out of school.' He studied Ted. 'You'll need to get something else to wear. A pullover and a shirt. And one of those jackets with patches on the elbows.' He paused. 'And maybe some glasses. We'll grab a cab from next door and meet you back here.'

Fin smiled at Joe. Joe smiled back, but it wasn't his usual cheeky grin. 'Let's go and get this Chris geezer then,' he said, trying to sound enthusiastic.

'He's all right, Joe,' Fin said, putting his carton in the bin by the door. 'You'll really like Christopher. He's great.'

'Yeah,' Joe's voice was completely unconvinced, 'I bet he is.'

TWELVE

All roads lead to Rome. The old phrase rattled around use-lessly in St John Golden's head as he wrapped the dark cloak over his shoulders and strode through the dirty streets. It wasn't cold exactly, but there was definitely a strange chill in the air. He followed the muddy track as it twisted and turned through the streets and alleyways.

In The Nowhere there was no Rome as far as St John knew, but all roads did lead to the Old Bailey House of Real Truths, after a fashion, at least: one path from each section of the city would lead the residents here without them having to veer too far into times and places that didn't suit them.

The Old Bailey House of Real Truths belonged to all the inhabitants of the city, and they could enter it whenever they so wished. Most days, though, it was quiet, if not completely empty. People were just too busy with the mundane business of living, until time, in whichever period they happened to exist, finally ran out and the everyday business then became about dying. Which kind of put a full stop to things, which-ever world you inhabited.

Still, though they might not visit it often – if ever – The Nowhere Londoners liked to know that the Old Bailey was there, that someone was looking after the important things. As he turned the final corner, St John smiled. It might have been a while since he'd been in The Somewhere, but people were people, wherever you went. They might lie and cheat throughout their short, miserable lives – a small fib here, a little white lie there, and then all the rest – but they still upheld the importance of *truth*. It was just that not many of them wanted to face real truths that often. It was much easier to stay away. That suited his purpose for the evening nicely.

The alley he was in opened out into a wider street, and although the day was becoming gloomy, St John kept to the walls. It didn't exactly matter if he was seen, but he'd found himself becoming far more cautious in recent days. Now that the final steps had been taken, he'd have to be on his guard until the stories were recovered and he – and his sponsor, of course – had control of all the worlds.

High above him, on the very top of the white stone building, the huge carving of a truth vial looked down over London. To a visitor from The Somewhere, the truth vial could easily be mistaken for an hourglass, though a truth vial was longer and slimmer, and although it did dip in the middle, the contents hovered in that area rather than slipping through on the way from one end to the other. A truth vial might look like an hourglass on the outside, but the brightly coloured fluid on the inside looked more like it came from a nineteen seventies lava lamp, he thought with a snide grin.

The carved copy that rose up from the top of the building was made of marble with gold edging. It was certainly imposing, but it could never be as impressive as the real things: the rows and rows of vibrant colours that were stacked inside the building like books in a library.

St John did not climb the stairs at the front to go through the main entrance but instead sought out the smaller door a little way down the left side of the building. He took the large brass key out of his pocket and unlocked it. He looked around to ensure the street was empty and no prying eyes were watching, then he viciously kicked both the door and the lock itself several times, until both were damaged, looking as if someone had broken in. He stepped inside and closed the door behind him.

The air around him was hushed, as if even nature was aware of the sanctity of this place. Perry Longman would be waiting for him upstairs, but before heading for the Storyholder's apartments he followed the corridor forward and peered through the open double doors on his right into the vast oval room. He didn't step inside – he had not the slightest desire to hear any real truths himself – but instead just stared into the massive room where lights glowed and twinkled in shelved rows from the floor to the high domed ceilings: a vast sea of glorious luminescence.

St John couldn't see or hear any of the general public on any of the various levels. There was no sound of laughter or crying, or shouts of angry denial that normally came with a visit to the House. The Old Bailey House of Real Truths was not a place for the faint-hearted, and most people didn't really want to know the absolute truth about themselves or the ones they loved. Ignorant bliss was far easier to live with.

The Archivers moved silently up and down ladders, carefully moving a vial from one place to another, deft fingers seeking out dulled colours that needed taking to the Vaults of Dead Truths or the Room of Myth and Legend. St John didn't worry about the Archivers causing him any problems. The Archivers were all deaf, blind and mute, with pale, almost albino skin, the only people that could work with real truths day in, day out, without going mad. They were so profoundly deaf they couldn't hear the truths, but the bright colours in some way penetrated their dark worlds of blindness, allowing them to identify each and keep it in its right place. They were a mystery to everyone in The Nowhere.

St John stared at the black-robed figures as they shuffled around the building, each oblivious to the others, and yet never even brushing another's arm as they passed. How they managed their work was a mystery to all. Every once in a while, two or three would just appear at the main doors of the Old Bailey where they would wait for admittance. As soon as they were redressed in the black uniforms and allowed access to the rooms, beautiful smiles would stretch across their pale faces and they would immediately start sorting and filing the real truths, as if they had been born for the job and trained all their lives – and maybe they had. It was thought they came from somewhere outside the city, but no one, not even the Prince Regent, could say for sure. St John's nose crinkled as he turned away. As far as he was concerned, they were just a bunch of freaks.

He followed the inner corridor until he came to the central atrium, where water trickled into a marble pond before being pumped back to start the loop out of the stone goldfish's mouth. A sweeping staircase curved upwards, clinging to the wall as it followed it round. St John took them two at a time, jumping the space at the bottom where Baxter had been murdered seventeen years before. Time was ticking on.

At the top of the stairs, the two high white doors were closed and St John knocked quietly, three times, then twice, then three again. The door opened a little, then widened as Perry Longman on the other side recognised him.

'I'm glad you're here. This place gives me the creeps,' said Perry. Although he was nearly thirty, his thin frame made him look younger. Of all his Knights, Perry was the only one that St John felt any disappointment in. He was brave and clever, no doubt about that, but there had been rumours that he'd been seen in gambling dens and casinos, in both The Nowhere and The Somewhere. St John knew there was nothing trustworthy about a man with a vice – but at least now he'd found a purpose for him.

'What are we doing here, anyway?' Perry looked around him at the pure white of the Storyteller's home. There was not a touch of colour in any of the furnishings, or the décor. 'We've got her, haven't we? All this white makes me feel grubby.'

St John smiled. He knew what Perry meant; how the place

stayed clean was as much a mystery as the working of the Archivers below them. 'Part of the Knights' role is to guard the Storyholder's apartments. To protect her.'

'But she's not here. We've got her. So why keep up the pretence?'

'Because the rest of the world doesn't know that, Perry.' St John spoke slowly, as if to a particularly simple child. He felt for the wooden-handled steak knife that he'd stolen from the local market earlier and hidden in the folds of his cloak. Now his fingers gripped it tight. 'And they'd hardly believe that we'd let someone take her without a fight, would they? The Knights were founded on the concept of honour.' His voice was soft.

Perry looked around, his hands on his slim hips, his Inner Council ring looking almost too big on his knuckle. 'So are we going to wreck the place then?' Perry grinned. 'You punch me and I punch you, so we've got a couple of bruises?'

St John stepped forward. 'I'm afraid it has to be somewhat more convincing than that, Perry.'

There was a brief moment of confusion on the man's face as St John closed the gap and embraced him.

Holding him firmly with one arm around his neck, St John pulled him in.

'I am sorry, Perry, but even you must see that you're the most expendable.' St John plunged the short knife upwards, under the thin man's ribs and straight into his heart.

Perry barely had time to let out a final shocked gasp before the light faded from his eyes.

Although the first blow had been enough to kill him, St John stabbed the dead man several times more before letting the body fall to the ground. He crouched, and using the hem of his cloak as a glove, pulled Perry's double-edged sword free of its scabbard and wrapped Perry's limp hand around its hilt.

He checked to make sure there was a fair amount of blood

splattered around, and once satisfied, he walked back out to the stairwell, leaving the doors wide open. He didn't bother looking through her apartments. They'd been through her things when they'd stolen her away in the middle of the night. There was nothing else there of any interest. What he wanted, the Five Eternal Stories, she kept inside her. That was her role.

He darted past the entrance to the Oval Room and crept out through the broken side door, pulling the cowl of his cloak up so that it covered his reddish-gold hair. His steps were quick and sure as he headed away.

As he rounded the corner, St John felt the first heavy drops of rain and as one landed on the back of his hand, he stared at it. Another landed alongside; both were dark and dirty, the colour far richer than if the cloud had been tinged with smog. Puzzled, he looked up.

This was black rain. He'd only ever seen it once in all his years in The Nowhere, and he'd not stayed for the storm it heralded. He'd waited that one out in The Somewhere. Watching the dark water fall, he thought of the Storyholder. She and the stories she guarded held the balance of all the worlds steady and although she'd never confirmed or denied it, everyone knew it was she who had caused the last black storm.

He wondered for a moment exactly how far away the prison on the other side of the mirror was. Maybe too far. He looked up at the uneven sky. Perhaps he needed to be less patient with her. Maybe it was time to take his gentlemanly gloves off and get the business done.

Movement in an alleyway across the street caught his eye. Looking up, he glimpsed the dark, swarthy face of the Magus staring back at him. After a second the other man disappeared back into the shadows. St John looked after him for a moment. The eyes in that leathered skin had looked afraid.

St John pulled his cowl further over his face and strode back towards the medieval quarter of Old Town. It was too late for fear now.

THIRTEEN

After ten minutes jogging through the silently respectable Surrey night, a far cry from the harsh concrete of the Brickman Estate, the boys finally came to the entrance to St Martin's. The large school sign stood proud and graffiti-free at the edge of the open gates, beneath the low branches of the leafy trees. Joe paused and peered down the wide, sweeping driveway that led a couple of hundred metres to the vast building that had once been a stately home and was now one of England's finest boys' schools. Yellow lights shone brightly, illuminating the stone façade.

'This is your other school?' Joe said quietly.

Fin nodded.

'It's shitting huge.'

'It's only a school.' Fin knew that probably sounded a bit lame to Joe, but it was true in a way.

'Yeah, looks just like Eastfields.' Joe snorted.

'Well, it's different, but the same.' Fin shrugged. 'It's my red trunk school.' There were some obvious differences between the two schools, but Fin figured they had a lot more in common, though those things were too subtle to explain quickly. He didn't have the time or the words to make them clear. He thought about the Judge putting him in the different types of schools. Maybe the differences between the worlds and their peoples were like that. Maybe you had to go there to understand.

'What time is it?' Fin asked, changing the subject, and Joe glanced down at his watch.

'Just gone ten.'

'Right. It's after lights-out for Christopher, but he won't be asleep yet. I don't think so anyway.' His heart pounded hard. It felt weird being at St Martin's and being on the outside. This year he didn't belong here any more than Joe did. Not that it probably felt that way to Joe. 'We'll have to be careful. Mr George, the housemaster, he'll be patrolling.' He smiled at Joe. 'Mr George is a bit like Boggy Marsh. He just *knows* when stuff is going on.'

'Gotcha.'

They were hidden under the line of oak trees in the grounds as they ran across the silent grass. Finmere had never really looked at St Martin's by night before. He had to admit there was something majestic about it.

They crouched behind a bench on the lawn while Fin got his bearings. 'Right, over there? All of that wing is the prep school.'

'Prep?' asked Joe.

'Yeah, the Junior and Middle School. You start at six years old here.' Fin looked up at the familiar windows. Ten years ago he'd been sleeping behind one of those. It was in his first year here that he'd decided to hide his blanket in case he lost it in all the moving around. He remembered cuddling it and crying into it before taking it to Postman's Park. He flushed a little at the memory. He'd been such a baby.

'We need to get round to the other side. The Upper Fifth dorms are on the first floor.'

'Upper Fifth?' Joe looked as if Fin was speaking a whole different language.

'Sorry. Year Eleven.'

'Oh.' Joe was trying to sound like he didn't care that he was only understanding one word in every three Fin was saying. That normally meant that he cared a lot.

110

Keeping low, they ran round to the side of the building. It was darker there without the lights that lit up the main entrance. Finmere smiled. He grabbed a few pebbles and took aim at the windows above. His first shot hit the wall and fell, useless, to the ground. The second came perilously close to hitting the window on the floor below. This wasn't as easy as he'd expected. Finally the third pebble hit its target and both boys flinched as it clinked on glass. Nothing happened.

Fin launched another stone, his eye in now, and it struck the glass bang in the middle.

'Get ready to run, just in case,' Fin said. It would be just his luck if Mr George was patrolling along the Upper Fifth corridor at that precise moment.

'If Mum hadn't taken my flipping phone, this would be a lot easier,' Joe said.

'No, it wouldn't. Phones are top of the banned list at St Martin's – immediate expulsion if you're caught with one.'

'No shit? I'd like to see them try to get away with that at Eastfields. No chance.' He let out a derisive snort.

A sash window above them rattled and rose and a boy's head appeared. Fin and Joe stood up and Fin waved. He couldn't see who it was.

'It's Finmere Tingewick Smith! I need to speak to Christopher Arnold-Mather,' he hissed, wincing as his voice seemed to echo loudly round the grounds. But it obviously wasn't that loud – that, or the boy at the window was a bit deaf.

'What?'

'I said—' he hissed again, and then stopped. 'Wait there,' he whispered to the boy, and trotted over to the building. With Joe close behind him, he ran up the fire escape, holding his breath with every clank of metal. The closest stairway was lined up with the dorm next door, and when they reached the second level, they crouched. The boy was hanging out of the window just a metre to their right.

'I'm Finmere. I go to school here,' Fin said. The boy looked back at him, puzzled. He was obviously new. 'Sometimes,' Fin qualified. 'Look, I just need you to get Christopher for me.'

The freckly boy stared at him for a second and then shrugged and disappeared. Fin and Joe stayed huddled on the fire escape, their breath steaming out after their run. A few moments later, some jostling and muttering on the other side of the window announced Christopher's arrival and he stuck his head out, his tall, lanky frame half-hanging over the sill.

'Fin!' he grinned, 'what the bloody hell are you doing here?'

'I need your help with something,' Fin whispered. 'It's really important.'

'Is this to do with your dad? Has one of his spying missions gone wrong? What is it we have to do?'

Joe had been peering through the railings at the grounds below. He looked up and stared at Fin. 'Your father's a spy, eh? He gets about a bit, doesn't he?'

Finmere prickled a little with embarrassment. Just like he'd told Joe his dad was a big master criminal because he'd figured that would most impress the Eastfields kids, he'd told Christopher and his friends at St Martin's that his father was a spy – he'd been six years old, and once he'd said it, he couldn't see how he could go back on his story.

'I can't explain here, Christopher. You've just got to trust me. We need to find your dad.'

The excitement on Christopher's face fell a little. 'What's my father got to do with anything?'

Fin was itching to be on their way. Mr George was always telling them that his nose could smell the slightest hint of mischief in the air, and that nose was probably leading him to the East Wing right now. 'Christopher,' he said urgently, leaning forward, 'we need to hurry. Just go and get dressed and come on!'

'And bring some cash. We're nearly broke,' Joe added.

Christopher stared at Joe for a moment before looking back at Fin. 'Am I going to be back for breakfast?'

Joe laughed a little wildly and Fin elbowed him. 'I don't think so, mate,' he said.

Christopher grinned. 'Good. Can't stand bloody porridge. Back in a mo.' He'd disappeared back into the dorm almost before he'd finished his sentence.

Ted had a minicab waiting outside the café behind Aldgate Station and the three boys piled into the back seat while Ted took the front. Fin barely recognised him. In the tweed jacket, cable-knit jumper and corduroy trousers, and carrying a battered brown briefcase, he looked every bit the harmless, slightly doddery old man Finmere wanted him to appear. Maybe there was a tiny chance that his plan might actually work. Now that they were back in the city, he was feeling decidedly less confident.

Fin sat between his two friends. Christopher had taken the fact that Fin's dad wasn't a real-life James Bond reasonably well under the circumstances, but that, together with the idea of a whole other school – and a whole other best friend – had been lost in the far more amazing stuff that Fin, with Joe interrupting here and there, had whispered to him on the cab ride back from Surrey.

Joe now sat quietly on the back seat, chewing his bottom lip and staring out of the window.

Ted twisted round in his seat and asked Christopher, 'So, where's your dad likely to be then, son?'

Christopher looked at Ted thoughtfully, and Fin wished his friend could see the old man in his proper blue uniform with all its brass buttons. Ted looked pretty impressive and invincible like that, no matter how old he was.

'All this stuff they've told me, about different worlds and that. Is it really true?' Christopher said.

113

'Yes, it is, son. And if we can get into the 'ouse of Detention, then we can prove it to you.'

Christopher grinned and nodded. 'Yes, I suppose you can. He'll be at Grey's. It's his club. It's in—'

'I know where it is,' Ted cut in softly. 'It was Harlequin Brown's club too. A good club to belong to, that one.' Turning back round he directed the driver in the direction of Westminster.

Finmere looked out at the lights as they sped by. The London traffic had finally cleared for the night, giving them a decent run. He didn't think he could have stood being trapped in traffic, not with this hanging over his head.

'So, Joe.' Christopher leaned forward, a thick dark curl from his mop of hair falling over his face. 'Do you play rugby at this other school – Eastfields? You look fast. Scrum half?'

Joe shook his head. 'Football – I'm a forward. Goal scorer.'

'Cool! Maybe after we're done with whatever it is we're doing I can teach you rugger and you can teach me football. We play it at St Martin's, but only for fun, in break. Rugby and cricket are our main sports.'

'I don't get cricket really,' Joe admitted, 'all that strolling around all day. It's a bit boring.'

Christopher laughed. 'I think so too. Old man's game.' He leaned back and stared out of the window for a bit, then elbowed Fin. 'He seems like a good sort,' he whispered.

'He is.' Fin could tell by the way Joe's shoulders had relaxed a bit that he was starting to like Christopher too, but Joe was always going to take more convincing. He wasn't as open or easygoing as Christopher was.

After a moment, Joe looked round from the window. 'So what about you, Fin? What do you like best? Rugby or Football?'

Fin looked at the innocent expression on his friend's face. Joe may not have been academically clever, but he was far from stupid. Fin smiled, knowing exactly what the question

114

was really asking, and it had nothing to do with sport. Christopher had turned at the question and was looking at Finmere too.

Fin shrugged. 'I like them both exactly the same.' He stared straight ahead, through the driver's windscreen.

FOURTEEN

Of all the capital cities of the world, none has as many gentlemen's clubs of fine reputation as London. Quietly revealing that you were a member at Boodle's or White's could open doors at some of the finest establishments across the five continents. Many of the older clubs were more respected than the British Government itself.

In guide books you would always find White's listed as the oldest club in London. Its membership was in the main drawn from the younger Royals and the gentry. The fact that the oldest gentlemen's club in the city was actually Grey's was one of London's best-kept secrets.

Grey's was *very* exclusive. Its membership was capped at one hundred, and unlike others of the city's most prestigious clubs, admittance to the hallowed portals depended less on what family a man came from than on what kind of man he was – although obviously the twenty thousand pound annual subscription fee meant its doors weren't open to just anyone. And Grey's could refer to itself as a 'gentlemen's club' with its head held high. Unlike many of its counterparts, Grey's had never opened its doors to lady members. It enjoyed its peace and quiet too much.

Finmere, Joe and Christopher tumbled out on the pavement while Ted paid the cabbie. The white Georgian house rose up clean behind the black railings, one in a long row of buildings that curved into an arc.

Fin looked at the shiny plaque beside the black glossed

door with the big brass handles. The streetlights in this part of London were in good repair, making it easy to read, even now when it was very nearly midnight. 'Grey's,' Fin whispered to himself. 'Established 1682. "Semper fidelis, Semper paratus" – *Always faithful, Always ready*.' Fin fought the urge to touch the perfect golden shine. There wasn't even the ghost of a smear on it.

Ted rang the doorbell and Fin elbowed Christopher forward. 'Remember the plan,' he reminded him. His heart rattled in his chest: *plan* was hardly the right word for his idea, which felt paper-thin – but there was no time for revising it now …

'Stop worrying, Fin,' Christopher grinned. 'I know how to play the old man. And anyway, he'll get us in there just to get me out of the way. He's always so busy.'

The door opened and a bald, thickset man in a smart suit eyed them from the hallway. He didn't smile. If you could pick a complete opposite to Jarvis, Fin thought, then this man would be it. He looked more like a nightclub bouncer than a butler.

'Can I help you gentlemen?' His voice was all gravelly East End even though he was pronouncing his H's and T's properly. How very strange. Fin had expected someone at least as posh at Jarvis – even as posh as Christopher, maybe.

'Yes, you can,' Ted said, not sounding very much like Ted at all. 'We would like to speak with Mr Arnold-Mather. It's a matter of some importance.'

'I'm his son,' Christopher cut in with that sense of authority he had always had; it always impressed Fin. He could have used some of that supreme self-confidence when he'd been speaking to the women at The Rookeries – in fact, he could use that confidence pretty much all the time. He'd seen the boys at St Martin's and the kids at Eastfields, and he'd decided that kind of confidence couldn't be copied or learned; it was inbred. It came from coming from the kind of life where it was drummed into you from the moment you were born that you were privileged and special – even if, as Fin had often thought while looking at some of the more unpleasant boys at St Martin's, you weren't.

'I need to speak to my father rather urgently and I know that he never leaves Grey's before one when he's in town,' Christopher said, drawing himself up straight.

The bouncer/butler eyed Christopher and then examined the rest of them, staring at each in turn.

'Well?' said Christopher, impatiently, an imperious note in his voice.

For a moment Fin caught a glint in the man's eyes that hinted at how enjoyable it would be to squash Christopher like a fly— And then it was gone and he stepped aside, letting them in before quietly closing the door.

'If you would just wait here, I'll see if the member is available.' He nodded curtly before disappearing through one of the three sets of tall doorways that led off the foyer.

Fin looked around. There were two large leather Chesterfield sofas, one red and one green, set at right angles, with a small corner table between them. Their colours made Fin think of his school trunks. He wondered for a second where his red trunk actually was. Maybe when this mad adventure was over they'd let him have it early.

None of them took a seat. The sofas didn't look as if they were meant for sitting on, just as the precisely folded newspaper sitting neatly on the table didn't look like it was meant for reading. A large grandfather clock ticked loudly. The bronze hands pointed at twenty-five to midnight. At some point Fin figured he'd feel tired and the day's events would catch up with him, but right then it felt more like the middle of the afternoon than the middle of the night.

A different pair of doors opened and the bouncer/butler came through, followed by a taller man with thick grey hair.

'Christopher.' Unlike the butler's accent, this man's voice was pure cut-glass. 'What on earth are you doing out of

118

school at this time of night?' He was dressed impeccably, his dark suit barely creased, his striped tie perfectly tied in an Oxford knot. Finmere was impressed; he had never managed to get his quite right for school, and it certainly never lasted for more than a few hours. And it was uncomfortable – why would anyone dress like that in a club that was meant for relaxing? What was the point – just to look a certain way?

'Father.' Christopher stepped forward and held out his hand. Mr Arnold-Mather took it and gave it a firm, but rather impatient shake.

'Well?'

'It's a school challenge,' Christopher said. 'We've got forty-eight hours to complete a project on a London historic site of our choice. And we really want to do the House of Detention in Clerkenwell. It's got such a great history and apparently there are ghosts there and everything!' Christopher didn't give his father a chance to interrupt. 'And the winners get a prize and the school will be awarding a new Independent Learners Trophy.'

Mr Arnold-Mather gave a cursory nod to the bouncer/butler. Fin could have sworn he saw a flash of disappointment wash over the man's face before he disappeared through one of the doorways. Perhaps he'd been looking forward to chucking them out on their arses.

'But what are you doing in London in the middle of the night?' When he frowned, his bushy eyebrows met in the middle.

'We've been trying to work out what to do and we only just had our idea – and there's only one day of the two-day research time left and then it's back to school.' Christopher pointed at Ted. 'This is Mr Mason. He's the support tutor supervising us.'

Ted stepped forward and shook Mr Arnold-Mather's hand. 'Good to meet you, sir. I do apologise for the lateness of the

119

hour.' His accent had disappeared again and Fin didn't like it; Ted sounded like a stranger.

'If we left our idea until tomorrow, you'd have been at Westminster and we'd never have got to see you!' Christopher's hands were planted melodramatically on his hips and Fin began to worry that his friend might be overdoing it a little.

'Yes, I see that.' Mr Arnold-Mather's low voice was sombre. 'But Christopher, it *really* isn't done, disturbing a man at his club.'

'I'm sorry, sir,' Christopher mumbled, looking down at his trainers.

Mr Arnold-Mather ignored his son and looked at Finmere and Joe. 'And you are?'

Fin held out his hand. 'Finmere Tingewick Smith, sir.'

The man's eyes widened slightly as he gripped Fin's hand. His skin felt rougher than Fin would have expected from a politician. 'So you're Christopher's best friend,' he said after a moment's pause. 'We've heard a lot about you. Sounds like you have led a most interesting life.'

Fin blushed, embarrassed. He guessed Christopher had told his parents about Fin's dad being a spy. Still, he had a name of a possible real father now – *Baxter* – and not even his embarrassing lies could dull his excitement over that.

His hand was finally released and Mr Arnold-Mather turned his attention to Joe, who stuck his hand out straight and firm. 'Joe Manning. Pleased to meet you.' It sounded more like 'pleezedta mee'cha' and Mr Arnold-Mather's eyes narrowed slightly.

'Joe's at St Martin's on a scholarship,' Christopher piped up, flashing his eyes helplessly at Fin behind his father's back. Fin admired his quick thinking: boys at St Martin's did not speak with strong London accents or drop their final consonants.

'Yes,' said Joe without hesitation, 'a sports scholarship.'

'And what is your sport, young man?'

Fin's heart thudded. If Joe said football, there was no way

120

Mr Arnold-Mather would believe it. It wasn't a St Martin's sport.

'Rugby,' Joe said loudly. 'I'm a scrum half.'

'Excellent.' Mr Arnold-Mather smiled tightly. 'Well done, young man.'

When he turned his attention back to his son, Joe winked at Fin and Fin grinned back. Joe definitely wasn't stupid.

'So, Christopher, exactly what is it you want from me in the middle of the night?' Mr Arnold-Mather asked.

'Well, the House of Detention is closed to the public—' Christopher started.

'Ah, now I see. You want me to let you in. Well, that I can arrange. I'll have someone meet you there in the morning.' He moved to get something from his inside jacket pocket, but Christopher stopped him.

'We'd really like to get in tonight, sir,' he said, trying not to sound desperate.

Fin's skin tingled with nerves. If they had to wait until morning then Christopher's escape would have been noticed, and St Martin's would report the missing student to his parents and their game would be up. The other boys could be pretty inventive when covering for people, but they could only fool the masters for so long.

'There's stories of ghosts and stuff,' Christopher continued, adding hurriedly, 'I mean, obviously *we* don't believe in any of that – but we think it's really important to include it in our project. And we have to head back to St M's tomorrow night, so tonight's our only night.'

'And we only had the idea to do the House of Detention this afternoon,' Fin jumped in.

'And we've got way more chance of winning than the other groups.' Joe was never one to be left out. 'They're all doing boring places like the British Museum.'

Mr Arnold-Mather raised his hands to silence the boys and he looked over at Ted and sighed. Ted smiled and sighed back

121

in that irritating way adults did when they were sharing an exasperated 'teenagers!' moment. Fin wondered if adults ever realised just how exasperating *those* moments were for the teenagers in question.

'Well, it's highly irregular, but I do approve of ingenuity. I suppose I could arrange for someone to meet you there and let you in. It's not exactly full of national treasures, you know.'

Christopher grinned at Finmere, who grinned at Joe. Looked like they were in!

'Are you planning to stay the night?' Mr Arnold-Mather asked.

'Yes, sir,' Ted said, adding, 'I shall be with them, of course.'

'Fine. I'm not a great believer in molly-coddling boys. A little lack of sleep won't kill them.' Mr Arnold-Mather reached into his pocket and pulled out a leather-covered memo book and a slim gold pen. He scribbled an address on a sheet of paper and handed it to Ted. 'Leave the keys at the reception desk there in the morning; that will serve.'

He looked at the grandfather clock. 'Not quite midnight. I'll call Hatcher now. He should be able to meet you there in thirty minutes or so.'

He looked at Christopher and smiled. 'Well, son, I'm glad to see that you're learning how to think things through. Work hard and behave. I shall be interested to see how this project of yours works out.'

'Yes, sir,' Christopher said, shaking his father's hand firmly.

Watching them, Fin decided they looked very awkward together, as if they were almost strangers. Maybe having parents that lived only in your imagination wasn't so bad after all.

Feeling as if they'd been dismissed, they shuffled past Mr Arnold-Mather as he opened the door to let them out, muttering their goodnights and thank-yous.

'Well, that went surprisingly smoothly,' Ted said as soon

122

as the door was closed behind them. His accent was thankfully back to normal. 'Not knocking your plan, Fin,' he added quickly, 'but given it's the middle of the night an' all—'

'I know what you mean.' Christopher glanced back at Grey's. 'He's not normally so obliging. Maybe he's winning at cards.' He paused. 'Or perhaps he just wanted to get rid of me – I mean us.'

He stumbled over the last words and there was an empty silence that no one knew quite how to fill.

'So where is this House of Detention place when it's at home then?' Joe piped up, breaking the moment.

'Clerkenwell – not too far from here,' Ted answered. 'We've got half an hour, so we might as well walk it.'

'As long as we're not running. We've done quite enough running for one day,' Joe muttered.

'So much for a being a pro footballer,' Fin laughed.

'Didn't you hear?' Christopher broke in. 'He's a scrum half now.'

Standing there between his two best friends, Finmere felt good. He was going on an adventure, and Joe and Christopher were coming with him. They'd be like the three musketeers, all for one and one for all, their double-edged swords at the ready ...

FIFTEEN

It started raining as they waited in a doorway in the quiet residential area of Clerkenwell. For a moment Finmere thought that the drops were black, but it must have been the way they looked in the streetlights against the darkness of the night.

A black cab pulled up and a short man in a long wool overcoat stepped out. He spoke to the driver for a moment before coming over to them. He was wearing a bowler hat. The boys looked at each other. None of them had ever seen someone actually wearing a bowler hat before.

He spotted them in the doorway and came over, then paused in front of them and peered over his glasses, studying them. 'This way,' he said finally.

Fin pulled his jacket closer around him, trying to block out the cold rain, as he followed Ted at a quick trot into a side-street. The man – Hatcher, Fin presumed – unlocked a gate in the railing, behind which were steps leading down into a gloomy well. Fin wasn't sure what he'd been expecting, but he'd expected the entrance to a prison to be somewhat grander.

The black cab growled while in front of them Hatcher fiddled with various locks and keys, muttering under his breath as he worked, just loud enough to make Fin certain they were supposed to hear. 'Dragged out of bed in the middle of the bloody night ... No explanations ... filthy rain ... death of cold ... bloody spoilt brats ...'

The door to the House of Detention swung open and

124

Hatcher leaned in and flicked the light switch. Yellow beams spilled out onto the street. He turned to them. 'Make sure you have the keys back promptly tomorrow morning,' he said coldly. 'This isn't a playground.'

Without another word he bustled past them and back to his waiting taxi.

'Thank you!' Fin called after him. Hatcher didn't turn round.

'Cheerful chap,' Christopher said.

'Um, can we go in now? I'm flipping freezing.' Joe jostled them forward.

Once inside, under the light, Finmere stared at the others. His eyes hadn't been deceiving him: where raindrops had splashed down his friends' faces, it looked like muddy tear tracks.

Joe stared back at him.

'Yuk! Wipe your face, Fin.'

'Yeah – right back at you.'

They used sleeves and a couple of ragged tissues to rub themselves clean. Ted used a handkerchief, and then stared at it thoughtfully. 'Black rain. That's not good. Not good at all.' He sniffed and then stuffed the handkerchief away. 'Right. We'd better hurry.'

Fin stared at him. The old man had quickly tried to cover up his horror at the sight of the unnatural colour of the rain, but he hadn't done it quickly enough. The look on his face was enough to make Finmere's bones shiver. How much wasn't Ted telling them?

'This place is creepy,' Joe whispered as Ted led them down to the second floor. The low ceilings were curved, and even though they were high enough to walk upright, even the boys hunched a little.

Finmere peered into the rows of gloomy stone cells. 'You were making that stuff up about ghosts, weren't you, Christopher?'

'Yes, of course.' Christopher didn't sound so confident.

'You might've made it up for your dad,' Ted said walking deeper into the underground building, not leaving the boys any time to explore, 'but there're plenty of stories of ghosts and strange noises in the 'ouse of Detention. Some ghost-watching TV show even came and spent the night 'ere, not so long ago. They left scared out of their wits.'

'Really?' Fin breathed quietly, and felt both Joe and Christopher pull in a little closer on either side. He didn't have any urge to push them away. There was definitely something spooky about the silent cells of the old prison.

'It wasn't no ghosts they heard, of course,' Ted continued, 'not ghosts like they imagined 'em.'

'Well, if it wasn't ghosts,' Fin asked, 'then where did the voices come from?'

Ted found a small stairwell and led them down, to what was obviously being used as a storage area. Mannequins that must have once been used in displays on the upper storeys were crammed, forgotten, into cells. Even the light was dirtier, and the temperature had dropped a couple of degrees as they'd gone deeper into the bowels of the earth. Ted turned left.

'Travelling's not as safe as you might think. Some people like me get really sick; I feel like I can't breathe, but for some others it's worse. And the effects can get you any time, not just on your first trip.'

He stopped and turned to the boys. 'I was going to 'ave this little talk with you at the doorway, but 'ere'll do.' He paused. 'Travelling to The Nowhere and back ain't without its risks. There are voices down 'ere; they're those unfortunate people who found the doorway and went through it, but never arrived on the other side ...'

'What?' Christopher broke in, 'where did they go then?'

Ted shrugged. His face was grim. 'No one knows. They're trapped somewhere, that's for sure. I've 'eard crying down 'ere meself. I don't think it's a place, not like any of the worlds. I

126

think they just exist somewhere in between. Like being stuck in space.'

'Oh, that's great,' Joe said with feeling.

'But,' added Ted, 'it's rare. Tends to happen to them as don't believe in what they're seeing. People with no imagination. It's as if their own brains stop 'em making that final cross-over, leaving 'em stuck half-mad somewhere in the middle.'

Fin smiled, slightly nervously. 'We'll be all right then. We believe.'

'There is something else. Time is funny in The Nowhere. It's all right getting there, but it can play tricks on you coming back.'

'How do you mean?' Fin was beginning to wonder if this was really such a good idea.

Ted paused and looked at Fin, as if considering how much he could take. 'The old boys at Orrery House,' he started, 'the ones you shave every year?'

Fin nodded.

'As it 'appens, some of them ain't so very old ... sometimes coming back from The Nowhere can suddenly age you. That's why being a Knight is such an honourable role. Some of those men you shaved? They weren't no more'n twenty-five or thirty on their last trip. They left there young 'n'ealthy, and they arrived back an instant later old and fragile.'

The boys looked at him, their mouths slightly open.

'After a few years, no matter 'ow 'ard they try to fight it, they tend to drift into a kind of catatonic state. They don't die early, mind. They're just old for a very, very long time. It's not to be taken lightly. The Ageing can 'appen to any Knight or Traveller, and there ain't no rhyme nor reason. No one's safe. Double-edged swords are treated with respect, and only used when absolutely necessary.'

The boys stood in silence. Fin could see the first glimpse of real fear in his friends' faces, and he felt it echoed in his own stomach. To get old, really old, just like that, in the space of a breath? That was much scarier than actually dying and he still hadn't really got his head round that either.

'Can't anything be done for them?'

Ted gave a tiny lift of his shoulders. 'Sometimes, just in the last moments before midnight, mostly on very special occasions, the Ageing will reverse. It don't 'appen very often, though – maybe once every five or ten years? But every night we get the old men shaved and presentable, just in case.' He let out a long breath. 'You can never give up 'ope, you see. If 'ope goes, then we're all lost.'

Fin thought of the hours he'd spent shaving the men at Orrery House. He suddenly felt very proud and humble to have been trusted with the task.

'So what you're saying is that could happen to us?' Joe's hand ran over his hair.

Ted nodded. 'That's about the long and short of it, yes.'

Fin looked at his friends. 'You don't have to come with me. Really. You've both done loads to help already. This should be on me.'

'It's different for Fin,' Ted said. ''e's already come back from The Nowhere once – when 'e was a baby. Some of his 'istory is in The Nowhere and some 'ere. You two on the other 'and, are Somewhere born and bred.'

Christopher and Joe looked at each other, their eyes wide, and then they both grinned.

'If you think we're going to let you off on this jaunt on your own, then you are very much mistaken.' Christopher slung his arm around Joe's shoulder. 'Right?'

'Too right.'

'But it could be dangerous,' Fin said. He knew what Joe was like for rushing in without thinking, and despite their different backgrounds, Christopher wasn't that different.

'No doubt about it, son,' Ted added, 'it *will* be dangerous.'

'All the best adventures are, aren't they?' said Christopher.

128

Joe rolled his shoulders like a boxer getting ready for a fight. 'Bring it on!'

They found the doorway behind the wall of the furthest cell. Ted switched on the light and the bulb flickered and hissed into life above them.

'Poor sod that got this one, back in the nineteenth century, 'e'd 'ave 'ad to be manacled – no one wanted 'em exploring and adding to the ghostly wails.' Ted ran his hand over the old wall. He found the brick he was looking for and tugged it, and a section of the wall opened out slowly, like a door.

'That is wicked!' Joe said excitedly.

Fin thought of the vase at Orrery House that opened up the door to that special room and then the bookcase at The Rookeries. 'The Knights are big on secret doorways,' he muttered.

Ted heard him and nodded. 'Some things are best kept 'idden.' He paused. 'Like this.'

In the gap, a view to another world had, quite literally, opened up. People bustled past, chatting and laughing, the women in long dresses and the men in frockcoats. Fin guessed they were going about their daily business, not en route to some high-class fancy dress party. There was something a little strange about the view: it looked two-dimensional, not real, and though there were shades of dark and light, there was no colour anywhere.

'It's like a black and white film,' he breathed eventually.

'All the tears an' rips look like that until you go through. The doorway is the same.'

The boys stared at the other side as Ted opened his brief-case. He pulled out the double-edged sword that had been thrust into Judge Harlequin Brown's chest. Fin recognised the glittering hilt, even though the rest of it was in a sheath attached to a leather belt.

'Put this on,' Ted said, undoing the buckle and handing it to Fin. 'You'll need it to get back. Fowkes will show you how to use it.'

Fin did as he was told, doing the belt up tightly around his waist. The sword felt heavy against his leg, but he adapted his balance so he could walk with it without even thinking. He was ignoring the gentle knocking in his head. Whatever was behind that mental door, he didn't want to know. He wasn't opening it. *Ever*. That knocking scared him in a way he didn't understand, and he was fine with not understanding it. Instead, he focused on the magic of The Nowhere.

Joe was staring through the open rift. 'Aren't we going to look funny over there? It's all oldey-worldey, like looking into the past.'

Ted shook his head. 'This ain't our world, son. I told you, time's funny in The Nowhere. There's bits of all times there, some like our own 'istory, some changed and made all their own. Most of the locals, they tends to stay living in the area of time that suits 'em best – you'll see what I mean. But they won't bat an eyelid over a pair of jeans or two. Remember, it's like our world, *but very different*. Don't ever think of it as our London, 'cause it ain't.'

The boys nodded and Ted pulled a piece of paper out of his pocket. ''ere's the address of a pub you can stay at for the night, and a letter for the landlady. Mrs Baker knows 'er; she'll see you right.' He rummaged in his other pocket and retrieved a few strange-coloured notes and a coin. ''ere's some money – there's plenty there.'

Fin stuffed the notes in his pocket, then looked down at the coin. It winked back at him. He turned it over between his fingers. A normal coin had a head's side and a tail's side, but this one didn't: it had a profile of a man on both sides, but he faced in different directions.

'That's different. That's not money,' Ted said quickly. 'No one's used this doorway for years, and even in the old days it was rarely opened, not once the Knights' swords were forged. But after all the problems we 'ad, what with people getting through all by accident, we installed a gatekeeper on the other side. I don't even know if there's still someone watching, but if there is, give 'im that. It'll show you're an intentional Traveller: one of the Order.'

'Okay.' Finmere swallowed. This was getting realer by the second.

''e should give it back to you, just in case you need to come back this way. Make sure 'e does.' He looked at the other two boys. 'I've only got one coin. There's more, but I don't know where they're kept. If you do split up, then think carefully about who gets it.'

'What about the brick wall?' Fin asked. He didn't fancy walking into that, doorway or not.

'It's designed to open automatically for Travellers coming the other way. You'll be locked in down 'ere until I come, but you'll be safe. I'll stop by a couple o' times a day to check for you.'

Christopher pulled a mobile phone out of his pocket. 'Give me your number and I can call you if we come back this way. It'll save you coming down here on the off-chance.'

Fin looked at the handset. 'So much for the rules, then.'

'Cool phone,' Joe said. Joe's phone had been taken off him by his mother the previous week after he was put on report by Miss East. He had another week to go before he was due to get it back.

Fin didn't have one at all. According to Judge Brown, *the world was noisy enough before the invention of the mobile phone* – he certainly wasn't having one, and that meant Finmere could live without one too. Fin had respected that decision, even though there were always cheap handsets for sale at school. Anyway, it had made his stories – his lying – easier, if he was out of reach when he was away from either school.

Ted looked at the device in Christopher's hand. 'Don't 'ave one, son.'

Looking bemused, Christopher put the phone back in his pocket.

Fin turned to Ted. 'Right. So we go in, find this address, and stay the night. Then we have to find Baxter's friend Fowkes, and tell him, "Something's happened to the Storyholder," and then he'll know what to do.'

'I 'ope so, Fin, mate.' Ted's words sounded heartfelt.

'Where do we start looking?'

'I don't rightly know,' he said, a little sadly. 'Fowkes, well, 'e gave up the Order when Baxter died; 'e got drunk and disappeared somewhere in The Nowhere. The couple at the pub; they might be able to 'elp you – maybe even know where 'e is. But my bet is you'll find 'im somewhere dark, the kind o' place people go to when they've given up, when they think they don't care much about life and death no more. The kind of place people can get lost or dead in very quickly.'

Fin frowned. 'They don't sound like good places.'

'They won't be.' Ted looked long and hard at Finmere. 'I told you it'd be dangerous, Fin. Now you don't 'ave to do this. No one will think any less of you if you don't.' He paused. 'But I truly think you might be our last and only 'ope.'

Fin smiled. 'I'll do it. I *want* to do it, Ted – for you, and the Judge, and Mrs Baker, and everything you've done for me. And for Baxter, too.' He added the last words softly. He stepped forward and hugged the old man, breathing in the smells of soap and tobacco and the ghost of lavender. 'I think I *have* to do this.'

'You're a good boy, Fin. The best.'

When they broke apart, Finmere thought the old man's eyes were glistening a little too brightly. Maybe it was just the light.

'Let's do it then,' Joe said quietly.

Fin nodded. 'Here goes,' he said, glancing at each of his friends. 'One for all, and all for one, and all that jazz.'

With a final smile at Ted, and gripping the coin tightly, he shut his eyes and stepped into The Nowhere.

PART TWO

The Nowhere

SIXTEEN

For a moment they just stood in silence. Fin had thought he'd feel something more when they'd stepped through the doorway, but there was no sense of anything momentous – it was just one ordinary step. The place they'd stepped into—? That was *far* from ordinary: no longer a dull black and white, now full of vibrant colour.

'I know it's raining,' Joe said quietly, 'but has anyone else noticed how warm it is?'

'Maybe it's summer here,' Christopher said.

They were standing in what looked like a wooden shelter built against a rough wall, looking at a tall wooden gate with a rusty iron chain holding it shut. The doorway was still there behind them, and when he glanced back, Fin could see Ted looking in.

They nodded at each other, then the black and white Ted raised his hand and gave Fin a thumb's-up and a big grin, then turned and walked away. Fin decided it was probably easier that way.

He looked out into the warm afternoon. The rain was muddy, like the rain had been back in their own London, and judging by the expressions on the faces of the quaintly dressed passers-by it wasn't any more normal here than it was at home. Christopher rattled the gate. 'What do you think? Shall we just jump it?'

Fin had been looking around. 'Hang on,' he said as he spied a small bell with a string attached above Christopher's head. He tugged, and they all flinched at the deep, resonant sound. They stared at the tiny brass instrument.

'Bloody hell!' Joe wiggled a finger in his ear. 'How does that tiny thing make so much noise?'

Finmere shrugged. 'I guess it's like Ted said. Things are different here.'

Christopher grinned. 'Excellent. This is going to be fun.'

'It's phat, man – that's what we say in Sauf Lunnon.' Joe exaggerated his accent and grinned at his new friend. 'Truly sick.'

Fin hoped they hadn't forgotten already how serious Ted had looked when he'd tried to explain how dangerous this mission might be.

A shadow fell across the uneven road in front of them and a man appeared on the other side of the gate. 'Well, I'll be,' he said, peering in between the rough-hewn planks. A dark rain drop hit the shiny bald patch that covered most of his head. He wiped his hands on the apron that was tied round his thick waist. 'Nothing's come through this doorway since I inherited the shop from my old dad.'

Christopher looked around, confused. 'I know things are different, but what on earth exactly can you possibly sell from here?'

'My butcher's shop's next door, son.' He dug around in his trouser pocket and pulled out a chain of old-fashioned iron keys. 'Well, I'll be,' he repeated under his breath as he found the key he was looking for. 'Never seen nothing like it.' He grinned, revealing dark gaps between rotting teeth. 'Now then: I believe you've got something to give me?'

'Oh yes.' Fin held out the strange coin. The sword banged against his leg as he moved and he saw the man's eyes narrow as they fixed on its jewelled hilt. He found himself gripping it with his free hand. 'I take it you're the gatekeeper?'

'That I am, my boy,' the man said, turning the coin over

138

between his thick fingers. 'Jacob Megram, that's me.' He looked up. 'This all looks in order.'

Fin held out his hand. 'Um … I think you're supposed to give it back.' He tried to sound as if he knew what he was doing.

Megram laughed, a throaty sound with rough edges. 'Right you are. I'm not too practised.' He handed the coin back to Fin. 'Me old man, he told me what to do ten years ago, but there ain't been no Travellers since he retired, so it's all a bit dusty in me head.' He opened the wooden gate, and the boys stepped out. A drop of rain hit Fin's hand. It was warm, like the air.

'Is the rain normally black in The Nowhere, Mr Megram?' he asked, slipping the coin carefully back in his pocket.

The butcher's face fell slightly. 'No, no, never seen the like before. Not in a long time, anyways. Maybe it's something blowing in from south of the river. Or them future blocks.' He looked up. 'There's a lot of scaremongering going on, even talk of the old Prophecy. Thought we'd ditched that when we banished the Magi. Me, I like to believe there's always a logical explanation. Can't tell the wife that, though. To her, it's all omens and signs. You know what women are like.'

He looked over to the right, where a small collection of women with shopping baskets were gathered at the front of the shop. 'At least this shower's passing, eh?'

The boys looked at each other. They were not really well briefed in polite conversation with grown-ups, not even Christopher – his parents tended towards the 'children should be seen and not heard' school of thought, even if he was sixteen.

'Well, I suppose we'd better get on and find this pub, then,' Christopher said. 'Um … I don't suppose you know where The Red Lion is, do you?' He looked up at the gatekeeper hopefully.

Megram held out his hand for the piece of paper and looked

at it thoughtfully for a while. Finally, he said, 'Don't often leave the shop, to be honest, boys. The street, well, there's a street of that name over by St Paul's – that's over that way.' He pointed to his left. 'I'd start there, meself.'

Fin held out his hand. 'Thanks, Mr Megram.'

'You're welcome.' He barely touched Fin's fingers, then slapped his hands on his thighs. 'I'd best get back to the shop.' Muttering, 'Well, I'll be,' again, he turned and started to move off.

'So, which way?' Joe asked.

Fin looked at the piece of paper Ted had given him. 'I don't recognise the street name myself, but Mr Megram said to head for St Paul's, so let's do that. We can always ask from there.'

'Let's go then,' Joe said, and led the way into the narrow street opposite.

SEVENTEEN

Courtiers were sitting or standing in various small groups in the Throne Room when St John Alexander Golden kicked open the double doors at one end. Perry Longman's body was hanging limply in his arms. His entrance was dramatic, as he'd intended it to be, and he smiled inwardly as a flurry of gasps ran through the huddles of powdered and pale ladies and gentlemen who had been giggling behind fans or playing a few hands.

The three musicians attempting to force out a decent tune on the harpsichordian stopped abruptly at the sound of St John's violent entrance. St John was relieved: the harpsichordian was the Royal instrument; that it was being played meant at least one member of the King's immediate family must be here.

The click of his heeled boots on the intricate mosaics of the marble floor echoed up into the high carved ceiling of the long room as St John strode up to the slight figure sitting on the golden throne. One white-stockinged leg hung over the side, the buckle on the black patent shoe glinting as it swung backwards and forwards like a metronome.

St John dropped the body on the red-carpeted stairs leading up to the throne, fell to one knee – elegantly – and bowed his head.

'Get up, get up!' The Prince Regent's unusually high voice sounded a little peeved. He turned from the window he'd been gazing through as St John rose to his feet.

'You are always so melodramatic, St John.' He waved a lace handkerchief at the body. 'I'm not sure this was entirely necessary.' He carefully moved his leg back over the arm of the throne and sat up straight. His highly rouged cheeks were accentuated by the whiteness of his heavily powdered skin and the high, stiffly curled white wig.

St John looked at him. The Prince Regent might dress like a dandy, with his ruffled necklines, bejewelled shoes and tightly fitting silk breeches, but St John had never been fooled by his appearance. The Prince Regent was not a man to be underestimated.

The Prince raised a hand and the room emptied, the two dozen courtiers scurrying away to continue their games and flirtations without either the glorious presence of their Regent, or the terrible cacophony of the harpsichordian. He waited until the great gilded doors had closed behind the last of them before he spoke.

'How did your Knight die?'

'Murdered at the Old Bailey House of Real Truths, Your Majesty,' St John said. He paused. 'We found him stabbed to death in the Storyholder's apartments.'

Only the slightest twitch at the corner of the Prince's plump rosebud-pink mouth betrayed any emotion; his voice remained clipped. 'And the Storyholder?'

St John hung his head. 'Gone, Your Majesty. Someone has taken her.'

The Prince rose to his feet and walked carefully to the large window. The palace had a lot of windows and mirrors. There was no problem with glass in this part of the city.

'This black rain is a bad sign.' He spoke so softly that St John had to strain to make out his words. 'It's moving across the city, sometimes raining here, sometimes there. You can see a lot from the top floors of the palace – more than the people realise, I sometimes think.' His small, thin fingers touched the pane of glass. 'I think there's a storm coming. A storm like that of seventeen years ago, perhaps even worse.'

'Someone has taken the Storyholder and murdered a Knight. There things are more serious than the weather, Your Majesty.'

The Prince arched a carefully plucked eyebrow and when their gazes met, his did not hold the familiarity and respect St John had expected. The Regent's dark eyes were cold. 'The last time a black storm struck was after a Knight was killed.' His mouth pinched. 'The Storyholder was involved then too, if you remember. Which I am quite sure you do.'

'This is different.' St John kept his head slightly bowed. 'This isn't the work of an angry mob—'

'The people had a right to be angry. The Storyholder should never have been touched! Not like that.' He spat the last word out.

'But to murder a Knight? *That* was unforgivable!'

The Prince's eyes flashed angrily. 'What he *did* was unforgivable! The Knights are sworn to *guard* her, not to *love* her!'

'He didn't touch her – she swore to it. The Storyholder doesn't lie.'

The two men stared at each other and finally the Prince raised his hands. 'But we had all these arguments seventeen years ago. I do not wish to have them again now.' He sighed again and sat down on his golden throne. 'My father the King wanted to finish with the Order after those dark days. He wanted to send you all back, and he would have, had it not been for Harlequin Brown. He persuaded my father of the Order's necessity; he reminded him that the men of old had *insisted* on the formation of the Order, even if their beliefs were now believed archaic.' He paused, and then, speaking so quietly he was almost whispering, said, 'It was Harlequin Brown who said that even if the Order had not been foretold, we could not judge you all on the actions of one man – and one man who had paid with his life. Baxter died for what he did, and perhaps that was justice enough.'

143

He looked up at St John. 'He is a wise and noble man, Harlequin Brown, and I think perhaps I should come to your Somewhere and meet him. He too must be deeply concerned by the Storyholder's abduction. He will understand the importance of this to all of us, more than most.'

'A King should never leave his kingdom, Your Majesty,' St John said firmly, 'especially at a time like this.'

Keeping his eyes on the Knight, the Prince spread his hands wide. 'But I am not a King. Merely a Regent.'

St John could feel the façade of mutual respect slipping away. He stood his ground. 'And I must respectfully remind you that I am Commander of the Inner Council of the Order of the Knights of Nowhere. I lead the Knights now. Harlequin Brown is all but retired.'

The Prince shrugged elegantly, barely wrinkling his tight satin brocade coat. 'There are leaders and there are leaders.'

The insult wasn't lost on St John, but he gritted his teeth and temporarily swallowed his pride. He needed the Prince Regent on side – for now, at least. 'If you truly wish to speak to Harlequin Brown, Your Majesty, then of course I can take you through. But you know there can be ... side-effects.' If the Prince chose to take him up on the offer, then St John would just have to get rid of him and damn the consequences.

The Prince sighed. 'I have heard of the Ageing. I am no coward though, St John Alexander Golden.'

'I would never be so foolish as to suggest you were.' St John looked out at the filthy rain streaking the windowpane. 'But if there really is a Black Storm coming, your people will need you here.'

There was a long moment of silence that echoed along the thirty-metre length of the Throne Room.

'I give you a week to find her. Someone will surely come forward with a ransom demand and you will find them. They will hang at Smithfield for this.' The Prince Regent looked out of the window as he added, 'She must be returned unharmed.'

If anyone had been looking at his face, they would have recognised how truly concerned the Prince was ... but he did not want the Commander of the Knights of Nowhere to see the depths of his fear.

He mastered his expression and turned back to St John. 'This crime is inconceivable. Only a madman would take her. The Five Eternal Stories hold all the worlds in place – who would be so mad as to try to change that? To what end?' He sighed, a small whisper of air in the vast room.

'People are talking of superstitions, Your Majesty,' St John said smoothly, 'of your world and ours bound together. They speak of the Prophecy.' His eyes hardened. 'But these things are of times long gone; I do not – *will* not – believe there is any truth in them today. We put them – like the Magi themselves – behind us.'

St John thought he could see fear behind the defiant dark eyes. Of course the Regent didn't want to believe in the truth of the Prophecy – if he did, then he'd have to accept that the Curse of the Kings would one day come for him. St John bit back a smile. It was all destiny at work. *The dark man to rule the Dark Age.* The words rang constantly in his head.

'We live in mad times,' St John said eventually. He thought perhaps the moment of chill between them had passed over, and he quietly congratulated himself on his ability to play any man in the world – in *two* worlds.

The Prince smiled coldly. He said softly, 'But it seems the Magi have come back. I have reports that one has been seen in the city.'

'A Magus?' St John let surprise colour his voice. 'But I thought they were banished?'

'They are – but if these reports are correct, then perhaps these events are connected.'

Although his face was straight, inside St John was sneering. *Of course* the two things were connected – he had organised them both, after all. It was irritating that the Magus had been

145

seen despite all his precautions, but it wasn't as if any of it would really matter for much longer.

'I'll have my men find him, Your Majesty,' he promised. 'If there truly is a Magus in the city and he has something to do with this terrible thing, then we'll know soon enough.'

The Prince Regent met his gaze and nodded. 'Perhaps we are on the same side, St John – or at least different sides of the same coin.'

'Of course we are, Your Majesty – we always have been.' St John stopped himself from adding that it was all written in the Prophecy.

When he came out of the palace he was smiling. A week was a long time. He'd have the stories by then, and the Prince Regent – primped-up fop that he was! – would have to bow to his commands. That's if he wanted to live, of course, which, St John had discovered over the years, most people did. The Prince would do as he was told. It wouldn't be in the best interest of his beloved people to do otherwise.

He thought of the Storyholder imprisoned in the mirror. The time for being a gentleman had passed. He needed to call the Truthfinders.

EIGHTEEN

The boys eventually found The Red Lion Public House at the corner of a busy T-Junction at the back of St Paul's. Back in their London, streets stank mostly of cigarette smoke and diesel fumes, but in The Nowhere the smells from various different kinds of hot food stalls were overlaid with the stagnant taste of the river. They'd seen the river on their walk – or rather, they'd seen its banks, and the thick layer of fog or something similar that rose a metre or more from its surface. There must have been boats out there somewhere, but Fin couldn't make out any shapes, and he was very glad that he wasn't trying to row or sail in that water. The smell from the streets was bad enough.

Someone knocked on the door and Fin turned.

'Coming!' Christopher got up from the narrow single bed he'd been sitting on and opened the door. The landlady – she'd introduced herself as Ida Harvey when she'd read the note from Mrs Baker – bustled through carrying a tray.

'There you go, boys.' She put it down on the dresser and smiled. 'A nice pot of tea and plenty of buttered toast. There's some homemade strawberry jam there too.'

'Oh, great!' Joe bounded across the room in a flash. 'I'm starving. Thanks, Mrs Harvey.'

Fin smiled. Joe was already smearing jam thickly onto a buttered slice. 'Oi, leave some for the rest of us, gannet!'

Mrs Harvey beamed. 'You tuck in. There's plenty more if you need it. And it'll be time for dinner in an hour or two.'

Her hair was set in firm curls and under her knee-length dress, she wore thick tan tights. They'd watched films about Britain in the Blitz at school, in history, and it was suddenly obvious to Finmere why Mrs Baker listened to all those old 1940s wartime records. And she dressed a bit like Mrs Harvey too, like something out of the Second World War. Maybe this was the place Mrs Baker had come from. He was having a bit of a hard time taking it all in. He'd just realised how blindly he'd been living all his life.

As if reading his mind, Mrs Harvey stepped back a little and put her hands on her hips as she looked at Fin. 'So, you're the boy Maggie's been looking after, eh?'

Fin felt a prickle of shy embarrassment at the back of his neck, and nodded.

'She always thought you were something special,' Mrs Harvey murmured. 'She said as much in her letters.' She smiled. 'Right fond of you, she is, our Maggie.'

Fin didn't know what to say. Once again he felt a twist in his gut when he thought about all the people who had looked after him for so long. He hadn't appreciated them at all. He made a silent promise to himself, for the thousandth time that day, that he would never be that selfish again.

'Here, Finmere.' Christopher handed him a piece of toast, munching on another himself. 'This jam is excellent, Mrs Harvey. Delicious.'

She preened a little, smoothing her dress. 'Me mum's secret recipe, rest her soul.' She walked back to the door. 'Now, you boys try and get a couple of hours' kip. I'll call you when it's time to come down for dinner.' She smiled at them all. 'Welcome to London.'

Once the enormous pile of toast was finally devoured, the boys lay back on their beds and talked quietly about the strange sights they'd seen on their short walk from the doorway to the pub. How much more was there to see? They couldn't really fathom it.

His stomach full and gurgling, Fin shut his heavy eyes and just listened to the quiet chatter between his two friends. Joe said something, about whether there was a premiership football league in The Nowhere, and Fin laughed, which somehow turned into a yawn. He glanced at his watch, then shook it. It looked like it had stopped just after midnight – just as they'd crossed over into The Nowhere. He stared at the frozen luminous hands for a minute. Maybe it would start working again when they went home. It wasn't long before even Joe fell silent and soon all Fin could hear was their deep sleep-breathing.

Within seconds, he joined them.

The bar of The Red Lion was busy and hot, and the air was heavy with cigarette and pipe smoke that made Finmere squint as they pushed their way through the heaving room. Men and women were laughing loudly with each other as they downed pints of what looked like thick beer, except for the grey froth that topped it off. It wasn't white, like Guinness; Finmere thought it looked pretty unappetising – but he figured it certainly had the same effect as ordinary beer, judging by the glowing faces of the crowd. The whole place was buzzing with people enjoying themselves.

'It looks like they like to have a laugh in The Nowhere,' Joe said as they grabbed one of the few empty tables and quickly sat down. 'I wonder what the laws are on underage drinking over here? I wouldn't mind trying some of what everyone else is drinking.'

'I'm sure you would, you little chancer!' They jumped as Mrs Harvey appeared out of the throng, as if summoned by Joe's words. She placed a large tray down between them all. 'But you can wait till you're seventeen, just like everyone else.'

There was a bowl of steaming stew and a crusty bread roll

for each of them, and large glasses of some red juice.

'Now, you boys eat up.' Mrs Harvey's hands rested on her ample hips. 'That's good home-made stew, that is – I saved it back for you, and just as well I did, there's been so many in. I'm surprised the noise didn't wake you up sooner. I was going to give you ten more minutes before I came and got you. But here you are.' She beamed at them.

Fin noticed her face was flushed from the heat, and he could see the man and two younger women behind the long wooden bar were being kept busy refilling glasses, washing dirty ones, and clearing away tables and ashtrays. He wondered if they'd find time to eat themselves, and started to feel guilty that Mrs Harvey was waiting on them instead of taking a break.

Christopher and Joe had no such reservations; they were both tucking into their food whilst watching the people around them. Most of the women had their hair in shoulder-length curls that barely moved. They were wearing knee-length dresses, and almost all of them wore vivid red lipstick that brightened otherwise bare faces. The men wore suits and trilby hats. Except for the three of them, there wasn't another pair of jeans in sight.

'It's like something out of an old war film.'

Fin wasn't sure if Christopher was just talking to himself, but he nodded anyway.

Most of the commotion was coming from round the other side of the bar and Fin stretched in his seat to see more clearly.

Three men, in their thirties, Fin thought, sat in the middle of a crowd talking loudly and setting off rounds of laughter or gasps of astonishment in their merry audience. Each of the talkers had three or four pints lined up and one in hand, and as Fin watched, a man came back from the bar and added another glass, nodding shyly to the biggest of them, who was enthralling his audience.

'They look different to everyone else,' Fin said with a frown. 'How come they're dressed like that?'

Joe, sitting opposite, tilted his chair so he could see. 'They look like they're dodgy. Like part of a Firm,' he said.

Fin could see what he meant. All three wore black polo-neck sweaters, and despite the heat in the pub, they had kept their leather coats on. It was almost as if they were dressed in a uniform of some kind. The biggest man, the one who was doing most of the talking, had a dark clipped beard and slicked-back hair. He looked like he spent a lot of time in the gym.

Mrs Harvey, who'd come back with more bread rolls, laughed at Joe's comment. 'Of course they're different, God love 'em! They're Traders – we don't get Traders in very often. That's why we're so busy tonight. Everyone likes to hear the Traders' stories, especially at times like this – even more especially when the black rain's been falling. We all need cheering up.' Her face clouded over slightly. 'There are legends about the coming of black storms, and none of them's good. Only seen it once before, and it lasted nigh on twelve months. A lot of people went into the river that year.'

She shivered, and then shook a smile back onto her flushed face. 'This crew just got back this afternoon.' Her eyes glassed over slightly as she looked at them. 'South of the river and back. Fancy that!'

'What's so special about going south of the river?' Joe asked.

Mrs Harvey looked down at him, her brow furrowed. 'Well, everything, lovey. Traders are the only ones who can cross the river safely, and you've got to be born into Trading. The water in the Times flows funny – and I don't mean funny ha ha, neither. That river will suck you right in if it gets the chance. If it doesn't take your boat under you, you'll end up lost in that mist until you'll throw yourself over the side rather than starve to death.'

She looked at each of them in turn, then said darkly, 'You go down to the bank and listen: you'll hear people calling for help. It's their own fault, mind – they should have been less miserable with their money and paid a Trader to do their business in the South of The Nowhere for them, or to take them across if they really had to travel.' She shrugged. 'But you can't teach common sense, now, can you?'

'Aren't there any bridges?' Fin said, still staring at the fierce-looking men. He wasn't sure he'd want to get into a boat in that river mist with anyone who looked that dangerous.

'Bridges? Blimey, sweetheart, you are green, ain't you?' She shook her head. 'There's only one bridge in the city, and that's the West Minster Bridge. And no one knows how that got there ... it's just always been there.'

The man behind the bar waved frantically, trying to get Mrs Harvey's attention – probably wanting her to help with the crowd all demanding drinks. Finmere thought Mrs Harvey was doing a very good job of studiously avoiding noticing him.

'There's rumours, of course, and most people say the Magi built it, right back at the beginning of everything.' She winked at Fin. 'That's where I'd put my money – but since the Magi have been banished from the city for more than a hundred years, I guess we'll never know for sure.'

She looked at all three of them, one by one, as if to make sure they were all paying attention. 'The only thing I can tell you, tell all three of you, is that the West Minster Bridge ain't safe for crossing, so don't be thinking to try it. You're still on the river, see, and the tides can still pull you in.

'They just do it differently,' she added ominously. 'They play with your mind, that's what people say. People do still cross it, though: desperate people, maybe them with people chasing after them, and those others who think these things only happen to other people, that they'll be fine. But the outcome is generally the same. They get halfway, then climb over the side and quietly jump.' Her voice dropped. 'You've got to be in a very, *very* good mood to try crossing the bridge. Otherwise the river will get you. Just you mind me, boys. Always pay the Traders.'

Fin nodded decisively, but at the same time, he was desperately worried. There was so much to learn about The Nowhere – why had Ted sent *him* to do this important job? He wasn't up to it, he had only just turned sixteen. He couldn't see how he could possibly avoid letting down all those people who were depending on him.

Mrs Harvey grinned, lightening the mood. 'Now you boys enjoy your dinner. It'll quieten down soon enough in here, and then we can have a good chat.' She finally acknowledged the sweating man behind the bar and, picking up a couple of glasses on her way, went back to help him.

Fin, Joe and Christopher got back to the business of eating. They strained to pick up fragments of the Traders' bawdy tales of the Southern women, and as they listened, Fin wasn't sure if it was the stew or the stories that were making his nose burn a bit.

NINETEEN

St John Alexander Golden, Commander of the Inner Council, pulled the blanket away from the mirror, and then poured himself a glass of wine from the silver-chased decanter sitting ready on the small round walnut table. He didn't offer his companion anything.

'I thought I told you to stay hidden. One of the Prince's informants has seen you – how did that happen?'

The swarthy man standing by the door shrugged. 'I have been careful. But—' He broke off and looked at St John for a moment. 'The black rain has made everyone afraid and suspicious. Including me.'

St John sighed. The last thing he needed was for the Magus to lose his nerve, especially at this stage. 'It's just rain. It will pass.'

'It's the start of a black storm,' the Magus muttered. His voice was guttural, his accent from far-away lands beyond the South. His silver earrings tinkled as he stepped closer to the mirror. '*We've* made the storm. I wish I had known what it was you intended when we started. I didn't think you would bring this blackness on us.'

'You didn't *want* to know.' St John could barely keep the disdain from his voice as he stared at the purple robes and weighty gold jewellery the Magus was wearing. He wondered why the man couldn't just dress like a normal person – or as normal as people got in The Nowhere. At least he covered his outlandish clothes with a heavy cloak when he was in the streets, but even so, Londoners in The Nowhere were just as savvy as those back home. They could always sense a wrong 'un.

St John turned back to the mirror. 'We didn't make this storm,' he said, gesturing, '*she* did. And if we don't get what we need from her soon, then the black storm will be the least of our worries – for *both* of us.'

The Magus glanced at the study door, looking as if he'd rather be safely on the other side of it. St John recognised that look. It was the look of a man who was wondering how on earth he'd let himself get himself into such a situation.

He smiled.

'Look, there's no going back now. In a few days it will all be done, and no one will even know that you were involved. Not that it will matter if they do.' He gripped his arm, a little surprised to find how strong it felt under the silk of his robe: all sinew and bone. 'Just think,' he added, softly, 'a few more days and you can return home a hero, ready to lead the Magi back into the city where they belong. And the Magi will be truly men of power in the new society, I promise you that.'

The Magus nodded, his eyes damp. 'Yes. Yes.'

St John looked at the mirror. 'For great change there is always a need for some kind of sacrifice. I need you to show me how to summon the Truthfinders. We can't delay any longer.'

'Tell me, St John Alexander Golden,' the Magus said quietly, 'what makes you think you can hold the stories? You know the Prophecy.' He paused before whispering the words that had been echoing in St John's own mind: '"*Eternal stories held unready shall bring black tempest and madness, a battle for King.*"' He paused. 'Your mind is unready, I think.'

'What makes you so sure?' St John's smile was a bitter slash across his face. 'And remember, the Magi never could see the outcome of the Prophecy. Perhaps the Dark Age will be a good thing ... and perhaps the Prophecy is just an old riddle that means nothing.' The Knight's low voice dripped menace. 'You Magi know no more than the rest of us.'

He was tired of talking. Despite his apparent unconcern, a black storm was coming, there was no denying that, and he wanted this situation taken care of before it arrived. The Magus could keep his fears and regrets; St John had no place for such things. The time for walking away was long past. 'Now fetch them,' he said quietly.

The Magus smiled wryly, acquiescing, and as he turned his attention to the mirror, small drops of sweat formed on his dark face. He took a deep breath and shut his eyes, ready to summon a magic that was beyond the Knights, the Regent, even any King in any world. This was the true curse of the Magi: an understanding of powers that mere man could not comprehend, and would always resent.

St John turned back to his wine as the Magus commenced his strange chanting. As he listened, the Commander of the Inner Council couldn't help but wonder how the Magi had allowed everything to be taken away from them so suddenly. It was not something that was discussed much amongst the Order; according to the Knights' records it was generally regarded as none of their business. He smiled slightly. Soon everything in all the worlds would be the Knights' business.

'They're here,' the Magus gasped, and as St John spun round he wondered briefly if perhaps he should make an effort to pay more attention to the man's spells and incantations. But then, it wasn't as if he had any intention of shutting the mirror prison down again; it would prove very useful, especially in the early days of his new regime. A little fear could go a long way in a confused society.

He stepped towards the grey surface as the Magus moved slightly back. 'From now on,' the banished man whispered, 'whenever you want to call them, just knock on the centre of the frame at the top, three times. They'll come.'

'It's as simple as that?'

'It is now, yes.'

St John nodded, the Magus almost forgotten. The Truth-finders were here! He felt almost nervous, despite being safely on his side of the reflection. His head was aching slightly as he peered into the murky gloom. On the other side, looking as if they were both standing close to the mirror and at the same time disorientingly far away, stood two figures. St John flinched. Their pale, bald heads were smooth, with veined skin stretched thinly over their skulls.

They had no eyes – the skin was pulled tight across the large empty sockets – and yet he still had a terrible feeling that they were looking right inside him. He thought that if there were more colour in the prison, the flesh that dipped slightly in those hollows might be a deep red, and mottled, like a scaly scab.

Their thin bodies were hunched over, their shoulders crooked, and although they were wearing black trousers of some kind, their skeletal chests were left bare. The same patterns carved around the edges of the mirror were etched across their abdomens, and like those carvings the shapes moved and rippled, sliding up their arms and disappearing over their shoulders before reappearing around a narrow side or a hip and rejoining the constant swirl of movement.

St John stared. 'How can that be? How can … ? Unless—' He paused. 'Are they part of the prison, or mirror, or whatever this contraption is?'

'Yes.' The Magus had backed up against a large desk. 'That's why they are so effective. They cannot be bribed or corrupted by anything from any world. They and the prison are one.'

'How very interesting.' St John sipped his wine nonchalantly, trying to ignore his trembling hand.

The two creatures stepped closer, moving as one, pulling their lips back and clacking sharp, pointed teeth together, sucking in hisses of air as they did so, almost as if they were tasting it.

The one on the right leaned forward, his neck stretching slightly. He licked his lips and tilted his head. 'You seek some reluctant truths?' His voice was like a bitter wind cutting through an abandoned tunnel. There was no warm life in it. It wasn't a voice that St John could ever imagine laughing. But then, neither was it a face he could imagine smiling.

'Yes. Yes, I do.' He tugged the chain roughly and pulled the Storyholder into view from the dark place that held her on the other side. She was thinner than she had been the previous day, but there was still fire in her eyes. 'From her.'

The second figure chattered its pointed teeth and jerkily circled her. St John watched as she ignored its repulsive presence, instead gazing at the Magus, who was cowering behind him. There was no disguising the disgust in that look.

'What truths do you want her to tell?' the Truthfinder asked sibilantly.

St John smiled. 'She knows the five stories – the Eternal Stories. I want her to tell them to me ... to me *alone*.'

As the creature bent forward to bow, St John could see blue veins running like a spider's web across its skull. His teeth clacked, and as he grinned, he drew his lips back to reveal high gums and a long tongue. 'As you wish. We will return.'

Without warning or farewell, the creatures and the Storyholder were sucked backwards into the world on the other side of the mirror until they were just a tiny dark speck at the centre of the oval of grey, and then they were gone, leaving the murky surface empty and the chain at St John's feet pulled taut. He hoped it was strong enough to hold.

The prison was apparently huge, with its never-ending hallways and cells of pain and eternal anguish. The Magus had suggested it might be a universe in itself, and the one thing St John hadn't been too sure about was how to summon prisoners to the surface. If the chain broke, the Storyholder – and more importantly, her stories – could be lost in there forever.

But the chain would hold, St John was sure of it. Nothing as insignificant as a rope of steel could possibly interfere with his destiny.

'This is no good! This is no good – what have I done?' The Magus paced in a small circle, wringing his hands. 'I have done such a wrong, such a *great* wrong—' He looked up at St John. 'This is a terrible thing I have helped you to do. If I had known – if I had thought beyond my own anger ...'

St John handed the man his cloak. 'Stop worrying. I have everything under control. Now just concentrate on not being seen.'

His worried muttering was interrupted by a loud knock on the door, and at St John's brusque call, Kane and O'Regan appeared in the study.

'There's a man here to see you, sir,' Kane said. 'He says he's the gatekeeper.'

'Send him up.' He turned to indicate the Magus. 'And show this gentleman out.' He slapped the cloaked man on the back.

When Kane had taken the Magus out, St John pulled O'Regan close. 'Follow him, kill him and bring back the body. His whining is starting to annoy me, and if we don't deal with him now, I think he'll be going running to the Prince Regent himself before long. Do it fast and clean, but it needs to look like he was attacking you.'

'Not a problem, sir,' O'Regan said, his face expressionless.

St John watched as he followed the other two men out. His thick body was all muscle. Back in their own world, O'Regan had been a soldier before he'd become a Knight. Killing was something he was particularly effective at. And St John liked soldiers. They were good at following orders.

The mirror was covered and the door to the small study locked by the time the gatekeeper arrived upstairs. St John was sitting at a table next to Conrad Eyre.

The man stood in front of him, his cloth cap clutched in his hand, shuffling from foot to foot in front of him. 'Jacob Megram, sir,' he said, trying not to sound nervous. Although he still wore his work clothes, he'd attempted to smarten up by adding a tatty jacket to his ensemble. He glanced at the laptop in front of Conrad Eyre for a moment and then licked his lips nervously as he waited for St John to speak. He was sweating already.

'So you're the gatekeeper?' St John was quite impressed, despite Megram's scruffy appearance. It took a lot for someone to leave their part of the city in The Nowhere, and the man was probably feeling the tiring effects of being in a different Borough. 'I'm afraid I can't remember if we've met.'

'No, sir, no, we haven't,' Megram said. 'There's not really been a need since my father's day. I was worried I wouldn't be able to find you. I didn't really want to ask too many questions, if you know what I mean. Then I found this address in some of my father's effects, along with your name.'

St John suspected all the head-nodding that was accompanying the man's stilted speech was not helping his travel sickness one little bit. Poor sod.

'And now you've found me.' He smiled, but his patience was thin. It had already been a long enough day. 'So what is it you had to tell me so urgently?'

'Well, I'm sure you already know, your Lordship, but the missus, well, she thought I should come and tell you anyway, what with all this black rain and everything, and the missus, well, the missus lost her father in the madness during the last storm, so she thought it was best to be safe rather than sorry.' He paused, sucking in a breath. 'It's just that – well, three young lads come through the doorway this afternoon, and since no one's used it in years, it just struck me as odd, your Lordship ...' His voice petered out and he stood there twisting his hat and looking desperately uncomfortable.

160

The rising boredom St John had been feeling melted away. 'Three boys?' He glanced over at Conrad, who had leaned forward in his chair. 'And you let them in?'

Megram looked around helplessly, as if searching for the right answer. 'Everything was in order, your Lordship, they had the two-headed coin. Even knew I was supposed to give it back. They knew where they were too. Didn't show no surprise.'

'What did they look like, these lads?'

He thought for a moment. 'Not too old, I reckon – good age to be butcher's boys, maybe fifteen or so? One was black. One was tall and thin and a bit of a gent, I'd reckon, by the way he was speaking, if you know what I mean. The one with the coin, he was blond, a bit smaller than the other two. He seemed to know more than the other two. He did most of the talking.'

St John thought of the folder Conrad Eyre had brought back from Harlequin Brown's apartment at The Rookeries. Surely this was too much of a coincidence, three teenagers suddenly turning up in The Nowhere through the doorway?

'There's another thing, sir.' Megram interrupted St John's train of thought.

'Yes?' he said coldly.

Megram blanched, but went on bravely, 'The blond boy, your lordship: he had one of them swords, like yours.' He looked at Conrad. 'And his. And the gentleman's down-stairs.'

St John's eyes narrowed. 'Are you sure? It might have been an ordinary blade.'

Megram shook his head. 'Nothing wrong with my eyes, your Lordship. One of my few talents, sharp-seeing: this was a Knight's sword, a double-edged sword, sure as eggs are eggs. It had jewels on the hilt, like yours, and he had the ring too, like all you Knights do.' He frowned, as if something had just occurred to him. He looked at St John, then Conrad, then

161

said slowly, 'That ring: it didn't match his sword, not like yours do.'

He looked down at the floor as if he'd finished speaking, and then added, 'Oh, and they were trying to find a pub. Somewhere near St Paul's, I think it was.'

St John's heart thumped angrily in his chest. It had to be this wretched youth, this Finmere Tingewick Smith. He was obviously important in some way – had someone had sent him here against the Knights? Who could have done that? He clenched his teeth. That old bastard Ted Merryweather, Defender of The bloody Somewhere? It had to be him …

A silent growl raged in his throat. He'd deal with Ted bloody Merryweather personally when this was done. It had been so long since he'd been back in his own London that he'd almost forgotten the other man even existed.

Finally he looked up, and realised that Eyre and Megram were staring at him.

'Have I done the right thing, sir? Coming to see you?' The gatekeeper was sounding a little frightened.

St John liked the sense of power that gave him and let the gatekeeper stew a little longer before getting to his feet. He undid the small cloth purse that hung from his belt and tipped out a handful of gold coins.

'You did, Megram, you did indeed do the right thing. The Order has an excellent gatekeeper in you. Here, take this.' He held out the money.

'Oh no, I couldn't sir.' Megram's eyes glazed over at the sight of such largesse.

'Oh, but I insist.' He nodded, and this time the butcher took the coins, his eyes wide.

'Thank you, sir. You're far too generous—'

'There is one more thing, Mr Megram. No one else is to go in or out – do you understand? When I can spare one I'll send a Knight down to help guard the doorway, but for the time being it will be up to you and you alone. Yes?'

162

Megram drew his stocky body up tall. 'Yes, sir, your Lordship. You can rely on me, sir.'

'Good man. Now, if you'll excuse us …' St John didn't have to finish the sentence; Jacob Megram was already backing out, bowing as he did so, as if St John was an emperor or a king.

When he was certain the man had gone, St John frowned and asked out loud, 'What *are* they playing at, those fools at Orrery House? And what makes this kid so special they think they can send him against us?' He kicked the chair he'd been sitting on.

'Do you think it's the same boy from the file I gave you?' Conrad asked, keeping a safe distance from St John.

'Finmere Tingewick Smith?' he said with a sneer in his voice. 'No such thing as coincidence. Of course it is.' St John paced a little. 'I want him found immediately. You take charge of that.'

'Finding them shouldn't be too hard,' Conrad said. 'Do you want all three?'

'I think so: we don't yet know which of them is Smith. I definitely want the blond one with the sword alive. My money's on him.'

'I'll leave Paul Kane and Malachi O'Regan and take the other four. We'll have them here in no time,' Conrad said, just as O'Regan came back through the door.

He hadn't knocked this time, and now he stood there panting, his head low.

St John stared at his empty arms. 'Where is the Magus?' His voice was cold. 'I think my orders were clear: bring him back *dead*. And I'm not seeing him, either alive or dead.'

'That was the problem, sir,' O'Regan said, still wheezing a little.

'What was the problem, exactly?' St John resisted the urge to pull out his sword and kill the Knight where he stood. The

Inner Council were few enough as it was, and he'd already sacrificed Perry Longman.

'I couldn't see him. One minute he was in the alleyway a few metres ahead of me, and the next— Well, just as we turned the corner into Temple Chambers, he disappeared!'

St John's eyes blazed. 'You lost him.'

'No.' O'Regan raised his head. 'No, I didn't lose him; he *vanished*. I watched him disintegrate into thin air.'

There was a long moment of tense silence.

Eventually Conrad Eyre broke it. 'That's the problem with the Magi, I suppose,' he said. 'They're very good at magic.'

St John sighed. He had to believe O'Regan. The man wasn't a liar – he didn't have the imagination. He swallowed his frustration and smiled. 'We can find the Magus after you've found the boys.'

'Boys?'

'I'll explain later.' Conrad flipped the laptop open and let it whirr through its start–up processes. He smiled, satisfied. 'The system's working. There should be only three red dots showing when we're gone: you, Kane and O'Regan. If anyone breaks in, you'll see them on here, and it'll give you plenty of time to decide whether to fight them, or cut through to The Somewhere and take the mirror.'

'Good.' St John thought of the secret doorway in his office: it led down to the street from the back of the next-door house. He'd cut through to hide the mirror if it were absolutely necessary, but he had no intention of going himself. Those secret stairs would serve him well enough.

He wondered what his Knights would make of his fear of Travelling. He didn't think anyone had realised just how long it had been since he'd actually been home for anything other than the unavoidable annual council gathering in the Whispering Chamber, and the follow-up report at Orrery House. They wouldn't be impressed, he guessed. They definitely wouldn't continue to follow him.

He often reported his imaginary trips at interminable length – since the Order didn't keep a record of Travellings, and no Knight would dare to ask pointed questions of him, it had ensured his phobia went unnoticed. It helped that things had been quiet between the worlds; that had made his plotting so much easier. He shivered. He'd been there when the Ageing had hit Lucas Blake; no way did he want *that* happening to him. Once he had the Stories, things would be different. Who knew how much power he'd have at his command then? The true extent of what the Storyholders could do had never really been tested. He fully intended to be the one to find out what those limits might be.

'The gatekeeper said they were seeking a pub near St Paul's,' he said to Conrad. 'There can't be too many in that area. We'll search them all.'

Conrad pulled his cloak from the back of a chair. 'And he said pub, not inn, so they were probably heading for one of the more modern Boroughs.' He strode to the door.

'Keep in touch, Conrad Eyre,' St John said, and turned to look out of the window at the city. He could see the part-wood, part-stone dome of St Paul's from here, though the bomb-blasted hole on the other side wasn't visible from this angle. It was a strange place, the cathedral. Perhaps that was why the original Inner Council had chosen it for their meeting place. Maybe he'd call a gathering of the Knights when this was done – but not in the Whispering Chamber of The Somewhere St Paul's, no: he'd have his meeting here. It was time for a change. He was sure he could hear the ghosts of Knights gone by in that strange whispering of the wind. It was time to lay those ghosts to rest.

He smiled. As night slowly fell outside, lamps and candles flickered into life across the city. In the distance, the strange shapes of Future Block glowed like a faraway moon. A cool draught tickled the back of his neck, and he turned and stared at his locked study door with rising excitement. The

Truthfinders were back. He could feel it. It was time to finish this.

He took a small torch in with him and lit three of the lamps along the wall, brightening his view of the dull, rippling surface, before pulling up a chair. The monstrous creatures were standing on either side of the Storyholder, who was lying crumpled on the ground. 'Not so powerful now, are you?' St John muttered, a small wave of triumph rising in his gut. She was broken, that much was obvious – and that meant the Stories would be his, and within a matter of moments. He shivered in anticipation, wondering how different he'd feel when they were inside him ... when he was the most important person in existence in all the worlds.

He smiled. 'That was much quicker than I expected.'

The Truthfinder clacked and clattered his teeth for a couple of seconds before finding his hollow voice. 'Quick and slow have no meaning here. One moment and eternity are all one.'

'How interesting,' St John said, not finding it very interesting at all. The inner workings of the mirror prison didn't matter to him one bit, just as long as the prison itself was effective – and it appeared it was, otherwise why would the Truthfinders be back so soon? He found he was salivating slightly.

'She's ready to give me the stories?' he asked, trying to hide the tremor of excitement in his voice.

Patterns swirled across the monster's pale, concave chest. 'She cannot,' he said, his voice echoing around the small room.

St John had so been expecting a 'yes' that it took a long moment before he realised that wasn't what he'd heard. 'What?' He cleared his throat and forced some sound from it. 'What do you mean, "she cannot"? *Why* can't she give them to me?' His voice was beginning to rise in pitch as his fury seeped into it.

166

'She does not have them to give. She has hidden them.'

St John stared at the Truthfinders, completely dumbfounded. If anyone other than a Truthfinder had told him that, he wouldn't have believed them, not for a moment. A Storyholder separated from her stories? He hadn't even thought that was possible – not when it was the Storyholder's sole purpose: to guard the Five Eternal Stories, to keep them inside and alive … *That was how the worlds remained in balance!*

He stared at the broken figure, loathing washing through him, eating him up. She'd always been difficult, this one, right from the start. First there was the terrible business with Baxter – though that had, admittedly, helped serve his own purpose. Now there was this. He gritted his teeth and thought about his Knights. He had promised them success, and he had trained them to be ruthless. He did not care for the idea of them losing faith in him. He started to shake when he realised his silent partner wouldn't be too pleased either. And, of course, there was his own burning desire for the power the stories would bring him: that hadn't changed at all …

'Where has she hidden them? And how?' he hissed, his rage slowly bubbling up inside him.

'You did not request that information.'

His temper finally cracked and as he stood up he kicked his chair out of the way. 'Well, I'm bloody requesting it now!' His skin burned an angry red, clashing with his golden hair and beard.

'Then we shall find your answers.' The empty voice remained impassive despite St John's fury.

The Storyholder moved for the first time. She lifted her head, and her loose hair fell about her shoulders. 'No,' she whispered, and even in her despair, there was such beauty and strength in her voice that it dispelled the darkness around her. 'No, you will not have your answers.'

St John stared, a little confused, as she lowered her head and, hidden by a curtain of hair, started jerking from side to side. Muffled yelps came from her until, finally, she spat something onto the ground. A low, wet howl gurgled from her throat and she collapsed even further, as if she'd sacrificed her last strength. Her face was still hidden as she mewled in agony.

St John crouched by the mirror, his heart thumping loudly in his chest. 'What is she doing?' he demanded of the Truthfinders, 'what is she doing in there?'

The Truthfinders stood impassively. Even the clacking of their sharp teeth subsided slightly, until one said, 'She has taken the Right to Silence.'

'The what?' St John shouted as he looked into the foulness of their crimson-covered sockets.

'She has taken the Right to Silence,' the monster repeated. 'It is open to every prisoner, although few are strong enough to take this route.'

'But you're *Truthfinders*,' he spat, his fury palpable. 'You can still get my answers, can't you? The Magus promised me you could get me what I want.' He suddenly felt as if all the plans he'd made were as fragile as a house of cards and now, after all these years of careful building, the delicate structure was wobbling. How had this happened? 'He *promised* me,' he repeated.

Their mouths clicked and hissed in unison, their tongues darting out over their sharp teeth, and although St John knew that humour was beyond them, he had this nasty feeling they were laughing at him.

'We make prisoners speak the truth,' one of them said eventually. 'If they cannot speak, then we cannot retrieve information.'

'What do you mean, *if they cannot speak*?'

The Storyholder finally raised her head and looked at him. Her eyes were glowing, defiantly victorious, and St John realised he'd been foolish to think they'd broken her spirit. He stared at her face, appalled. Her mouth hung open, as if

168

it was too painful to close, and thick, dark blood coated her chin and ran down her neck, staining her long yellow hair. Never taking her eyes from his, she spat a mouthful of hot red liquid to the floor.

'She cannot speak without a tongue.'

St John's own mouth fell open at the enormity of what he was hearing. 'She's bitten off her own tongue?' he whispered.

'That is the only way to access the Right to Silence.' The Truthfinders were fading, melting into the greyness, their moving tattoos lingering slightly before they too vanished.

'Where are you going?' St John leapt to his feet again, his anger overriding his shock as it pumped through his veins. 'You *cannot* go!' he screamed, 'I have *questions*! There are things I need to know!'

'We cannot ask them. We are done.' By the time the last sentence was finished, the dead echo of the Truthfinder's voice was all that remained of them.

For a second all St John could hear was the rush of his own breath in his ears. This couldn't be right. *This couldn't be right at all*. This was *not* how it was supposed to play out.

St John and the Storyholder stared at each other, separated by centimetres and a universe.

His jaw twitched as rage and hate built to a crescendo, bubbling up through every cell in his body.

Eventually, his vision filled with red, and he snapped. He stormed over to his desk and started kicking the thick wooden pole that went through two great metal links and anchored the chain that was wound around one of the desk legs. He screamed out his frustration, sweat dripping from his forehead, as he kept pounding away at the wood, until the thick stave started to splinter and crack. Finally it broke and fell from the two links, and the chain started sliding heavily away, scraping across the rough wooden floorboards as it was inexorably sucked into the mirror.

St John, panting, stared at the Storyholder, who was drifting away. With no anchor for the chain that was cuffed around her ankle, she was falling deeper and deeper into the dark world on the other side.

'Enjoy your hell, Storyholder!' As he spat the words out, she was swallowed up by the gloom, then lost …

TWENTY

The pub had finally quietened down after the Traders had left, stumbling drunkenly back out into the street, still talking and laughing as loudly, if less coherently, than they had been at the start of the evening. Many of the other drinkers had stayed for one more drink, chatting quietly in the residual excitement for half an hour longer, but after a while only the regulars were left, the normal steady flow of customers who were easily managed by the two girls behind the bar.

The food had been filling, and by the time Mrs Harvey had time to come and sat down with them, even Joe had finished, leaving three crusty hunks of bread still in the basket. The thin man came behind the bar to join them.

'This is my husband, Albert,' Mrs Harvey said, taking one of the two pints he'd brought over. 'Thanks, love.'

Fin thought the grey foam on the surface looked like the dishwater at the end of washing up duty at St Martin's. He was surprised to see a slight steam coming off the surface.

'My feet are killing me.' Albert Harvey took a long sip of his drink and smiled. 'Oh, that's good.'

From a distance, and rushing around behind the bar, Albert Harvey had looked like a young man, but now Fin could see that he was the same age as his wife, maybe even a bit older. His hair was still dark, but he had a large bald patch at the back of his head, and his face was lined above his slightly sagging chin. But his eyes sparkled with humour, just like Mrs Harvey's – and Mrs Baker's. Fin decided he liked him.

'So,' Mrs Harvey said, her plump arms resting on the table, 'Maggie wouldn't have sent you here for no reason. But I'm surprised she's sent boys on her business, especially with the kind of company she keeps. Not that she tells me much – and not that I want to know much,' she added quickly.

'Something bad's happened, or it's happening, isn't it?' Albert Harvey gently interrupted his wife.

'Yes,' Fin started, 'it's the Knights. They've—'

'Stop there.' He raised his hand. 'We'll do anything we can to help Maggie – and the Order – but we don't need to know the details. To be honest, the less we know the better. I remember the Great War—'

'The First World War?' Christopher cut in. 'But that was ages ago.' He frowned. 'And it was in *our* world. Were you there?'

He shook his head. 'No. No, I don't know much about your world, but maybe the Great War came out of one of those leaks between our worlds? Here, it was more than fifty years ago now; my father fought in it.' His face darkened. 'But I remember him saying then: we can only betray with what we know. I didn't really understand it back then, being a kid and all, but I do know now. It means if you don't *know* anything, you can't *tell* anything.'

Finmere looked at Christopher and Joe, who both nodded. He wondered if they too were starting to feel a touch nervous. It was all sounding so *serious* – which of course it was, he knew that … but he wished they could just treat it like some kind of an adventure and ignore all the more sinister stuff. He thought they might do better that way.

'Do you have a lot of wars in The Nowhere?' Joe asked.

'No, that was the last one; that's why it's called the Great War. It was terrible enough for us to well and truly learn our lesson.'

Fin thought of all the wars still raging at home.

Christopher obviously was too.

172

'Our Great War changed its name to the First World War. That says it all, doesn't it? I suppose we didn't learn our lessons.'

Mr Harvey nodded. 'I've heard that about The Somewhere. That it's an angry place.'

'No, it's not,' Joe said, 'not always. It's—'

'The Knights can't be trusted,' Fin said, cutting Joe off even though he was defending their home. The best way to defend all their homes was to get on with what Ted had sent them to do. It didn't stop Joe from scowling at him, though.

Fin didn't look at him, but continued, 'We've been sent to find someone called Fowkes and give him a message.' Fin was working hard to limit the information as much as he could, whilst still finding out what they needed.

'The Knights can't be trusted?' Mrs Harvey repeated Fin's words incredulously. 'What, none of them?'

'None of the young ones,' Fin said.

'Except this Fowkes,' Joe added.

'That's why we have to find him,' Christopher finished.

All three of them looked at the Harveys.

'I knew something terrible was happening,' Mrs Harvey whispered. 'The black rain doesn't lie.'

'Fowkes, you say?' Albert Harvey smiled wistfully. 'Now there's a name we haven't heard in a long time, eh, Ida? I'd quite forgotten him.'

Ida flushed a little. 'That Andrew Fowkes was quite a Knight. Funny the things you forget. Life just moves on and the memory goes.' She paused. 'And they was bad times, so easier to forget than remember, if you know what I mean.'

Finmere wasn't sure that he did know what she meant, but he'd come to expect that from the adults around him. 'We need to find him, fast.' His heart thudded. This wasn't looking too hopeful.

'Blimey, he vanished a long time ago,' Mr Harvey said, snorting through his nose like a horse. 'Don't think I've even

173

heard stories about him, not for the best part of fifteen or sixteen years.'

He looked at his wife, and then in unison, as if they'd shared the same thought, they both spoke one word: 'Savjani.'

'Savjani?' Fin repeated. He wasn't sure whether it was a place or a person.

'Exactly!' Mrs Harvey beamed. 'If anyone knows where to find him, it'll be Savjani.'

'Is he a Knight too?' Christopher asked.

'No,' Mr Harvey laughed, 'though would've been if he was Somewhere-born, I reckon. But he wasn't, and us Nowhere men, we don't travel so well.' He smiled wistfully, and for a moment he looked as if he were lost in the past. 'Back in the old days, he was always hanging around with Fowkes. And Baxter,' he added softly.

The mention of Baxter made Fin's stomach knot and he was suddenly aware of the weight of the ring he was wearing: a dead man's ring; maybe even his father's ring.

'So where's this Savjani now?' Christopher broke in.

'He's an artisan. A clothcrafter,' Mrs Harvey said. She looked at the boys' confused expressions and added, 'He makes clothes. He's done well for himself, mind. Everyone's heard of Savjani these days. He kits out people all over London, any Borough no problem. I've heard he even makes clothes for the Prince Regent now.'

'Where can we find him?' Fin grinned at Joe, who smiled back. Perhaps they had a chance of success after all.

'Hang on.' Albert Harvey went behind the bar and after much noisy rummaging about, reappeared clutching a scruffy folded-up document. 'Here's a map of London – don't know how reliable it is, mind, but it should give you a general idea of where you're headed.' He handed it to Fin, who tucked the map into his back pocket with a word of thanks.

'Right now,' he continued, 'to get to Savjani's you need to go up past Convent Garden. You'll see the walled gates on your right, I think, and then head up to The Circus. He's got a big workshop on the corner of the crossroads there. There's always good business to be found at a crossroads in The Nowhere. You get traffic from all the Boroughs.'

'I don't know if it's just me,' Joe said, draining the last of his juice, 'but this Nowhere place gets more and more confusing, the more I hear.'

'That's life though, isn't it?' said Albert Harvey, 'confusing. And it doesn't change as you get older; you just get more used to it. Anyway,' he added, 'it's easy for you lot from The Somewhere; you can move between Boroughs without it bothering you. It's harder for us Nowhere blokes. Not many can move around without side-effects.'

The noise in the bar suddenly dropped, and Fin looked up as someone leaned over and whispered in someone else's ear. Some people who were leaving looked around, over at their table. Another woman frowned, and leaned in to share what she'd just heard with the man beside her. He listened, and then they got up and left. Fin stared. What was going on?

He didn't have to wait long to find out. One of the two barmaids came and crouched down beside the table. 'Sorry to disturb you, but I just heard something I thought you should know,' she said quietly, looking behind her nervously.

'What's that, Tilda?' Mr Harvey asked, his voice calm.

The girl's eyes kept flicking to the door. 'Someone's just said that a group of men are scouring the pubs in the area for three strangers. Young lads.' Her eyes flitted onto Fin. 'They've just been in the Green Man. Quite loud they was – they scared Mrs O'Connor, and that takes some doing.' Her voice dropped even lower. 'They said they were on the Regent's business. They had swords and everything.'

She looked at Fin, Joe and Christopher again. 'Just thought you should know,' she repeated softly.

Mrs Harvey patted the back of the girl's hand. 'You're a

175

good girl, Tilda. Now you get yourself off home; tell Jane too. We'll clean up tonight, Albert and me.'

The girl looked deeply relieved and scurried away, and within moments she and Jane had disappeared out of the door. They hadn't even stopped to pull on their coats.

The jolly atmosphere of earlier was truly dead now. Only a few customers remained, valiantly raising their pint glasses. Fin suspected they were probably just too inebriated to realise that the party was over.

'You three have to leave, now.' Albert Harvey was already on his feet and ushering the boys away from the table. 'Out the back, now – the Green Man's only two streets away.'

The boys hurried behind the bar and into the back of the pub. Mrs Harvey unlocked the door and peered out. 'It looks clear out here,' she whispered. She squeezed each boy's shoulder as she pushed them urgently into the embrace of the night.

From the right, sounding through the damp air, they heard a man's voice barking an incoherent command, quickly followed by the sound of heavy feet breaking into a jog. Fin's heart shifted to somewhere in his throat. It was the Knights – it had to be.

'Now hurry! And take care!' And Mr Harvey had disappeared back inside before he'd finished speaking, ready to face the Knights heading into his pub.

'Thanks for everything,' Fin whispered.

'Will you be okay?' Joe asked Mrs Harvey.

'We'll be all right if you three are all right.' She smiled, but all three boys could see the fear in her eyes. Fin had seen that same fear on Mrs Baker's face when they'd found her beaten up in her own kitchen. Mrs Harvey gave them one last smile, and then closed and bolted the door on them.

For a second the three of them huddled where they stood, then Christopher whispered, 'This isn't safe for us or them. Let's get the hell out of Dodge.' They wove their way between the empty barrels and crates that were stacked up in the paved yard to the waist-high brick wall that separated the property from the street. Pausing in the shadow of a pile of boxes they peered cautiously over the wall.

Quietly heaving sighs of relief when they saw the pavement on the other side was clear of people, they hopped over one by one, staying close to the bricks, as if they could provide some sort of camouflage against unwanted attention. The entrance to The Red Lion was round the other side, and if the Knights had sent someone to check outside, they hadn't made it round to the back. Yet.

'Let's go this way.' Find pointed left. 'We'll get clear, a bit away from here, and then we can check the map.'

One either side of Finmere, the boys jogged up the pavement away from the pub. The night was warm and muggy, the threat of hot, dark rain hanging in the air. Fin's heart ached a little for the crisp cold of his own London, that he understood, at least a little. He frowned to himself: if Ted was right, then he belonged here as much as there. It certainly didn't feel like it, not yet.

The pavement seemed to be getting thinner, and closer to the level of the tarmac, which in turn looked less smooth and dark than it had a few moments before. Maybe they were coming to the edge of a Borough? Fin couldn't deny he was curious to see how things would change at the next corner.

'Do you think they'll really be okay?' Joe asked again.

'Of course they will,' Christopher answered, his voice somewhere between a whisper and a pant as they ran. 'They know what they're doing.'

Fin didn't say anything as he rounded the corner and leaned against the rough wall to get his breath back. He wasn't at all sure that anyone knew exactly what they were doing any more. He just figured that maybe you got better at pretending as you got older, which was a different thing entirely.

He pulled the map out of his pocket. At least they had

a destination: they had to get to Savjani's. What had the Harveys said? Go past Convent Garden and up to The Circus. As he unfolded the thick paper he peered up at the dark walls around them. 'Can either of you see a street name?'

Beside him, Joe laughed. 'Look.' He pointed at the strange map, which was like nothing any of them had seen before. As the sheet opened, the buildings stood up like holograms, transparent and ghostly, even in the night gloom. Finmere realised he was actually looking down on sections of the city. As his eyes rested on each building, the name of the street it sat on appeared like a speech bubble above it for a moment or two and then disappeared.

Fin looked at where Joe was pointing. Where the rest of the map stood up from its surface in the sepia-brown tones of old photographs, a small red finger moved up and down slightly over a short, narrow street not far from the river, and a bubble rose and popped above it, repeatedly stating: YOU ARE HERE. Finmere looked up at the others and grinned. 'At least we'll know if we're going the wrong way.'

The three of them pored over the map until they'd located Covent Garden, then Fin handed the map to Joe. 'You're in charge of directions,' he said, and they set off, following the strange map, and disappeared into the night.

Conrad Eyre stood at the bar, his dark cloak pushed back over one shoulder, the jewelled hilt of his sword clearly visible. George Porter was on his right, and the rest of the men had spread out, kicking aside anything in the way. The noise of wood scraping on wood was loud and harsh. The last two customers picked up their coats and left, their heads bowed low, their drinks unfinished.

No one had been very surprised to see them. That hadn't surprised Conrad; in big cities, word had a habit of travelling fast.

'Quiet night?' He stared at the thin man carefully wiping the bar down. A woman – his wife, presumably – was collecting glasses.

'We were busy earlier. Some Traders were in.'

'Rushed off our feet, we were.' Conrad didn't miss the flash of annoyance that the man sent his wife. Despite the humid warmth, the atmosphere in The Red Lion had dropped several degrees.

'So what can we do for you?' the landlord asked, casually.

Conrad nodded to George Porter, who strode behind the bar and into the private living quarters of the house.

'We're on the Prince Regent's business,' Conrad said. 'He's asked for our assistance in tracking down three teenage boys. We think they're in a pub in this area.'

The landlord shrugged. 'Like I said, we were busy earlier. I didn't see any lads though – not that I'd've served them.' He paused. 'But they grow up so quickly these days, it's sometimes difficult to tell the boys from the men.'

Conrad stared at the man and wondered if this scrawny middle-aged publican could really have meant that last statement to sound like an insult. Surely a Nowhere nobody would never insult one of the Knights? The Knights were rarely seen, and they had the allure of otherworldliness – they were held in slight reverence by most of The Nowhere residents. That business with Baxter was mostly forgotten; seventeen years was a long time, after all, even in The Nowhere, where time could be a bit odd.

'What's your name?' he asked coolly.

'Albert Harvey, sir. And this is my wife, Ida.'

'What about you, madam?' Conrad turned to the matronly woman. 'Have you seen three boys? Perhaps strangely dressed? Needing directions?'

The landlord burst into a derisive laugh before the woman could answer. 'Her? She's been at her bloody friend's all day, doing God knows what. Probably spending more of my hard-earned bleeding cash, when she should have been here helping me.'

The woman shot her husband a furious glance and Conrad smirked a little. He'd seen that look fly between his own parents plenty of times in the long years before the divorce: the kind of look that had ruined his childhood. If it hadn't been for St John Golden and the Order, he didn't know where he'd be now.

George Porter appeared quietly behind the wife. Conrad looked at him for a moment, and then at Albert and Ida Harvey. 'So neither of you have seen any boys around here?' he said softly.

The couple shook their heads.

Conrad smiled, but there was no humour in it. 'Well then. Perhaps you can explain how those came to be in your possession?'

Porter placed the neat folded pile of clothes on the bar in plain view. Fin's favourite hoodie was on the top. Ida Harvey opened her mouth, but she was cut off quickly by her husband. 'I let them in when she was out.' Albert's voice was strong. 'Can't trust her to keep a bloody secret.'

Conrad stepped up close to the bar so that he was looking down on the thin man. 'Where did they go?'

The man shrugged. 'They didn't say.'

Conrad waited, his whole body still, his eyes staring into those of the other man. Eventually he saw it: the twitch of the Adam's apple in that scrawny neck as Albert Harvey nervously dry-swallowed.

'I need that information,' Conrad said, pleasantly.

Albert didn't reply.

'Suit yourself.' He glanced at Archer. 'Lock the doors. And let's get Mr Harvey here a seat.'

TWENTY-ONE

A light drizzle was falling as Fin, Joe and Christopher walked past the high walls of what the map called Long Acre. It didn't look anything like the Long Acre in Finmere's own Covent Garden, with its trendy boutiques and outdoor cafés leading down to the glorious Opera House and the Apple Market.

Instead they walked along a high brick wall the length of what should have been the busy road. Every few metres they passed a nailed-up sign that read: **YOU ARE IN CONVENT GARDEN, THE HOME OF THE STORYHOLDER ACADEMY. PLEASE REMAIN QUIET SO AS NOT TO BREAK OUR CONCENTRATION**. On a smaller line underneath was added, as if it were an afterthought, **AND PLEASE KEEP OUR BOROUGH TIDY**.

Christopher laughed out loud at that and for a minute or two, as they travelled through the night, Fin and Joe joined in. That line looked so ordinary, coming after the extraordinary statement before it. Or maybe they just needed to laugh. The weather soon knocked away their high spirits, however, and the clothes Mrs Harvey had left them gave very little protection against the hard, heavy drops that Finmere knew, even in the darkness, would be black. After a while, the boys fell quiet and kept their heads down, despite their curiosity to see more of their new surroundings.

Eventually they reached the end of Convent Garden and emerged into an almost Georgian street. Christopher sniffed. 'What time to do you think it is?'

'Don't know,' said Joe. 'About eleven?'

'Don't you think there's still a lot of people out and about for this time?'

Fin looked up, wrinkling his face against the rain. A man in a suit nudged him as he pushed past on the pavement, obviously eager to get somewhere dry and warm. 'Maybe. But London's always busy, isn't it?'

'And,' Joe added, 'this isn't our world, however much it seems a bit like it.' He looked up at the bronze gargoyles that sat awkwardly out of place on the front of the tall white Georgian houses. 'There's clues everywhere to how different it is.'

'I know what you mean,' Christopher said. 'It doesn't feel like home at all.'

'Hey look.' Fin smiled, shaking raindrops from his face. 'I think we're at The Circus.' The crossroads ahead of them opened out into a large square. Somewhere at its centre Fin could just glimpse a statue, but it was barely visible through the hubbub of the market that filled every square inch of the open ground.

'Shit,' Joe breathed, and for a moment the boys just stared. There were lanterns and lamps hanging from the corners of each covered stall, an orchestra of different lights coming from candles, oil lamps and bulbs, creating a halo that reached a metre into the night sky and lit the square as brightly as if it were daylight.

Despite the rain the stallholders were still selling loudly, hawking their wares to the men and women browsing, calling out an offer here or a not-to-be-missed deal there.

'That just about covers it,' Christopher said softly, letting out a low whistle. From somewhere at the far side of the square, behind the never-ending stalls oozing with the exotic and ordinary, came the strains of something that sounded a little like an Irish folk tune, though it was hard to be precise over the sea of sounds in front of them.

'No wonder they call it The Circus.' Fin scanned the visible shops that made up the walls of the square. 'There!' Over to their left a large, ornate sign hung above a huge corner storefront of glass and stone. *Savjani's* was printed on the gold background in curly purple letters.

'Great. Let's get out of this rain.' Joe grimaced. 'It tastes strange.'

In order to avoid getting lost amongst the maze of stalls they took the longer route, sticking to the pavement. Fin kept his lips pressed shut, trying to avoid getting the black rain in his mouth, but with the way it was pouring down, he hadn't been completely successful. Joe was right. The water was muddy, and sickly-sweet. It didn't taste like rainwater at all.

'Black rain here and black rain at home,' Christopher muttered, folding up the map. 'I'm finding that slightly freaky, I don't mind saying.'

'Me too,' Fin said. *Along with the black space trying to open up inside my head*, he almost added, but he bit that thought back instead. That was something they didn't need to know, not yet at least. And anyway, that door was staying closed for now.

'But I guess that's why we're here,' he said instead. 'This Fowkes will know how to stop it.'

'We hope,' Joe added, quietly.

Inside, Savjani's wasn't quite what Finmere had expected. Instead of racks and racks of clothes on hangers, all ready to buy, the vast space was filled with mannequins coated in different styles of outfit, the dummies fat and thin and short and tall, and a whole mixture of sizes in between. There was no rhyme nor reason to their arrangement that the boys could see. The colours and different cuts confused Fin's eyes, making him squint a little.

'I guess you don't come here just for a T-shirt,' Joe whispered. They stayed together, walking carefully between the lifeless but beautifully dressed figures that crowded round them, further into the shop. Eventually they came to a long white counter where a plump man in a purple turban that perfectly matched the colour of the sign outside was bowed over a piece of paper, making swift gestures with the pencil in his hand.

He tutted and swept the drawing off the counter and onto the floor where it landed on a pile of previously discarded sheets. 'No, no, no,' he muttered, before immediately beginning sketching on a fresh piece of paper. He didn't look up at the three figures dripping water into a dark puddle on his sparkling clean floor.

'Um ... what are you doing?' Joe asked, clearly fascinated by the plump man's precise strokes. The heavily jewelled hand paused, and slowly the turbaned head rose, revealing a smooth brown face. A moustache curled outrageously above his pointed beard and a purple gem sat amidst the combed and clipped hair, exactly at the centre of his chin. His midnight eyes widened, not at the presence of the boys, but at the absurdity of the question.

'Why, I am designing. What else could I be doing?' He shrugged his silken shoulders. 'I am Savjani. I *design*. I *create*. I turn the ordinary into the *exquisite*.'

Finmere glanced sideways at Joe and Christopher. Christopher's eyes rolled slightly, and Fin knew that Savjani's mannerisms were now logged into his friend's memory banks for later regurgitation. Christopher was an excellent mimic; he could send an entire room into the kind of laughter that doesn't stop until you really think you're going to wet yourself, or because the ache in your face just hurts too much to carry on.

'Mr and Mrs Harvey at The Red Lion sent us to you, Mr Savjani.' Fin spoke slowly, praying that the flamboyant little man was at least partially listening, even though the turban had descended again and the pencil was once more incising

184

lines on the clean sheet. 'They thought you'd be able to help us find someone we're looking for. A man called Fowkes?'

The pencil stopped.

The turban slowly rose.

For the first time Savjani actually appeared to see the three boys standing in front of him. 'The rain has made your clothes dirty.' His accent remained thickly eastern, but some of his exaggerated mannerisms fell away.

'It's black rain,' Christopher said. 'There was some at home before we left as well.'

'It's disgusting, whatever it is.' Joe brushed water from his arm. 'And it's getting worse.'

'Home?' Savjani's eyes focused on Finmere's sword. 'You look a touch young to be carrying a weapon like that.'

'It's not a weapon.' Fin felt as if the tailor was testing him in some way, and maybe he was. Maybe he'd heard that bad things were happening in the worlds. 'It's not meant for killing people with.'

Savjani's fat, perfectly manicured fingers twirled the tips of his moustache, his various rings and bracelets sparkling. 'I know very well what this sword is for. I've seen several like it. But not recently. Now tell me why three boys' – and he looked at Joe and Christopher – 'who I don't think belong in this world, might be looking for a man who has been forgotten for longer than perhaps they have been able to balance on their own two feet?'

Fin thought carefully. 'We have good reasons to see him. But I think perhaps it's best if we don't say too much.' He tried to remember exactly what it was that Mr Harvey had said. 'It's only with what we know that we can betray our friends.'

Savjani stared for a moment and then laughed aloud, clapping his hands together. 'Yes, yes! Exactly! Very good! Oh yes.' He sighed.

'So you can help find Fowkes then?' Joe sniffed.

'Perhaps.' He nodded. 'Perhaps, yes I can, but it has been a long time even since I have seen him.' The tailor shook his head. 'He was a good man. We were good friends.' He smiled sadly. 'The best of friends. Perhaps like you. Three best friends.'

The door behind them blew open a little, pushed by a gust of wind, and Christopher jumped slightly. All three boys turned to make sure there was no one there.

Fin was deeply relieved to see the doorway was still empty, but his heart thumped as he looked back at Savjani. 'Do you have any idea where he is? We've got a map. If you could just give us an address then we could get on. You see, there might be some people following us, and if they catch us before we've done what we came to do ... well ... things could get a whole lot worse—'

Savjani held a hand up to stop him. 'The black rain is turning into a storm, I think. And the storm never lies.' He looked past the children towards the door and said softly, 'The worlds are unsettled. And there are not many who can cause such a thing.' He tutted again, as he had when he'd been drawing, then rang a small bell attached to the wall behind him. It tinkled merrily and set off a chain of similar sounds past Savjani and through a door which Fin presumed led to a workshop, or maybe a flat above the shop.

'I don't have an address for him. Men are not found by their address in the place he has retreated to live – in fact, they are rarely found at all.'

'Can you give us a general direction or something?' Joe asked.

'You will need more than that.' Savjani smiled. 'And I can provide better than that map.'

The door behind him flew open and a girl stood there, one hand on her hip. She looked decidedly irritated. 'What?' she asked, ignoring the boys completely. 'You can't possibly have more deliveries for today, surely? I'm in the middle of a really good book. And anyway, this rain will spoil your clothes.'

Savjani's eyes twinkled. 'This is my daughter, Mona.'

Mona looked around at the boys. Although she had thick, plum-coloured hair, her eyes were a match for her father's. She stared frankly at Finmere and then Joe and Christopher. All three boys shuffled from foot to foot, suddenly slightly embarrassed.

'I think she is about your age. Fourteen years.'

'Nearly fifteen, actually,' she added from the doorway. 'I'm probably older than them.'

Fin was about to point out how wrong she was, then stopped himself. Something in Mona Savjani's voice reminded him of Kayleigh Trent at Eastfields: she had that same blunt confidence, and Finmere was getting the distinct feeling from the looks they were getting that she wasn't too impressed by them so far. There was no point in winding her up any further.

'Great,' Joe muttered, 'just what we need. A mouthy girl.'

'I heard that.' Mona folded her arms across her chest and threw her father an impatient glance.

Savjani smiled. 'She is just like her mother. Strong-willed.'

'And speaking of Mum' – Mona tossed her hair behind her shoulder, revealing large gold hoops hanging from her ears – 'she's wondering when you're going to come upstairs.'

The gold earrings and bangles should have looked all wrong with her tracksuit-style baggy trousers and zip-up stretchy shirt, but somehow it all worked. And despite the jewellery, at least Mona Savjani didn't look like an overly girly girl, which came as something of a relief to Finmere, who was totally baffled by all that pink stuff and giggling. At the same time she definitely looked like a girl, and she was definitely pretty. She was, he decided, confusing.

'It does seem quite late to have a shop open,' Christopher added. Mona's definite prettiness wasn't lost on him either – but the girl just sent him a withering look.

187

'What are you talking about? It's not that late. It just looks late.' She frowned. 'Are you simple?'

'Mona!' Savjani said crossly, 'our guests are not from London. They have come from far away – further than even you have ever been. Be polite. Or there will be punishments.'

Mona didn't look even a little bit scared, but she did stay quiet.

The tailor shrugged at the boys. 'Time is strange here. For the past two weeks we have awakened to find it the afternoon. Afternoon, evening, night, and then afternoon again. No morning.'

'What?' Joe stared. 'No morning? But that can't be right.' He looked at the others. 'I mean, the sun and the moon and everything – it can't work that way. You can't just skip mornings—' He paused. 'Can you?'

'Perhaps our mornings are going somewhere else at present.' Savjani smiled. 'I'm sure they will return to us when they are ready.'

'Does that kind of thing happen a lot?' Christopher asked.

'Just often enough for no concern to be caused.'

'Not like this rain.' Mona came through the doorway and stood beside her father. Like him she was petite, but she definitely didn't have his roundness. 'They're talking about the rain wherever you go.'

Savjani wrapped an arm around his daughter's shoulder proudly. 'My Mona is different to other children. She has made our family's wealth. She is one in a thousand.' He leaned towards the boys. 'The city doesn't affect her. She goes wherever she wants, with no tiredness or headache.' He laughed a little. 'She's like a sewer rat!'

'Dad!'

'Ah, daughter, it is true!' He turned back to the boys. 'When she was small, it would infuriate us when she ran off to explore. But now? Now I can guarantee delivery to anyone anywhere in the north of the city, for the cheapest price. I am not bound to the extortionate chains of carriers through each Borough, nor must I risk thievery from those who find themselves in financial difficulty so that my clothes never arrive. She has made me the most successful clothcrafter in London.'

Mona looked up at her father fondly. 'I think that's due to your talent, Dad. Not my feet.' They smiled at each other, sharing a moment, and watching them Fin realised that neither he, Christopher or Joe had ever had a moment like that in their lives. Joe's father was long gone, Finmere had never known his, and he'd seen the awkward hand-shaking between Christopher and Mr Arnold-Mather.

Mona hugged into her father's chest. 'So what do you want then?'

'I need you to take our guests somewhere.' Savjani stroked his daughter's hair. 'And you must be very careful.'

'Where do they need to go?'

'The Crookeries.'

Mona's face lit up, and her father sighed. 'I thought you would like that. I think you, with your wandering feet and fearless heart, you will make a very good Trader when you are grown.'

Even though her nose wrinkled, Fin could see that she was proud. 'I'm not spending my life sitting in that stinking mist. Yuk.' She looked up. 'What exactly are we going to the Crookeries for?' For the first time she looked at the boys as if they might be interesting after all.

TWENTY-TWO

Mr Harvey's thin face was quite swollen with bruises, and as he slumped in the chair he was breathing hard and sweating. Conrad took the seat opposite him. Why were people so stubborn? Why couldn't they just answer the questions put to them? There was no need for ordinary people to go through this. They weren't *involved*. They should stay that way.

'What I need from you is quite simple. What are the boys here for? Are they looking for something? And most importantly, where are they now?'

Mr Harvey stared back from under the lid of a red eye. 'I don't know nothing. I told them not to tell me nothing. Thought you'd be along.'

Conrad studied him. He could believe that of this man who was proving to be a whole lot tougher than he appeared. 'They must have asked you something.' He was getting impatient for answers. If they left it much longer the boys would be too far ahead and St John would have his guts for garters. And more than that, the Commander would be *disappointed*. St John was the closest thing to family that Conrad had; he always felt a complicated mix of love, admiration and a healthy dose of fear whenever he thought of St John Golden. It was enough to keep him on his toes.

He leaned forward and spoke softly. 'You're going to have to give me something.' He turned to Archer. 'Bring the wife.' Conrad stared coolly into Albert Harvey's beaten face, not even looking up as Ida Harvey was pulled into the bar, her indignant words of protest turning into a sob as she saw the state of her husband.

Albert looked at his wife and then at Conrad, and the Knight knew that he didn't have to say another word. Albert Harvey understood. And so did Ida.

'Albert, don't you dare—'

But she was cut off in full flow by Archer's hand firmly covering her mouth.

'Well, that's a thing I never thought I'd see.' Albert Harvey's voice was still strong, despite the beating he'd taken. 'The brave and *honourable* Knights of Nowhere threatening a woman.' He paused and ran his tongue gently over his split lip. 'You should be ashamed of yourselves.'

'Sometimes the end justifies the means. And I can live with that.' Conrad didn't even flinch.

'Savjani's.' The word fell from Albert Harvey as softly as a leaf in a forest. 'They wanted to go to Savjani's.'

On the third floor of Orrery House, Ted Merryweather lifted the vase from the small alcove and hoped for the best. Nothing happened. He sighed. He hadn't really expected any different. The room wasn't there. It wasn't there most of the time – in fact, Ted had only ever been in it himself once in his whole lifetime, when he was a boy, just at the end of the Great War. His dad had kissed his mum good-bye, left his cigarette tin on the mantelpiece, and never come back. It had helped him then, in its own way, just to be shown how much *more* there was out there – that there was really magic in the universe, and sometimes it was worth fighting and dying for. That was all so long ago, but he'd hoped that it would be here to help him again. To give him just a little bit more strength for what was coming.

The muscles in his neck and shoulders were stretched as tight as a drum, and he wished more than anything that

Judge Harlequin Brown would come around the corner of the silent white corridor and chastise him for foolish dreams. He missed his friend, but he needed him, too. They needed a proper leader, and right now Ted felt his own clumsy inability only too strongly.

As it was, Freddie Wise appeared in view, leaning heavily on one stick. 'There you are, Ted,' he said. 'What are you doing up here in the third-floor morgue?' His sharp eyes spied the alcove. 'Ah, I see. I take it the room's not there?'

Ted shook his head. 'And don't call the bedrooms a morgue. They ain't dead, Freddie.'

'No, no, they're not.' Freddie's voice was crisp, like dry winter twigs snapping. 'But they might as well be.' He raised his other hand, holding up a slim can. 'And what is this godawful stuff you've given us to drink?'

Despite his heavy heart, Ted grinned. 'It's supposed to give you wings.'

Freddie took a long sip of the caffeine-laden drink and grimaced. 'Tastes foul – almost like bubblegum – but it does the job. I'm definitely feeling somewhat more awake.'

'Good. Keep drinking it. How are the others?'

Freddie leaned against the wall and shrugged slightly. 'They're younger than us.'

Ted laughed. 'You ain't that old under the skin, Freddie Wise – what are you now, forty-five?'

'Fifty. Old enough. Wise enough.' He paused. 'Harper Jones and Cardrew Cutler are doing their best to get as many of us awake and functioning as possible. Lucas Blake is working out a battle strategy for when they come.' He shook his head. 'A battle of old Knights against young. Who'd have thought it?' He smiled a little.

They stood in the soft silence for a moment, both thinking about what lay behind and what lay ahead.

At last, Freddie said, 'You're doing a good job, Ted.' He sounded matter-of-fact. 'Harlequin would be proud.' He sighed and for a moment a trickle of silence ran between them.

He hesitated, then went on, 'The dark rain's on every weather report, though it's only falling in London so far – they're looking for some kind of industrial explanation.' He stopped and looked at Ted, then said softly, 'There've already been some incidents. A man running a homeless shelter went out last night and killed four destitute people with an axe. It was on the news. He can't explain why. And some people are saying they've seen cracks in the sky; but so far they're being dismissed as UFO nutters. Thankfully, London is full of lunatics and we're used to not taking them seriously,' he added dryly.

Ted stared at the blank canvas of the wall opposite. Neither of them needed to state how bad things could get; they were both well aware that if the madness of a black storm came to The Somewhere, it could mean the end of civilisation. There was too much anger and too much danger in this world of nuclear bombs and germ warfare, not to mention all the missiles and tanks and grenades and guns and knives, and all those people, suddenly full of rage and hate … It might only be raining in London for now, but if the rain turned into a tempest, God only knew how far it might spread. Even in the bad times all those years ago, the black storm had never made its way into The Somewhere.

He thought of young Finmere and his two friends. He hadn't had much of a chance to really prepare them for what they might find themselves up against. There must have been more he could have done to keep them safe, even in that short time.

He gritted his teeth. 'Golden will send 'is men to deal with us, and we'll be 'elpless against them.'

Freddie nodded. 'Yes, that's true. But that doesn't matter. What matters is that we stand and fight.' He took another swig. 'And who knows – maybe young Finmere Tingewick Smith and Fowkes will come up with something.' He slapped

Ted on the back in a gesture of uncharacteristic good cheer. 'Stranger things have happened.'

There was nothing about the fussy-looking man in the purple turban that Conrad liked. He particularly didn't like the way he had barely looked up from his drawings when the Knights had come in.

'Three young men, you say? Boys?' Savjani muttered, before shaking his head and crumpling up the piece of paper and tossing it to the floor.

'Yes, that's what I said.' Conrad took a long breath, trying to keep his temper in check. 'Three times now.' Behind him, Maxwell and Archer prowled the rows of mannequins, but Conrad was pretty sure that their air of menace was lost on the fat little tailor.

'We are on the business of the Prince Regent!' he repeated loudly. He was beginning to almost believe it himself.

'Three boys.' Finally, the tailor looked up and twirled his moustache. 'Yes, I've seen three boys. They came in and asked for work and then I sent them away.' He shrugged, an elaborate gesture that made his various necklaces jangle. 'I see many boys wanting work. Every day, five or six of them.'

'They wanted *work*?' Conrad stared at the round face. He didn't believe the tailor, not for a moment. There was something in the straightness of the gaze that convinced Conrad that Savjani was bare-faced lying. 'These boys were *not* looking for a job.'

'Then perhaps the boys I saw were not the boys you seek.'

Conrad leaned across the counter, making sure his wet coat sleeve rested on the pile of papers. 'One of them was wearing a sword, like mine.'

'I don't recall a sword. I don't recall them. I barely looked up from my papers. I am trying to create something spectacular for a most valued client.'

194

'You're lying to me,' Conrad said, gritting his teeth. 'You've seen these boys. You know exactly who I mean. Now, you listen—'

'—you are on the Regent's business, you say?' Savjani brushed drips of dark water from the expensive paper. 'Well, I shall be seeing him tomorrow when I personally deliver his new frockcoat.' He waved a chubby finger in the direction of a glittering white outfit on one of the closest mannequins. It was topped off with a ridiculously high and powdered wig. He smiled.

'He is one of my best clients. We are almost, you could say, friends. If I remember something that I now cannot recall, I shall make sure I tell him directly.'

Conrad bit back his anger. The insinuation in the tailor's words was not lost on him. Savjani had the protection of the Prince Regent; Conrad would not be able to bully the information he needed out of one of the most influential businessmen in London in the same way he had a nobody pub landlord. Savjani knew something, that was for sure, but it didn't look like Conrad would be getting it from him.

'Make sure you do.' He frowned. 'And remember, little tailor, power can change hands very quickly.'

'True,' said Savjani, no longer smiling. 'But often not as easily as people would think.'

Conrad had neither the time nor the inclination to get into a battle of riddles with the irritating man. Instead he turned and stormed back out into the wet night, wondering what St John Golden was going to make of this.

TWENTY-THREE

Standing in the middle of the destroyed rooms of the Story-holder's apartments, St John Golden started barking expletives that turned somehow into an indecipherable roar of spit and rage. The vein in his temple throbbed as he finally stopped, panting, trying to get his breath back.

This was *not* how it was supposed to be. He should have had the stories by now. *The worlds should have been his.* The Dark Age should have arrived before anyone even realised it was coming.

Instead, he'd torn through her rooms like a hurricane, ripping apart her possessions with no care in the search, while below him the Archivers moved quietly around the building, quite unaware of the torrent of noise and anger above them.

She was gone, lost in the depths of the prison, and she wouldn't be coming back.

And he'd found nothing. He was not even sure what he was looking for. He'd never heard of the stories and the Storyholder being separated before. As far as he knew, a Storyholder kept them inside her until they became too much to bear, and then she would pass them directly into her successor. So if they weren't inside her, where on earth could they be?

His head started to hurt, a stabbing pain behind his left eye, and he sat down heavily on the edge of the bed, his shoulders slumping forward. God, how he longed for a proper morning. He did his best thinking in the mornings. Waking up with the sun already high in the sky left him feeling as if he had missed out on something important, and he really didn't need that, not right now.

He looked out of the window, where only the black night was visible. Water pattered against the arched glass; regardless of whether it was morning or afternoon, it didn't look like anyone would be seeing the sun any time soon. A black storm was coming, unless he could stop it. He shivered. Despite his bravado, he knew madness came in a black storm; he'd heard the stories of the last one, after Baxter's death. Anything could happen in a black storm.

Heavy footsteps pounded up the curved staircase and St John's practised hearing picked out the heavy rattle of a sheathed sword against a man's leg.

'I'm in here, Conrad,' he called wearily.

He waited until the younger Knight was standing in front of him before asking, 'Well? Have you found them?'

Conrad Eyre, ignoring the wrecked possessions around them, bit his lip. 'They've been to a pub called The Red Lion, and from there they went to Savjani's at The Circus.' He stopped to shake some dark raindrops from his cloak.

Sitting there in the defiled purity of the Storyholder's home, St John could smell the odour rising from the drops: something like the river, but worse: murky, and sickly-sweet, with the hint of something rotten underlying it.

'Savjani wouldn't say where they went, and I couldn't get the information out of him any other way. He made it very clear that he was a friend of the Prince Regent's,' Conrad finished.

St John's brain forced old memories to the surface. His left foot softly tapped on the carpet. Savjani's ... why would this boy that Harlequin had been so protective over go to Savjani? The tailor's name tasted important in his mouth. What did he have to do with ... ?

'Fowkes!' He interrupted his own thoughts, spitting the word out almost unconsciously, 'they're looking for Fowkes.'

197

'Who?' Conrad Eyre sounded puzzled. St John could barely see him; his own anger at himself was blurring his vision. How could he possibly have forgotten *Fowkes*? His face burned red and he fought to control it. He didn't need Conrad to see him losing control. There'd been enough of that already.

'Before your time,' he said quietly. 'Fowkes was a Knight. He was Baxter's best friend.'

'Baxter?' Conrad breathed the word. 'Wasn't he the one who—?'

St John smiled grimly. 'He died here, murdered by the mob at the bottom of the stairs, for the grievous sin of falling in love with the Storyholder. He crossed the line.' He looked at Conrad. 'Although the Storyholder declared in the House of Real Truths that he'd never touched her.'

'Jesus.'

'Yes.' St John raised an eyebrow. 'Very unfortunate for poor Baxter, and it nearly ended the Order. Savjani used to idolise those two Knights. That must be why the boys went to him. They're looking for Fowkes.'

'I've never heard of him,' Conrad said.

'Everyone remembers Baxter, and yet we all forgot Fowkes. Funny that. He was a good Knight – he could have challenged me for the post of Commander if he hadn't vanished.'

St John smiled, almost wistfully. Conrad was a boy when Fowkes vanished. Fowkes and Baxter were a different breed. The smile hardened at the edges. And that's why St John and his men would win. His breed were tougher.

'The Crookeries,' he said suddenly. His eyes were once again the colour of sharp steel. 'That's where he'll be, I'd put money on it. Kill him when you find him.' He paused. 'And kill those wretched youths too. I want this situation dealt with.'

Conrad disappeared as swiftly as he'd arrived, leaving St John alone once again in the sea of white. Fowkes. He should have thought of Fowkes. From his pocket he pulled out an embossed silver cigarette case. He flipped it open, took out one of the French cigarettes inside and lit it.

He inhaled deeply and stared at the case. It had been tossed through a cut he'd made between the worlds a week earlier. He'd forgotten to throw it back to his elusive Somewhere partner. What would that man make of all this disruption to the plans, he wondered? St John took a long last look at the expensive case, at the carved eagle on the front, before throwing it to the floor. It landed on the crumpled bed sheets he'd ripped from the mattress earlier. He felt better without the weight of it in his pocket, as if he'd been released from at least one small pressure.

The sickly smoke made his head swim and it burnt his lungs. He needed to give up. Smoking was a sign of weakness; a clue to others that he was feeling the stress. But sitting there amongst the chaos that hinted that perhaps he hadn't planned quite as well as he could have, suggesting that perhaps he wasn't the dark man to rule the Dark Age after all, St John Golden couldn't bring himself to stub it out.

TWENTY-FOUR

Mona led them back to St Paul's by a different route, taking them down to the Embankment and along the dark road by the river. Even with the steady patter of raindrops falling around them, the stinking high mist still crept up over the wall and reached for them with long tendrils that seemed desperate to wrap around something alive and cling on. Eerie laughter and the echo of wailing almost oozed from its foulness.

'That smells disgusting,' Fin whispered, although he didn't know why he was whispering because there wasn't anyone around to hear them. The place was completely deserted.

'We should bottle some.' Joe's voice came from the inky blackness behind Fin. 'Take it back to Eastfields. Sell it to the Year Eights. It'd be way better than any stink bomb they could get off the market.'

'They say the Traders spend a whole day in the bath when they come in from the river.' Mona was striding out in front of them like a proud Indian princess. 'They sometimes have to burn their clothes, that's how strong the mist is. People don't want to be around you if you're covered in that stink. And besides,' she added, 'the mist can make you crazy. No one wants to be touched by the mist.'

The boys took a few cautious steps away from the river walls.

'So what on earth are we doing here then?' Christopher muttered.

Mona smiled at him. 'We're making sure we don't bump

into the men who were following you. No one comes down onto Times' Parade unless they really have to.'

Fin watched in the gloom as Christopher grinned back at Mona. He couldn't see in the night, but he was pretty sure Christopher was blushing. He watched for a moment and then looked back at the revolting but fascinating river. If he said that girls didn't make him feel a bit uncomfortable sometimes then he'd be lying, but spending every other year at Eastfields, where they made up half of the pupils, he was pretty used to them. But there were no girls at St Martin's. Watching Christopher's reaction to Mona was like going back to Year Nine again, when the differences between the girls and boys really started to show and most of the boys started going a kind of red-from-sitting-by-a-radiator-too-long colour if someone like Sophie Becks sat next to them a little bit too closely.

'We're nearly there.' Mona turned her attention back to the road and Fin felt slightly relieved. They could do without Christopher turning into a love-struck muppet right now. 'This way is quicker.'

Following her lead, they veered inwards from the river and headed back into the maze of London streets and alleyways. The ground underneath their feet was turning to mud in the constant downpour, and the pavements were disappearing. The occasional oil lamp hung from an uneven window, and children in rags sat on doorsteps, sheltered slightly from the rain, staring at the four teenagers as they passed. Most had dirty cloth tied round their feet for shoes and the girls' hair hung in matted dreadlocks from a lack of brushing. From inside one ramshackle dwelling a woman shouted angrily at someone, and Fin was sure he could make out the words '*thieving little tyke!*' just before a loud yelp.

'Is this the ghetto or something?' Joe stayed close to Fin.

'This is Poor Town, the last step before the Crookeries. Keep hold of your valuables, boys. And don't look scared!'

201

Fin thought that being told not to look scared was likely to have the opposite effect on most people, but he kept his mouth shut.

'All ri-i-ght!' Joe said, 'just like walking through the estate. I'm an expert at bowling it.' As evidence, he pulled himself up tall and started to move with the exaggerated swagger that most of the gangs used. Fin always found it vaguely ridiculous to watch, but he had to admit that Joe didn't look scared, which was something at least.

Christopher didn't imitate Joe's walk, but he did stand tall himself, and kept his eyes straight ahead. 'Well, I might not come from an estate, but we all have to be tough sometimes,' he murmured, 'just in different ways.'

Finmere, standing between them, gripped the hilt of his sword and checked that the money Ted had given him was still safe in his pocket. He'd leave the feeling tough bit to the other three; they were all doing a better job at it than he ever could.

'We're here,' Mona said as they turned the next corner, and Fin looked up. Ahead of them a handmade wall of nailed-together bits of wood rose up as tall as Christopher, right across the width of the street. There were occasional gaps big enough for a cat or small dog to get through, and a small half-open doorway in the middle. Behind the wall several large tenement buildings rose up, and Fin guessed there were even more tucked away behind them, though it was impossible to see. They were so closely packed together that you could probably climb from the window of one building across to the next with hardly any effort at all.

'Is it just me, or is that block leaning slightly to the left?' Christopher's eyes were wide.

'Probably. These are all condemned buildings. They should be knocked down, really, but the Prince can hardly do that with all these people living in them and refusing to leave, even if they are just Crookeries dwellers.'

202

'What's that supposed to mean?' Joe wasn't impressed. 'People can't always help being poor.'

'Of course not – but it's not the poor living in the Crookeries, is it?' She sounded very matter-of-fact, as if everyone knew this. 'It's *crooks* who live in the Crookeries – murderers, thieves. Women of loose morals. That kind of person.'

Fin looked at the words carved in a crooked line across the fence: *Refuge of the Destitute, Sanctuary of the Disorderly*. And this was where they were supposed to find help? He squeezed the hilt of his sword, pressing the ring on his finger into it, gold against gold, and thought of Ted, Mrs Baker, the Harveys and Savjani. They couldn't all be wrong about Fowkes, could they? And after all, how much could someone change over seventeen years?

He wasn't convincing himself. Seventeen years seemed like a bloody long time to him: a year longer than he'd even lived. He sighed.

'Follow me.' Mona stepped through the small gap in the doorway and the boys did as they were told. On the other side, a large bonfire burned and spat under an awning, the flames high despite the rain that had turned the night into a murky gloom. Beside the fire were two men, rummaging in hessian sacks, examining things that occasionally caught the light and flashed in shades of metal. One of them looked up. His wide face was scarred and dirty.

''ere, you!' He stabbed a filthy hand at them. 'What the bloody 'ell d'you want?'

The second man looked up too, and Fin felt as if they were being studied by two growling Rottweilers, fierce and wild – and ready to pounce.

''m looking for Jack Ditch.' Mona wiped her nose on the back of her hand. Though none of the boys had noticed quite when, somewhere along the way she'd taken off her jewellery. She was still pretty, but now she just looked like any ordinary girl. 'I done some pocket work fer 'im today.' Her accent had changed too, into a creditable Cockney twang.

The first man scowled. 'Jack and 'is bleedin' brats.' He nodded behind him. ''e'll be at Mary's place. Fourth block back, one over, second floor up. And you tell 'im: next time I sees any of 'is kids in this part of town, I'll slit their fucking throats. The Crookeries ain't no place for visitors.' He nodded at Mona. 'You tell him Old Ringrose said that, you 'ear me?'

'Will do, mister. But if I don't bring 'im me earnings, then *'e'll* slit me throat, right an' proper. Seems me throat's done for whichever way it goes down.' Mona grinned at the swarthy man, and after a second or two he burst into a raucous laugh.

'You'll do all right, you will.'

Mona scampered past the men and the boys ran to keep up.

Fin felt confused by the cacophony of sounds that poured from the damaged buildings all around them. Somewhere a baby cried while a screaming match carried on around it, and further down the sodden cinder path that served as a road, a woman belted out a loud, tuneless and very slurred song as she hung out of a third-storey window. She squealed and laughed as out-of-sight hands pulled her back inside. Everywhere there were rough, shouting voices.

Fin felt lost: here they were, in the slums of some part of London's history; though he'd read about times like this in History, and seen some Dickens and other stuff on telly, he'd never imagined it would be anything like this: so *filthy*, so *dangerous*, so *pitiful* ...

He didn't know quite what he had expected.

He counted buildings, and pointed to a rough wooden door. 'Second floor, did he say?' He pushed the door open, managing to get it past the swollen lintel, and Mona stepped inside. The building smelled of alcohol, stale sweat and some rank candlewax, and a myriad other scents that Fin's nose couldn't identify, but it was better than being out in the stinking rain.

Joe nudged him and pointed. In the shadowy corner of the hallway, a man and woman, both looking well past forty, were kissing. They were oblivious to the new visitors. The woman's dress was pulled apart at the top, and the man was fondling the heavy breasts that were hanging out.

'This is the Crookeries,' Mona whispered, catching the shocked and embarrassed looks that passed between the boys. 'Get used to it!' She reached the stairs and started up.

If they had thought it hot and sweaty on the ground floor, once they were inside Mary's it was like being at the heart of the furnace. The door opened onto a large open room, with a crudely built bar counter in one corner. A huge fire roared in the stone hearth that took up almost the whole wall, and each of the several wooden tables crammed into the space had five or six occupants around it. In what little space was left people were standing or leaning or crouching, all talking nonstop, as far as Fin could make out, while women in low-cut dresses were weaving expertly in and out, delivering metal jugs of what he presumed was the local beer.

Behind the bar, a hugely fat woman with untidy red curls piled up on her head and wearing far too much lipstick laughed raucously with the group of men surrounding her, though her eyes were constantly darting around the rest of the room. Fin didn't need anyone to tell him that this was Mary.

'Wait here.' Mona was on tiptoes, scanning the room. 'I'll find Jack and ask him where this Fowkes chap is. Jack knows everyone in the Crookeries.'

Fin was tempted to ask how a girl like Mona knew a man like Jack, but then he figured that very little about her would actually surprise him. He watched as she darted into the crowd. He, Joe and Christopher moved to the side and leaned against a pillar, trying to be as inconspicuous as they could.

205

They were already drawing a few strange looks from the more sober of the clientele, and none of them were friendly. A few tables away they could see Mona, crouched down beside a totally bald man whose ear was badly scarred. Jack Ditch, Fin presumed, and he was wearing what might have been a soldier's uniform of some kind. Fin saw a flash of something bright, and then Jack leaned forward and whispered something before patting Mona on the back and turning back to the equally intimidating men he was drinking with.

She shimmied back to them, grinning. 'Well, that was easy,' she laughed.

'Did you give him one of your bits of jewellery?' Fin grabbed her arm as they headed back out of the bar.

Mona shrugged. 'Just a bracelet. You don't get something for nothing, especially here.'

Fin felt bad. Her bangles and necklaces looked expensive. 'But I've got some money. You could have used that.'

'He believes I robbed the jewellery. If I gave him cash, then he'd want to know where I'd got it, and that would have caused way too many questions.' She glanced back. 'As it is, he's probably already forgotten we were here.' She ducked through the crowd towards the door.

'Well, you take the money, then. It's only fair.' Fin started to rummage for it, but Mona grabbed his hand.

'Don't be silly. My dad would kill me. If you agree to help someone, then you just get on and help them, regardless of the cost. It's a matter of honour. And don't *ever* pull out money in a place like this – that's just asking for trouble!'

They stepped outside, into the marginally cooler air, and waited for Christopher and Joe to catch them up.

'Does your dad know how well you know people like Jack Ditch?'

Mona grinned. 'Of course not. But what he doesn't know won't hurt him, right? And I mean, what's the point of being able to travel across the city if you don't put it to good use?

206

Do you think my dad's the only person in London I make deliveries for?' She shook her head. 'Where'd be the fun in that?'

She winked at Fin and touched her nose – *our secret* – just as the other two finally made it out of the bar.

'So, where did he say Fowkes was?' Despite her explanation, Fin still felt awful about Mona's bracelet; he'd buy her a new one as soon as he got the chance. That was a matter for *his* honour.

'Ditch reckons he's in the block two doors down. There's a gambling den on the top floor, Fowkes is tall, with dark hair. Ditch said there was a game on earlier and this Fowkes wanted in on it, so he should still be up there.'

Christopher peered back at the sagging stairs. 'Well, if that building's anything like this one, at least if it collapses we won't be underneath it. That's some small comfort.'

The building was one of the tallest in the slums. It was nine and a half storeys high, and as they ascended, the noise subsided a little more on each floor – though the increasing quiet was not necessarily a good thing. On the lower floors they could hear a lot of women's voices and drunken male laughter behind the closed doors, but as they climbed higher, each landing felt slightly more ominous, and by the time they'd reached the eighth level, they'd passed all manner of nefarious-looking groups, from people buying and selling what were obviously stolen goods, to men looking suspiciously like enforcers, maybe even assassins, with their cold eyes and vast array of weaponry. Various groups whispering together kept a close eye on the foursome as they passed, checking to make sure their plotting had not been overheard. All of them kept their eyes very firmly on the steps in front of them. None were under any illusions; these people would have not the slightest hesitation in slitting their throats, or even just chucking them into the river, their bodies lost forever in the evil bubbling mist.

The eighth floor had a fog of its own: a sweet-smelling fug of smoke that drifted out from the open doorways.

'What's in there?' Fin asked.

'Flower smokers.' Mona crumpled her nose up. 'Hold your breath until we get upstairs. Flower smoke makes your head go funny; it makes you sort of useless. Don't you have it where you're from?'

A thin, pale man in a jacket that was too small for him staggered out into the hallway and leaned against the wall, looking like he was about to be very sick. He frowned when he saw them on the stairs, as if not entirely sure they were there at all, and the effort of moving his facial muscles caused his legs to crumple under him until he was sitting cross-legged on the floor, still staring vacantly in their direction.

Fin looked at the man. 'We have some drugs that are similar, I think,' he said, and continued up the stairs. 'Don't the police try and arrest these people or anything?'

'They don't even try. The Crookeries is off-limits. Maybe the Knights can get in here, but they're not exactly police and they're not interested in what goes down here. When Crookeries dwellers step outside the fence, then they're fair game.'

Fin didn't say anything after that. There were parts of his own London that weren't that different – plenty of the Brickman Boys should be locked up, but no one ever saw the police hanging around that estate, did they? It was as much a no-go area as the Crookeries. As he rounded the corner, Fin heard the man below him throwing up. He hoped he'd managed to miss his own lap. He didn't look like the kind of man who would own two jackets.

Finally, they reached the ninth floor. The stairs continued up for another half a flight, but Mona stopped them on the landing, in front of a half-open door. No noise drifted out, not even any hushed whispering. It was silent. They looked at each other.

'At least we won't have to fight our way out of a crowd,' Fin murmured as he peered through the gap. After a second he pushed the door open. The others gathered round him and stared.

'This is the guy who's supposed to help us?' Joe looked at Fin. 'I think we're in deep shit, mate.'

Finmere couldn't disagree. He walked over to the card table, where the remnants of some card game were still scattered across it. The four tankards were empty, as was the jug in the middle, carelessly tipped over on its side. Alongside it rested a pair of large feet, dressed in threadbare grey socks that might once have been white.

'Where are his shoes?' Mona grimaced slightly.

'At least he's got the rest of his clothes on,' Joe said.

'I supposed we should be grateful for that,' Christopher agreed.

Fin could hear the disappointment in all their voices, and it was echoed inside his own heart. This was the best that Ted could come up with? This was the man who was going to stop the Knights and deal with whatever was causing the black rain and put the worlds back to normal?

As he stared at the comatose figure, his feet propped up on the table, his hands hanging limply at his sides, his head hanging back over the chair and his mouth open, Fin found it very hard to believe this man was capable of anything – even waking up without a hangover. He reeked of alcohol.

He grunted a little in his sleep, and that prompted Fin to action. 'Oh well. Here goes nothing,' he said, and gently shook the man's arm. When nothing happened, he shook him a little harder, but though he wobbled, and his grunting got a bit louder, his eyes stayed firmly shut.

Finmere was suddenly overcome with a wave of anger. They needed this man – they *all* needed him – and this just wasn't fair on the Judge, or Mrs Baker or Mrs Harvey, or anyone else.

All the pent-up emotions way down deep inside him released, and Fin shoved the man hard, sending him tumbling to the ground.

That did it.

'What the f—?' Finally the sleeping man's eyes opened as he landed with a thud on the dusty floorboards.

'Well, that worked!' Christopher grinned.

The man looked up blearily at the small group surrounding him, and then down at his socked feet with an equal amount of confusion.

'Are you Fowkes? Andrew Fowkes?' Fin asked urgently.

The man pulled his knees up under his chin and rested his arms on them. After a moment of blankness he finally focused his eyes on Finmere. They weren't friendly. 'Who wants to know?' he asked hoarsely.

'My name's Finmere Tingewick Smith, but you don't know me,' Fin started, the words tumbling out. 'Ted sent me here to find you, if you're the someone called Fowkes.'

'Ted?' There was a momentary flash of recognition in his eyes, but he shrugged. 'Never heard of him. You must have the wrong Fowkes.'

'Yeah, right,' Joe said, 'there must be dozens of them here.'

The man reached up and clasped his head with both hands, then ran his fingers through his dark, wavy hair, trying to wake himself up. It didn't make him look any tidier. He dragged himself to his feet, righted his wooden chair and sat down heavily. He looked down at himself, taking in the scruffy shirt hanging out of his black trousers. 'I can't believe I bet my bloody boots,' he muttered. 'I loved those damn boots.'

Fin glimpsed a small dagger wedged into his belt, but he couldn't see any Knight's sword. 'You need to listen to this,' he said urgently, 'the Knights have gone bad. They've murdered Judge Harlequin Brown, and they hurt my landlady badly, and I don't know if you're the man we're looking for but—'

He raised his hand to stop Fin speaking and then dropped it. 'I'm Fowkes,' he said at last. 'I'm the right Fowkes – well, I was once, anyway.' He looked around at Mona and the boys for a moment, then returned to Fin, scanning the sword at his hip. Then he shook his head wearily.

Fin stared back at him. There was something vaguely familiar about the dark man, but he couldn't figure out what it was. He hardly looked like anyone Finmere knew – definitely not like any of the teachers, not at either of his schools. Outside of that, Fin's knowledge of adults was pretty limited. Where could he know him from?

'I'm sorry to hear about Harlequin. I really am.' He rubbed the dark stubble on his chin. 'But it's not my fight, boy, not any more. The Knights haven't been part of my business for a long time. I'm sorry.'

Joe looked at him crossly. 'Whatever they've done, that's what's causing this black rain. And it's in our world too.' Joe sounded as desperate as Fin felt, and for the first time Fin was glad his friend had seen Mrs Baker and the sword still covered with the Judge's blood. He probably understood how desperate their situation was, even more than Christopher could.

Fowkes let out a small cough of laughter that turned into a kind of a sigh. 'I didn't even know it was raining.' He shook his head and stared at his feet. 'Like I said, I can't help you. You're looking for a man who no longer exists.'

'I don't believe you.' Fin didn't move, but his fists clenched. 'People don't change that much – not really. Not deep down.'

'And what would you know about it? You may think you're all grown up, but you're just a kid.'

'They all believe in you, whoever you are: Ted, Mrs Baker,

the Harveys, Savjani—' Fin was clutching at straws now, but he couldn't give up, not yet. 'They can't all be wrong, can they?' His heart thudded. Maybe they could. This drunken, bootless man wasn't exactly what he'd been expecting.

'And *we* believed in you too,' Christopher added, and there was no hiding the bitter disappointment in his voice.

Fin's memory jolted. 'Oh, and there was something else – it's actually the main message. Ted said to tell you that they've done something to the Storyholder.'

Finally, Fin had said something that made Fowkes look up properly.

'Tova?'

Fin shrugged. 'He didn't say a name.' The knocking was back against the locked door in his head, but he angrily ignored it. 'He just said that they'd done something to the Storyholder and you'd know what to do.'

'If you're lying—'

'I'm not, I sw—' But Fin never finished his sentence, for there was a frantic pounding up the stairs and a short, scruffy man burst in.

'Jack Ditch sent me over,' the man panted, looking at Mona, 'says to tell you as how you ain't the only ones looking for this fella. There's some blokes in Mary's, asking questions about him and three lads. Knights, they are. Jack says you owes him one.' He barely waited long enough to finish his sentence before scurrying away again.

Mona, Christopher and Joe looked at Fin, and then all four turned to Fowkes. His eyes were still locked on Fin's, as if not sure whether to believe what he'd been told.

From way down below them in the building they heard a man call out,

'Hey, you there! Where've you been up there? I saw you sneak out of Mary's.'

'The Knights!' Fin's heart was thumping in his chest again. 'We've got to get out of here—'

212

'Yes, but how?' Joe looked around for a window.

'I don't understand,' said Mona. 'My father would never have told. *Never.*'

Fin believed her. 'Maybe someone saw us – or perhaps someone just figured out we had no one else to go to except for Fowkes.'

'Um ... Really not that important right now.' Christopher was at the doorway. 'There are men coming up the stairs, and they're coming quite fast.'

Fowkes groaned and stood up. 'Okay, okay, follow me. And stay close.'

Fin grinned. 'You'll help us?'

'Let's get out of this mess first. We'll talk about the rest of it after that.' He led them out into the hallway and up the last few stairs that appeared to lead nowhere. Just out of sight in the corner of the wall was a half-door, cut into the old brick.

'God, I should have kept my bloody boots,' Fowkes muttered, kicking it open with his stockinged foot. He crouched and squeezed his large frame through, out into the night. 'Come on, then.' He pulled Mona through first, then the boys. Fin was last and the hard slap of feet pounding up the stairs was sounding very close behind them.

'Be careful.' Fowkes squinted against the rain. 'It'll be slippery up here.'

Fin closed the door tight and latched it before following the others. He wondered how much good that small bolt would do against determined Knights of Nowhere ... Fowkes led them quickly up a short ladder, on to the roof and onto a narrow gantry that ran alongside the tiles that rose steeply at their side. Although the rain itself was warm, it was being carried on a driving wind. Fin leaned into it. Ahead of him he could see Mona's hair whipping around her face, but she moved confidently, like an acrobat from the Chinese State Circus, or like an Olympic gymnast on the high beam. Fin wished his own feet felt so secure.

'What are all these pathways?' Fin wondered aloud. The slatted path sloped a little under him and he clung to the wooden railing, though it didn't feel quite as steady as he'd have liked. It wasn't that he was particularly scared of heights; he was more afraid of the whole falling-off business.

'Residents in the Crookeries often need quick getaways.' Fowkes' voice drifted back. 'Like our one, for example. If you're a local, you'll find the gantries link the buildings.' He paused. 'Be careful at this bridge. The third plank is missing, so keep your eyes down and your wits about you.'

Behind them, there was some banging and crashing, then the half-door flew open. Fin looked back to see a man climbing lithely out onto the ledge, a cloak blowing out behind him in the wind. His eyes met Fin's for a moment, and then he called something back into the opening.

'They're coming!' Fin yelled, moving so fast he almost collided with Christopher. They all broke into a run, more afraid of their pursuers than the slippery wood beneath their feet.

'Remember the bridge!' Fowkes cried as he disappeared round the edge of the next building. Fin kept his head down as the gantry crossed the small gap between the tenements, squinting to focus his eyes. The street below was dark. Whatever light and sound there was in the Crookeries was obviously kept inside. Then they were at the bridge, and like Christopher, he felt with his foot for the first plank, then the second, then took a deep breath and a large step across the hole where the third should be.

'Hurry!' Christopher hissed. Fin didn't need to turn round to know why: he could hear the men's footfalls, loud and heavy, and horribly close behind. Once safely across the bridge, he spat some rain from his mouth and ran.

As he reached the corner he heard a yell of surprised frustration, and he allowed himself a moment's pause to peer back. The first man, the one with the cloak, had run straight into the gap and was wedged up to the hip, with one leg dangling into the air below. He was cursing in frustration as two shadows tried to pull him up.

'Get after them! Get after them!' the man was shrieking, but his long torso was blocking the way for the others. Fin didn't hang around any longer, but he allowed himself a quick grin. Maybe luck was on their side after all.

Their head start secure, Fowkes led them through the maze of gantries that covered the buildings as intricately as a spider's web. When they reached the last tenement, right at the back of the buildings, they were no more than four floors from the ground. A rope hung down from the roof ridge, and Fowkes pulled himself up until he was straddling the peak. Mona was second, and she immediately lowered herself down the other side until she was out of sight. Joe and Christopher followed.

Finally it was his turn. Fin gripped the coarse rope and dragged himself up, his feet trying to find purchase on the wet slate. He leaned outwards, as if he was abseiling upwards. At the peak he paused for a moment.

Even from the lower height, the view was incredible. The mist on the river glowed an uncertain blue, and within it he could see tiny pinpricks of light. Maybe they were boats, slowly making their way across the treacherous water. And he could see buildings of all shapes and sizes, standing proud and firm against the wind and rain, their shadows cutting into the dark night sky. For a moment Fin was so absorbed in the magical sight that he forgot Fowkes was standing beside him.

'Whenever you're ready,' came the soft voice, and Fin turned to look at him.

'It's beautiful, isn't it?' Fin smiled.

Fowkes sniffed. 'I suppose it has its moments. Now get down to the ground before that lot catch us up.' He nodded backwards. Fin thought he could just about make out two dark shapes a few buildings back, they were moving on the

215

gantries a lot more slowly than they had been, and without the boys to show them the way, it looked like they weren't quite sure where they should be going.

With a glow of warm satisfaction, Fin took the rope and slid down to the muddy ground below.

They came to another tall wooden fence, much like the one they had entered the Crookeries through. Fowkes pushed open the door at its centre. As he stepped through, Finmere was surprised to find he vaguely recognised the layout of the streets.

'Hey' – he stopped and peered around him at the medieval buildings – 'are we in Clerkenwell?'

'This is Old Town,' Fowkes said, 'but yes, if you were at home you'd be in Clerkenwell.' He didn't stop moving, and he was starting to sound distinctly grumpy. 'But you're not at home, and I really need to find some shoes, and something to get rid of this blasted headache – preferably another drink.'

They turned into the next sloping street. It was quite deserted. It looked like the rain had finally forced most of the residents inside.

'Look at that!' Christopher pointed. 'It's an old-style well.' He ran over to it and peered in over the side of the thick stone walls. Finmere joined him, though it was too dark to see the water.

'That's Clerke's Well,' Mona called from the other side of the road where she was peering into a small shop window with Joe. 'It's a wishing well. It's—'

She didn't get to finish her sentence.

'So you must be Fowkes.'

Fin looked up as a man appeared a metre or so ahead of them and stopped. 'The Knight who ran away.' He sneered unpleasantly. 'You're not exactly what I was expecting.'

Fin pulled Christopher down a little so that they were slightly hidden by the well, but the man wasn't looking at them at all. He was staring at Fowkes, who was still a little

216

way behind them and trying to pull a muddy sock from his foot.

Fowkes straightened up slowly, wobbling slightly.

'I am afraid you have the advantage. I don't have a clue who you are.'

The other man laughed. 'That's because you've been away too long.' As he took a step closer, Fin could see that he was a lot younger than Fowkes. His slim face was wrinkle-free, and although he was tall, his shoulders were narrow and boyish.

'My name is George Porter. I'm one of St John Golden's most trusted Knights.' If he'd seen the boys on either side of Fowkes, they didn't appear to be of any concern to him. His polished boots shone, even in the darkness, and as he pushed his cloak to one side they could see his white shirt was spotless. Everything about him was perfectly clean, despite the rain and the mud. Fin stepped a little away from the well and looked back at Fowkes, who looked decidedly shabby and distinctly unsteady.

'St John Golden and trust?' Fowkes snorted. 'I wouldn't put too much store in that if I were you.'

Porter pulled his sword free. The metal sang, a sharp note, as he did so. 'You're an embarrassment to the Order and it will be a pleasure to kill you. You're pretty much dead already.'

Fowkes tugged his own small dagger free from his belt.

Porter laughed.

'Is that the best you can do?'

'Size isn't everything, you know.'

Finmere looked at the well-booted Knight with the gleaming sword and then back at the hungover and ill-equipped Fowkes and felt a rising sense of dread. The older man had no chance. Anyone could see that. Sweat tingled on his palms. He looked over at Joe, and his friend looked back. Fin's eyes slid down to Joe's skilful feet. Porter had barely even registered that they were there. His pulse quickened as his mind raced.

217

Maybe there *was* something they could do – something that he'd seen Joe do plenty of times on the football pitch.

He gave the signal, and Joe winked, grinning.

'Get ready to push,' Fin whispered to Christopher.

'What?' Christopher had no idea what Fin was talking about, but he said, 'Okay, with you.'

The Knight had started striding up the street towards Fowkes, who couldn't stride at all, because his bare feet sank into the mud with every step. Instead he filled the air with a mumbled string of expletives. Fin slipped backwards, keeping to the gloom of the walls, and then doubled back until he was slightly behind Porter, who was completely focused on Fowkes.

Just as the Knight became level with the well, Joe shot out of the darkness, his nimble foot darting forward and tripping Porter up before he'd even seen the boy. He lost his balance and started staggering uncontrollably, and Fin and Joe gave him a hard sideways shove towards the well a metre away.

As he tumbled forwards, Fin voiced his plan: 'In the well!' he shouted, 'in the well!'

They had to move fast, before Porter regained his balance and his composure, but there were four of them and only one of him. Mona and the boys were already tilting the Knight over the rough edge when Fowkes shouted,

'His boots! Get his boots!'

Porter's eyes were bright with panic as he realised what was happening to him. 'No!' he shrieked, 'No … no—' He dropped his sword into the black pit, and as he reached for it his desperate hands met only empty air. Mona stepped back and as the three boys gave him a last hearty push, Fin and Joe grabbed his boots and clung onto them as their wearer fell away and disappeared into the inky blackness far below.

The vanished Knight screamed and the sound echoed up to them for several long seconds before dying away. There was no splash.

'It can't be that deep, surely?' Christopher panted.

Fowkes joined them and took the boots. 'Good work.' He examined the soles. 'And about my size too.'

Finmere peered down into the well, a slightly sick feeling in the pit of his stomach. 'Why can't we hear him hitting the water?' he asked.

'Water?' Mona sounded confused.

'Yeah, water. That's what wells have in them, isn't it?' Joe looked as nervous as Fin felt. What exactly had they done to the Knight?

'Not in Clerke's Well. That's why it's the wishing well. It's bottomless.'

'Bottomless?' Christopher said. 'How can a well be bottomless? How can anything be bottomless? Deep, yes, but—'

'What I *mean* is, the bottom's never been found.'

'It'll come out somewhere.' Fowkes struggled to maintain his balance while pulling on a boot. 'Everything always does.'

'Funny kind of wishing well.' Fin thought of Porter falling and falling for ever. He'd thought the Knight would just end up treading water and calling for help. This was a bit more ... well, *final* than he'd planned.

Fowkes laughed. 'Bet he's wishing he hadn't let any little toe-rags push him in it.'

'Well, you couldn't have dealt with him. You're drunk. We've probably just saved your life.' Christopher sounded as if he might be wishing they hadn't.

'It's all a matter of perspective.' With Porter's boots now firmly on his feet, Fowkes walked away from the well. 'I've been drunk for more than fifteen years, so that makes being drunk normal. God knows how incompetent I'd be sober.' He paused to get his bearings at the T-junction.

'Well, can we at least try and find out?' As he followed Fowkes, Finmere wished Ted was there. He'd not be completely out of his depth; he'd know how to deal with this messed-up man. 'Anyway, Christopher's right: we've just saved your life,' he added. 'Doesn't that mean you owe us?'

Fowkes' only answer was a withering glance.

'Um, Fin,' Joe started, 'if it wasn't for us, his life probably wouldn't have been in danger—'

'At least your friend's got some brains,' Fowkes muttered.

Fin glared. 'You do owe us for your new boots.'

Christopher and Joe laughed out loud, and even Mona smiled. Fowkes continued to ignore Fin, until he eventually stopped outside a dark door.

'You four wait here,' he said. 'I'll be out in five minutes.'

Before anyone could answer, Fowkes was inside the house, leaving them standing out in the street. A light went on above them.

'Do you think he'll come back?' Christopher asked after a minute or two. Fin and Joe looked at him. the same thought had crossed their minds.

'Yes.' Mona peered up at the shadows moving behind the glass. 'He may be a drunk but he's a man of honour. My father wouldn't be so fond of him if he wasn't.'

Even if he wasn't so sure himself, Fin agreed: he had to trust all those people who did have faith in Fowkes. 'I hope he hurries up,' he said after another couple of minutes. 'It would be nice to be somewhere that isn't wet.'

Ten long minutes later, the door re-opened.

They all stared.

Fowkes had not only washed, but he had shaved off his stubble. He was wearing a sparklingly clean white shirt under a dark cloak, just like the clothes Porter had been wearing. A large gold clasp kept the cloak done up at his neck, and under it, hanging from his belt, Fin could make out the glint of a jewelled hilt. His heart finally started leaping, and he grinned.

'Okay, let's get out of here – quickly!' Fowkes pushed them as a huddle back into the street.

'Are the Knights here?' Fin's feet almost gave way under him.

'No, worse than that—'

A window above them screeched open and a bucketful of dark liquid came flying out from it. It fell right where they'd been standing. Fin decided he didn't want to think about the contents of the bucket.

'And don't you bloody well come back!' A head of long blonde hair appeared in the space. 'You can't bleeding well treat me like this!' The window slammed shut.

'Women,' Fowkes muttered.

Joe laughed. 'Why would you throw a bucket of water out at someone in all this rain? You're going to get soaked anyway.'

'There's no indoor plumbing in this part of town. That wasn't water.'

Fin was glad he hadn't stopped to think about the bucket.

'Oh,' Joe said, and then as he realised what Fowkes meant, made a face. 'Oh eugh! That's disgusting!' he grumbled, looking up to make sure nothing else was heading their way.

The overhead sky was turning to an overcast grey by the time they got to Fowkes' secret destination. Morning – or afternoon – would soon be arriving, but whichever it decided to be, it was still going to be raining. As it got lighter, they could see the thick cloud was like a blanket across the sky, with no hint of an edge or a break in it. Fin had never seen anything like it, and it filled him with a dread he didn't understand.

He'd tried to talk to Fowkes while they were walking, but the Knight had ignored most of Fin's questions, except for the occasional grunt of yes or no.

In the end, he'd given up and fallen silent, trudging onwards with his head bowed down against the rain. Even though the falling water was warm, the constant attack was making his

221

bones shiver, and he could see the same discomfort on the others' faces as they walked alongside him.

Finally the road they were on opened out into a square. There in front of them highly polished white steps led up to a huge, elegant building.

'Is that an hourglass? Christopher stared up at the carving sitting on top of the building.

'It's a truth vial.' Mona sounded tired, and Fin wondered if the constant rainwater was getting to her too. 'This is where the Storyholder lives – amongst other things. This is the Old Bailey House of Real Truths.'

Fin froze and stared. 'The Old Bailey?' His voice came out as a whisper.

'Yes.' Fowkes' voice was low. 'And be careful. It's likely there will be Knights here. Stay close.'

Finmere couldn't take his eyes from the building. *The Old Bailey House of Real Truths*. Apart from the obvious differences on its top – the truth vial replacing the Lady of Justice and her scales – the place was almost identical to the Old Bailey in his own London.

Fowkes turned. 'I said stay close,' he hissed. 'What's the matter with you?'

'Fin was found on the steps of the Old Bailey back at home when he was a baby,' Joe said. 'He's probably just a bit freaked. This place looks exactly the same apart from that thing on the top.'

'Sorry.' Fin dragged his eyes back to his companions and caught them up. Fowkes stared at him for just long enough for Fin to start feeling uncomfortable before turning away. 'When I say stay close, I mean it,' he growled.

Fin didn't even look down at the second step as he walked up it. This *wasn't* his Old Bailey and he had to remember that.

It became much easier once Fowkes pushed open the two heavy oak doors and ushered them in out of the rain.

'Why isn't it locked?' Christopher's voice dropped to a whisper.

'The House of Real Truths is always open – not that many people ever really come here,' Mona said.

Standing in the oval foyer, all pink and white marble, Fin's eyes were drawn to the double doors ahead. They were open a few centimetres, and he left the others and peered round the edge. He gasped, and said, 'Hey, come and look at this! It's amazing!' He looked all around, fascinated by the vials lining the walls from floor to ceiling, all glowing in a myriad colours. Strange men in black were moving silently between the rows. It was a sea of beautiful rainbow brightness, and Fin moved his head further in to get a better look.

As his chin crossed the threshold, however, everything changed. The men in black all paused, exactly in unison, and turned, staring with piercing pink eyes in his direction. Weirdly, they were all albinos, every one of them, and as their bodies froze like statues, so their mouths dropped open in identical 'o's of wonder. The beautiful colours drained from each vial, which instead glowed such a vivid gold that Fin thought every glass might smash from the pressure of trying to contain that glorious light.

His own mouth dropped open too, and he felt a terrible emptiness in his ice-cold stomach. It was the void: the void in his head was opening, and in that instant nothing existed apart from the gold glow and the silence.

The truth. The truth was coming for him and there was nothing he could do to fight it.

A hand grabbed him roughly by the collar and yanked him back before the door was kicked shut.

'This isn't a sightseeing tour,' Fowkes growled.

'I'm sorry ... I—' Fin's head was a whirl. What had happened to him? Something had taken over; something had tried to force that door in his head open. The awful feeling was slipping away almost as quickly as it had come, like a bad dream dissipating on waking. He continued to shiver for a moment longer.

'Don't go in there. Don't *ever* go in there.' Fowkes' face was so close to Fin's that he could feel the anger in his breath. 'In fact, don't go *anywhere* I don't tell you to, do you hear?'

Fin nodded, his face flushing. 'Sorry,' he mumbled again. Fowkes granted him one more scathing look and then turned away. 'And that goes for the bloody lot of you.'

As the last of the strangeness dribbled away from him, Finmere sheepishly followed Fowkes as he opened a smaller door and led them down a narrow corridor towards the back of the building. They emerged at the other end into another huge foyer, this one completely tiled with white marble. A sweeping staircase curved up around a goldfish-shaped fountain on one wall which was tinkling away tranquilly.

Fowkes stopped at the bottom of the grand staircase, one hand on the banister. His face had darkened.

'Are you okay?' Finmere asked.

Eventually, Fowkes nodded. 'Yes. It's just been a long time.' He didn't look at Fin. 'God, I need a drink,' he added, before skipping the bottom step and going straight onto the second.

Fin found himself doing the same.

They stood in the doorway of the apartments, staring at the sea of white mess inside.

'Looks like my bedroom on a good day,' Joe said, quietly.

Fin gave him a half-smile he didn't really feel. He knew his friend was just trying to ease the awful atmosphere that had fallen over them.

Fowkes finally took a step inside and they followed. What Fin had glimpsed through the half-open doorway downstairs, that had been magical. But there was something almost spiritual about the pure white surroundings of the Storyholder's home,

something even the boys from The Somewhere could feel tingling in their bones. But then, Fin thought, carefully placing
his feet and trying not to cause any more damage, there was
no reason they shouldn't feel it: Ted said what she did kept
their world in balance as much as The Nowhere. Seeing all
her things wrecked made his soul shake a little.

'This is very, very bad,' Mona whispered, staring at the
devastation around her.

Fowkes moved from room to room, calling that strange
name: 'Tova? Tova?' But the white walls gave him no answer.
He disappeared into a room on the left of the entrance door.
After a minute, Fin followed him.

Fowkes was sitting heavily on the side of the bed, surrounded by feathers from the ripped-up mattress and pillows.

'Have the Knights taken her?' Christopher stood in the
doorway behind them.

Fowkes nodded. 'Yeah. They've taken her.' His voice was
soft and sad, despite his fierce looks. 'I just don't understand
what they were looking for here? Why do this?'

'Maybe they wanted to make a point or something?' Fin
could hear Joe and Mona starting to tidy up in the lounge,
just like Joe had done at Mrs Baker's. Maybe he should go and
help them. He felt lost. He couldn't begin to guess at what
the Knights were up to. He wasn't up to this – he was barely
sixteen. What could he possibly do against these men?

'Someone else, maybe, but that's not St John Golden's
style.' Fowkes rubbed his newly shaved chin. 'Golden's too
detached.'

At the foot of the bed, Christopher bent down and picked
up something from the tangle of bed sheets and quilts. His
brow furrowed as he turned it over in his hands.

'What's that?' Fowkes peered over at him.

Christopher didn't answer, but flipped open the case. Fin
saw a glint of silver. Nothing else in the apartment was anything other than white. 'Christopher?'

225

His friend looked up. 'Sorry.' He held the item up. 'It's a silver cigarette case.' He tossed it to Fowkes, then bent again and gathered up the bedclothes from the floor.

Finmere sat on the bed next to Fowkes and they looked into the case. 'These are French cigarettes,' said Fowkes. 'Gauloises.' He handed Fin the case. 'One of the Knights must have left it here.'

'Do you think it could be St John Golden's?' The silver felt heavy and expensive.

'Maybe. I'd be surprised though. From what I hear' – he turned and looked at Fin – 'and although I may be drunk most of the time, I still can't avoid everything – anyway, I hear that St John doesn't Travel much these days.' He frowned, focused on Fin's hand.

'Where did you get that?' He grabbed Finmere's wrist and pulled his hand up so he could get a closer look at the ring on Fin's middle finger.

'It's mine,' Fin said quickly, 'Judge Brown *gave* it to me. He said it was in my cardboard box—'

'Your cardboard box?'

'The one Ted found me in when I was a baby. On the second step of the Old Bailey.' He tugged his hand free. 'It's mine. You can't take it. It's all I have that's really mine other than the blanket I was wrapped up in and now the Judge's sword, and that's not really mine.' He stumbled over his words, realising how childish they must sound, but desperately needing to get them out.

'But that's Baxter's ring.' Fowkes looked intensely at Finmere, which made his cheeks burn slightly, although he wasn't sure why.

'I know. Judge Brown told me.' He paused. 'Maybe Baxter was my father. That's what Ted thinks, anyway. And the Judge did too. They think maybe my mother brought me through and left me here – there. They said it was about a year after Baxter died.'

226

Fin stared at Fowkes, hoping to see some sort of recognition in his eyes, some memory of his friend having a woman he loved, a woman he might have had a baby with. A woman – a *mother* – who might still be alive ... Fin's heart ached for it too badly to even think about it.

But instead of recognition, all he saw was shocked confusion.

'But—'

'Well, that's all very touching,' Christopher said, folding his arms across his chest, 'but shouldn't we be getting on with finding the Storyholder? That storm outside is getting worse.'

Fin looked up at Christopher, shocked. That kind of cold outburst wasn't like him at all.

'*She's* causing the storm.' Fowkes moved on from whatever it was he'd been about to say to Finmere. 'She caused the last one too. At least it shows she's still alive.' He paused. 'Tova was always special. She's the strongest of all the Storyholders that have ever been. The other girls at the Academy, they used to say she had Magi blood in her. They probably said it out of jealousy, because they all knew that she was always going to be the one to take over, but I wouldn't be surprised if there was some truth in it.'

His stood up and threw some cushions back on the bed. 'They say that the last storm was caused by her despair.' The words came out like a deep sigh. 'Storyholders must retain personal emotional emptiness, you see. If she doesn't, then the stories work *for* her, instead of her being simply a vessel for them.' He shook his head. 'I never really did understand it. But the problem with black storms is that they tend to take on a life of their own, and when that happens – well, I doubt if even she can control it. Especially if—' He stopped and looked down at his feet for a while. 'Especially if they hurt her,' he finally finished in a low voice.

'So what do we do now?' Christopher peered out through

the alcove window at the rain splattering darkly on the glass.

'We'll go and see the Prince Regent. In the meantime, you kids should get a couple of hours' rest. I think it's going to be a very long day.'

'Can't we just go now?' Christopher's voice was dull. 'Let's get whatever we have to do done, and then we can all go home.'

Fowkes stared at him, irritated. 'We *could* go now, but as the Prince won't be out of his own bed for at least another two or three hours, we'd only be waiting around in the rain getting fed up and even more tired. So just do as you're told.' He strode through to the other room.

Finmere looked at Christopher. 'You okay?'

Christopher left the window, and walked over to the slashed bed. He lay down on one side and stared up at the ceiling. 'Yes,' he said, eventually. 'Sorry I snapped. It's just all this black rain. I keep thinking about how it's falling at home too. If anything terrible starts to happen over there—' He paused. 'I'd want to be with my parents, that's all.'

'It won't come to that.' Fin lay down alongside him, hoping he sounded more convincing than he felt. 'We'll have it all sorted out by then.'

'Oh, of course we will!' Christopher sounded slightly more like his normal self. 'One drunk and four teenagers, one of whom is a *girl*. How could we possibly fail?' He grinned at Fin, who smiled back, relieved.

'Thanks for coming, Christopher. It means a lot.'

Christopher grinned. 'That's what friends are for.'

Mona and Joe came through from the other room and Joe bundled onto the mattress, taking up the remaining space.

'Ha! Here's yours!' He lobbed a cushion at her that she just managed to catch.

'I thought in situations like this it was normal for the men

228

to sleep on the floor and give up the bed to the lady.' She sounded most put out.

'That may be the way you do it in your world, but in ours it's the other way round.' Joe's face was perfectly serious.

'Really?' For the first time since they'd met, Mona seemed slightly unsure of herself.

Fin sat up slightly and leaned on his elbows. 'Oh yes – on buses and everything. Women always give their places up to men. It's the polite way.'

'And honourable,' Christopher added. 'It's not really a rule or anything, but it is a matter of respect. People who value their family's honour and stuff' – he yawned widely – 'they always abide by it. But hey, if you want to do it your way, then that's fine.'

'No, no.' Mona rearranged some of the cushions that were scattered across the carpet. 'The floor's fine for me.'

Fin started laughing quietly alongside Joe. For a moment he felt almost calm. He was lucky to have such good friends, and now they had Mona too, and they'd found Fowkes. They'd make Ted proud. Fin was sure of it.

His eyes eventually slipped shut, and when he dreamed, he dreamed of the void trying to suck him down forever into its icy, silent darkness.

TWENTY-FIVE

The Prince Regent stood in front of his throne as the group walked up towards him, their heads bowed. Fin's heart raced. Before this, the closest he'd ever come to meeting royalty had been when the Queen's cousin had come to open the new wing at St Martin's, and even then he'd been third row back. He'd just cheered away with the rest of the prep school boys. This was completely different. He was actually inside a palace. He was actually about to meet a real live prince, face to face.

Joe hadn't said a word since they'd entered the palace and been shown into an opulent antechamber. Even Christopher had looked slightly intimidated during the five-minute walk down the incredibly over-the-top corridor to the throne room.

Mona had been very quick to tell the powdered courtier who had come to collect them that her father made most of the Prince Regent's clothes and that they were practically family friends, but the clipped smile and condescending look he'd given her had quickly shut her up. Like the boys, she too was looking more and more overawed every time they passed another portrait of a long dead king or queen, or another piece of expensive looking sculpture.

Finally they reached the other end of the throne room, and Fowkes fell gracefully to one knee. Finmere, Joe and Christopher did the same, far less elegantly. Mona sank into a curtsey.

'Your Royal Majesty,' Fowkes said, his head still bowed.

Fin let his eyes wander upwards. The Prince Regent was very small, not what he'd been expecting at all. If he hadn't had that huge purplish-white wig on, he wouldn't be anywhere near Fin's own height, and Fin himself wasn't exactly tall for his age. Though he might not be a big man, still, even Fin had to admit the Regent did look pretty impressive. His ivory-coloured coat glittered with a frosting of tiny diamonds, and underneath it the frills down the front of his shirt hung in tight pleats. His face was perfectly white, but above his rouged lips, his eyes were darker than Fowkes'.

The marble floor was hard under his knee, and Fin was relieved when the Prince gave a tiny flick of his wrist and Fowkes stood up again.

The Prince stared at Fowkes for a moment longer.

'Well, isn't this funny.' When the Prince finally spoke, his high-pitched voice didn't sound amused at all. 'I see not a single Knight for years and years, and then I see two in as many days.' He paused. 'But then I forget. You're not a Knight any more, are you, Andrew Fowkes?' His eyes scanned the man opposite. 'Although I see you still carry a sword. As does one of your young friends, I see. And that does rather surprise me.'

He sat carefully on his throne, his delicate fingers spreading his coat evenly under him. 'So, what brings you to me? The last time we met was on the eve of a black storm that raged for a full year, bringing madness and despair to my people. I hope you are not here to tell me to prepare for another one?'

'You are right, Your Majesty. I am not a Knight any more.' Fowkes stood tall under the Prince's scrutiny. 'And right now, I'm truly glad of that fact, or whatever shred of pride I might have left would be gone.'

'You have no dignity, just like that friend of yours, Baxter. He had no honour and he died like a common criminal at the hands of my people. And you? You ran to hide and drink

231

yourself to ruin in the Crookeries, instead of staying to defend your friend's memory.' He frowned. 'In many ways you are worse than him.'

As the Prince spoke, Finmere's face burned. Baxter *hadn't* been like that – he *couldn't* have been. Surely Ted would have told him if Baxter had been such a terrible man?

'Yes, I am.' Fowkes' voice dropped, but there was no anger in it, only bitterness. 'I am worse than him in ways you couldn't even begin to understand. But at the moment, I'm the most honourable of the Knights who are left – the young ones, at any rate.'

The Prince stared. 'St John Golden came here yesterday. He brought with him a dead Knight, the guardian of the Storyholder's apartments. Did you kill him?'

Fowkes shook his head. 'No, Your Majesty, most certainly not. I imagine St John probably did it himself. He's the one who's taken the Storyholder. He's got Tova.'

Under his mask of make-up, the Prince Regent looked visibly shocked. 'You lie!' he whispered.

'I almost wish I did – but I do not,' Fowkes said, growling. 'No. Her home is wrecked and she's gone. He must want to take the Stories from her. It's the only explanation. He's after the power, and the Knights of the Inner Council are with him. I think he's gone crazy.' He paused. 'I think he's started to believe in the Prophecy.'

The Prince stood up from his throne. 'The Prophecy is nothing but legend: an old wives' tale.' He looked down on Fowkes, and dropped his voice again. 'And perhaps you will tell me why should I believe you over St John Golden? How do I know you have not taken her yourself? That you are not the one who has gone power-mad?'

For the first time, Finmere heard real emotion in the Prince Regent's voice.

He paced over to the window and gestured widely. 'Look at this,' he said angrily, 'as if I need old legends or interlopers from another world to tell me that there is something wrong. Only Tova could cause a storm like this.' He glared back at Fowkes.

'I detest you and your Knights, coming here and causing trouble. There is not an honourable man amongst you. We have been fools to trust you for all this time. *I* have been a fool!'

No!' Fin shouted, as surprised as everyone else to hear his own voice echoing around the huge room. 'No,' he said again, more quietly this time. The Prince stared at him, shocked. Finmere stepped forward, level with Fowkes.

'You're wrong, sir.' Fin's heart thumped in his ears.

'And who are you? You're just a boy.'

Fin swallowed. This was it. 'I'm Finmere Tingewick Smith. I'm the one who was sent from The Somewhere to find Fowkes and try and put everything right. And these are my friends Joe and Christopher who came to help even though this is nothing to do with them.'

'And I'm Mona, Savjani's daughter, and I'm helping too.' If Mona was expecting some kind of recognition, she was disappointed.

The Prince stayed focused on Fin.

'They sent someone not even nearly a man yet? This is all the care they have for our world?' There was a sneer in the Prince Regent's voice. 'If he were half the man my poor deluded father thinks he is, then Harlequin Brown would have come himself!'

'He can't,' Fin said, heat searing his insides, 'he's dead! They killed him and I found him dying, stabbed through with his own sword.' He knew he was shouting but he didn't care. 'And you can't talk about them like that! I don't know anything about any Prophecy but I do know Ted's doing all he can, and they hurt Mrs Baker and probably Mrs Harvey and other people as well, and the only reason they had to send me instead of anyone else is because all the proper Knights

233

are old and in wheelchairs and not even awake, their whole lives taken by coming in and out of your world, but they all thought it was worth it and they all still love the Order and would die to protect The Nowhere!'

Fin was on a roll; he couldn't have stopped, even if a double-decker bus had crashed through the wall and run him down. 'So *don't* say they have no honour, not ever! Don't you *dare* say that!' He was panting now, the sound of his breath rushing in and out filling the vast hall, until he managed to get hold of himself and calm down a little. He didn't have to look around to know that everyone was staring at him. He could feel their eyes, burning into him.

'I'm sorry,' he said, quietly, 'but you can't blame everyone because of a few. It's not fair. Adults always forget that.'

'Do not apologise, young man.' The Prince came down a step, the poise in his voice completely restored. 'You should never apologise for speaking with passion. There is honesty in such emotion.'

He stared at Fowkes for a very long time before he spoke again. 'It appears that I have no alternative but to trust you.'

Fowkes let out the breath he hadn't realised he'd been holding. 'I need the address of the Inner Council's lodge, Your Majesty – seventeen years is a long time, and St John will have set up a new place when he took over. I presume your spies will have told you where it is.'

'It is in Old Town. In the House of Charter's Lane.'

Fowkes gave a wry smile. 'Of course it is.'

'I believe it is the largest south-facing building.'

'I know it. It's on the same piece of land that Orrery House stands on in The Somewhere.'

The Prince Regent turned to his throne and sat. 'You must restore the honour of the Order and return the Storyholder. Prove the Prophecy false.'

Fowkes nodded. 'For once, Your Majesty, you and I are in complete agreement.'

'There is one other thing that might interest you.' The Prince crossed one leg over the other and leaned back in the huge gilt chair. 'There's a Magus in the city. I have had too many reports of it for it not to be true.'

'I don't see what that has to do with this matter—' Fowkes was interrupted by a loud rumble of thunder from outside, and they all looked at the window for a long second.

'The Magi can reverse the Ageing,' the Prince said softly. 'If you can find one, then perhaps you will have a chance.'

Fin skipped a breath. Reverse the Ageing? Ted hadn't said anything about that. He looked at Fowkes, who looked dumbfounded. He obviously hadn't known anything about it either.

The Prince let out a long sigh. 'The most important thing is the safety of the Five Eternal Stories; that has to be the highest priority. If those are safe, then no man or Magus can do too much damage to any of our worlds.' He looked at each of them. 'No one comes before the stories. Not even Tova herself.'

The Prince Regent leaned forward and rested his arms on his knees in an uncharacteristically manly gesture. 'I loved her too, you know, a long time ago. But unlike Baxter, I did as I must. I kept my love only in my own heart.' He turned his head back to the gathering fury on the other side of the glass.

'Now go.'

The Prince maintained his composure until the echo of their footsteps had died away and he was completely alone. After the far doors had thudded shut he pulled off the heavy wig and dropped it carelessly to the floor beside him. He lowered his head into his hands, ignoring the itch of his shortly cropped afro. Quiet tears cut tracks through the white paint of his make-up, revealing the chocolate-brown skin below.

235

After a while, he unfurled his elegant body and peered up at the stained-glass windows high above, forgotten by almost all except those unfortunates whose job it was to climb up and clean them every evening while the court slept. He sighed, wishing that his tears would blur his dark eyes so he didn't have to see the images so clearly. Not that he needed to see them; they were burned on his retinas from a lifetime of looking. The story was all there: the Age of Reason that led to the banishing and the curse on a King who hanged a Magus at Smithfield for no reason other than wanting to stay in his home.

The Prince Regent wondered for a moment at the depth of injustice that his long-ago family had done to that Magus, and how they were still paying for it. A hundred years of the curse on his line, and less than two years left until he reached the age it would claim him. *The madness of Kings*. Somewhere in a far wing of the palace his own father, the king, danced and sang and drooled, the very picture of insanity, as he had since the end of his fortieth year. And just as his father had done before him, and his father's father ...

The coloured glass shone brightly, daring him to look away, but the Regent refused. Did they truly deserve it? Was it even a curse? He'd thought that by having no children of his own he might break the hold of the old magic, even if it claimed him. But now, standing small in the vast room, his scalp burning from the heavy wig he was forced to wear each day, the decision of his youthful self seemed unwise. If dark times were truly coming, The Nowhere would need a strong king, or at least a strong regent. For the first time in his thirty-eight years, he heard his own body clock ticking. And it sounded like a bomb.

They had to walk fast to keep up with Fowkes as he strode down the long corridors of the palace. 'So what are we going to do?' Fin asked breathlessly. 'Are we going to the Knights' house?'

'I'm trying to figure it out. Time is against us. We'll have to go there for our best chance of finding Tova, but we've got no chance of beating St John and the Council without the Magus, so we need to find him too.'

The answer was obvious to Finmere. 'We need to split up. That way we can do both in half the time.'

'No. That's not happening.' Fowkes glowered at the ground. 'I can't send you lot wandering around this London. Never mind that with Golden and his brutes after you it's insanely dangerous, you'd never find him.'

'I'm not from The Somewhere.' Mona spoke up from behind them, and Fowkes stopped.

'I know London like the back of my hand, and I know of the Magi,' she said. 'My dad used to tell me stories about them when I was little – almost as many as he used to tell me about you and Baxter.'

'If Fin gives me that double-sided coin,' Christopher joined in, 'then I can go with Mona and when we find the Magus then I'll just get back home through the doorway and take the cure to Orrery House.'

Fowkes looked from one to the other. 'What if you don't find him?' he asked.

Christopher shrugged. He'd been quiet all morning and his unusual seriousness remained. 'If we don't find him, then we're probably all up shit creek. Like the Prince said, the main thing is getting the stories safe.'

'Anyway' – Mona's hands were planted defiantly on her hips – 'we *will* find the Magus. There's only one place the Magi would go in London, especially at the start of something so rare and strange as a black storm.'

They all stared at her, even Fowkes, and she rolled her eyes. 'Well, it's obvious, isn't it?'

'Of course,' Fowkes breathed after a moment.

The man and the girl spoke in unison. 'West Minster Abbey.'

Having given Christopher the coin and a share of the money, Finmere, Joe and Fowkes watched from under the shelter of the huge stone archway at the palace entrance as he and Mona scurried out through the high iron gates. The rain came down heavily, falling in large puddles and drumming into the ground.

'Will they be okay?' Joe asked.

Fin didn't answer. It felt weird splitting up like this, and once again the seriousness of what they were doing hit him. He had another flash of the dying Judge behind his eyes. Would they even see Christopher and Mona again? His stomach tightened. He couldn't think like that – first, because it was almost impossible to imagine, and second, because it wouldn't do them any good.

As his friends disappeared around the corner, he sent them a quiet wish of good luck.

He looked over at Fowkes. 'I suppose we should head off too.'

Fowkes smiled. 'We're going to take a quicker route.'

'How do you mean?' Joe asked.

Fowkes looked at Fin. 'I think it's about time you learned to use that sword of yours,' he said with a fierce grin.

'But it's the Judge's really, and—' Fin began, a swirly feeling starting in the pit of his stomach.

'Not any more it isn't. It's yours now. And you wouldn't have it if Ted didn't want you to use it. Anyway, you need to understand it, just in case anything happens to me.'

Fin didn't want to think about that possibility, but he had to admit Fowkes had a point. 'Okay,' he said after a moment.

'But this normally takes a grown man at least a couple of

weeks to master, so don't get too excited because it might not actually work.'

'Fin will be able to do it,' Joe said. 'Fin's good at just about everything.'

Fin wished he felt even half as confident. As he pulled the sword free of its sheath, the gold gleamed brightly against the dark backdrop of the rain. Another wave of thunder rolled above their heads. 'So what do I do then?'

Fowkes pulled them into the far corner of the archway, out of sight from the few guardsmen who were valiantly trying to exercise their disgruntled-looking horses despite the worsening weather.

'Start by holding the sword ready, like this. Use both hands, at least to begin with.' Fowkes demonstrated, pushing Fin's hands so he was holding the sword straight out, level with the ground. 'Now you need to think of a place in The Somewhere where it'll be safe to open a hole into,' Fowkes started.

'Somewhere like Orrery House?'

'No, not there – for all we know St John Golden has already sent his bastard Knights there. Think of somewhere else: somewhere you know there's not likely to be anyone around who might see us. The most important rule of travelling is to have a place fixed firmly in your head. You have to be able to see it clearly – and not just *see* it. You have to know the sounds and the smells of it, too.'

He bent down so he was looking into Fin's eyes. 'If you haven't got that secure in your head, then the rift could just open up anywhere, and that's the last thing we need. So choose carefully, okay?'

'Why does where the rift opens matter as long as it's in London?' Joe leaned against the wall.

'Because what if the rift opens on the fast lane of the M25? Or in front of a speeding tube train? Firstly, we'd all be flattened, and secondly, that's something neither world needs.'

239

Fin's heart sank. 'Don't give me any ideas. Now all I can picture is Piccadilly Circus!'

'Try closing your eyes.'

Behind the darkness of his eyelids, Fin tried to stay calm as he racked his suddenly empty brain. There must be somewhere safe that he knew well. He gritted his teeth. Mrs Baker's house was out because the Knights already knew about it. St Martin's never had any private or quiet places, except for maybe the toilets, but he could just imagine cutting through to one of the chilly cubicles to find someone already sitting there, staring back through the rift at the three of them.

Finally, just as he was getting annoyed with himself, he had a thought.

'I've got it.' He kept his eyes firmly shut, not wanting to break his concentration. 'The back row of the reference section of the library at my school, Eastfields.'

'Okay. Now place yourself there,' said Fowkes. '*Really* there.'

Fin squeezed his eyes tighter. He could see the spines of the books in front of him, even down to the small squares of paper with the reference numbers typed on them taped two centimetres up from the bottom. This was his quiet place; he came here when Joe was in detention, or when he just wanted some time by himself, especially during his first year at Eastfields. Back then, he'd sit on the carpet that smelled like a strange mix of dust and industrial cleaning fluid, and lose himself in a book for a precious half-hour or so.

'I'm there,' he whispered.

'Now for the tricky part.' Fowkes' voice tickled his ear. 'Keep yourself in that place in your head, but at the same time you need to feel for the electricity in the sword.'

'The electricity?'

'That's the closest way I can describe it to you. The swords somehow tune into the vibrations in the layers of the worlds. You've got to feel for it, Fin, and then it'll find you.'

Fin's hands were sweaty around the hilt, and his arms were starting to ache. Maybe he couldn't do it. Maybe he wouldn't be able to. He shook the doubt away and squeezed his palms tighter as he thought of the library. At the same time, he imagined the double-edged sword to be a part of him, an extension of his arms, the tip of its blade like his own fingertips. His nerves reached into it and after long minutes, he gasped.

'I can feel it,' he whispered. A warm tingling ran over his skin, even deep within his bones, and he smiled. It almost tickled. Forgetting Fowkes and Joe were there, Fin lost himself in the sensation. It felt as if it were running round his head; now it was getting stronger, buzzing in his teeth, down to his feet, feeling warm and curious, as if it were exploring him. The library walls grew in his mind.

'I said I can feel it,' he repeated. There was a long pause.

'We know,' Joe breathed, and Fin opened his eyes.

'You're a fast learner.' Fowkes was looking at him in that same odd way he had back in the Storyholder's white apartment, but Finmere barely noticed. His mouth had dropped open.

'*I did it.*'

Directly in front of him was a grainy black and white image: a shelf of books. He recognised some of them; they hadn't been taken out by a student in years. It was the last row of the reference section of the upper floor of the library at Eastfields Comprehensive, that was for certain.

'That is *totally* cool,' Joe grinned.

Fin smiled back. 'I didn't even know I'd done it.'

'Doesn't look like there's anyone around.' Fowkes peered into the rift. 'Let's get across quickly, in case Fin can't hold it.'

The tingling was running in a loop, tiny shocks hopping round Fin's body, down to the tip of the sword and back round again. It felt pretty strong to him. Somewhere inside he already knew he could keep the rift open for ages if he needed to. He wasn't even feeling the weight of the sword any more, and he took one hand off the hilt.

'You ready?' he asked.

Joe stepped forward. 'So when I step through there I might come out the other side, like, eighty or something?'

'That's the risk,' Fowkes said, 'and I can't pretend that might not happen.' He grinned. 'But sometimes there's nothing like a bit of danger to make you feel alive.' His face clouded over. 'And I should know. I've been feeling dead for years.'

Joe looked at Fin. 'Well, I'm up for it.'

Fin wasn't surprised. Joe never backed down from anything.

Fowkes took the first step through.

'What will be, will be,' Fin said softly, and Fowkes' head turned.

'What did you—?'

The rest of his question was cut off as he reappeared on the other side. Finmere and Joe looked at each other, took a deep breath, and followed him through together.

To suddenly be back in Eastfields after all the strangeness of The Nowhere was disconcerting, especially seeing Fowkes dripping black rain, surrounded by tatty zoology reference books. And the double-edged sword looked pretty out of place too. The library was dark, with only the humming glow from the emergency exit light breaking through the gloom. So it was night in The Somewhere. Fin glanced around him at the familiar surroundings that felt so odd. The Knights must get some kind of jetlag going from one to the other all the time. You'd never know if it was time to get up or go to bed. His watch was once again ticking merrily. It read 3.15 – but 3.15 when? The same night they'd left, or a different night? If it was a different night, how many nights had passed? Fin wondered if he'd ever get his head round it all.

Joe finished checking his hands for liver spots and wrinkles. 'So we made it okay,' he whispered, 'what now?'

Fowkes looked intensely at Fin. 'Did you say, "What will be, will be"? Just before we came through?'

Fin had almost forgotten he'd said it. 'It's just a saying,' he started to explain. 'I must have heard it somewhere.' He remembered thinking that same thing back at Mrs Baker's, when he was looking under the bed and his hand went all funny for a moment. The way Fowkes was looking at him was making him feel uncomfortable and he didn't know what he was supposed to say. *It came from this weird dark space in my head, but don't worry, I've locked it up?* No one would understand that – he didn't understand it himself. Time to change the subject. He looked at the rift. 'Like Joe said, what now?'

The Knight stared at Fin a moment longer before saying, 'Closing it is easier than opening it – not that you had much of a problem with that. You just need to unthink it.'

'Unthink it?' Joe sounded completely confused.

Still feeling the hum in his fingers, Finmere knew exactly what Fowkes meant. He also knew that it was even easier than that: he just had to break the connection with the sword. He took a breath and pushed the fizzing sensation back into the metal, and the hilt and his sweaty palm became two again, instead of one fused entity. He shook out his hand, shaking away the remnants of the electricity, and the rift closed as if an invisible hand were zipping up a jacket over a bulging stomach.

'That is *so* cool,' Joe breathed. 'I need to learn to do that.'

'All in good time,' Fowkes said. 'I wouldn't have wanted Fin to learn it yet if he didn't already have the sword. Sometimes you can be too young.'

'You reckon? I always think you can be too old.'

Fowkes laughed out loud, and the warm throaty sound surprised Fin. They'd never heard him laugh before. So far, scowling had been more his thing.

'You may have a point, Joe.' The Knight pulled his own sword free. 'Now let's see if I can still do this.'

'Um,' Joe said, 'why didn't we go straight to this house if you know where it is? Surely you could have just cut a thingy through to it?'

'I needed to know you two could get home.' He stared at his sword. 'And I needed to know that whatever happens next, there will be the potential for the Order to survive.'

Fin looked at the dark, troubled face. 'If you care about the Order so much, then why did you leave? Why did you disappear?'

The man sighed. 'Sometimes you can care too much.'

'That doesn't make sense.'

Fowkes shrugged. 'It does to me.' The purple jewel glinted in the gloom as he raised the sword against the quiet ordinariness of the library. 'Anyway, it's done now. It's all done now.'

His eyes lost their focus for a brief second, and then with barely an intake of breath the blade cut a slice between the worlds, opening up a bloodless wound back into The Nowhere. 'Come on. Before someone sees us.'

No one looked back at Eastfields Comprehensive's library's reference section as the Knight led them back into their adventure.

The warm rain lashed against his skin, forcing Fin to catch his breath. It was falling even more heavily, though they'd been away just a few minutes. There was definitely a storm coming; it didn't need a weatherman to figure that one out.

As soon as Joe's foot was through Fowkes closed the rift behind them, just moments before a stocky woman in a soaking cotton bonnet and sodden grey dress scurried past them. She was carrying a bundle of washing and muttering under her breath as she went.

'That's the house.' Fowkes gestured across the lane. Fin held a hand up to protect his eyes from the foul water and stared at it. Unlike the narrow, uneven houses on either side of it, this building was large and sturdy. The front was a mass of dark timbers in all sorts of patterns, as if an early Tudor builder just hadn't known when to stop. The downstairs windows had been blocked up; from here it looked to Fin like they'd used some kind of mud.

'It doesn't look as if anyone lives there,' Fin said. 'What's happened to the ground floor?'

'Nothing; there are no proper windows in this part of town,' Fowkes said. 'The glass disappears, so most people have stopped trying to fit it. Instead, people fill the windows in to make it harder for burglars.' Fowkes tilted his head. 'Although in this Borough the thieves' windows have no glass either, so there tends to be a truce.'

Once again, Fin found himself wondering about the strangeness of this place. The palace was full of glass, yet here there was none. Where was the logic in that? Joe sighed, and Finmere figured he was equally confused about The Nowhere.

They trotted across the muddy ground and when they reached the rough-plastered wall, Fowkes looked up. 'We're going to have to get in to the second floor. We'll have to hope there's no one in there.' He frowned. 'I don't understand why the place isn't more heavily guarded. I expected to see one Knight on the door at least.'

Fin wondered what they would have done if there had been a sentry. He thought about the other Knight, George Porter, and how they'd tripped him into the bottomless well. Was he still falling?

'Maybe they're all out looking for us,' he said, though that thought wasn't particularly comforting. Neither was Fowkes' response.

'Or they've got The Storyholder somewhere else.'

'How come you didn't cut through to inside the building?' Joe asked. 'That would have been easier, wouldn't it?' He sniffed. 'And drier.'

Fowkes reached up, grabbed the thick wooden beam above him and started to climb. 'I've never been inside so I can't see

245

it in my head. Now, come on,' he grunted down at the boys, 'even in The Nowhere, three people climbing up the side of a building is generally considered slightly suspicious.'

Fin was a few centimetres shorter than both Joe and Fowkes, and he had to stretch his legs desperately wide to get him from beam to the next, but he managed it, thanks in the main to the complete lack of design that had gone into the façade of the building. The timbers looked like some sort of maniac trellis covering the whole surface of the building.

Fin watched as above him, Fowkes swung his leg over the windowsill and cautiously pulled back the curtain or what-ever it was that was keeping out the rain. He disappeared inside and the boys held their breath until he leant back out a moment later and hissed, 'Quickly!'

Fin pulled himself up the last few metres, with Joe right behind, and Fowkes hauled them both safely inside. They looked around while they were getting their breath back. Candles burned in holders against the rough walls, and in-stead of carpet, some sort of dead plants covered the uneven floor. 'So those are reeds,' Fin muttered to Joe, 'maybe I can hand some in to Settle instead of an essay!'

A wooden four-poster bed was pushed up against one wall. The thick curtains that hung down around it were pulled open.

A door slammed downstairs and footsteps thudded up towards them. Fowkes pulled the boys back behind the heavy curtain covering the open window, but the heavy boots went straight past their room and continued upwards.

'We timed that well,' he muttered. All three sets of eyes followed the sound of the heavy boots as they came to a stop somewhere above their heads. There was the creak of a heavy chair being pushed back.

'Well,' Fowkes kept his voice low, 'at least we know where everyone is. Let's go and surprise them, shall we?'

246

TWENTY-SIX

'You're not really very chatty, are you?' Mona peered up at Christopher from her side of the umbrella. He ignored her, keeping his eyes firmly fixed on the road ahead.

'Which is a little bit odd given that you volunteered to look for the Magus,' she continued. 'You could be more cheerful about it. I'm excited. I've never met a real-life Magus before.' She grinned at him, and despite the black mood that had been on him all day, he couldn't help being curious.

'Are the Magi dangerous?'

Mona steered the umbrella down a side-street. 'Depends on your definition, really. They do magic, and I guess that could be dangerous. It's why they were banished in the first place, being able to do stuff other people couldn't.'

'I don't believe in magic,' Christopher muttered. The streets around them were eerily quiet, as if most of London had decided not to bother venturing out that day. 'It's nearly always just tricks and deception.'

Mona looked at him. 'Maybe in your world, but not here.' She paused. 'At least I hope not, because I'm sure people who can trick and deceive others easily are probably far more dangerous than those who do magic.'

Christopher could smell the stagnant stench of the river long before it came into view, and by the time they were walking alongside the misty blanket that spread protectively over the water, it was truly pungent. His nose crinkled and he tried to breathe through his mouth. 'I'm sure that's got worse than yesterday.'

'It probably has. The mist can't rise because of the rain, so it's just getting thicker.'

'And nastier.' For a second he thought about plunging himself over the side, being sucked into all the rottenness there: that was probably where he belonged. Everything about him felt rotten and worthless. Would it have the slightest effect on anyone's plans if he disappeared? Or was it already too late for them? His jaw clenched. He wouldn't disappear. That would just make it too easy for—

'The Magi have been banished for more than a hundred years.' Mona's cheerful voice cut through his bitter thoughts. 'If one gets caught in the city, then that's an immediate death sentence. It's straight to Smithfield for them.'

They walked quickly along the embankment, as much in a hurry to escape the smell as to get to West Minster.

'What were they banished for?'

'The Magi used to be one of the most respected groups of people in London, almost revered. They'd been members of the King's Council for ever. They had their offices at West Minster Abbey – in fact, the whole of the Borough of West Minster belonged to the Magi people. It's where they lived and raised their families, right on the bank of the river. They're like the Traders. The Magi aren't afraid of the Times. Most people think the Traders have some Magi blood in them.' She drew herself tall under the umbrella.

'There's probably some in my family too, that's probably why I can move around the city so easily.'

Christopher thought that even though the Magi were banished, Mona looked a bit pleased about that possibility. 'How come the Magi are so different?'

Mona shrugged. 'No one really knows. My dad says he thinks it's because they were here first, long before the rest of us. He calls them The Nowhere's indig—' She stopped, trying to remember the word.

'The Nowhere's indigenous people?' Christopher finished off her sentence for her. 'I know what that means: they're the native people here, like the American Indians.'

Mona looked lost. 'Whatever. Anyway, my dad reckons that the Magi have always been here, but the rest of us haven't.'

'So where did the rest of the population come from?'

'Who knows?' She sniffed, and flinched from the smell. 'They might know more outside the city, but no one goes that far apart from the Traders, and even they don't normally go much beyond South London. Maybe we came through doorways like you did.'

'So you're all from our world originally then?' Christopher stared.

'Not necessarily. The Somewhere and The Nowhere aren't the only worlds, you know. It's true we're most linked with yours, but we get stuff from others too. We've probably got bits from all of them. Maybe that's why we don't travel well.'

'Very American,' he said with a snigger.

Mona looked surprised. 'Very what?'

'Doesn't matter,' Christopher said, 'just a stupid joke.'

The sky darkened and a bolt of black shot down from the ominous sky. They stopped, and looked up, their hearts pounding.

'I've never seen black lightning before,' Christopher breathed.

'Neither have I,' Mona said, softly.

Thunder rolled and cracked over their heads and they flinched again and moved a little closer to each other. For a moment a grey void opened where the lightning had split the sky: a great empty space. Christopher thought that if he looked into it too long, he might just veer off into the river …

And then it was gone.

'We're nearly there,' Mona said quietly. 'The empty Borough of West Minster is just round the next bend.' They picked up their pace, desperate to be out of the noxious rain, which was seeping into everywhere now.

'Finish telling me about the Magi,' Christopher said, trying to fill the silence.

'Well, for a long time things just kind of went along, with the royal family and the Magi running things together. The kings were always happy to have them around because – well, because they were magical and useful, and they made good ministers. And then when the Knights came, they brought stories of revolutions and the executions of traitors and even the murders of kings – which actually went a long way to explaining the odd head or decapitated body that used to appear occasionally in the old days. I mean, as much as we're used to odd things turning up, body parts of any kind are always going to be rather revolting.' She pulled a face. 'Glad that doesn't happen so much these days.'

Christopher grimaced. 'Stick to the point, Mona.'

The road ahead was starting to curve.

'Okay, okay!' She looked a bit irritated. 'Don't be so moody or I won't tell you at all!'

'Sorry,' he muttered.

'Forgiven,' she said with a wide grin. 'So where was I? Oh yes, anyway, the first Knights told all these stories, as well as some about burning witches and people dying for belief in some being who couldn't even be seen, which always sounds a lot like witchcraft to me, so I've always been a bit confused about why the believer people were always so against the witches, and my dad keeps trying to explain it every time he tells this story, but I think, to be honest, that it sort of confuses him too.

'But then, The Somewhere is a lot more violent than here, and that probably makes people a little bit funny in the head.'

250

Christopher glared at her, although put the way she had, religion did seem rather odd. But people had to believe in something, didn't they? Or else they'd feel … well, probably like he was feeling right then. Faithless. Empty. Hollow.

Oblivious to Christopher's strange mood, she went on, 'Over a couple of hundred years, the royal family stopped trusting the Magi, who were eventually all banished to the South. They were told that there was no place for old magical ways and superstitions in The Nowhere any more.'

'Didn't anyone speak up?'

Mona shook her head. 'The royal family have spies everywhere – they're still around today, keeping the Prince Regent informed about everything that goes on in the city. There's some in every Borough; it's just no one knows who they are. King Joshua IV sent the spies out to start rumours about the Magi and by the time he banished them, no one in The Nowhere was sad to see them go. '

Christopher wondered if anyone was ever decent when they grew up. Maybe it was only the young who were honest. 'He doesn't sound like a very good king,' he muttered.

'He probably wasn't,' Mona admitted, 'but then, you know what it's like. My dad says that's how people learn to hate: through what their parents before them distrusted. I guess the royal family aren't that different.' She paused. 'I reckon when there was Magic in the city it must have been much more fun than all this Reason. I wish I'd seen it.'

'Maybe the royal family are anti-fun,' Christopher suggested.

'Maybe. They probably are now after a hundred years of the Magi's curse.'

Christopher's feet stopped as they rounded the corner and he gasped. He'd thought that very little else in The Nowhere could surprise him further. He had, he'd just realised, been in a constant state of surprise of one sort or another since he'd

251

arrived. The view in the rain reminded him that there was always room for more.

Mona stumbled to a halt beside him. 'What's the matter?'

Christopher shrugged, unable to find the words. The grey buildings petered out at the edge of the road, and a small pile of rubble separated the houses from the wasteland that lay to his right. 'It just ...' He didn't know quite what to say. 'It just changes so suddenly.'

Beneath his feet the cobbles were dark and solid, a road patterned from well-worn stone, and unless you looked closely they appeared to be one vast dirty block, rather than so many smaller ones cemented together. Beyond where he and Mona stood, however, the individual stones were obvious, each fighting to keep its tenuous grip on the earth below it as weeds and grasses burst up around it. Some of the plants were knee-high or taller, reaching up into the gloomy light.

On his left the bridge rose up and disappeared quickly into the mist that enveloped it, rather like a plane flying into a dense cloud. Christopher shivered.

He could see why you might throw yourself over the side ... The idea of crossing that vanished bridge and walking over the water pattering out that unpleasant song where the black rain hit its surface made his soul shake, and he didn't know why. Maybe it was just the madness Mrs Harvey had talked about, reaching out in the tendrils of mist creeping into the abandoned part of the city. Maybe it could see the blackness inside him and was calling out to it. He turned back to the land. It was safer.

'No one goes to West Minster.' Mona looked up at the huge stone building standing with battered pride amidst the overgrown land, its four spiked towers still impressive despite the smashed windows and the heavy doors long broken from their hinges. Her voice had softened, as if she was really looking at it for the first time, rather than rushing past, eager to get to some place fuller of life and excitement, as if she shared Christopher's awe.

'Why?' he asked at last.

Mona shrugged. 'Who would come here? Travelling's too tiring for most people, even those in the closest Boroughs.' She stopped. In the few steps they'd taken into the rough land the rain had started coming down harder than ever. Or maybe it was the deathly stillness of the place ...

'And I suppose ...'

Now she sounded a little hesitant, and Christopher thought he could hear the faintest trace of fear in her words.

'Most people think there's a curse on it. Some magical spell left behind.'

'I wouldn't blame the Magi if there was, from what you've told me.' He wiped wind-driven rain from his face. 'Why haven't the Traders taken it over? I'd have thought it would be the perfect place for them.' He moved forward, his damp feet carefully picking out spaces between the slippery plants.

'The Traders don't like to live by the water. They can travel on it, but they don't like the smell. And I think maybe they have a kind of respect for the Magi. Who knows? Maybe they see them on the other side of the river, out past the borders of South London.'

Something scuttered off into an overgrown hedge surrounding an area that might at one time have been a lawn but was now a jungle home to whatever was left alive in West Minster. In the brief glimpse Christopher had got it had looked beetle-like ... if beetles were the size of kittens. He kept his eyes firmly on the ground as they headed towards the open doorway of the large church.

'So, what was the curse they put on the royal family?' he asked.

'The curse of madness.'

He didn't think he was imagining that Mona had moved closer to him. He could feel the arm of her jacket brushing his as they walked. Her voice wasn't much louder than a whisper either. Whatever excitement she'd felt earlier at meeting a real live Magus was evaporating now that they'd actually arrived. He didn't mind. Even with his own black mood, part of him liked the idea of her standing so close they were almost touching. He wasn't relaxed around her like Fin and Joe were. Girls weren't a feature at St Martin's. He was starting to wish they were.

Christopher stopped at the uneven bottom step of what must have once been a breathtakingly grand staircase. The walls towered above him, fifteen metres into the sky, a mass of stone and glass, and mossy eyes peered down suspiciously as the gargoyles on the towers stared at them. He frowned. The gaping doorway ahead revealed tattered shards of wood at its edges. It looked like an enormous dark mouth, filled with broken teeth.

'That man we went to see at the palace. He was the Prince Regent, wasn't he? Not the King.'

'Yep.' Mona took the next step up so that she was nearly as tall as him. 'All the kings since the banishing of the Magi have gone mad in their fortieth year.' She took the final step to the doorway, and stood in the entrance.

Christopher joined her. He shook out the umbrella and closed it up as she spoke.

'People remembered how the Magi had once been, and they remembered what had happened to them. It made sense to think they'd cursed the king. And who knows, maybe they did. There's a curse on them one way or another, and the Magi are the only people that can do magic.'

They turned together and walked into the gloom. Just inside the doorway stood two large stone candleholders, one on either side, that came up to Christopher's waist. Strange markings, like a foreign language, were carved into their sides, a little worn away from the weather over the years.

'So they were all kicked out of town, when they'd never

done anything except serve the King?' A metre ahead was another pair of wrecked arched doors, and Christopher was glad when they reached them. He needed a break from the heavy air that tasted of the rain.

'All except one, who refused to leave. He was executed at Smithfield. After that, their homes and this place, the symbol of all the Magi had once been, were wrecked.'

'I thought people here couldn't move around the city?' Christopher crouched to step through the second set of doors. Part of the heavy wood was still miraculously attached to the hinges.

'Oh, they can get around.' Mona sounded distracted as she followed him. She clambered through herself, then straightened up. 'It just has unpleasant side-effects, so they don't bother. In exceptional circumstances the mob will get going, like what happened to Baxter.' She let out a low whistle. 'Gosh – just look!'

Despite the ivy and other climbing plants that had forced their way in through the broken windows and spread over the walls, there was something more overwhelming about West Minster than there had been about the Prince Regent's palace that morning. Maybe it was that very sense of dereliction?

Carefully, he walked forward into the huge main hall. The three wide balconies with fancifully carved railings that ran along the sides above them did nothing to distract from the sweeping grandeur of the impossibly high ceiling. Somewhere up there a bird fluttered, disturbed by their intrusion.

Beneath their feet the large black and white tiles made the floor look like a chessboard. Embedded in the thick stone of the walls were circular metal plates with more of the strange symbols carved into them. The broken remains of ornate tables and chairs littered the place.

Christopher wandered over to take a closer look at the metal plates, though when he looked closer, he decided it wasn't like any metal he'd seen before. It shone like mother

255

of pearl, with hints of blues and purples and whites all rolled into one. His head throbbed a little and he tasted copper in his mouth. He turned away.

Mona, looking sad, righted a chair on the other side of the vast space.

'I thought you said it was *us* who were violent.' Christopher was speaking softly, but his voice echoed loudly, as if the place was happy to have live sound in it again. He gestured around. 'All this? It's terrible.'

Mona sighed. 'I didn't say that we were perfect.' She looked up. 'In your world they'd probably have killed all the Magi. At least here we just banished them.'

He looked at her. 'Oh, so that makes it all right then, does it?' He wondered if any people were ever capable of anything truly good. Not even love was good all the time. He thought of his father and his stomach turned slightly. Did he love Christopher at all? He used to think so, even under all the awkwardness, but now he wasn't so sure. His face burned. 'Just look at this! How could people do it?'

Mona shrugged uncomfortably, and under his hot, angry skin Christopher wondered if he looked frightening to her. He couldn't stop the words welling up; he needed to let something out, and it might as well be a small amount of rage.

'Look at it!' he shouted, 'this place was obviously special. And beautiful – the people who wrecked it, they didn't even *take* anything, as if the whole building was worthless! You lot are as bad as us! The Magi didn't even do anything wrong, and you just booted them out. They were here first: all this belonged to *them*!'

Mona didn't meet his gaze. She tucked her hands into her pockets.

Christopher didn't really know why he was shouting at her; it wasn't as if she'd done this herself. He *liked* Mona, and she wasn't the King or the mob or even his own father. He let out a long sigh and his shoulders slumped. He looked around at the walls and the floor and the plant life.

'Why didn't they fight back, Mona?' he asked quietly. 'Why didn't they fight back?'

'I have often asked myself this.'

The deep voice was laced with a strange, almost exotic accent. It floated to them from the balcony above, making Christopher and Mona jump. They looked up to see a man wrapped in purple robes peering down at them. He wore jewellery, gold and silver, and huge hoops dangled from his ears.

'All the power the Magi have, and they didn't use it. They just meekly accepted the judgement and left. It became an obsession for me, to avenge this wrong.' He hung his head. 'But no true good can ever come from vengeance.'

Mona's mouth had dropped open. She struggled to get it working again. 'Are you a Magus?' she managed, eventually.

The man nodded slowly, his hands still gripping the banister as he leaned forward.

'We need your help.' Christopher hoped that those railings weren't in as bad shape as the rest of the building. The Magus tumbling to his death in front of them wouldn't do anyone much good.

Dark eyes bore into them from above for a long moment, and then the Magus stepped backwards out of sight. Mona and Christopher waited, their hearts still beating hard, until he appeared on their level, walking through the wall a little ahead of them. Their eyes widened as he approached.

'Did I really see that?' Mona breathed. 'Did he just come through that solid wall?'

Christopher didn't know what to say. 'It can't be.' Even his constant surprise at the topsy-turviness of The Nowhere didn't mean he could believe in the truly impossible. A wall was solid. *No one* could walk through a solid thing. Physics and maths were his best subjects; he wasn't going to start doubting them now, despite how it had looked.

'It must be a trick. It's not possible.' Christopher looked at the lined face of the man who had stopped in front of them. 'How did you do that?'

'Maybe it was magic.' Mona took a tiny step backwards. 'He *is* a Magus.'

'No one can walk through solid stone. It can't happen.'

The Magus smiled, his teeth bright white against his dark skin, and wrinkles appeared in a network across his face. 'Perhaps, in this case, you are right, young man.' He waved a hand adorned with too many rings to be comfortable, and the section of wall he had appeared to walk through vanished, leaving an archway leading to a curved staircase. He flicked his wrist for a second time and the stones closed over the opening again.

'An illusory spell. The wall does not exist.' He smiled. 'Except in your minds.'

'That's very good.' Mona was obviously impressed. 'Maybe you can teach me something like that. People say I must have Magi blood in my body, you know. That's because I can—'

'The Prince Regent said you know a way to reverse the Ageing,' Christopher said quickly, cutting Mona off before she could reach her full flow.

The Magus' smile disappeared as quickly as it had come. 'And why would you want to reverse the Ageing? Do the Knights not have enough power?'

'The Knights have rebelled. They've taken the Storyholder, and we need to make some of the old Knights back in The Somewhere young enough to fight back. Otherwise—' He stopped for a moment and swallowed hard. 'Well, otherwise, I'm not sure how bad things will get. We're getting this black rain stuff back in our world too.'

'*Your* world,' Mona said, 'I'm very much a Nowhere girl, thank you.' She looked up at the Magus and her smooth

258

forehead furrowed. 'And what exactly are you doing back in the city anyway?'

The Magus visibly crumpled in front of them, the strength sagging out of his shoulders, and he sat down on the remains of what had once been a beautiful table carved from a solid tree trunk, but which now leaned awkwardly on its side, one leg smashed away a hundred years before.

'I have been foolish,' he said finally, his rich voice hollow.

Christopher and Mona exchanged a glance, but stayed silent.

'All my life I have heard the stories of London, the city by the river that was once ours. All my life I heard the stories of the men who took it from us. The Elders talk of these men with pity, but I felt no pity for them.' His fingers pulled a string of shiny beads from his pocket and he worried them as he spoke.

'I wanted these men to suffer for the humiliation they dealt to the Magi.' He smiled softly. 'But I could not act alone. I was not brave enough. And then, one day, a messenger came to our desert citadel and said a man was in the South of London: a Knight of The Somewhere, and he was asking about the Magi.

'As if it were Fate, the Elders sent me to investigate.'

'What did the man say?' Christopher crouched beside him, but his eyes were lost in the past. He let out a small, cynical laugh.

'Of course he said everything I wanted to hear. He promised me revenge. He promised me that the Magi would return to the city more powerful than ever. And all he wanted was one thing, one small thing in return.'

'What was that?'

The man's sad eyes finally met Christopher's. 'A mirror – not just any mirror, but the Incarcerator: the dwelling-place of the Truthfinders.'

'You're not making any sense,' Mona said.

'Perhaps not to you, and the detail surely doesn't matter.' He rubbed his chin. 'What matters is that my madness is now lifted. I have done a terrible thing, and I must help put it right.'

Christopher's heart thumped. 'You'll tell us how to reverse the Ageing?'

'I will explain it to you. And then, perhaps, we will proceed.'

Mona grinned. 'Excellent.'

Something about the intensity with which the Magus was staring at him made Christopher's own smile die before it reached his lips. Their gazes locked and the boy felt as if he were diving into the dark, endless ocean of the man's soul. The Magus didn't blink.

'Your friend must wait outside,' he said at last. 'This isn't for her to hear.'

Christopher nodded.

'Wait a minute! I—'

'Just do it, please, Mona.' His voice was soft but firm. For a moment she hesitated, then she slowly took a step backwards.

'Well, if you're sure. But I'll be right outside the door. If you need me just shout.'

'I will.'

'Thirty minutes,' the Magus said. 'That is the time we need, That is, of course, if we choose to go forward.'

He heard Mona's footsteps patter out to the doorway. She may have peered back at him before stepping outside, but Christopher didn't check. He was focused entirely on the Magus. The man was looking at him as if he were an adult; Christopher reckoned he had a good idea what that meant.

'This reversal of the Ageing doesn't come for free, does it?'

The Magus shook his head sadly. 'No, my friend. Nothing of any value ever does.'

Christopher sat down cross-legged in front of him. 'So tell me. What's the price?'

TWENTY-SEVEN

'Where are Kane and O'Regan?' Conrad took off his soaking cloak as thunder roared outside. 'I left them here.'

St John glared at the younger Knight. 'Where are the rest of the Knights you took with you?' It would do Conrad Eyre good to remember who was in charge here. He turned his back on him and stormed into the smaller room, ignoring the useless mirror as he passed it. At least there was a fire in his private room.

St John stood in front of the flames, feeling in desperate need of something to keep out the chill that had taken hold inside him.

'They're doing as you asked.' Conrad followed him in, clutching the laptop. 'They're ripping the town apart looking for Fowkes and those boys.'

'I've sent Kane and O'Regan to Savjani's. I want him brought here.'

As the small computer whirred into life, Conrad's fingers paused over the keys. 'The Prince Regent won't be happy about that,' he said softly, not raising his head from the screen.

St John rubbed a hand over his beard. It needed clipping. Another day and it would start to look untidy. He almost laughed. *Everything* was getting untidy. 'There will be a lot of things the Prince Regent won't like.' He bit the inside of his mouth. The Prince Regent was the least of their worries.

'Why is the chain unlocked?'

St John could feel Conrad's eyes in his back. He took a

261

moment to regain his inner steel before facing him. The men had been his a long time; their loyalty would last through this – especially Conrad's. He drew himself up tall and turned around to meet the younger man's eyes.

'She's hidden the stories somewhere.'

A breath's silence passed.

'She's *what*? But I thought—'

'They're not inside her. And as she's no longer in a position to tell us where they are I've left her in the prison to rot.' He poured himself a goblet of wine and took a sip. To give Conrad his due, he didn't say any more, even though St John knew he would be thinking that regardless of the stories they should have kept the Storyholder where they could reach her. And worse, he was right. How had he let his anger get the better of him like that? The wine was warm.

He'd been stupid. She was a figurehead; the people loved her. He could have used her to secure himself as their leader, once he'd eventually found where she'd hidden the stories – and he *would* find them. He had to. Still, he felt the world unravelling through his fingers. He needed somewhere safe for him and his Knights to go and ride out the storm. Orrery House was the only place.

'You need to gather the Knights, all of them,' he said quietly.

'But they're all over London! They're not due to check in for at least another hour.'

'Then use that hour recalling Kane, O'Regan and Christian France. He's at the doorway with the gatekeeper.'

'Shouldn't we leave that—?'

Conrad Eyre's questioning tone was irritating him. It was as if perhaps he no longer fully trusted St John's judgement – or maybe he was just becoming paranoid. Orders. Action: that's what Conrad needed to keep his questioning mind occupied, and Conrad loved him, he was sure of that. Maybe some of the others he had to watch out for – he was the one who had trained them to be ruthless, after all.

'We have to take back Orrery House.' He paused for effect. Aside from the need for a safe haven, that decision should make his Knights happy; they had wanted control of the home of the Order for quite some time, but he had held off, not wanting any suspicion to fall on him until they'd got the Storyholder and the stories. A twinge in his gut frightened him: the mere *idea* that he could fail ... He shook it away.

'Once we have that secure' – he was glad to hear his voice was strong – 'we will have bought ourselves time to find the stories.'

Conrad nodded. 'The men will be pleased with that.' Something flickered on the computer screen and Conrad frowned. 'We've got company. Three people.' He scowled. 'That can't be right.'

'What can't be right?' St John didn't need any more surprises. His body was a mass of aches and tension.

Conrad pointed. 'They're coming up the stairs. One's unidentified, but the program has identified the other two from the ring information I stole from Orrery House. One's Fowkes—'

'Excellent.' St John smiled. Something was finally going in his favour.

Conrad looked up.

'But it says the other one is Baxter.'

St John looked down at the three dots on the screen. Baxter was dead; he knew that for certain, even if his body had never been recovered. He'd seen the mob attacking him on the stairs. He'd started to fight his way through to help, before he'd realised the advantages to be gained by Baxter's death. Instead, he'd returned to his own flat in The Somewhere and waited it out. Most of the Council still believed he'd tried to save his fellow Knight; it had secured his own election as Commander. He doubted he could have done much for

Baxter even if he'd tried. The mob had been too large and too angry.

The rumour was that the Storyholder had taken the body and buried it in secret, where no one could desecrate it, and St John believed it. The black storm that followed was the outpouring of her grief, and it had tormented The Nowhere for a full year. That was what was said in the taverns and cafés whenever the skies darkened and people were reminded of darker days. *Stories, tales, legends and folklore*: that's what the worlds survived on.

'Someone's wearing Baxter's ring,' he said at last. 'Now that is interesting.' He looked towards the door. Baxter's ring had gone with his body. How exactly had the Order retrieved it?

'Let's get ready to welcome our guests, shall we?'

Conrad positioned himself by the door, his sword ready. St John didn't need to look at the computer screen to know where the intruders were. The floorboards in the room next door were old and creaked with every step, however lightly they were trying to walk.

The door flew open, and St John smiled.

TWENTY-EIGHT

Thunder rolled loudly above the old building, sending the birds nesting in the ceiling cawing and fluttering deeper into the rafters. Somewhere in the city the black lightning struck and Christopher wondered what would happen if it hit you – would you die outright, or would it just blacken your soul? Maybe it would leave you feeling as numb as he did now.

He and the Magus were sitting cross-legged, facing each other, and as Christopher stared at the black and white checks he could feel the other man's thoughtful gaze on him. But he wasn't ready to talk just yet. He needed to think.

How had he got here? He'd thought it was just chance, the sheer luck of being Finmere Tingewick Smith's friend, and maybe that was partly it, but now, looking back, he was beginning to wonder how much of anything was chance, and how much they had been pushed together unknowing.

Tears stung at the back of his eyes. Everything was a lie. *Everything*. He'd been used and his heart hurt.

The Magus saw his damp eyes and misunderstood.

'You have a choice, you know. This is much to ask from someone just starting out on their adult path. You probably do not even understand properly.'

'It's not that.' Christopher sniffed, and when he knew the tears were under control, he looked up. The Magus had said that no good came from vengeance, but if he did this, it wouldn't be like revenge as such; it would the opposite, a small way of trying to put something right – it might not be his wrong, but he certainly felt that he was part of it. He wanted to be like Ted and the good Knights and have honour. He didn't want anyone to question which side he'd been on after all this was over. That would be unbearable.

'What will happen if we don't do this?'

Neither pair of eyes flickered as the next crack of thunder exploded right above their heads. It was as if, just for this while, they were outside of normal events.

The Magus sighed, and this time it was his turn to look down at the tiles. 'Who knows? Maybe the end of everything. Maybe nothing at all. But this storm ...' His voice drifted for a minute as if his words were being stolen away by the wind and rain sweeping across The Nowhere sky. 'This storm holds a dark promise.' His tongue clicked against the back of his teeth like part of a strange, long-forgotten language. 'There is trouble ahead.'

Ahead. The word held new meaning for Christopher, and he tried to get his head round it. He'd never really thought about the future before, not beyond the long summer holidays or getting through double Latin. Not in terms of years, *his* years, with death at the end of them. He was only just sixteen; everything was about the moment. A month in the future might just as well be a lifetime.

'If I could give it all myself, then that is what I would do.' His shoulders drooped further. 'I will give all I have.'

Christopher met his heavy gaze and in those dark pools he could see the man's guilt and inner shame. It made Christopher think once again about what he'd seen in the Storyholder's apartments and his own black mood bubbled to the surface, followed by a wave of rebelliousness and anger and hurt all rushing together. How bad could this be? It couldn't be worse than feeling as he did right now. He figured that was what the Magus thought too.

In that moment he felt closer to the strange foreign man from a different world than he could ever remember feeling for his own family. He attempted a half-hearted grin. 'Well, who knows? Maybe I'd have been run over by a bus at forty-five. And thirty-nine's pretty old anyway.'

'Give me your hand,' said the Magus.

Reluctantly, Christopher did as he was asked. His palm was slightly sweaty; the Magus's skin felt as dry and cracked as the desert. The Magus trickled his fingers across the lines on Christopher's pale skin. 'You have to give with knowledge,' he whispered.

Christopher's mouth dried, his heart thumping in his tingling chest. 'What? What do you see?'

'You would live a long, long life: until your eighty-fourth year.'

Eighty-four. Another sixty-eight years. Christopher's head spun. He couldn't even imagine himself at twenty, or having a job and a wife and all that stuff, let alone wrinkles and aching limbs and grandchildren of his own. *Eighty-four.* It was such a long way away.

'And if I do this, then I die at thirty-nine?'

'At some point in that year, yes.'

He shrugged. 'It's still pretty old,' he repeated.

'That is a matter of perspective.' The Magus released his hand.

Twenty-three years away was both far in the distance and not so long at all, all in the same instant. He felt sick, but he'd made his decision. 'How many will we be able to reverse?' He stared at the Magus' face, and wondered at the deep wrinkles that covered it. He realised he himself would never get lines like that. It was a very weird feeling, but not as awful as the dark shame that was eating away at the pit of his stomach.

'Three.'

'Oh.'

'Three will be enough.' The Magus smiled, and from within the hidden folds of his silk robes his deft hands pulled a glass bottle in a filigree silver holder. He took out the stopper, placing it carefully on the black square between them. From somewhere else a small brown bag appeared. He untied the lace that held it closed and tipped out a handful of strangely coloured metallic waxy candles. They were short and stubby, no two the same size.

Christopher swallowed. 'Will it hurt?'

'No. No pain.' The Magus looked up. 'I will put you in a trance. When you wake up, you will find the bottle is full. Make sure the stopper is on tightly and take it quickly where you need to go. Share it equally between three. Do you understand?'

'Yes,' Christopher said, puzzled, 'but why are you telling me now?'

The Magus leaned forward and squeezed his hand. 'For me, there will be no *after*. I will be dead.' He smiled again. 'I am giving everything I can.'

Christopher's breath caught in his throat. The Magus had said that earlier, but he hadn't really understood; he'd just thought that the Magus would be … well, just *older*.

'Are you sure? Can't you—?'

'Shhh, young man. I have to do this, to atone for my terrible mistakes, and the price that I am costing you.'

More tears threatened to come. Nothing was supposed to have been like this. It was just supposed to have been a stupid *adventure*, and now everything had changed. He thought of the cigarette case and gritted his teeth. Nothing had changed; not really. It was just that his eyes were open now.

'Let's get started then.'

Thunder racked the heavens above then and Christopher closed his eyes.

TWENTY-NINE

There was a moment of complete confusion after they'd burst into the room. It took that moment for Fin to realise that someone was holding a sword to Fowkes' throat and that the Knight had gone from running to standing very, very still, very quickly, leaving Fin tumbling into the room ahead of him and clutching at what looked like an old-fashioned picture frame to steady himself. As the Knight who had Fowkes in his grip eased him to one side, Fin saw Joe, still standing in the doorway, his eyes wide. They stared at each other for a moment. *This was not the way it was meant to go.*

'Welcome.' The man in the middle of the room closed the laptop with a careful click and smiled. He was tall, his skin pale under a golden beard, but his face was starting to wrinkle around the eyes and forehead.

'It seems our computerised security system is fully operational, Conrad. Congratulations.'

Fin's heart raced. This was him: St John Golden, it had to be. And *he'd* caught *them*.

'You seem to have lost your touch, Andrew Fowkes.' Golden picked up his goblet and took a measured sip.

'And you seem to have lost your mind, St John Alexander Golden,' Fowkes growled, despite the sharp blade at his throat. 'What the hell do you think you're playing at?'

'All in good time.'

Just as Fin thought the men had forgotten him and Joe, the Commander of the Knights turned to face him. Trying to at least appear brave under the scrutiny, Fin stuck his chin in the air and glared in what he hoped was a defiant way, despite the trembling in his legs.

But St John Golden wasn't looking into his face, but down at his sword, and at the hand with which he'd protectively covered the hilt.

'This must be Finmere Tingewick Smith. The mystery boy old Harlequin Brown was so interested in.' He raised an eyebrow and looked back at Fowkes. 'And he's wearing Baxter's ring – a family connection, perhaps? Is he Baxter's boy?'

'Baxter didn't have any children. I don't know who the hell he is.' Fowkes didn't even look at Fin as he answered curtly, and Fin gripped the strangely carved metal surface tighter. It made his head hurt, but he decided that that was all right. It was better than feeling like he wasn't there at all: as if he were back to being nothing.

Baxter didn't have any children. He pushed the words away. Maybe Fowkes didn't know everything. There *was* some link between him and Baxter. He'd felt it ever since he'd first heard that name. In fact, he'd felt weird ever since he'd seen the double-edged sword, and that *had* to be the reason.

Conrad had a firm hold on him, but Fowkes still struggled. 'What have you done with Tova? She's causing this black storm – why?'

Given his throat might be cut at any minute, Fin couldn't doubt Fowkes' bravery. He suddenly seemed very far removed from the bootless drunk they'd found in the Crookeries.

St John Golden laughed, a reedy sound empty of warmth. 'Oh yes, your precious Storyholder.' He moved away from the desk and came closer to Fowkes. Fin looked over at Joe, standing forgotten in the doorway and nodded at him, trying to make him back off slowly and get away. It was stupid for them both to be stuck there, and none of this was really any of Joe's business. Joe just scowled and shook his head. Fin glared at him again, but to no avail.

'She's lost in the mirror,' St John purred at Fowkes.

'The what?'

Golden pointed to Fin, and Fowkes stared.

'She's in *there*?'

Fin peered round the edge of the purplish-bronzy carved metal that shifted hotly under his hand. The surface didn't reflect anything at all; it looked like muddy water.

'It's called the Incarcerator. I got it from the Magus.' St John Golden turned his back on Fowkes and went back to his wine. 'It's a special and terrible kind of prison that goes on for eternity. It makes you give up your secrets. I hoped that I wouldn't have to use it.' He shrugged casually. 'Unfortunately, she's lost in there now. And she'll never find her way back.' He raised his glass and grinned, victoriously. 'Cheers.'

Fowkes' eyes narrowed, then after a few seconds he let out a sharp bark that Fin could only guess was a return volley laugh. 'But she didn't give them up, did she, St John? Otherwise you wouldn't have wrecked her apartment that way.' He laughed again, and while the sound was restricted by the arm at his neck, it was still very evidently mocking. 'You don't know where the stories are, do you? You've done all this for *nothing*.'

Fin almost smiled when he saw the other man's grin freeze.

'What do you know about where she's hidden the stories?'

'More than you imagine.'

Fin stared at the surface of the mirror. It looked cold and dark and empty on the other side. The Storyholder was lost in there, forever. He stroked the strange metallic frame and the grey skin rippled liked the clouds outside. The Storyholder was key to everything. She was the one causing the storm. His mouth felt dry as his fingers tingled. She couldn't be lost forever, she just couldn't.

Thunder clapped so loudly above the house that everyone

flinched. The storm was getting worse. Fowkes and St John stared at each other in the flickering candlelight, the rest of them forgotten.

'It wasn't Baxter she loved, you see,' Fowkes spoke softly. 'It was me.'

Even the man holding the sword to Fowkes' neck drew in a small, sharp breath at that. Forgetting the mirror prison for a moment, Finmere stared – and so did St John Golden.

'When the mob came, Baxter was just waiting downstairs,' Fowkes continued. 'He kept them from us, even though he thought what we were doing was wrong. It was me they should have killed. He was completely innocent.'

Fin's blood rushed and pounded in his ears. *The Storyholder, Baxter, Fowkes* ... it felt like a web wrapping round him. If Baxter wasn't his father, then maybe Fowkes was – but why would he have been found with Baxter's ring? And why in The Somewhere if Fowkes was in The Nowhere? Confusion overwhelmed his fear. He'd thought he'd been getting closer to answers, and now he felt like he'd been shoved further away than ever. He'd been so sure there was a link between him and Baxter – he'd felt it, somewhere behind that closed mental door. Had it just been his mind playing tricks on him all the time?

He dipped his fingers into the grey surface of the mirror. It was cold on the other side – not like water, or even a cold wind. This was an empty chill that sucked at him. He pulled his fingers out and stared at them, feeling the coolness running up inside his veins.

'Well, well, well.' St John finally spoke. 'Not so honourable after all.'

Finmere didn't bother to turn round, but he listened to the conversation through the jumbled confusion in his own mind. He needed to think. The Storyholder couldn't stay in there: she was causing the storm, and the storm needed to be stopped. His head hurt.

'But that's not the point, St John.' Fowkes was calm.

'And what is?' He gently swilled the wine in his cup.

'The point is that I know where she hid the stories.'

For a second, Fin thought he would be able to hear a pin drop. Even the storm fell silent, as if it too was holding its breath. He frowned and fought the urge to turn back to the events in the room. The muddle in his head was clearing. He dipped his fingers into the grey filmy surface again, shivering on contact. *The Storyholder was in there and someone had to get her back.*

'Tell me where.' Golden's voice was as cold as the strange prison beneath Fin's fingertips. Careful not to be noticed, Finmere lifted one leg and stepped over the mirror's gilt frame, biting his lip to stop from crying out at the shock of being half in one place and half in another.

'Let's settle this like the honourable Knights that we used to be. Let these boys go and I'll meet you in St Paul's and we'll duel.'

St John laughed. 'St Paul's? What, the Whispering Chamber? You are such a romantic.'

'Not St Paul's in The Somewhere. Here.'

Fin gripped the edge of the mirror as he lifted his second leg. His teeth were chattering. He sent Joe a grin, and this time his friend nodded and backed off. Fin watched until he was sure Joe had run out through the second room and started down the stairs. He smiled even wider: Joe wasn't running because he was afraid; it was just that he was smart enough to know that Fowkes wouldn't have any chance of getting Golden where he wanted him if the Commander of the Knights could use either of them as a hostage.

Joe's footsteps clattering down the creaking wooden stairs made all the Knights look up. One boy running might have caught their attention, but it was Finmere that held it.

'Fin! No!' For the first time Fowkes sounded afraid.

'Don't do it, boy,' Golden growled, stepping forward. 'I want answers—'

'Someone has to get her back.' Fin forced the words out between lips that were turning blue, and just as Golden's hand reached out to grab him, he met Fowkes' dread-filled gaze and smiled, released his hold on the frame and disappeared inside.

St John Golden's hands clutched at air. Finmere was gone.

THIRTY

Joe had not run very far at all. He figured it was enough that they thought he'd gone, and after all, it wasn't as if he had anywhere to run to. Christopher had the weird coin they needed to get back, and he was with the Magus, and Fin had ... well, as far as he could tell, Fin was now lost in that mirror thing.

After he slammed the main door shut, he carefully started climbing up the front of the building again. The rain was coming down much harder and he struggled to keep his grip on the slick wood, but with his face set in the kind of grim determination he normally felt only during County Cup Final matches, he pulled himself beyond where they'd stopped earlier and up to the third floor.

The sky had started to turn from grey to the blue before sunset. Joe felt as if they were all being swallowed up by the night. The rain tasted foul in his mouth and grimacing, he spat it out before silently bringing himself up to rest on the thick stone opening that was the strange old-fashioned windowsill. He carefully leaned backwards and let his muscles rest, determined not to look down. Three floors up was a long way to fall.

Heavy drapes separated him from the men on the other side, but he could still make out the occasional snippet of conversation.

'*Meet at St Paul's ... one hour ...*'

There was a moment's pause and then there were only the

two strangers' voices. Fowkes must have cut himself a hole through to somewhere else.

'*I'll fight Fowkes ... easy ... out of shape ... get the Knights back ... Orrery House ...*' Joe knew he didn't have to be the school brainbox to figure out what they were planning: they were going to kill Fowkes and fight the old men at Orrery House, regardless of whether they had any chances of getting those stories or not.

The room fell silent and after a few moments the door far beneath him opened. He risked a peek downwards and watched the two cloaked figures disappearing in different directions into the gloom, before very thankfully letting himself tumble back into the room.

It felt odd to be alone in The Nowhere. He thought of the strange map stuffed in his pocket and wondered for a moment if he should try to find Christopher, or even try to get through the doorway back to his own world without the coin and warn Ted and the others, and then he thought of Finmere. He stared at the mirror. Despite its strange carvings and beautiful purplish-bronzy surround there was something that chilled the soul about it. And Finmere had gone inside it.

He ignored the wine and the laptop and walked over to the mirror prison. He sat down cross-legged in front of it. If Golden had told the truth about the Storyholder being lost inside, then how the hell was Fin supposed to find his way back? He ran one hand over his short curly hair – and stopped.

He brought his hand down, staring at it as he turned it this way and that. Suddenly he knew what he had to do. He slipped one arm inside the mirror, cursing at the sudden change in temperature, and stretched his hand out. If Fin got lost, he could just reach for Joe and he'd pull him out. He felt the awful chill penetrating his veins, but his eyes were determined. He would wait.

THIRTY-ONE

From the mouth of the darkening alleyway, Christopher looked at the doorway. Rain hammered at the ground now, a black blur against the encroaching night sky. Hidden in the shadow he watched Jacob Megram pacing up and down, muttering to himself. He squeezed the bottle in his pocket one last time and rummaged for the coin.

'What are we going to do?' Mona whispered. It was the first time she'd spoken since she'd ignored the instructions the Magus had given her and crept back inside the huge hall just as Christopher was covering the husk, all that was left of the old man's body, with his purple robes and tears. He'd ignored her questions as he stoppered the bottle tightly.

He wished she'd understand that it was better for her not to know, rather than he just didn't want to tell her, but she was a girl and he figured that wasn't the way their brains worked. Girls always wanted *to talk things through*. Boys – well, boys thought letting things lie was often the best way.

The past hour felt surreal, as if maybe it hadn't happened at all. Rain trickled down his face and in a moment of defiance he opened his mouth and caught it on his tongue. The sickly-sweet rotten taste was now tinged with bitterness. Those sixty minutes had happened, though, and now he had to make sure all those years hadn't been given up in vain.

'Mr Megram!' He left the shelter of the alleyway behind and ran across the road, Mona beside him.

The butcher turned, jumping slightly. 'There was a Knight

here. He was helping me guard the doorway.' He stepped back a little, his eyes wary. 'He says I'm not to let you through.'

Christopher shook his head. 'Please. You've got to listen to me. It's the *Knights* who are bad.'

'They've done something to the Storyholder.' Mona grabbed the gatekeeper's arm. 'They've taken her.'

Jacob's eyes peered at her. 'You're not one of them as came through first. Where's that other lad? The one with the Knight's sword?'

'I don't know.' Christopher bit back his frustration. '*Please*, Mr Megram, we've been through loads trying to get here, and this storm—'

'I've never seen the like.' Megram glanced fearfully upwards. 'Not for years. I reckon maybe the wife's right: there's bad times coming. She's certain it's whipping up to be a black storm, all right.'

'She's right: it is,' Christopher cried. 'It's the Knights – this black storm is all because of them.' He was trying to shield his eyes from the driving rain. 'You really have to believe us – we need to stop them! That's why they want to stop me going back—'

'Oh, I don't know.' Megram stopped pacing. 'I just don't know—'

'It's true.' Mona stepped under his umbrella and right up close to him. 'I'm not one of them, I'm like you, from right here in The Nowhere, so you can trust me.'

Megram looked from one to the other and then let out a long sigh. He fumbled for the keys. 'Well, they have left me here on my own, and you do have the coin ...' He looked up. 'You do have the coin, don't you, son?'

Christopher pulled it free from his pocket.

Megram sounded more decisive now. 'Well, I am the gatekeeper, and I do believe my job is to let persons with such a coin through, so that's what I'm going to do.' After a moment's fiddling with the gate, he unlocked it. 'And have mercy on me if I'm wrong.'

Christopher grabbed the gatekeeper's hand and shook it vigorously. 'You're not wrong. Thank you. Thank you so much.'

All three of them stepped into the shelter of the wooden hut and stared at the rift and the gloom on the other side.

'Shall I come with you?' Mona asked, her voice soft.

'No, I can do this by myself. You and Mr Megram here' – he looked at the stocky butcher – 'you need to go back to the Prince Regent, explain what's happening and tell him to be prepared. Who knows what the Knights will try next?'

She bit her bottom lip. 'Take care, Christopher.'

'I will.' He pulled her in and hugged her. She felt warm and soft and his stomach tingled. Embarrassed, he stepped back and was surprised to see tears in her eyes.

'Are you okay?'

'Yeah.' She sniffed. 'It's just the rain. You'd better go.'

He gripped the bottle in his pocket and turned his back on them, looked into the rift. Well, at least if going back through aged him, he'd be able to get what was left of his life back. He took a deep breath and stepped through to The Somewhere.

Inside the mirror the world was grey – or at least something *like* grey. It was some kind of shade that Finmere had never seen before: a grey with all the colour stripped away from it. It was grey in an *absent* way.

For a moment, he looked back through the mirror and could just make out Fowkes' mouth open in a desperate 'No!' and then he saw St John Golden's hand reaching for him. Both men were rippling and trembling through the surface. They were hard to see clearly though, as if a universe separated them rather than just a thin layer of glass. *A void.*

He turned and wobbled slightly, his legs suddenly unsteady

as his heart thumped with surprise in his chest. He was stood on a thick stone ledge less than two metres wide; the mirror was embedded like a window in the wall behind him. Beside him was another such ledge and window a foot or so away, and next to that another, and another, and so on, all the way round the vast cylindrical room. And above him and below him were more circuits of ledges and mirrors ...

Fin peered cautiously over the edge. The stone floor was at least thirty metres down, and he couldn't even begin to count the rows of mirrors and ledges between him and it. His head swam with a sudden rush of nauseating vertigo. How the hell was he supposed to get down? Climb? His hands were clammy. There was no way he'd be able to grip the ledge for long enough to lower himself to the next one, and then he'd fall ...

No sooner had he had the thought than he was suddenly sucked back from the ledge, pulled away by an invisible wind, his feet waving frantically in the air as he tried to find some purchase. Still looking back at the mirror and the ledge and The Nowhere beyond, Finmere plummeted away.

He landed on his feet, completely unharmed, in the centre of the stone circle below, as if he'd been carefully placed there at the last minute by an invisible hand. He took three deep, shaky breaths, forcing his racing heart to slow down. Even though the air was freezing, no condensation formed in front of his mouth. It was strange, as if he wasn't even breathing at all.

He looked at the rows and rows of mirrors and ledges lining the high circular walls, going upwards for what looked like for ever and his heart fell. How was he supposed to remember which one was his? Had he been about halfway up?

Concentrating, he thought his way through the fall and then fixed his eyes on one ledge. That one was his; he was sure of it. He began to let out a small sigh of relief, but it caught in his throat. Something was happening. A groan echoed through the very fabric of the building, making the worn stone beneath Finmere's feet grumble. His heart thumped. What now?

The walls creaked and suddenly the mirrors and ledges were spinning and shifting themselves around like a Rubik's cylinder. Fin desperately tried to keep his eyes fixed on what he thought of as *his* mirror as it slid into new spaces, but before long they were moving too fast and with no distinguishing features to separate it from the rest, it became part of the blur. Finally, they all came to a stop.

His eyes wide, Finmere turned slowly, gazing up at the mirrors that surrounded him. There must be hundreds, no, thousands... Maybe even more. His mouth dried. No wonder Golden said the Storyholder was lost in here forever. Without the right mirror, no one could possibly find their way back.

He gripped the sword, but the metal felt cold. There was no answering hum of warmth in it, no life. Getting out of here wasn't going to be as easy as cutting a hole through to Eastfields Comp's library. For a second, panic threatened to overwhelm him. What had he been thinking, leaving the others and going into the mirror? What had he thought he could do? The walls closed in on him slightly as he struggled to breathe.

Fin gritted his teeth. Panicking wouldn't help him now. It wouldn't avenge the murder of Judge Harlequin Brown, or help Fowkes, or Ted, or the Storyholder. He let out a very long breath and waited until he was breathing normally again.

Find the Storyholder. That's what he'd come here to do, because she was key to getting everything back to normal. That was why he'd stepped into the mirror: to help save the world for everyone else? Or was it because somewhere deep down he thought she could answer unlock the mysteries of his life? *Maybe she was even his mother.* It was the first time he'd allowed himself to think such a thing, but if Fowkes and the Storyholder had been in love, then maybe Fowkes was his father and she was his mother. Maybe it was his Storyholder blood that was making his head feel funny. *Mother. Father.* It was too much to even imagine, but he couldn't help himself. Maybe he did have parents, more than one … Even though he was so nearly grown-up, the childish longing was unbearable.

He scanned the chamber again and finally spotted a small archway in the smooth curves to his right. He trotted towards it. Having learnt his lesson with the mirrors, he didn't step straight through, but poked his head carefully round the side. A maze of low stone corridors branched off it, and dull moans and cries floated through them like ghosts in the chill air. The pathways were identical, even down to the way the bricks were laid.

Finmere bit his lip. It was bad enough that he didn't know which mirror was his; if he couldn't find his way back to this chamber, then all hope for them really was lost. He needed to leave a trail of some sort to help him keep track of his route. He rummaged in his pockets and pulled out the notes and the handful of change Ted had given them. There were maybe twenty coins – how far would that get him? Maybe a few hundred metres, and that was only if he spread them meagrely.

As they were exposed to the awful prison atmosphere, the coins dulled and turned to the same shade of empty grey as everything else. Fin's spirits sank. So not only would he not get very far, he'd have a hard time even seeing them. A sorrowful cry echoed up to the mouth of the chamber and stopped in the doorway. It made Finmere shiver. What kind of people were kept here? He couldn't get lost. Surely being stuck in this prison would drive anyone mad. There was definitely insanity in that cry.

As he put the coins back in his pocket, his arm brushed the double-edged sword and he paused, an idea slowly forming in his head. He pulled the blade free and stared at it. Although

282

the warmth had gone out of it, the sword still fought the gloom with its shine. The sharp edges glinted. Turning his free hand over, Fin looked at his smooth palm. He had nothing else he could leave a trail behind with.

He squeezed his eyes shut and pressed one edge of the sword into his open hand and then swiftly pulled it back. He gasped, pain shooting through him and sending a wave of nausea from his fingertips to his stomach and up to his mouth. Through his watering eyes Fin gazed down at the gash running across the meaty pad of flesh next to his thumb. It was deeper than he expected, and he was sure that if the light was better he'd be able to see the exposed bone underneath. But then, what had he expected of a blade that could cut between worlds and had killed someone as strong as Judge Harlequin Brown? After wiping the sword awkwardly on his trousers, he put it back in its sheath. Unlike the coins, his blood glowed red brightly against the dullness of his trousers. It looked like the first application of colour made by an artist on a blank canvas: out of place and separate from the uniformity of the rest of the surroundings.

Finmere waited for a moment as he cupped his hand, but the crimson stayed vivid. He tilted his arm and let a thick drop land at the join of the paths and the chamber, and then stepped across.

THIRTY-TWO

The wall on the other side of the doorway must have swung open as he first stepped into the rift. As he came completely through into the House of Detention, Christopher was surprised to see that the low yellow lights were all on, not only in that cell but further along the corridor too.

As the wall ground shut behind him, he looked down at his hands. They looked normal, none of those stringy veins and brown spots that old people got. Well, at least one thing was going right. Now he just had to get out of the prison and back to that house in Charterhouse Square where Ted was.

The bottle still felt safely heavy in his pocket. He reached the bottom of the staircase and started climbing to the next level. A shadow cut across his path and then disappeared, as if someone were moving above him. Maybe it was Ted – maybe he'd actually lucked out and got back exactly when Ted had come to check.

'Ted?' he called softly, but he got no answer. He peered cautiously round the side. Footsteps were climbing up to the ground floor level. Maybe Ted hadn't heard him. If he didn't catch up, then he could end up locked in for hours, and by then it would probably all be over, one way or another.

He sprinted to the next flight and bounded up them two at a time.

'Ted!' he shouted, 'Ted, wait! I'm here!'

The familiar figure at the other end of the corridor stopped and turned. It wasn't Ted. For a moment Christopher just stared, before taking a small step forward in case his eyes were playing tricks on him.

'Father?' he said eventually. 'What are you doing here?'

'Oh, thank God,' Justin Arnold-Mather said as Christopher walked slowly towards him. 'Your teacher was supposed have brought the keys back this morning and they never turned up. I was worried about you.' His dark eyebrows hooded his eyes and in the pale yellow light it looked to Christopher almost as if his father's sockets were empty.

'We're fine,' he said.

'I tried ringing the school, but this blasted storm has been playing havoc with the phone system.' Mr Arnold-Mather looked past him. 'Where *is* your teacher? And that friend of yours, Finmere?'

'And Joe,' Christopher said, 'I had two friends with me.'

'I do remember, Christopher. Where are they?'

'They're outside. I just had a funny feeling I'd left some lights on.' Christopher started walking towards the exit.

'Really?' As he fell into pace beside Christopher, his father frowned. 'That's very odd. I've been here at least twenty minutes. How strange I didn't see you.' He paused. 'And the doors were locked.'

For a moment father and son just stared at each other, neither expression readable, but both looking for something in the other. Christopher pushed the outside door open.

'That's probably Joe and Fin playing a joke on me,' he said, eventually. 'They must have locked me in.'

'That must be it. Although I did go downstairs. I'm surprised I didn't see you,' Mr Arnold-Mather repeated.

Christopher shrugged and gave a half-smile. 'Well, I'm here now.'

They stepped out into the rain and in his already damp clothes, Christopher shivered as fresh drops hit him, the wind beating into his side as it whipped down the narrow street. The storm wasn't as bad as it was in The Nowhere, but it was definitely worse than it had been when they'd left. While his father locked the door, Christopher's feet itched. He had to get to Orrery House, and fast.

A black cab chugged ominously on the pavement. Mr Arnold-Mather turned and smiled. 'Jump in, son, and I'll drop you off wherever your friends are.'

Christopher shook his head, backing away slightly. 'It's okay. I'll run and catch them up. They've probably gone on ahead of me now.'

'Without locking up? And where *are* the keys?' His father frowned, and Christopher could feel his fragile story crumbling.

'Look, I've got to go.' He started to move away, and not a moment too soon, because someone else stepped out of the taxi: the large East End butler – or bouncer – from Grey's. *What was he doing here?*

His father reached for him, but Christopher dodged out of his way, eager to get past the taxi before the heavyset man could grab him. His lungs burning as he tried to keep his footing on the slick pavement, Christopher darted round the corner and on to the main street.

'Come back!'

They had taken too long to start chasing, but though Christopher knew they wouldn't catch him, he didn't slow up. Nor did he look round.

'Come back, Christopher!' his father shouted. 'Come back, damn you!'

The last words echoed in his ears and Christopher pushed his legs faster, wanting to be lost by the time they got back in the cab and came after him. *Damn you.* The first time in his life he'd managed to raise any emotion in his father and that's what he got. Not *I love you*, but *damn you*. He gritted his teeth. And damn you right back, Father, he thought, for the first time feeling bitter about the bottle in his pocket and what it had cost him. Damn you right back.

Finmere had been walking for what felt like hours and his hand was throbbing. The initial flow had slowed and occasionally he had to squeeze the cut to make the blood fall in large enough drips to create a secure trail.

'Tova?' He spoke quietly. 'Storyholder?' The air swallowed up his voice, taking its energy and leaving it hollow, unlike the cries that drifted out from the cells on either side of him. He'd shouted at first, but it had caused too much of a reaction from the inmates, some screaming at him to go away, others repeating what he'd said back to him, still more shouting nonsense phrases in languages he didn't understand but whose harsh sounds frightened him.

Another fork loomed ahead and he dragged his tired feet forward. This was hopeless: the stone dungeons went on for ever. And the temperature was dropping too. Goosebumps covered him, and his wet clothes were just getting colder instead of drying.

'Storyholder?' he called down one, 'Storyholder?'

'*Sweet blood ...*' The words hissed at him.

Finmere jumped away as thin, dirty fingers scrabbled through the small gap at the bottom of a cell on his left.

'*Hmmm, sweet, innocent blood ...*' The voice gasped slightly. 'Double *blood! Hmmm, double blood!*' A long tongue followed the fingers, unfurling a dozen centimetres across the cobbled stones towards Finmere, stretching for the last fallen drop. Fin watched in disgust as the tip desperately sought out the crimson spot, which was a centimetre too far for its owner to reach it. Whatever was on the other side let out a low moan of despair.

Fin was tempted to stamp on the hideous tongue, but he couldn't bear to come into any contact with it. Instead he hurried into the next tunnel.

'*Feed me!*' the prisoner howled after him. '*Blood! I need the blood! Feed me!*'

Finmere broke into a run, wishing he could block out the sound, and his heart beat faster, pumping his blood faster round his body, and crimson splashed from his cut as his arms swung. He imagined that awful tongue, and bony fingers growing and following him, getting stronger with each taste of his blood until they were powerful enough to tear free from the cell.

His breath rushed in his ears as his feet picked up the pace. Once he'd got a few hundred metres away he allowed himself a quick peek behind, but there was nothing there but empty gloom: no monstrous creature was coming after him, hissing and whining for his blood. Maybe he was being childish and stupid, but he wasn't sure anything was impossible in this terrible place.

But they were locked up. He smiled with relief. They were all locked up. He looked down – and frowned as something caught his eye. There were blood patches on the ground *in front* of him. They were darker than his, probably because they were older and drier. He looked at the wall, and saw a smeared hand print on one of the doors. Someone injured had come this way, and it can't have been too long before.

He held his palm of his good hand over the mark on the door. They were almost the same size. Excitement flickered in his stomach and his tiredness evaporated. Whoever had left that print wasn't too tall and didn't have very big hands. He grinned to himself. It was a woman's handprint, he was sure of it.

'Tova?' he called more loudly this time, no longer caring about the jeers and caterwauls that his voice elicited in the residents. 'Storyholder? Are you there?'

The trail of blood she'd inadvertently left for him led Fin round three more corners before he found her, curled up against the wall, knees under her chin and her head hanging forward, her yellow hair glowing slightly, fighting the grey emptiness around them. A long piece of chain was attached to one scabbed ankle.

Suddenly shy, Finmere slowed down. It was her. He'd found her.

'Excuse me,' he whispered, crouching down a short distance away, 'are you the Storyholder?'

A slim hand trembled as it rose and pushed the long, loose hair back. Her face was still covered by her arm, but her eyes looked into his. They were the most beautiful eyes Fin had ever seen, and even in the awful, neutral nothing that seeped into everything, he could see flecks of blue and brown and violet in her irises.

'I'm Finmere Tingewick Smith. I've come to try and get you out of here. I've left a trail for us to follow.' He didn't mention the slight problem when they got back to the chamber of mirrors. She looked exhausted, and her eyelids were slipping slightly shut, as if she was forcing herself to stay awake.

He'd deal with getting them out once they were back in the mirror chamber.

'Let me help you up.' He held his good hand out. Her eyes widened and she stared at the ring, before slowly touching it with her own bloodstained fingers. He shrugged, feeling awkward. She looked so fragile that he knew the answers he wanted would have to wait.

'I was found with it when I was a baby,' he said gently.

Her gaze stared into his and her head lifted. Finmere couldn't hold back a small cry, and she pulled her hand back quickly to cover her messy blood-caked mouth. He stared. *What had they done to her?* The cut that throbbed on his palm seemed like nothing now.

Ashamed at his reaction, Fin hung his head slightly.

'Are you okay?'

She nodded and tried to smile, but it turned into a flinching grimace. It was her tongue, Finmere realised with horror.

Something had happened to her tongue.

'Can you walk? It'll take us about an hour. Can you manage that?' She nodded again. He thought it had been an hour; maybe it would take them longer to get back. His watch wasn't working, and he was sure that time in this place had its own rhythm, just as it did in The Nowhere.

Slowly, carefully, he pulled her upwards. She was only a couple of centimetres shorter than Finmere. She was willowy slim and beautiful, even with the terrible wound in her mouth. She was unsteady on her feet, and he lifted the heavy chain over his shoulder and then took her arm.

'You can lean on me if you'd like,' he said softly.

And she did.

THIRTY-THREE

Mitesh Savjani climbed through an uneven hole in the damaged wall of St Paul's and then unclipped his cloak and shook the rain from it. He was dressed from his turban to his curling shoes in black silk, and only the purple gem in his beard shone occasionally in the shadows, betraying that he was there. Even the scabbard at his side was midnight black.

He sighed and tried to shake away the fatigue that crept into his bones. He found moving around the city easier than some, but it was still exhausting, and if it hadn't been for the adrenalin pumping madly through his body he would have fallen asleep on the spot. And that, he thought, would be no way to greet an old friend after too many years.

Sitting on the bottom step of one of the stone staircases that spiralled up the walls, Savjani wished that one day he could see the St Paul's in the other London. His good friends Fowkes and Baxter had told him of it when they were young men together. Maybe if he'd seen that place, then he would be able to understand why they were so fond of this one. As it was, he was somewhat confused.

He looked around at the various planked walkways that ran above his head from one side to another, left over from when some optimists had tried to repair the strange structure, which of course they'd never been able to do. It was one of the unbuilt structures of London, and they were notoriously difficult to interfere with.

There were houses that were planned and put up by

residents; they were more compliant, but places like this, and those weird Future Blocks – they had just appeared. St Paul's was the strangest. It came the first time as one small section in flames, which had perplexed the Londoners, but as the flames never spread, it didn't really cause too much concern. Like some of the other more interesting places in The Nowhere, St Paul's sat on a crossroads of several Boroughs but, unlike the others, instead of forming a strange but new amalgamation from the Boroughs on which it sat, St Paul's kept distinct features of each.

Above and to his right, a huge hole in the domed ceiling let the black rain through to patter on the ground. The only function St Paul's served in this London was as a landmark. People had tried to find a use for it, but could never agree on one, and with the holes in its side and in the roof it wasn't even safe enough for children to play in. The only people that Savjani knew who considered it significant were the Knights. And everyone in The Nowhere knew how strange those Travellers were.

He waited and listened and didn't allow himself to doubt that he'd come to the right place. He knew his friend. He knew where he would come.

And he was right.

Twenty minutes later the rift opened and a figure stepped through, quickly closing it up behind him.

Swiftly getting to his feet, Savjani emerged from the shadows and smiled.

'Andrew Fowkes.'

The Knight had already put up his sword at the first sound, and now he paused for a second until recognition dawned.

'Mitesh Savjani?'

The clothcrafter shrugged. 'I thought perhaps you could use a little help.'

The two men smiled.

'It's been a long time,' Fowkes said. 'I see that baby daughter of yours has all grown up.'

'Oh yes. I knew she would find you.'

As he looked into his old friend's tired face, Savjani wished that they could just wander back to his home above the shop and eat and talk and remember, perhaps healing some wounds along the way. But there was no time for that right now.

'So, who are we expecting?' he asked.

'St John Golden. He thinks I know where Tova has hidden the stories. I've told him if he comes and fights me here and wins I'll tell him.'

Savjani twirled his moustache. 'He believed this?'

'He didn't really have any choice. He's sending the rest of the Knights to kill the retired Knights at Orrery House. I've just been and warned them. Maybe if the boys find the Magus, then there might be a chance.'

'A Magus?' Savjani fluttered his fingers with sudden curiosity. 'No matter. You can tell me later.' His eyes twinkled. 'When we have won.'

Fowkes smiled back. His expression was hard, but Savjani was pleased to see that there was some spirit in it. He remembered how broken his friend had been the last time they had spoken. Perhaps time did heal a little – time, and the opportunity to make some amends.

'The odds aren't in our favour, Savjani.'

Savjani pulled his own sword free. 'It is always more interesting that way. Now, let us be ready!'

Fowkes nodded, and touched the tip of Savjani's sword with his own. 'Let us be ready.'

THIRTY-FOUR

'You've done good, young Christopher. You've done really good.'

Christopher left a trail of muddy footprints on the perfect carpet as he followed Ted through the bright elegance of Orrery House. As they reached the staircase, a tall man in a crisp butler's uniform and white gloves appeared silently in the corridor beside them.

'Get the others to the Oval Room, Jarvis,' Ted said. 'The lad's got some news. And can you get 'im a change of clothes?' He looked down at Christopher. 'A nice thick sweater, at least.' His arm wrapped round Christopher's shoulder and it felt like the first dry thing the boy had touched in forever. 'You'll soon warm up 'ere, son.'

Ted wasn't wrong. The heat in the house tingled in his bones. 'The Knights are going to be coming here,' Christopher said quickly, not wanting to wait. How much time did they have? What if the Knights came through before he'd had time to reverse the Ageing?

'I know.' Ted was grim. 'Fowkes just cut through on 'is way to meet Golden; 'e told us. We thought they'd try as much, and we've been getting prepared. Who knows? It's looking grim but we might just 'ave a chance.'

'I've got something.' Still shivering despite the delicious warmth of the building, Christopher pulled the bottle out of his pocket. 'It'll help us. I got it from the Magus.'

*

Twenty minutes later, and the few retired Knights who could move were seated around the long table in the Oval Room.

'There you go, dear.' Maggie Baker put another cup of tea in front of Christopher. He stared for a moment at the bruises on her face. They looked painful, although she showed no sign of hurting. It was hard to realise that what was happening in The Nowhere was just as much part of his real world as it was of that one. He chewed the inside of his mouth. It was beginning to look as if it was more connected with his own real life than he could ever have imagined.

Damn you!

The words echoed in his head, but as he let the hot liquid scald his mouth, he shook the dark thoughts away.

At last he was slowly warming up. The jumper Jarvis had given him was thin, but it was made of the finest cashmere and it was trapping his own body heat in its soft weave. He wondered for a moment which of the comatose Knights it belonged to. Over his steaming mug, he looked at the old men sucking mints and sipping coffee and Red Bull alternately. No one touched the plate of biscuits on the table. It was hard to believe that some of them were still quite young, in their twenties, even. The shiver that ran through him was nothing to do with the cold.

It was only when Maggie sat down that the men began to speak. A wizened man whose hands were wrapped around the end of a walking stick leaned forward and peered at the small glass and silver bottle that Christopher had put on the table.

'If it's a new variety of those awful caffeine drinks Ted's been forcing on us,' he said dryly, 'then I think I shall have to decline.'

'Likewise, Freddie.' An old man wearing bifocal glasses laughed as he looked over the top of them. 'I was never that keen on Red Bull when it first came out. Didn't sleep for a week, first time I drank it.' His humour subsided suddenly. 'How things change, eh?'

295

'This is different.' Ted hadn't sat down, but instead stood beside Christopher's chair. 'Gentlemen, I'd like to introduce Christopher Arnold-Mather, one of our Fin's school friends; 'e's been over in The Nowhere 'elping Finmere and Fowkes.'

Christopher could feel himself flushing. 'Pleased to meet you,' he said quietly. The men around the table nodded and gave their names. Christopher tried to cement each to its face in his head: *Simeon Soames, Lucas Blake, Freddie Wise, Harper Jones, Cardrew Cutler.* He smiled at each. He didn't think he'd be able to remember who was who once they'd left the table; people that old all looked pretty much the same to him.

'So what is it, Christopher?' Harper Jones' eyes twinkled in his sagging face. 'What is it that you've snuck back from The Nowhere?'

Christopher took a deep breath. 'It reverses the Ageing. There's enough for three of you. No more.'

His face burned in the silence that followed. He'd half-expected at least one of them to make a grab for the bottle and try to drink it all, but not one of them moved. It made him feel strange inside. These were men of honour; Ted hadn't been lying about that: true Knights of Nowhere, not like the corrupt ones who had chased after him and Fin and Joe.

Freddie Wise leaned back in his chair. 'A cure for the Ageing? Well, well, well. Now that *is* interesting.'

'We need to choose three of you,' Christopher repeated, 'and we don't have much time.'

Cardrew Cutler tilted his head and looked right into Christopher. 'How did you get this?'

'We ain't got time for that now, Cardrew,' Ted cut in, 'not with the Council coming for us.'

Christopher was relieved. He didn't want to lie, but the secret of the cure was his burden. He was afraid they'd make him drink it himself if they knew what he'd done, and tempting though that was for a small, scared part of his soul, he couldn't allow it.

'I say Freddie, Simeon and Cardrew get it.' Lucas Blake spoke first. 'We need your brains, Freddie – and you three have been Aged longest.' He looked over at Harper Jones. 'Sorry, mate.'

Harper shook his head. 'No apologies needed.' He smiled. 'If I was still a younger man I'd probably punch you for it, but hey, those days are gone.'

Listening to the old men talking was strange, thought Christopher: Lucas Blake and Harper Jones looked so old, but when they spoke, he could hear an echo of their true ages in their reedy voices.

Freddie Wise smiled. 'Ah, the arrogance of youth. I'm afraid that's not your decision to make, Lucas.'

'Why the hell not?' Lucas glared at him.

'Because, young man, this kind of decision needs to be made by the most senior members of the retired Knights, and ratified by Ted here as our Defender.' He raised an eyebrow. 'And if I remember right – and I do! – *you* are not amongst that particular group.'

'But—'

''e's right.' Ted looked at Freddie and nodded. 'So, who do you reckon, Freddie? You know 'em all best, and you know what's coming. Harlequin would want me to defer to you.'

Christopher watched as the old man sipped his coffee and pondered the question. The one thing he hadn't expected was to find the Knights fighting over why others should have the cure over themselves.

'There really isn't any debate to have.' Freddie Wise's voice was clear and strong. 'Lucas Blake and Harper Jones must take it.' He raised his hand to silence their protests. 'If my Ageing were reversed, I'd still be too old to be much good in a fight. You've both served under Golden, been part of his Inner Council, and you both know the men who are loyal to him. And they know you. Seeing you back the way you were might well unsettle them.'

297

'Jolly good thinking,' Cardrew Cutler added, taking a strong mint from the tin in front of him. As he popped it in his mouth and started sucking it he added, 'And they're both rather handy in a fight.' He looked up at the two men. 'I remember one time when you'd both got rather the worse for wear and I had to come and bail you out, and Harlequin—'

'Not now, Cardrew.'

'Yes, of course.' He settled back down in his chair. 'Sorry, Freddie.'

'And who will be the third?' Ted asked.

'Simeon Soames or Cardrew Cutler? I'm sorry, gentlemen, but we may need to decide that one on the flip of a coin. I can't choose between two such fine Knights.'

'Oh, that's got to be Simeon, no contest,' Cardrew piped up cheerfully, and his gums grinned at the man opposite. 'Anything to stop you grumbling on about that blasted wheelchair.'

'That's no way to make a decision!' Simeon erupted.

'It's as good as any,' Cardrew countered, 'and anyway, I've got used to these old bones.' He looked over at Freddie Wise. 'I served beside you when we were both Inner Council. I think I'll just carry on a little bit longer.'

There was a long pause.

'So it's decided,' Freddie said. 'Jarvis, would you be kind enough to take the bottle and help Lucas, Harper and Simeon to one of the rooms. I think this is something the gentlemen should do in private, don't you?'

The Oval Room seemed very empty when Lucas Blake, Harper Jones and Simeon Soames had gone. Although their heads were high, Christopher was sure he could see some small disappointment in Cardrew Cutler's and Freddie Wise's eyes. A clock ticked away in the background, the minutes slipping by: one, two, three, four, five, until ten had passed with no one speaking a word. Rather than meet the gaze of the men, Christopher stared at the table, and for the first time he noticed the words carved into the old wooden surface. He frowned.

'Is that the Prophecy everyone keeps talking about?'

'Yes,' Ted said. 'If you look at it from the other end you'll be able to read it the right way up.'

Christopher continued staring at the shapes of the words, without trying to get any meaning from them. 'Doesn't matter. I think I've already had my own Prophecy from the Magus,' he muttered quietly.

Ted stared at him thoughtfully. 'No one ever really knows what the future 'olds, son. Even the Prophecy means different things to different people. Fate's a funny bugger – it's got an 'abit of shifting on you.'

Christopher smiled softly, but he didn't look up. He'd said too much. The last thing he needed was to be cross-examined by the old men who weren't so very old really, because he was quite sure they were all far sharper than they looked. He waited for their barrage of questions, but none came, and after a few minutes that felt even worse.

He grabbed a biscuit and crunched it, despite his stomach's protest at the food. He needed to break that awful silence.

'Chocolate digestives.' Cardrew winked at Christopher. 'Now *that's* a good idea: just what I need. Pass 'em over, lad.'

Christopher pushed the plate across the polished wood towards the old man's fingers, and before long there were two mouths munching loudly.

The terrible quiet dispelled, Ted looked over at Mrs Baker. 'How are the preparations coming along?'

'I think we've finished almost everything Lucas suggested.' She took one of the biscuits herself and nibbled carefully, taking small bites so her healing lip wouldn't split again. 'Nearly all the bedrooms are rigged so that something heavy will fall on the heads of whoever opens the doors, and we've set up strings attaching the door handles to the bell pulls by the beds, so that when they're opened, the service bell downstairs in the pantry will ring. Any of the old boys' rooms not booby-trapped will be locked.' She looked down at her biscuit, then added quietly, 'There wasn't time to rig them all.'

'Good work. We'll guard this room, if you're up for it, Maggie?'

'You got a sword for me?'

Ted clicked a button somewhere and a section under the table slid open, revealing five slim silver swords shining in a rich mahogany tray. He pulled one out, ran his eye appraisingly over the blade and handed it to her. 'You be careful with that now, Maggie.'

She gave him an affectionate smile. 'You be careful yourself, old man.'

'What about me?' Christopher asked. 'Do I get one?'

Ted smiled wryly. 'I can't go giving swords to youngsters, mate. I know you're sixteen, but that's not old enough, not yet. That would be no good.' He sighed. 'You need to get somewhere safe, out of this house for starters.'

Christopher shook his head. He wasn't running away. He hadn't done all this to be packed off somewhere out of the way at the last minute. 'I'm not going. I'm—'

His words trailed off as the doors to the Oval Room flew open. Three young men, strangers, stood in the doorway, hands on their swords. Two were blond, with hair cut short back and sides, framing their strong faces as they stood tall and proud. The one in the middle had short dark hair that spiked up fashionably. His chest was broad and powerful, and in his black trousers and white shirt he looked every inch a Knight. He grinned and threw a pair of bifocal glasses onto the table.

'Well, I don't know about the rest of you,' Lucas Blake said, 'but I'd forgotten just how handsome I am.'

Christopher's mouth wasn't the only one that had fallen open.

'Well, I'll be damned,' Freddie said eventually. 'Maybe we shall have a chance after all.'

THIRTY-FIVE

The Storyholder had torn a strip from her dress to make a bandage for his cut hand and then they stumbled forward together, following the crimson patches that glowed against the dirty grey ground. The corridors curved and split endlessly as the two figures slowly made their way back.

By the time they'd been walking for half an hour Finmere's shoulder ached from supporting her weight and carrying the chain, but he ignored it and spoke softly as they walked, telling her everything that had happened since his sixteenth birthday. He wasn't sure that she was listening, and occasionally when he glanced over, her eyelids were slipping shut, but he thought that anything was better than listening to the achingly desperate noises from those incarcerated around them.

Finally, when he thought his shoulder was going to pop from its socket, the archway appeared ahead of them.

'We've made it,' he whispered. 'We're back at the chamber. Look!'

Finmere wasn't sure why he felt so excited. It wasn't as if he knew which mirror was theirs – but at least he'd be able to get her out of here. Surely going through any mirror would be better than staying in this awful place.

The Storyholder raised her head and gave a half smile as they stepped into the cylindrical room.

'Now I just have to remember which one I came through,' Finmere muttered once they'd reached the centre, feeling at once helpless and hopeless. Tova leaned in against him and he could feel her hot skin: she was running a fever and he needed to get her out of here right now. He gritted his teeth. Even if he had any chance of recognising the mirror they came through, how would they climb up to it? He stared harder. There had to be a way; people had to get out of here somehow. He scanned the rows, turning slowly, hoping the Storyholder wouldn't collapse. His hand still throbbed and his shoulders hurt and he was exhausted. Despite her fragility, if she fell he might not have the strength to get her to her feet again.

His eyes stopped and he stared. There was something different about one of the mirrors about four rows up. Finmere squinted. And then he grinned. Was that really what he thought it was?

'It's Joe,' he whispered, and then he laughed. 'It's Joe's hand poking through – look!' His aches and tiredness gone, he held on to the Storyholder and pointed. 'There, look – can you see?'

She looked up, following his fingers and then the world slid beneath them, and Finmere clutched at her, disoriented, as they fell upwards. As they landed on the ledge, Fin gasped, glad to feel solid stone beneath him. He didn't pause to look down or even wonder at the physics of it. He smiled at the Storyholder. Her skin was dreadfully pale, especially in contrast with the blood that stained her mouth, and her golden hair hung lank across her shoulders, but Finmere still thought she was the most beautiful woman he'd ever seen in his life.

She was staring at Joe's slim arm, her expression hidden by strands of matted hair. 'Ark … an …' she whispered, not looking up at Fin.

Fin looked at her, not sure what she meant, and then he squeezed her arm. Whatever it was, it could wait until they were safe.

'Come on,' he said. 'Let's go.'

He gripped Joe's hand.

They tumbled onto the floorboards on the other side, Fin landing heavily on Joe, the Storyholder falling through after him and landing beside them. The yellow glow of the candles made Finmere squint after that dreadful grey absence of light in the prison, and the air was rich and warm. Fin sucked it in, filling his lungs. It tasted sweet.

'Blimey.' Joe sat up, spitting out a mouthful of reeds and dust. 'I wasn't expecting you back so soon.'

'Soon?' Fin frowned. 'I've been gone hours.'

'No you haven't,' Joe said. 'Fowkes and Golden have gone to fight at St Paul's – the one over here, not ours.' He looked over at the door. 'We need to get out of here fast. That other bloke will be back soon. He's gathering the rest to go and fight at Orrery House.'

The Storyholder pulled herself up so she was sitting and Joe stared at her, his mouth open. Fin, scared he was about to say something about her tongue, glared at him. Joe's lips wobbled a bit and then latched on to some different words.

'What are we going to do, Fin? This storm is getting worse.'

Fin took the Storyholder's slim hand. 'We need you to get your stories back. We need you to stop the storm.'

She stared at him with her strange multi-coloured eyes, and then studied Joe for a long moment time before looking back at Fin. She nodded and tried to speak, but all she could manage was a painful gurgle. Finmere looked desperately around the room. 'Can you see anything she can write with?'

Joe jumped to his feet and rummaged around the desk. 'Got a pencil.' He waved it in the air. 'There's a file here.' He paused. 'Fin? It's got your name on.'

'Just bring it over here.'

304

The Storyholder's eyes were drooping again and Fin was worried that she would fall unconscious before they could get her to help. Joe crouched next to him and handed her the pencil. Her fingers trembled and she slid a little to one side with the effort of gripping it. Her face concentrating, she pressed the lead into the buff cardboard folder, carefully spelling out a word. Fin watched. *Somewhere*. She stopped. Finmere looked up at her.

'You've hidden the stories in The Somewhere?' She nodded.

Fin looked at Joe. 'We have to go back. We'll take her to Orrery House.'

'Will she be all right travelling?' Joe looked worried. 'I thought they said people from The Nowhere didn't travel so well.'

'We don't really have a choice. And anyway, if she's hidden the stories over there, then she must have been before.'

'Okay.' Joe gently took the Storyholder's other arm and helped Fin lift her to her feet. 'You'd better do your thing, then.'

Fin pulled the sword out of its sheath and it started humming immediately, tingling through his arm and up to his heart. He could sense its energy as if it were a racehorse just let out from the stable, raring to gallop in the open air. He closed his eyes and thought of white: the pure white carpet of Orrery House. He could see the hallway stretching out ahead of him to the staircase, so clearly it was almost as if he was there. He smiled. 'What will be, will be,' he whispered.

When Conrad Eyre arrived back twenty minutes later the room was empty. He glowered at the folder and pencil lying on the floor. Picking it up, he read the one word: *Somewhere*. He looked at the file and then the mirror and then at the file again, before tossing it back on the desk. All his questions would be answered soon enough.

He turned to face the Knights who came up the stairs behind him. For a moment they all stood in silence, and then he drew his sword.

'Let us be ready,' he said.

Metal clanged as the others raised their own.

'Let us be ready!' they answered in unison.

THIRTY-SIX

With Ted and Mrs Baker's help they took the Storyholder down into the kitchen and sat her beside the roaring fire. Mrs Baker rummaged in one of the large drawers and pulled out a packet of painkillers, and made Tova swallow them with some water.

'She's in a bad way, Ted.' Mrs Baker looked up.

'When this is all done Jarvis will be able to look after 'er. Just do your best for now.'

'What about the Oval Room?' Mrs Baker carefully wiped the Storyholder's face, just as Fin had seen Ted do to hers back at her house.

'This is more important. I'll keep 'em away from the map, don't you worry.' He frowned and looked at Tova. 'She should be somewhere safer, though.'

The Storyholder glared at him, and Finmere wanted to smile. She was still strong inside, and just like Fin, she wanted to be involved in the fight. Ted turned to Finmere.

'You boys stay 'ere. A battle's no place for teenagers, and you can 'elp Mrs Baker.'

Finmere looked over at Joe and Christopher, who both raised their eyebrows.

'I mean it,' Ted growled, 'there's going to be enough to think about without worrying about you lot on top of it. So just stay put, all right?'

'Okay, Ted.' As much as he wanted to help where he could,

Fin didn't want Ted to think they were in the way. 'And good luck.'

'Good luck to all of us.' Ted ruffled his hair. 'Old Harlequin would be proud of you, Fin.'

Finmere fought the urge to hug the old man. If he did that it would be like admitting that he was scared that he wouldn't see him again, that they wouldn't win the battle. If he allowed that thought to take root in his head it might jinx them all.

A sound crackled on Ted's hip and he pulled the walkie-talkie free and spoke softly into it.

He turned. 'They're 'ere,' he said softly, and strode out of the kitchen.

Fin's heart raced to his mouth and his palms turned sweaty. For a moment there was silence, then two of the servants' bells in the long line on the far wall started ring, and from somewhere up above came a loud yell of pain and frustration.

Mrs Baker looked up. 'I'd say the old iron warming pan just landed on someone's head.'

'Are we really going to stay here and do nothing?' Christopher asked.

Fin looked at him. Since coming back through from The Nowhere he hadn't had five minutes to say even say hello to his friend, let alone find out about his adventure with the Magus. Something about him was different, though, and Finmere couldn't put his finger on what it was.

'Ted said ...' His voice trailed away. Ted had said what he had because it was the honourable, the morally right thing to do. He couldn't ask them to fight; they were too young and unprepared. But Finmere figured that Ted and the retired Knights were going to need as much help as possible if they were going to win it.

'Is there a lock on this kitchen door?' Joe asked. 'It looks pretty solid. If it was locked they wouldn't be able to get in too easily.'

'Not unless they cut a rift through,' Fin said.

'The Knights don't come down here.' Mrs Baker was watching them. 'Jarvis wouldn't have it. No Knights belowstairs; he's very old-fashioned like that.'

The three boys looked at each other. 'That's settled then. If we lock it behind us then the Storyholder and Mrs Baker will be pretty safe. The Knights can't cut through if they can't picture it,' Fin added, before looking around. 'Now we just need to find some stuff we can use.'

Fowkes stood on the uneven ground of St Paul's and peered into the gloom. His nerves tingled and he pulled his double-edged sword free. Its hum was electric, as if even the metal could feel the tension in the night air. Somewhere behind him, Savjani was pressed against the wall halfway up to the next level, his own sword ready. It was good to have someone standing beside him again, even if it did make him feel a fresh ache for Baxter. He just hoped Savjani was up to what he'd asked him to do.

'Come on in, St John,' he said softly. 'I can hear you there.'

The tall figure stepped into the open space and unclipped his dark cloak, letting it tumble to the floor. He smiled, his white teeth shining in the darkness.

'All that drinking hasn't completely dulled your senses, I see.' St John Golden slid his sword out and held it casually aloft.

'I think you'll be surprised.' Fowkes raised his own, and took a step forward, nearer to the bottom step. 'Although perhaps not altogether pleasantly.' He smiled too.

'You over-estimate yourself, Fowkes. You always did.' St John matched Fowkes with a step of his own. 'Conrad's despatching the retired Knights as we speak. Soon Orrery House will be ours. The Storyholder is gone. The Prince

Regent is a puppet.' He shrugged. 'Are you catching my drift? Why not just give up now?'

Fowkes grinned fiercely and backed up to the first step. 'But you don't have the stories, do you? You haven't got the first idea where those are. And how long do you think your men will stand with you without those?'

St John's face darkened. 'I'll get them.' He darted forward and Fowkes jumped back up onto the first step of the stairs. 'But you won't be around to see it!'

St John lunged, and their double-edged swords clashed.

Mona was no longer nervous of the Prince Regent, and as the thunder and lightning battled in the sky she glared at him. Somewhere behind her Jacob Megram was clutching his hat and dozing off in a chair, the journey to the palace having proved too much for him.

'Look, there must be something you can do! Can't you send your spies to the Knights' house or something?' It was difficult hearing herself over the awful music that was being valiantly attempted on the Harpsichordian. 'We need to find out where Finmere and Fowkes and the others are!'

The Prince Regent's dark eyes seemed devoid of emotion, but his delicate fingers drummed on the soft velvet arm of his throne. He flicked his wrist and the music stopped. The musicians gratefully scurried out through one of the side doors.

'Thank mercy for that,' Mona muttered. The storm outside raged against the wall of windows, the sound even more spooky without the awful royal music covering it.

'These Knights,' the Prince Regent said eventually, 'always causing damage. This is their problem. Let them clean it up.'

Mona stamped her foot in sheer frustration. 'But this is *our* world! And what if they *can't* clean it up! What about your people?' She paused. 'What if it's the Prophecy coming true? Are you just going to sit on your backside and let it happen?'

The Prince Regent raised an eyebrow. 'You really are very rude.'

Hands on her hips, Mona raised her own eyebrow right back at him. 'And you really are very infuriating.'

Finmere hadn't been prepared for the total confusion of a battle in such a confined space, and as they crept up the stairs from the kitchen all three kept as low to the ground as they could. The sound of metal on metal echoed down from above them, and the sound of heavy boots thudding despite the soft carpet.

Something crashed and broke and voices called out to each other:

'*Christian France! Check downstairs!*'

Finmere flinched, and then his heart stopped.

'Someone's coming!' he muttered. Up through the banisters he could see a dark shadow moving towards them.

Joe darted past him to the wall on the other side of the stairs, unravelling the ball of twine they'd found in one of the kitchen drawers and wrapping the excess around his palm. Behind Finmere, Christopher did the same with the other end.

Fin pressed himself against the wall and waited. The line they'd run was invisible against the pure white of the carpet, but should be just high... .

Fin held his breath as the footsteps got louder.

'What the f—?' The footsteps stumbled.

'Gotcha!' Joe cried as the Knight who had tripped over the twine tumbled to the ground.

'Get him!' Christopher yelled, leaping up to join Joe, and Fin dived in the middle. All three landed on the man, who looked up, shocked and angry. 'Get off me, you bloody hooligans!'

Fin sprayed the bottle of kitchen cleaner straight into the Knight's eyes and his indignant ranting was cut off with a scream. While Joe and Christopher pinned the man down, Finmere released three more hefty squirts into his mouth, and almost felt sorry for him as he writhed and coughed, gasping for air.

'One down!' He pulled the Knight's sword out from its holder. 'At least we know he won't be going anywhere.'

'Damn, we're good,' Joe panted, squashing the Knight's attempts to move by bouncing heavily on him.

Fin peered upstairs. 'Can you two get him tied up?'

Christopher smiled and pulled a roll of brown tape from his back pocket.

'How come you didn't just stab him with the sword?' Joe held the Knight's arms behind him as Christopher wound the tape tightly round his wrists. 'I mean, I know it wouldn't have been nice, but—'

'Double-edged swords aren't designed for killing.' Finmere smiled softly. 'I'm only going to use it if I really have to.'

'Yeah, that makes sense. Anyway, who'd want to stab someone up with all that blood and stuff?' Joe pulled a face. 'Gross!'

On the second-floor landing Conrad Eyre gritted his teeth and kicked another white door in. A box of books tumbled from above and landed where he would have been standing. He frowned. These defences should have been laughable – and perhaps they would have been, if Orrery House had been as he'd expected it to be, with just Ted and Jarvis and a few old men. It should have been easy. They should have all been *dead* by now.

How had St John Golden not known that they would be

facing a proper fight here? Could it be that their leader wasn't as well-prepared as he'd led them to believe? First the fiasco with the Storyholder, and now this. Doubt grew like a cancer in his mind, and he felt ashamed of it.

He trembled with anger and a fear he didn't want to admit to as he stepped over the scattered books and towards the wheelchair. There were young Knights here – not novices or amateurs, but fully trained young Knights, and he was sure that he'd spotted Lucas Blake amongst them. But that couldn't be: Lucas had Aged five years ago, and surely if there'd been one of the rare reversals they'd have heard about it.

Faced with an old man whose milky eyes stared at nothing, Conrad felt a wave of revulsion. What he was doing was probably humane – it's what he would want for himself. And regardless of whether his faith in St John was turning out to be misplaced, there was no going back now.

'Time to die,' he muttered and raised his already bloody sword. Something hit him hard on the back of the head and, wincing, he turned.

'I don't think so,' the old man said dryly as he lowered his walking stick. 'You should be ashamed, Conrad Eyre.' He raised his own sword. 'We had such high hopes for you.'

'Freddie Wise?' Conrad laughed. The back of his head throbbed, but not enough to even daze him. 'Fine, I'll kill you and then I'll kill him. It's time to make way for the new order.'

'Over my dead body.'

Conrad stared at the old man. 'If you insist. Don't say I didn't warn you.'

Their swords clashed and Freddie moved backwards, tottering down the corridor. Conrad could feel the man's weakness as they parried. There was not strength enough in his arms to hold the sword, let alone wield it properly. They passed the doors that he'd already kicked in and despite his obvious disadvantage Freddie shook his head, pityingly.

313

'Is this how you thought it would be, Conrad? When St John talked to you about power?' Freddie wheezed. 'Did you think you'd become a murderer of brave men? Helpless men?'

Conrad laughed. 'It's a means to an end.' He thrust forward, sending Freddie sprawling onto the next flight of stairs, and his sword tumbled out of reach. Conrad stood over the old man and smiled. 'And for some of you, it's a mercy.' They locked eyes. 'Say goodbye, Freddie Wise.'

'Not so fast, Conrad Eyre.'

Conrad looked up to see where the voice had come from. His sword froze. *It couldn't be ...*

'You took your time,' Freddie muttered, wriggling out from under Conrad's blade.

Conrad had forgotten the old man as soon as he'd seen the other. Shock ran like fire through his body. 'Lucas Blake,' he spat out.

The dark-haired man grinned. 'Surprised? There's a couple of other familiar faces upstairs too.' He looked down at Freddie and then back at Conrad. 'It looks like you've gone off the rails in the past five years, Conrad.' He tutted. 'Honestly – fighting old men?' He raised his sword and tilted it. 'Why don't you pick on someone your own age?'

Feeling his frustration and anger rising inside him, Conrad turned. 'With pleasure,' he growled as their swords clashed.

Sweat ran down the back of Fowkes' neck as he thrust and parried, matching St John blow for blow. For all his own brave words he could feel the lack of practice in his aching muscles and shaking bones. He was holding St John off, but the other man was in control of the fight. Fowkes knew he was just playing a defensive game; now he needed to find his confidence. He had always been a better fighter than Golden. Golden didn't have his instinct for it. If he could just tune into that again, then he could defeat him.

314

He sucked his side in and hopped backward, just avoiding a glancing blow, and St John's eyes gleamed.

'Still confident, Fowkes? Or are you just the same coward you were when you let Baxter die for you?'

Red anger rose up, and Fowkes fought to control it. He needed to stay calm. He needed to stay a true Knight if he was going to win this, not only for himself but for Baxter too. He thought of his old friend's ready smile and quickly twisted himself round and brought his sword down hard. Golden's victorious expression wobbled and Fowkes grinned. So he still had some of the old magic after all.

'Don't count your chickens, Golden.' He ducked, easily avoiding the strike. Behind him he could feel Savjani, preparing to take over his side of the fight. 'You always were too damned cocky.' He started to visualise the Oval Room of Orrery House. As he grinned, he rolled to one side and Savjani stepped into his place.

'Hold him!' With one quick slice in the air a rift appeared. He didn't look back to see the Commander's shocked face, but he did hear Savjani's laugh as they clashed blades. As he leapt through the rift he didn't worry about St John Golden trying to follow him. He'd see the fear in enough Knights' eyes in his time. Golden was scared to death of the Ageing, too afraid to travel – if he wasn't, then he would have been there now, fighting side by side with his men.

Finmere made his way up the stairs to the top floor, ducking between the fighting men. Cardrew Cutler stood on the landing next to a line of wheelchairs. The loose skin around his chin shook as he smiled and shook his head.

'I thought Ted told you to stay somewhere safe.' He wiggled the metal chair he held out in front of him as if it held an invisible passenger. 'I almost lobbed this down the stairs at you. Good job I've got my glasses on.'

Fin peered back down over the banisters; he could see the wreck of one chair on the landing below. 'You're throwing *wheelchairs* at people?'

'Most fun I've had in ages.' Cardrew grinned. 'Now shoo.'

Fin made his way to the Oval Room at the far end, leaving the old man to guard the stairs. When he stepped inside, his heart thumped and almost stopped, before starting to pound furiously. Fowkes was standing in the Oval Room talking to Ted. He could see the sweat on his forehead. Unnoticed by either of the men, he listened.

'Mitesh Savjani's holding him. How are things here?'

The walkie-talkie gripped firmly in his hand, Ted paced up and down. 'Better than I could've 'oped. If it weren't for that cure Fin's mate brought back we'd be well lost, but I think we're 'olding our own. We've lost some of the old boys, though.' He looked up. 'Don't you kill Golden, Fowkes. You're better'n that.'

Fowkes nodded grimly. 'It'll be hard though.' He gave the older man a wry smile. 'And that's if he doesn't kill me first.'

'We need him and Eyre alive. The others'll give up without them.'

'We've got company!' Cardrew Cutler's voice carried along the corridor, shortly followed by the sound of metal crashing against the banisters as a wheelchair crashed down the stairs. Ted and Fowkes both looked up, their eyes falling on Fin, who froze in the doorway.

'Finmere? What the 'ell are you—?' Ted started, then, 'Oh, never mind. There's no time.' He slapped Fowkes on the back and grabbed a long steel pole from the table. He passed Finmere and went out into the corridor.

On the table something shifted in the wood and Fin stared. Words carved on its surfaced glowed golden and then streams of light erupted upwards from each one like a laser show,

316

forming their shape in the empty air. Something inside him sang back to them, as if deep down he already knew the letters and the words they formed. His mouth dropping open, Fin looked at Fowkes through the rhyme. The Knight seemed unaware of the beautiful poem hanging between them. How could that be?

> *When life and death are bound in one,*
> *The balance of all will come undone,*

The lines in the middle glowed brighter than the rest, and staring at them, Fin felt the same fear that had gripped him when he first touched the sword. The locked door in his mind strained to stay shut as the bright words sought entry. He couldn't open it; he *couldn't*. Whatever he was hiding in there terrified him too much. It was a *bad thing*, he knew it: a *wrong thing*.

Fowkes stepped forward and grabbed Finmere's arm, bursting the words into a spray of colourful petals that drifted back to their places in the quiet wood.

'Stop gawping and get under the table and hide.' Fowkes glared at Fin before turning and cutting a rift back to The Nowhere. Fin stared at it, and then the table, and then the rift again, and then before he really knew what he was doing, he squeezed his eyes shut and dived through behind the Knight.

As he landed in a clumsy roll, the cold wet ground knocked Finmere's breath out of his lungs in a hard gasp. He ignored the pain in his chest and was on his feet in a moment, standing by Fowkes' side, panting but with his sword already drawn, if a little unsteadily.

Fowkes stared at him. Fin looked up at the wrecked ceiling of the strange Nowhere St Paul's where the rain raged into the gloom. From the level above them came the sound of metal clashing against metal. On the unsteady walkway, Savjani grunted, and they could see one arm hanging lame at his side, and red blood dripping from it.

Fin could see that the injured tailor was badly parrying the attacks from the agile St John Golden, who whirled elegantly around him, making the clothcrafter look completely out of time with the rhythm of their fight.

Finmere raised his sword and grinned at Fowkes. Where the next words came from, he had no idea; they just tumbled out of his open mouth, in his voice and the echo of another.

'Let us be ready.' He touched the tip of his sword to Fowkes', making the metal sing.

'Let us be ready,' Fowkes whispered, and they moved as one up the stairs, Finmere keeping time with Fowkes as they took the steps two at a time. Fowkes slipped round to the right and took Savjani's place with a fluid movement, his strong sword replacing the weaker one, and the tailor stumbled down a few stairs and then collapsed against the wall, his face pale. Fin thought for a moment that he might slip and fall all the way down, or over the edge of the stairway, as there was no railing or banister, and he scrambled up the few steps to catch him.

'Are you okay?' Finmere pushed the heavier man so that he was sitting more steadily on the stone step.

The tailor winced and then smiled. 'Just a flesh wound.' He winked. 'And luckily I have plenty of flesh.'

Fin looked at the injury in the man's shoulder and the thick, shiny liquid pumping from it. 'We need to cover it up. You're losing a lot of blood.' The gash in his own hand was a paper-cut in comparison.

He tore off his shirt, crumpling it into a ball and pressing it hard into the gaping wound. Behind him, Fowkes swore and St John Golden laughed and Fin fought to ignore the urge to turn and try and help. Even though he'd put it back in its sheath, his sword was humming eagerly and he could feel it tickling against his hip.

Blood was soaking through his balled-up shirt far too quickly and the tailor's face had turned a sickly shade of pale green. This wasn't looking good. 'Have you got a belt?' he asked.

Savjani nodded. 'You may have to undo it for me. My hands are cold.'

His own fingers frantic, Fin fumbled under the tailor's black top and the curve of his heavy belly until eventually he found the buckle. The tailor's skin felt too hot, as if he was starting to run a fever – or something worse.

'Maybe I should cut a hole for you to go back to your shop.' Fin pulled the leather belt free. 'You need to be somewhere safe.' With shaking hands, Fin slipped the leather around the man's back and then did it up tightly over the stab wound. Savjani let out a small yelp and Fin flinched.

'Sorry,' he mumbled. 'It has to be tight to stop the bleeding.'

The tailor stroked Fin's head. 'Do not fear for me, Finmere. A little pain and a little blood loss I can live with.'

'Still, we should get you somewhere safer.' Fin reached for the blade that sung through his bones, but Savjani's sweaty hand stopped him.

'My place is here. Give me a moment, and then I will be well enough to fight again.' His eyes were strong. 'I will not leave Fowkes.'

Despite his reservations, Finmere nodded. He knew exactly how the tailor felt. He wouldn't leave Fowkes either, regardless of what happened.

The fight was coming down the steps now. Fin looked up, and was surprised to see that Fowkes was the one in control, pushing Golden further down the stairs. Their swords were a whir of flashing metal.

Still crouched by Savjani, Fin gripped the hilt of his own.

How could he help Fowkes without getting in the way? Despite both his body and the sword screaming at him to join in, Fin's brain knew that he was likely to be more of a hindrance than a help. What did he know about sword fighting?

'George Porter!' Fowkes suddenly called out.

'Porter?' St John may have been the one being forced down the stairs, but he didn't sound nearly as out of breath as Fowkes. 'What about him?'

Fin's eyes widened, his heart thumping in his chest. Very slowly he straightened up, fully aware of the message in the Knight's words. Fowkes wasn't talking to Golden. He was talking to *him*.

Leaving Savjani, he clung to the wall and crept up three stairs, so close to the fight that he could feel the blades cutting through the air. *George Porter.*

With a loud grunt, Fowkes pushed forward, maybe not as elegant as Golden's lunge, but equally efficient. Golden stepped backwards, confidently reaching for the step below.

Finmere stared at that highly polished boot, and for a moment time slowed to sticky molasses. Golden's foot hung, a mid-air snapshot in the grey night, and then Fin saw his own trainer-shod foot reaching forward and catching the back of the man's heel.

They seemed to stay like that forever, and then Fowkes' voice cut through, spinning everything back to normal speed: 'Push!'

Above him, Fin saw Golden's free arm flailing as he tried desperately to regain his balance. No slow-motion this time, Fin kicked out again and caught the Commander's remaining leg, buckling him at the knee. Finmere leapt forward, grinned and did what the Knight had ordered. He pushed.

There was nothing elegant about the way St John Golden tumbled over the edge of the stairs and down to the floor below. He landed with a heavy thud, his sword clattering on to the buckled concrete floor a metre or so away.

For a moment there was no sound but the black rain on stone.

Finmere and Fowkes peered down at him.

'Do you think he's dead?' Fin whispered, really hoping that he wasn't, despite everything that he'd done.

A groan wafted up to them.

'Doesn't sound like it.' Fowkes raised an eyebrow. 'But I think that leg is definitely broken.'

Savjani hauled himself to his feet and joined them. Fowkes wrapped an arm around his old friend to keep him upright.

'That will serve him right for ruining my shirt.' The tailor's voice was weak but full of humour. Fin was pretty sure that he would make a full recovery.

The wall behind them rumbled.

'What now?' Fowkes muttered as heavy feet stamped into the cathedral somewhere below them. Fin reached for his sword.

A familiar head of purple hair ran into view and Mona cried, 'Dad, Dad!' She looked around, then caught sight of them all. 'Are you okay? I got some help!'

A group of armed men surrounded St John Golden.

'So I see.' Savjani smiled at his daughter.

From within the small posse of uniformed soldiers, their heads covered with old-fashioned steel helmets, the Prince Regent's dainty figure stepped out. He carefully picked up St John Golden's sword and turned it over in his hands for a moment before looking upwards, his dark, unfathomable eyes seeking out Fowkes.

'We will guard him for you.' His delicate voice wafted up towards them. 'Perhaps you should return and assist the others. Show the rebels this.' With what looked like inordinate ease, the Prince tossed up the heavy sword.

Fowkes caught it. 'Yes, Your Majesty.' He winked at Finmere, waved his sword, and then, within a breath, they were both gone.

THIRTY-SEVEN

The battle was over pretty quickly after that. With Conrad Eyre caught by Lucas Blake, and others subdued by Simeon Soames and Harper Jones, all three filled with the vigour of returned youth and ably assisted by the young, the elderly and a barrage of wheelchairs, it only took Fowkes to arrive with St John Golden's sword in hand for what remained of the Inner Council's resolve to crumble.

Most looked quietly relieved to be able to surrender; many had found it difficult to be faced with old comrades whom they had thought lost to the Ageing.

While Finmere and Joe stayed with Ted and the Storyholder, Christopher went with Fowkes back to the Knights' house in The Nowhere.

He stood there now, a vague sickness in his stomach, feeling somewhere between a child and an old man alongside Lucas Blake, Fowkes and Harper Jones as they stared at the mirror in the dimly lit room that had until recently been St John Golden's private rooms.

He hadn't been quite sure why they'd been so easy about letting him come with them, but then he'd seen something in Harper Jones' eyes, a kind of wondering pity, as if perhaps they knew that the cure he'd provided had come with a personal cost. Christopher wondered if maybe he was marked as damaged in some way that he couldn't see.

Yellow light flickered from the flaming lamps in the wall and Christopher stepped forward to take a closer look at the man attached to the other end of the chain that ran from the heavy leg of the desk and disappeared into the surface.

St John Golden no longer looked so imposing. His thin face was as grey as the gloom that surrounded him. His eyes looked too large, the hollow bags under them too big and heavy, the sockets too bony, and there was very little trace of his previous natural arrogance. Behind him, Christopher could hear the Knights discussing the possibility of summoning the Truthfinders, to seek the names of any further traitors who might be hidden amongst them. They had forgotten that Christopher was there, if just for a moment or two.

He crouched and leaned forward. 'Do you know my name?' he whispered into that eternal gloom.

Golden's eyes narrowed.

With a bitter smile Christopher whispered some more, his mouth so close to the surface that the prison sucked his breath in. He felt both halves of his heart ache as the words poured out of him until Golden pulled away. Christopher stared at him.

'It's the only way to survive.' The words were barely even a whisper, but were formed clearly enough for Golden to see. By the time Fowkes and the other Knights turned back round, Christopher was standing against the wall, as if nothing had happened.

It was after the bell rang out across the city, signalling that Conrad Eyre had been hanged in Smithfield Market that St John Golden bit his own tongue off, screaming in agony as he did so. Before the Knights could stop him, Christopher took advantage of their shock and reached for the chain, deftly turning the key in the lock and freeing it from the desk.

As he watched Golden disappear into the depths of the world of the mirror, despite Fowkes' best efforts to catch the chain and pull him back, Christopher sat back on his heels and felt a cold, black satisfaction in his soul. He hadn't lied completely. It *was* the only way to survive. But no one would be coming to save St John Golden. No one would take the risks that Finmere had to bring the traitorous Knight back, and Christopher thought that Golden was a fool to have believed him. Or maybe he was just desperate. Either way, Christopher had done what he needed to do. He'd got rid of Golden and protected his own place with the Knights.

If they knew the truth, then they'd probably want nothing to do with him, and then what would he have left? Where would be left for him to go? For a moment he wondered if his insides would ever lose the chill they'd felt since sitting with the Magus at West Minster Abbey.

Fowkes grabbed both his arms and shook him. 'What did you do that for? Why would you do that?'

'That's exactly what he did to the Storyholder,' Christopher said. 'An eye for an eye.' He looked up. 'A tongue for a tongue. An eternity for an eternity.'

The grown men stared at him and then at each other, but he didn't look at them. He just wanted to feel better. Maybe he'd start feeling better now. Maybe.

Finmere didn't know what Ted, Fowkes and the others planned to do with the Knights they had locked up in some of the rooms of Orrery House. In the main the adults had taken to talking quietly together behind closed doors. He wondered why they weren't more celebratory, all things considered, and he was glad to be outside and leaving them to it for a while.

The Storyholder looked strange in jeans and a jumper, her long hair pulled back in a ponytail. Fin guessed she had to be nearly forty, but her skin was fresh and clear, and in normal clothes she looked even younger than she had in The Nowhere. A scarf was wrapped round her neck and high across her nose, protecting her damaged face from both the bitter wind and curious on-lookers, and only someone who knew how weak she was would see the tiny wobble in her posture as she kept herself steady.

On the corner of Charterhouse Square, Joe stamped his feet and peered through the drizzle for a taxi. 'So, where are we going?'

Fin looked at the Storyholder. 'Where did you hide the stories? Is it near here?'

She shrugged, her eyes twinkling a little and she pulled the notebook she'd come to rely on from the pocket of her coat. Raindrops splashed on it, but at least they were clear, or nearly so. There would be no black storm, not this year, at any rate.

She scribbled a single word on the top sheet and held it out for Fin to see. He stared at it, and his mouth opened a little. She watched him, and he saw so much care in her eyes that he thought he might cry.

'Blanket.' He read the word out loud. '*My* blanket?'

She nodded.

Questions whirled in his head so fast that they blurred into a mess that he couldn't figure into complete phrases, let alone ask.

'You put the stories into *my blanket*?' he eventually breathed. 'You brought me here in it? *Wrapped in the Stories?*'

She nodded again.

'There's a cab!' Joe called, and whistled loudly for it.

Finmere's heart felt as if it had been eaten by his stomach. 'How did you know I wouldn't lose it?'

She shrugged and scribbled another word.

Faith.

The cab chugged to a halt. Joe pulled the door open for them.

'I don't understand. Are you my mother?' The words were out before Fin could stop them, and the Storyholder's shoulders sagged slightly, her brow furrowing.

'Come on!' Joe shouted, but Fin couldn't bring himself to move.

'I need to know,' he whispered.

Yes and no. She pressed the scribbled sheet into his hand and then climbed into the cab.

Fin felt sick. Yes and no? What did that mean? That wasn't an answer; that just brought up a thousand more questions. *Or maybe an answer you don't want to think about.* The dark space in his head and heart oozed the words into his mind and he pushed them back. They could go away. The dark space could go away. He'd locked it up behind the door, and it would stay strong, of that he was sure. They'd saved the Storyholder and everything was going to be right again, hopefully including his head. He stared determinedly out of the taxi window, focusing on the solidity of the London he loved.

Twenty minutes later and the three of them were standing in Postman's Park, Fin and Joe supporting the Storyholder's arms. Finmere wasn't sure if it was the strain of being in The Somewhere or whether it was her injury, but she had definitely weakened since they'd left Orrery House.

The cold and rain coming on the back of the recent awful weather had kept most of the tourists away and other than an old woman sitting on a worn bench and staring into the fountain behind them, they were alone in the small park. The rain splattered on the roof of the small wooden walkway that ran alongside the plaques.

The Storyholder stepped away from Finmere and Joe and looked up at the painted ceramic rectangles, reading each one, her eyes wide with awe. Occasionally she reached up to run a hand over the smooth, cracked surfaces. When she looked back round at the boys, she was crying.

So many beautiful stories of self-sacrifice, she wrote. *You hid the Five Eternal Stories here?* She stared at him as if his choice of hiding place made perfect sense to her.

Fine nodded, suddenly feeling awkward, and then stepped over to Olive Jones' plaque, furthest along the wall. He found a damp twig on the ground and worked one end under the ceramic until it caught on the plastic bag wedged between the stone wall of the church and Olive's memorial. He dragged it downwards until his fingers could get enough purchase to pull the bag free.

Joe and the Storyholder stood close as Fin pulled the old hand-knitted checked blanket out into the open air. It felt strange, having others look at it. For a moment he pressed it to his face, sucking in the memories of a childhood of longing, mixed in with the damp and plastic odour that was embedded into the fibres.

He stared at the faded colours and frayed edges. For such a long time it had been the only thing he had that was truly his own, and it felt strange to give it back, even though it was the Storyholder who had put it in his box with him. Maybe this was part of growing up: saying goodbye to childish things.

Tova's soft, pale hand gently covered his, and he found that it wasn't so very hard to relinquish the blanket into that touch.

The colours crackled as sparks of electricity started running along each and every thread.

'That's beautiful—' Joe stepped back, watching in awe as the stories she'd so carefully knitted into the blanket broke free, released by her touch: a swirl of rainbow light rising up and out of the wool, forming a helix of whirling brightness reaching from the blanket into the air up to the wooden ceiling.

Fin thought every shade of every colour that he had ever seen was in that dancing light: the hues of autumn leaves and icicles and late-spring blossoms and sticky toffee pudding and low summer sunsets and crisp green apples and juicy red apples, and every other beautiful shade that he could imagine. He found himself giggling aloud, his hands clasped over his mouth as he stared in wonder, just like Joe on the other side.

As the colours twisted faster and faster, the shades merged into five distinct colours; red, green, blue, black and white. They rose in thick cords, winding around each other: ghosts of life, finally released.

The Storyholder let out a low moan, her knees buckling slightly, and Fin grabbed her. The lines of colour unfurled, their strands standing separate and proud from the blanket that was now just white wool with the stories drained from it.

The Storyholder reached for them with stretched-out hands. First the blue line trembled, then it disappeared into her fingertips, as if she had sucked it inside her. Her eyes flew open and she gasped. The green followed the blue, and then the strip of white began its journey. It was still half there when it shivered, and so did she, before with an anguished yell, she sucked it inside her.

She fainted, becoming a dead weight in Fin's arms, and as he fell to the ground with her the blanket slipped free. The two remaining colours, the black and the red, hovered uncertainly in the air. Terrified that they might be lost into The Somewhere, Fin stretched out his own hand to touch one of them. The black strand danced in the other direction, as if Fin and it were magnets fighting each other. Fin reached for it again, and it darted easily out of his reach. He looked desperately over to Joe.

'They can't get away!'

Joe wasn't listening, but was staring instead at the two columns of pure rich colour that had stopped in front of him.

Fin cradled the Storyholder in his arms, watching: the black and red had fled from his touch, but they were drawn to Joe and were now hovering patiently centimetres from his face. Slowly Joe raised his hand and reached forward. The colours leapt aggressively into his fingers and Joe cried out as they burst their way into him, striking him like lightning.

And then the air was empty.

When Fin looked up, it felt like all the colour had drained from the world, not just the pale blanket crumpled on the ground beside him. Joe's shoulders shook with deep, dark sobs that seemed to echo from his soul. The anguished sounds didn't belong with Joe, who had the cheekiest laugh at Eastfields and who never thought beyond the next prank or the next football match.

Fin reached out with his free arm and pulled his friend close, wondering why he felt that something terrible had just happened.

EPILOGUE

The midnight sky was clear over London as the circle of men gathered in the Whispering Chamber of St Paul's Cathedral. Stars twinkled above the blaring horns of the traffic and the glowing neon lights that filled the streets; everything was back to normal after the strange weather of the week before. To the ordinary eye it would probably look like all was well in the world ... but then, to the ordinary eye there was only one world.

The Knights spread themselves evenly around the Gallery, as the Knights had always done before a meeting, but this time there were too many empty spaces. Looking at the gaps made Andrew Fowkes feel hollow.

'What about the Stories?' Lucas Blake's voice echoed around the room as if the words were being repeated a fraction of a second after being spoken, over and over again. The effect was strange; daytime visitors often giggled, hearing their own words whispering back at them, making conversations hard to understand. In the middle of the night, however, and to the secret few who met here, the layers of sound added to the weight of their words. 'They shouldn't be in a boy. Who knows what they'll do to him?'

'We'll just have to wait and see. As soon as Tova's stronger she'll take them back. He's with her at her apartments, and she'll be helping him cope. She'll do her best to look after him, despite her own injuries.'

Fowkes sighed. The teenagers should never have got

involved so deeply. This adventure had affected them all in ways there was no going back from. He'd seen something dark in Christopher's eyes that worried him, and now Joe had the stories in him. And then there was Finmere. What were they to do about Fin? He'd asked Tova over and over where the boy had come from, but she wouldn't tell him anything. She wouldn't even look at him.

Fowkes wished he had more answers, and thinking of Tova made him wince a little. He hadn't seen her in seventeen years, but the pain in his heart for her and for Baxter remained as fresh as ever. He'd lost them both that dark night, in different ways. He gritted his teeth. The pain and guilt were always going to be there and he was just going to have to learn to deal with it. His weak days were done. The Order needed him – because as much as they might want to ignore the Prophecy, it was beginning to look as if they couldn't.

'The stories are now held in one unready.' Freddie Wise was voicing Fowkes' own thoughts. 'Are we going to talk about that? Maybe we need to study the table more closely.'

Each of the old man's words felt like a punch to Fowkes' stomach, but he pulled himself up tall. 'Maybe, but the Prophecy is all a riddle. Lots of it doesn't make sense, and I'm sure we could find all kinds of meanings in it if we tried.' The weight in his words almost dampened the whispered echo of them as they danced through the chamber. 'What we need to concentrate on now is rebuilding the Order.'

'And what about Fin?' Ted asked. 'The boy's been acting funny: keeps 'aving these quiet moments, as if something's on 'is mind that 'e don't want to talk about.'

Fowkes had noticed it too, and he'd noticed a few other strange things about Fin during the course of their adventure that he didn't want to think about too much yet. Things he knew that he couldn't possibly know.

'He's been through a lot – they all have. It's bound to make them a bit quiet from time to time.' Fowkes figured that wasn't entirely a lie, more avoidance of the question. The boys *had* been through a lot, and they'd all come out of it changed, anyone could see that.

'If you say so.' Ted didn't sound convinced, but then neither did he sound as if he was going to argue.

The rest of the men stayed silent, and in that moment Fowkes realised something. He was the next Commander of the Inner Council. The vote hadn't been taken yet, but he knew the outcome. He could hear it in the silence around him. Someone was obviously about to give him the keys to the Rookhaven Suite. He sighed.

Justin Arnold-Mather sipped very expensive brandy from the cut-glass crystal and reflected on his life-long friendship with Harlequin Brown. Life-long for Harlequin, at any rate.

The amber liquid burned elegantly in his throat. It had never ceased to amaze him how much trust Harlequin had placed in that schoolboy friendship. But then, Harlequin had always been like that: private, but full of honour and fidelity. For a man so exposed to the wickednesses of the world, Harlequin had never lost his childhood loyalties, even though Justin had shed his own as soon as he realised that the adult world didn't work that way. Harlequin had apparently never noticed.

It was Justin in whom he had confided when the baby – Finmere Tingewick Smith – had turned up in the cardboard box, less than a year after Christopher had been born. Harlequin had told him everything: about the Knights, The Nowhere, the stories, the Ageing. Everything.

Justin had stayed true to that childhood bond, at least as far as Harlequin was concerned. He had claimed no interest in this other world, only in helping his friend where he could. Even when his first wife had died and Harlequin had offered him a place in the Knights, Justin had declined. He'd said his place was here, in The Somewhere. Poor Harlequin had believed him, never seeing Justin's calculated judgement – he wasn't afraid, not like Golden had been, but he didn't care for the odds. He'd always kept his hand in, though, kept an eye on things. He'd stayed close to Harlequin and made sure Finmere went to Christopher's school. The red and green trunks had been his idea, inspired by the sofas at Grey's. Harlequin had smiled at that.

But now Harlequin was gone, Golden had overplayed both their hands, and Christopher had surprised him at the House of Detention. He'd seen knowledge in his son's eyes, but as yet, no one had come for him. And now it appeared there was a cure for the Ageing and it was his own son who had found it. And Christopher was still friends with Finmere. Finmere Tingewick Smith: *that elusive boy around whom so much was carefully wrapped.*

So many players.

Justin Arnold-Mather smiled to himself as he sipped his brandy, staring into the fire that blazed eternally in the oldest gentlemen's club in London. There was still much to be won in this battle of the worlds, but he'd stay in the shadows.

Just for a little while longer.

ACKNOWLEDGEMENTS

The biggest thank you must go to my brilliant friend Adrienne Smith without whom this book would most certainly never have been written. Her birthday walk around 'The secret village of Clerkenwell' inspired all the adventures in these pages and books to come. It was a perfect day with wonderful friends, so Adrienne, Mike, Christopher and Jo, thank you all for this book and more. Another thanks must go to Mike Smith for coming up with the name Finmere Tingewick Smith while driving around Milton Keynes during Adrienne's pregnancy. Little Hayden will thank you forever that you gave the name to me instead of christening him with it!

More thanks are due to all those whose names I have stolen – with their permission – for the characters in this book – you made my teaching days far more fun than they should have been. Big shout outs to Andrew Fowkes, Adam Baxter, Simone 'Mona' Mather, James Arnold, Jimmy George, Charlotte East, Mitesh Savjani to name a few. I hope the adventures of your lives are less hectic than the fictional ones I've created for you!

As ever, I must thank my lovely agent Veronique Baxter for all her hard work and faith in me, and my Beloved Editor, Jo Fletcher for her enthusiasm for my work and her self-control over my never-ending grammatical slips! The Gollancz team rock; Jon Weir, Mark Stay, Charlie and Gillian especially for helping Jo sell me.

Beth, Clappers, Jules, The McNally clan and the Turnham Green massive – thanks for good times and believing in me. You all bring magic to my world.

And thank you, whoever you are, for reading all the way to the very end including this page!

Turn the page for a sneak preview of
the sequel to *The Double-Edged Sword*

THE TRAITOR'S GATE

Available now

PROLOGUE

The smell of blood, sweet, warm ... everywhere. The air was thick with it under the sludgy stink of life. The air was ... familiar. It had been such a long, long time that sometimes he didn't even remember who he was. What he was. Tongues and teeth and heat flashed behind his eyes. He shuddered. He wasn't there, not anymore. That nightmare was over. He'd clawed his way back. His torn and bleeding fingernails were testament to that.

Blood.

So sweet.

His mouth watered as he wandered through the dark, cobbled streets. It was night but unlike where he'd been, there were lights here. Lights, and life, and laughter. The human sounds hurt his ears and tugged at his heart as his feet shuffled along the dirty road. He squinted in the yellow glow of the gas lamp. Everything was familiar: not quite home, but almost. He thought he might be crying; it was all so confusing. He'd been gone for an eternity. He thought perhaps he'd half-become one of them, he'd lived like them for so long. He'd eaten like them. If he wasn't crying then he thought he should be.

'Night, Albert,' the young woman called as she stepped out into the street right in front of him. He ducked into a doorway and peered cautiously round the side of the rough stone.

A disembodied arm, cut off just above the rolled-up shirt sleeve, waved the girl off.

'Night, Tilda. See you tomorrow.' A man's voice, with a soft East End London accent.

London. That's where he was. Of course.

'I'll be sharp.' The young woman smiled over her shoulder.

The pub door closed and he heard the hard squeal of a metal bolt being drawn across it.

Blood.

The girl's blonde hair shone in the light from the pub windows, the curls carefully styled so they still fell neatly onto the collar of her coat, even after having worked behind the hot bar all evening. She was pretty, and her low heels clicked on the stones as she passed him and turned down the narrow alley opposite.

Blood. He smelled blood.

His feet slithered after her. It was night after all. And his tongue was growing.

ONE

If the ground floor of Orrery House was always slightly too warm, the third floor was a virtual sauna. Jarvis had hung up Fin's jacket downstairs, and as soon as the door was shut behind him the teenager stripped off the thick sweatshirt and long-sleeved top he was wearing over his T-shirt to keep him warm against the icy December blasts; in Orrery House they were definitely surplus to requirements.

His face was still flushed with heat as he looked around. This had been Simeon Soames' room. It was less than two months since Fin had come to shave that old man's face, just one of the old boys who filled the house. It felt like a lifetime ago – but time was a funny thing, as everyone around him was so fond of saying. Simeon Soames was no longer confined to a wheelchair by the Ageing, and he had moved out to a flat close by. Whole new worlds had quite literally opened up for Finmere since that night, his sixteenth birthday, though they hadn't stopped Ted and Fowkes packing him back off to Eastfields Comprehensive for the remainder of the term. That had been an abject lesson in how time could slow itself down when you least wanted it to. Fin hadn't needed to do any Travelling to find that out. Still, school was done now, and the holidays were here. It was Christmas and there were two whole weeks before he had to think about Eastfields again.

He tugged the stiff window open slightly, allowing a small, sharp breeze to cut through the oppressive heat, and stared out at the dark evening. Fairy lights twinkled on the trees and

5

bushes that lined the square, and through one of the windows opposite – the offices of some bank or business – he could see a large, heavily decorated Christmas tree. The colours were simple, just red and gold, nothing too gaudy for a work environment, and the tree was strung with pearls instead of tinsel, but it was beautiful all the same. Normally the sight of any Christmas tree was enough to make Fin smile – a blend of holiday excitement and festive good cheer – but this time he found there was also a tiny kernel of sadness mixed up in all that traditional warmth.

He looked down at the ring on his middle finger and the jewel that glinted at its centre. Even in the short time that had passed it was fitting more snugly than when Harlequin Brown had handed it over. Another sign that he was growing up. Funny, he'd always thought that when you got older you got more answers, but that didn't appear to be true. His world was still full of questions. He still didn't know who he really was, or where he'd come from. If only the Storyholder—

'Your sword's under the bed.'

Fin jumped slightly at the sudden intrusion on his thoughts.

'You know, for if you want to visit Joe. And your friends. And there ain't no reason you shouldn't 'ave it when you're 'ere, is there?' Ted smiled from where he stood in the doorway. 'And it's good to 'ave you 'ere, Fin. For Christmas. It really is.'

'Thanks.' Fin smiled. The old man was no longer a once-a-year-almost-stranger, and the strange bond between the boy and man had grown into something strong. Until he knew anything different, Ted was the only family Fin had, as close as, anyway. It *was* good to be at Orrery House for the holidays – the first he'd ever spent there – but it also felt like another sign of the changing times, and as much as his old life frustrated him, sometimes Fin couldn't help but be afraid of where his new life might lead him. Ted, dressed in his nightwatchman's uniform, looked just the same as ever, though. There was always something comforting about seeing Ted.

'How have things been?' Fin asked. 'Is everything okay now?' The past few weeks at Eastfields had not only gone by tediously slowly, but he'd had very little information about events in The Nowhere. It was as if, now that his adventure was done, he was expected to just slip back into school life as if nothing had changed. How was *anyone* supposed to do that? Especially as Joe hadn't been there to keep him company.

Thinking of Joe, Fin's heart tightened and he felt slightly sick. More than that, he felt slightly ashamed. What was he whining about anyway? He'd dragged his two best friends into the madness of his strange life and neither of them had come out unscathed.

'So-so,' Ted said. 'Fowkes is Commanding the Order now. I think Harlequin would have approved of that.' The old man's eyes softened at the memory of Judge Harlequin Brown, Fin's erstwhile guardian, and Fin gave him a small smile. He wanted Ted to know that he felt the Judge's loss too.

'Joe's still with the Storyholder. They're 'aving some problems getting the stories out of 'im, but they'll get there.' Ted's smile was kind. 'Things could've been worse, you know, Fin. You did good – we *all* did good.'

Fin crouched down and pulled the heavy double-edged sword out from under the single bed. The metal was warm, and he felt the familiar tingle running through his veins. Ted was right, of course: things could have gone a whole lot worse. St John Golden was beaten, lost in the Incarcerator Mirror, and the Knights were regrouping. For the moment the Black Storm had disappeared. So why did he have this feeling that perhaps they were all celebrating a little too soon? And was that feeling coming from the black space behind the locked door in his mind? He was tired of it, whatever it was. The Christmas holidays were finally here and he fully intended enjoying them with his friends, his *family*, the Knights of Nowhere, and all those who had helped them in their fight against St John Golden and his gang. If *they* weren't worried, when they knew far more about all this Somewhere and Nowhere business than he ever would, then why should he be?

Fin lifted the sword and turned it this way and that, catching the soft light in the room on the edges. It felt good in his hands, and he had to fight the urge to slice open a doorway to The Nowhere. His fingers tingled. The sword was as eager to be used as he was to use it.

'One of the finest, that sword,' Ted came further into the room and let the door shut behind him, 'and you're a natural with it, that much is clear. You'll make a fine Knight one day, Fin, and that'll make this old man very 'appy.'

The ruby embedded in the hilt winked at Finmere, and the boy looked from the sword to the ring on his finger and back again. At the centre of the black and gold ring sat a sparkling jade-coloured stone. Unlike everyone else who wore both sword and ring, his two stones were different colours.

'I wonder where Baxter's sword is,' he said, the thought slipping out of his mouth before he could stop it.

'It'll turn up when it's good and ready.' Ted leaned on the desk beside the bed. 'These things 'ave an 'abit of doing that. My guess is the Storyholder's got it safe somewhere. She'll give it back when she thinks the time's right.'

'I wish mine matched, that's all. Like all the others.'

'But you're not like all the others, mate.' Ted smiled, wrinkles creasing his face as he did. 'So maybe everything's exactly as it should be.'

Fin put the sword down next to his holdall on the bed and shook the tingles out of his fingers. Nothing felt like it was as it should be. He wished that niggle was as easy to shake away as the sword's tingle.

'Is Fowkes here?' he asked.

'No, 'e's over at The Rookhaven Suite. Got a few things to do.' Ted's eyes darkened slightly. 'But 'e'll be along later to say 'ello. You know, if all 'is business gets done.'

Finmere wasn't surprised. He got the feeling that Fowkes didn't like him very much, and he wasn't sure exactly why. Sometimes he caught the Knight looking at him oddly out of the corner of one eye, and it felt like Fowkes *chose* every word he said to Fin, rather than just talking to him naturally. It was weird. Maybe Fowkes just didn't like that Fin had Baxter's ring. After all, they'd been best friends, back in the day. Still, whatever it was that made Fowkes act odd around him, Finmere was pretty sure it wasn't his fault, and that made it worse, because he didn't know how to make it better. Grown-ups were hard work. He was happy to stay a teenager for a while longer.

The strains of 'God rest ye Merry, Gentlemen' drifted through the open window and both Finmere and Ted stared out. The small Salvation Army band had taken up position in the square and were singing at the door of Orrery House. The brass instruments blew the wind aside as they blasted out the tune and the singers – many much older than the true ages of the men they were singing to – held up sticks with old-fashioned lamps attached. Watching them and listening to the soft blue notes of their carol made Fin feel happy and sad all rolled into one.

'They come every year,' Ted said quietly. 'There might be no sign outside, Fin, but some folk knows we're 'ere.'

Fin almost smiled. Outside, it was nearly Christmas, a time of good cheer. Why couldn't he feel that?

'Jarvis will be getting some mulled wine and 'ome-made mince pies ready to take out to 'em. Why don't we go and give 'im an 'and?' Ted's kind eyes twinkled. 'I could use a mince pie and a drop o' something warm meself. And then of course we've got the tree to decorate.'

'I didn't see a tree.' Fin's mood lifted slightly.

'We was waiting for you. There's always a tree. Who doesn't 'ave a tree at Christmas? What kind of thinking is that?'

Fin smiled, and this time he felt it in the pit of his stomach.

'Unless, of course,' Ted said, 'you're too old for decorating a Christmas tree—'

'You can never be too old for that, Ted. You going to help?'

''course I am, son. Now let's go before that lot out there eat all the pies.'

Grinning, Fin followed the old man out into the heat of the third-floor landing and towards the stairs. He glanced over at the inconspicuous little alcove behind which, not so long ago, he'd found a secret room. Where there had been a vase of lilies then now stood an arrangement of holly and berries. Fin wondered what would happen if he reached out and moved it. Maybe later, he thought, as they took the spiral stairway down into the heart of the house. It was Christmas, after all.